Hopelessly addicted to e
Kristine Lynn pens high
wee morning hours befo
Oregon college. Luckily,
dire. When she's not grading, writing, or searching
for the perfect vanilla latte, she can be found on the
hiking trails behind her home with her daughter and
puppy. She'd love to connect on X, Facebook, or
Instagram.

Sue MacKay lives with her husband in New Zealand's
beautiful Marlborough Sounds, with the water on
her doorstep and the birds and the trees at her back
door. It is the perfect setting to indulge her passions
of entertaining friends by cooking them sumptuous
meals, drinking fabulous wine, going for hill walks
or kayaking around the bay—and, of course, writing
stories.

Also by Kristine Lynn

Accidentally Dating His Boss
Their Six-Month Marriage Ruse
A Kiss with the Irish Surgeon
Nine Months to Marry the Princess

Also by Sue MacKay

Paramedic's Fling to Forever
Healing the Single Dad Surgeon
Brooding Vet for the Wallflower
Wedding Date with the ER Doctor

Discover more at millsandboon.co.uk.

HOW TO RESIST YOUR ENEMY

KRISTINE LYNN

PARISIAN SURGEON'S SECRET CHILD

SUE MacKAY

MILLS & BOON

All rights reserved including the right of reproduction in whole or
in part in any form. This edition is published by arrangement with
Harlequin Enterprises ULC.

This is a work of fiction. Names, characters, places, locations
and incidents are purely fictional and bear no relationship
to any real life individuals, living or dead, or to any actual places,
business establishments, locations, events or incidents.
Any resemblance is entirely coincidental.

Without limiting the author's and publisher's exclusive rights,
any unauthorised use of this publication to train generative
artificial intelligence (AI) technologies is expressly prohibited.
HarperCollins also exercise their rights under Article 4(3)
of the Digital Single Market Directive 2019/790 and expressly
reserve this publication from the text and data mining exception.

® and TM are trademarks owned and used by the trademark owner
and/or its licensee. Trademarks marked with ® are registered with the
United Kingdom Patent Office and/or the Office for Harmonisation in
the Internal Market and in other countries.

First published in Great Britain 2025
by Mills & Boon, an imprint of HarperCollins*Publishers* Ltd,
1 London Bridge Street, London, SE1 9GF

www.harpercollins.co.uk

HarperCollins*Publishers* Macken House, 39/40 Mayor Street Upper,
Dublin 1, D01 C9W8, Ireland

How to Resist Your Enemy © 2025 Kristine Lynn

Parisian Surgeon's Secret Child © 2025 Sue MacKay

ISBN: 978-0-263-32516-4

08/25

This book contains FSC™ certified paper
and other controlled sources to ensure responsible forest management.

For more information visit www.harpercollins.co.uk/green.

Printed and Bound in the UK using 100% Renewable Electricity
at CPI Group (UK) Ltd, Croydon, CR0 4YY

HOW TO RESIST YOUR ENEMY

KRISTINE LYNN

MILLS & BOON

To PC Samsonite
(and every other iteration)

'A new friend, which feels like a miracle.'

Your influence is on every page of this book.
Thank you.

CHAPTER ONE

"TAKE TWO ASPIRIN and check in with me tomorrow," Olivia Ross said. As team physician to the winningest Manchester Premier League football team, she'd seen her share of serious injuries. This wasn't one of them. She opened the medicine cabinet in the team's triage and rehab facility and sifted through the cotton balls, bandages and swabs they normally doled out. She handed a packet of meds to the young German football player on her table.

"Seriously?" Geoff Bilken, their striker, asked. The only part of him that was wounded was his expression.

She shrugged, biting back a smile. "Sometimes it really is that easy." When Bilken didn't budge, she sighed. Was this about his blow to the ribs or his ego?

"Did you get my roses?" he asked.

And there it was. She'd gotten his flowers. And broken out in hives. He'd have known to avoid that particular token of affection if he bothered to talk to her about anything other than football. It was fascinating how the men in her life and on her team saw her interest in football and conflated it with an interest in them. Or assumed that was what gave her depth, made her interesting.

"I sure did. They're beautiful, but horribly inappropriate— I'm your doctor and more than a decade your senior," she said, then directed his attention to the trash can outside the window where a dozen long, green stems poked out of the top like a macabre garden. "I'm also allergic. If I bring them home, I won't be able to see for a week."

"What about dinner? You're not allergic to pasta, surely?"

She took his empty pill packet and sighed. "I really think you should find someone your age. I'm not interested. And won't ever be."

Every evening there were women—hot, single, *young* women—lined up around the entrance to the training facility waiting for the German, a new addition to the team. It was sweet, his devotion to the one thing he couldn't have, but she wasn't issuing a challenge. She was laying down boundaries the striker crossed like it was the halfway line on the pitch.

"Bilken, you've got to go," she said, ushering him to the door. He was walking much steadier than he'd done on the way in. Go figure. "Head back to training and tell the manager I've cleared you to play."

He grumbled, "What will it take for her to say yes?" Which she ignored. Instead, she locked up the medical facility she was responsible for, noting how much was on her to-do list for the next day thanks to Bilken sucking up her last half hour.

The frequent advances from her players were annoying for more reasons than the work time they claimed. Bilken and his teammate Jonesie, a twenty-year-old defensive midfielder from Argentina, were the only two to ask her to dinner since Henri. Jonesie claimed he could be the supportive man Olivia needed despite the fact that she'd had to explain to him what a mortgage statement was and that he needed to file taxes *each* year.

And Henri was over a year ago.

What a disaster that had been, too. Rumors floated about him being out with a supermodel half his age and she'd confronted him via text since she was on the road. He'd ghosted her completely and she'd seen him and the model at the rooftop bar at Blaze two nights later.

At least that was better than Rian. That piece of work had the balls—or lack of—to break up with her because "How can I compete with a team of men you're with all day, every day, when I'm only one?" That was some bullshit. She'd translated the Greek businessman's lame excuse as *I can't compete with you, a driven woman who knows what she wants. It makes me feel small.*

Which, she smiled as she climbed in the back of the luxury sedan owned by the team, he was. Good riddance.

Still, as the city roared by her, the stadium where they competed coming into view on the horizon like a beacon home, she wondered where the good men had all gone. By all accounts, she was a desirable catch. Tall, blonde, curves she kept tight thanks to her gym membership and flaunted in luxury apparel... Oh, and she was the English Football League's most respected team physician. What she had to offer wasn't "cheat on me with a model" energy. She needed someone to match her drive, her passion.

Was there really no one?

Her phone buzzed twice. Neither message was from an intelligent, ambitious man wanting to take her to dinner. She rolled down her window and let the warm June night into the car. Some days her life felt more like a Greek tragedy than romance novel. She kept scrolling.

There was a message from Robert, the owner of the Manchester football club, about the tournament they'd be hosting in a few weeks' time. That, she was excited for. Fans would arrive en masse and while she wanted to keep everyone safe so they didn't need her services, she didn't hate the idea of a change of pace.

As much as she loved her job, it could be monotonous, especially since she'd worked with the manager of the team to help prevent training injuries.

Then there were another two texts from Robert asking

her to call him right away, and ASAP, in case she'd forgotten what right away meant.

And…

Olivia smiled. A text from her dad. She'd been on the road with the team the past three weeks and he'd gone radio silent. Since she'd started with Manchester, he was careful not to "interrupt the travel since that's where PFAs were won and lost," but she'd missed him. Hell, if she was being honest, she missed him even when she was in town and they checked in weekly.

Mostly because the check-ins seemed to be about the team and not her. The topics her dad was comfortable discussing were limited: team dynamics, medical protocols she'd implemented and club performance against other heavy hitters in the Premier League.

All benign. At least it was more than she'd had with him as a teen.

She just couldn't help the worry she was running out of time with him.

She called him back rather than send a text reply. She had ten minutes until she got to the newsroom.

"Hiya, darling. You're not at work?" her dad answered in lieu of a traditional hello. Nothing about their father-daughter relationship was traditional.

"Almost to the studio, actually."

"What's the topic about today?"

"A follow-up to the segment we did last month on player safety. Apparently some doctor from League One has opinions that are 'contradictory' and they think a debate-style taping will increase viewer attention before the tournament starts."

"Wow. Don't get yourself set about, hon. I don't like them setting you up like this."

"I'll be fine, Dad. I'm prepared and I've got eight more years with this team than the pundit they drummed up."

"Yes, but—"

"Enough about work, though. How are you doing? Tests come back okay?"

Her dad had a slew of exams to figure out why he wasn't sleeping at night and was losing weight, which was the root of her worry. Especially since the tests were two weeks ago and her father had been tight-lipped about the results.

"They're fine. Probably just need to eliminate stress. Which is why I'm sharing my feelings about this interview. From a surgical perspective, make sure you look at post-play statistics. There's research out there now about players' head injuries that are leading to subdural hematomas. I'll send it over."

"Thanks, Dad."

He promised to watch her show, said goodbye and hung up. Olivia pinched the bridge of her nose. She glanced at the call time. Less than two minutes and it was the first time they'd spoken in weeks. Of course, per usual, it was about work, too. Not her life—not that she'd had one outside work of late—but he'd also avoided talking about him, too.

The worry grew into something caustic and she swallowed heartburn back into her chest.

The town car pulled into the parking lot and parked at the entrance to the studio.

"Give me a minute, Frank," she told the driver.

"Yes, ma'am. Take all the time you need."

What she needed was another life.

Well, maybe not another life altogether, but something different, something that would shake things up a bit. One where she could practice the kind of medicine she wanted and come home to a love that supported and fulfilled her. Where men weren't intimidated by her success but she could still climb toward the heights she wanted to live at. Where her father loved and supported her outside of her connection to the Premier League.

Sure, she could quit the team and join a medical practice that wasn't spent most of the time on a crowded bus of sweaty men with too much money and oversize egos. On one hand, it might allow her time to meet someone special before she hit forty, when the chances of her having kids dropped significantly. But on the scales of her life, it would topple her off balance. Because the other side carried the heaviest weight of all—her father.

She'd be saying yes to some parts of life she'd dreamed of, but snapping the sinewy tendon tethering her to her dad. And besides, she really did love her job. Where else could she be in charge of an elite team's health and see the world whilst she practiced medicine?

Giving all that up didn't seem worth it, which was why she felt like a woman divided most days. But the last time she'd met her dad for lunch, he looked...old. He had lines where there hadn't been any before, and had lost weight. Coupled with his tests, it's no wonder she was worried.

And therein lay the rub.

If only she could have the job, the team, but not the travel. Because no Professional Football Award was worth giving up time with her father. Even if it was important to *him*, which was why she was still traveling with the team, still giving up her dreams of a family and stability, still taking gigs like talking on *Football Wrap-Up*.

It made him happy, and she could give him that, at least.

She glanced at her watch. Shoot. Speaking of *Football Wrap-Up*, she was late.

Robert would have to wait. She'd call him from the road on the way home. As she flipped through an email attachment her father had sent over with the latest medical research on players' postplay injuries that could be attributed to time spent on the pitch, she readied herself for a fight.

She knew what she was doing, and more importantly why she was doing it. As a woman, she might have a long way to go till she found her way, but as a doctor? She was top-notch and dared anyone else to tell her otherwise. Especially a nobody from a lower league.

He'd rue the day he let his agent talk him into airtime with Dr. Olivia Ross. And she'd get home in time to catch the latest episode of *Love Island* with a tumbler of whiskey to wash her day down.

She had to admit her life was pretty amazing—she had what others only dared to dream of. So, why didn't it feel like enough?

CHAPTER TWO

Mateo Garcia adjusted the mic on his lapel. It wasn't the device that was uncomfortable, but the starched collared shirt. Give him a polyester wicking blend any day. Preferably with his last name stitched on the back.

But those days were long over. Reflexively, he stretched his bad knee. It cracked, an audible reminder of the past that had catapulted him into the world of medicine from professional football.

"So, tell us, Dr. Garcia, what is it about football that's so inherently dangerous?"

Across the anchor desk, his counterpart smirked. He'd seen what Dr. Ross thought about injuries in their sport; she wasn't exactly quiet about it. In her mind, most injuries stemmed from training, when he'd seen the opposite in his experience. Game day, and the pressure to perform for spectators, led to overuse injuries.

He'd been fine with the idea of combating Dr. Ross at first. Even though this little debate his agent had conjured up to generate press ahead of the merger was his first and Dr. Olivia Ross was practically a staple guest on the football show. He knew his stuff.

But now…he wasn't so sure anything out of his mouth would sound intelligent enough to combat the nerves he felt all of a sudden. His throat was dry and his chest felt like it used to before a big match.

It was the woman across from him. Her eyes were crystalline blue, but even this far from her, he could see the sea green flecks in them. The depth they hinted at would have been enough to bowl him over, but then there were her full, red lips tucked into a smirk. Why couldn't he help from imagining them pressed to his? He'd never fixated on a woman like this before and it was pretty damn inconvenient he was unable to do anything else on this, his television debut.

She's just another physician, like you.

If he didn't get his brain in check, he'd lose the opportunity to finally work for a team that wanted real change. Olivia was the only thing standing in his way and it'd serve him well to remember that.

"Well, it's a sport that is increasingly hard on the body. It's a padless sport, aside from shin guards, but still sees a harrowing number of collisions."

"Harrowing?" Dr. Ross asked. "In an age of contact sports such as American football and rugby, it doesn't even compare. In fact, the total number of game-related injuries has gone down as you'll see from these graphs here. It's in practice and training where the real issue lies."

She'd done her homework. Good for her. But he knew those numbers, too. He also knew the true cost behind those stats to those affected.

Mateo's scar buzzed with tension. He was finally to the place he could go for a jog, or a long walk, without much of an issue. But it never went away, the sweet sting of pain from the toughened line of skin along his calf, thigh, and knee. Same went for the headaches from the three concussions he'd incurred—the last one "catastrophic," the physician said.

Career ending was what Mateo should have heard. Maybe then, he wouldn't have played that one last game. It sure as hell wasn't training that forced him out of the game he loved.

Mateo shook the Technicolor nightmare from his thoughts.

"Those numbers are encouraging," he said. Her smirk deepened into a smug grin and this time, he was able to ignore the pull of those lips. *Not yet, sweetheart.* "But what's troubling isn't solely the number of collisions. If Dr. Ross would have allowed me to continue before she shared numbers I too am fully aware of, I would have explained that the price tag for these injuries is still costing the league just shy of one hundred fifty million euros."

The anchor, a former player from before Mateo's time, whistled.

"That's not chump change," he said.

Mateo didn't give Dr. Ross the courtesy of a glance, though in his peripheral vision, her smile fell. He resisted the urge to shoot her a grin and shrug of his own. They'd be colleagues soon enough and he'd have the chance to show her his plan then. Or, rather, show the owner of the team why his approach to player safety was more cost- and personnel-effective than Olivia Ross's.

"No, it's not. And that's not even including the cost of replacing players that are sidelined due to injury, or the long-term costs the league is required to pay for extended-treatment plans after a player is dropped from the roster."

"In case you failed to notice, training is for working out the kinks, including safety protocols, and the matches are when the players are cut loose to put those skills to the test. They're supposed to be fun." She tossed her blond hair and the studio audience laughed. She was known for flippant comments, which were usually dead on as well.

Not today.

"Fun is all well and good, but not when it's at the cost of players' careers."

A small gasp from the audience said he'd hit a nerve.

"So, what do you suggest, Dr. Garcia?" Olivia asked. Looking right at her was a mistake. Her eyes, previously light and lined with a sexy blend of smugness and mischief, had hardened into icy blue stones. Stones she looked likely to throw at him if she could. "Are we supposed to outfit the players with pads and bubble suits?"

She snorted her derision but he held her gaze.

"That's not what I'm suggesting, though it would make for entertaining television to see Messi in a bubble rolling down the pitch, I'm sure."

The anchors laughed, but Olivia didn't crack a smile.

Good. He'd put the fun-loving princess of football medicine in her place. Her reputation preceded her, but it also worried him. How was he supposed to make meaningful change if she was to be his partner? She'd fought for the elimination of the third round of concussion protocol during matches because it "warranted no discernible results." Instead, she'd thrown the money Manchester spent on player safety to better boots, turf and shin guards.

As if the one to two players each season that were found to have mild to moderate concussions could be written off. He'd been written off and look where it got him. It sure wasn't his boots that cost him a career.

"I think the football world wants to hear what you plan to implement, because it's fine to throw out costs of injuries in matches, but did you know players spend four times the amount of time on the field during training than they do in matches? What will happen to those safety protocols when you suck the training money dry so you can make game changes across an entire league? They'll exceed the numbers you're talking about."

"Good questions, and an excellent segue." Mateo flipped his notes. He'd been alert before the show aired; everything he'd seen and read about Olivia Ross said she was a hard hitter, a rule bender and a woman who liked to be in charge. But she had a weakness he'd exposed in their ten minutes on air together. She liked being right. And in this case? She just wasn't. The data supported his initiatives, and he had no problem setting her straight. "I'm not a data analyst, but I *am* a doctor. And I wanted to show you the real-time cost associated with lowering preventative care for elite and professional footballers during matches."

He nodded to the producer behind the camera.

"What Dr. Garcia has for us seem to be photos of injuries. Can you talk us through them, Dr. Garcia?"

"Absolutely," Mateo said.

He stared at Olivia, at the red painting her cheeks. He'd underestimated how stunningly attractive she would be in person, and the blush juxtaposed against creamy skin and crystalline azure eyes made her even more so. Too bad he wasn't there to get a date, something his body finally seemed to realize. He was there to drum up discussion in the league about preventative game-time medicine for elite athletes before the biggest merger in the league's history took place.

"This first slide shows the extensive injuries to the frontal and temporal lobes of ten top players in the league over the past ten years," he explained.

"We've all seen these. And they're tragic, yes, but not damning. Look at the career-ending fractures and joint dislocations in players sustained in training. The numbers skyrocket. Adriano, Totti…they'll argue that there aren't differences between catastrophic injuries. A career ended is a career ended. Period."

Mateo nodded. "Sure. But are those ankle sprains and clean breaks preventing players from ever walking or speaking again?"

He'd minimized her data, which wasn't completely fair, but he wasn't there to play to her advantage. He was there to make change and keep his new job.

At all costs.

"Can you please show the next slides?" he asked.

The producers put up new images of three former players in wheelchairs. They were extreme cases, but all three had been almost fatally hurt on the football pitch when they'd played through a lesser injury.

"These are former Premier League players that have lost all quality of life thanks to brain injuries sustained during play. Not training, but a match."

"Where did you get these?" Olivia asked. Her lips were parted and she looked…surprised, if he had a guess. Interesting.

"I've got a study funded to look at these long-term effects of injuries sustained during matches and to make recommendations to the safety board of the league."

Did Olivia not know that her owner had taken such an interest in Mateo's research that he'd purchased it, along with Mateo's team? At first, Mateo had been worried. What if Robert Mansfield and the Manchester team were buying his research in order to silence it? But he'd had it put into his contract that they allow his research to continue for at least a year, and Robert had expressed how important it was to be a leader on the pitch and in the league's medical advances. Mateo had also thought both he and Olivia came to the TV taping with a shared understanding of where Manchester was heading. And that only one of them was keeping their position at the end of the trial.

"Anyway, you'll see that each of the players got significantly worse the longer they were subjected to play after injury. And before you ask, yes, this includes training."

The announcer and Olivia were both silent as he flipped through the CT scans of players pre- and postinjury. He took that as his opportunity to continue. They could get into semantics later.

"And you'll also see that, if a player is pulled from the

game after an impact and given ample time to rest, the same injuries clear up ten times faster."

He flipped through a second round of slides, a what-if of possibility he wished had been available to him. Maybe then, he'd still be playing in the game that got him out of Colombia, gave him a family when he'd had no one but his mother.

"Not all players are worst-case scenarios like those three. And that's who we're hoping to help."

Players like he'd been. Of course, he'd been lucky enough, adaptable enough, to have been able to make an interesting career pivot into medicine. He made good money now, and it was more predictable than football, more stable for sure. But the passion he'd had for the game hadn't been sidelined as he had been. Every day, the desire to run down the pitch, chasing a football and his dreams of the World Cup, ached like a phantom limb.

At least with Spain, as their physician, he'd been given the family part still. His only hope was that he wasn't about to lose it all because he'd taken a gamble with his research.

But he hadn't been able to sit on the side and watch as player after player headed toward his same demise—not when he could do something about it.

"So, what are you suggesting?" the moderator asked.

"It's a series of protocols, really. It starts with the training regimen Dr. Ross suggests, including proper rest days and equipment updates," he said.

Olivia rolled her eyes. "This may be revelatory in League One, but premier teams are already doing this." She sat back and crossed her legs. Her suit skirt had a slit that rode up, exposing her toned, tanned thigh. Whether it was to intentionally throw him off or not, he couldn't be sure. But he swallowed the lust that built in the back of his throat. It wouldn't do him a damn bit of good here.

"I'm aware. And yes, most are, but not all. It's also only

part of the solution. We, as a league, need to have backups ready to play if a first-string player is injured."

"We have that, too." More audience laughter, but less confident, especially as Mateo sat up and shook his head.

"You have second-string players waiting in the wings, but I'm talking about another round of first-string players warmed up and able to play at a moment's notice."

Olivia laughed. "A double roster?"

Mateo nodded. The moderator whistled again. Did he have any other way of showing emotion, or was that just the best way he'd found to gain audience attention? Mateo bet it wouldn't matter for today's program. It was tense enough without the theatrics.

"No one is going to buy that—it's too expensive to carry a double roster," Olivia said.

"It's too expensive not to."

"I can't imagine you pulling this off," she said. Her smile was more of a sneer. "It's not how we do things here."

"Want to know what I learned on the neighborhood field in Colombia?" She didn't reply. But she didn't avert her gaze, either. No, she held it like a challenge. "Anything goes on the football pitch."

She sat forward, leaning her arms on the desk in front of them. It took a Herculean effort for him not to stare at the shapely curves. Gazing at her confident expression, her eyes dancing with challenge, he was mesmerized. Damn. The woman was stunning, and a firecracker at that. Working in the same facility as her wouldn't be easy on many accounts, his body's reaction to hers topping the list currently.

"Well, good luck with that. I hope you find teams that are willing to play ball with these results. Because there's no way the Premier League will touch it."

The moderator opened his mouth, but Mateo shook his

head. "It seems a little unfair that you came to the show today without all the information—"

"I've got the same numbers you do," Olivia shot back.

The fire in her eyes turned the blue into pools of heat. Her gaze trailed over his features, his torso. It was a gesture he was familiar with, having seen it so many times before. It was almost unrecognizable on Dr. Ross, who was known for her playfulness, sure, but also her lack of desire to date, even casually. If he didn't know any better, he'd say she felt the same attraction to him as he did for her, physically at least.

Another complication to be dealt with off-air.

"You do, but you seem blissfully unaware that the Premier League has already made a move to support these preventative protocols in the hopes that the rest of the EFL will follow."

Olivia sat forward in her chair. Every bit the professional, he caught a slight tic in her jaw that belied her nerves. He half hated to be the one to break this to her. On the other hand, it gave him a leg up he wasn't used to having, especially coming from League One.

"Who?" she asked. One word laced with fear.

"Manchester."

Olivia's plump lips flattened into a thin line. "Are we done here?" she asked.

The moderator nodded. "I want to thank Drs. Ross and Garcia for joining us today and for talking through this important issue around league safety. Join us next week when we bring on three retired players to talk about what they're doing now. You won't believe it until you hear it here, on *Wrap-Up*. Until then, 'leave your mark,' football fans."

Olivia was up and out of her seat, tugging her mic off, before the moderator had finished with the *Wrap-Up* slogan.

When they got the all-clear, Mateo chased her down the hall. "Olivia, wait."

"You baited me in there."

"It wasn't my intention." But she was right; he had. "And that's not a way to get off on the right foot. Especially when we'll be working together. Or at least, I'd like to."

She barked out a humorless laugh. This close, he was privy to the flecks of green in her eyes, giving them a Mediterranean glow. He was also close enough to catch a hint of her perfume, a thick, seductive aroma that wrapped around his good sense and choked it.

He reflexively took a step back.

"We won't be doing any such thing."

"It's that or give your boss what he wants—a 'healthy competition that will make the team better one way or another.'" He used the same air quotes as Robert Mansfield had, and it felt just as hackneyed as it had a week ago when Robert had done it. It felt even worse now that Mateo could see the person on the other end of the competition. A real woman who would really lose her job if Mateo kept his. There wasn't anything good about this scenario.

Except for one key item.

Mateo would be given a chance to change league safety for everyone and then, maybe down the road, he would be able to start a scholarship to bring safety measures to underserved places like Colombia, where he'd grown up. That was worth the risk, worth everything.

"Robert wouldn't dare."

"Listen," he tried to explain, running a hand through his hair. Regardless of the opportunity this gave Mateo, he had a thing or two to say to his new owner for not giving Olivia a proper heads-up about the merger. "I'm sorry you were blindsided. I honestly thought you knew."

Her eyes darted between his. She looked like a caged animal desperate for escape.

"So, what, Robert bought your research? He's going to be adding to the team roster?"

"More than that. He bought my whole team, Olivia. The whole Leganés League One team."

Her eyes got wider, if that was possible. "Which includes—"

"Me."

She paced outside the TV offices.

"So Manchester is going to have two team physicians, along with two full teams? That's not financially viable."

Jesus, she really didn't know anything, did she? A wave of pity washed over him.

"I don't think he plans on keeping the whole team, just the ones who will cover positions that are most impacted by injury. Strikers, goalies, midfielders. And no, Robert doesn't plan on keeping both docs. Especially not when we have different approaches to safety. Which is why I'd like to talk to you offline about finding a way to collaborate. Maybe we could convince Robert he does need us both."

Olivia stopped pacing and wheeled on him. For a moment, he imagined her as she was right now—a black skirt suit that hugged her curves, with a pink button-down blouse unbuttoned just enough to show off her femininity, heels that highlighted her shapely calves and toned legs—but meeting her in a bar or restaurant. Maybe he'd have wanted to know why there was a hint of sadness behind her fiery gaze, or why she fisted her left hand so tight when she seemed nervous. Maybe he'd have liked to see how those lips tasted. But not meeting her as he had, at the other side of a negotiating table.

"I've got no plans to go anywhere," she said. Her finger poked at his chest. "And how can I work with you when you and Robert betrayed everything I've worked for? You might have what you think are the answers, but I know what I'm doing, too."

"I know. And I'm sorry this caught you unaware, but

Olivia—Dr. Ross—I've worked too hard to let this go without a fight. This cause matters to me more than you know."

"Is this just a cheap ploy to get up to the big leagues?"

Mateo shook his head. "If I wanted that, I'd only have to wait two years—we were going to be promoted either way."

She likely knew that if she, like other team docs, kept tabs on the competing teams and schedules. Spain's team was the strongest anyone had seen it in years. Decades even. No small measure of pride filled the space in his chest that had been empty since having to relegate his own football career just as it was getting started. He'd helped make them strong by switching out players before they were subject to overuse or preventable injuries. His protocol would keep others from the same fate, and no woman, no matter how alluring, was going to keep him from that.

"So why, then? Why are you hell-bent on coming into my team and disrupting my medical practice?"

"Because it *needs* disruption. You have one of the highest overuse injury stats in the league."

"So talk to the manager. Convince him to give the guys time off. I've built the strongest safety protocol in the league when it comes to training, but he has to follow it. Why am I being punished for his lack of follow-through?"

Mateo took another step back, but Olivia followed as if they were locked in a ballroom dance—if ballroom partners wanted you dead, that is.

"I will. Believe me, I'm going to start there and then build back with or without you. This isn't just a single-system approach, Olivia. I know you don't know me from the next guy, but I've done the research and time and I know what I'm doing. And like it or not, your owner agrees."

"Then why does this feel personal?" The wounded lilt to her question hit Mateo like a midfielder hurtling at him without slowing.

"It is to me, but I didn't mean to involve you. One of those scans I showed this morning? That was *my* traumatic brain injury after my last concussion. I asked to be kept out of the game, but my coach said he didn't have anyone else to put in who could do what I could do."

"You're that Mateo Garcia," she said.

"If you mean the player whose head injury had him barreling down the field too fast, too out of control to stop before he collided with the goalpost, giving him a truly career-ending knee injury, then yeah, that's me."

"And you became a doctor to prevent that from happening to anyone else?" Olivia asked.

He'd shown his hand, and maybe too soon. But the look on her face, the softening around her eyes, said maybe it was worth making this human connection. He nodded, swallowing hard as she leaned in close. She was near enough that he only needed to dip forward half a breath and he'd be locked in a kiss with the alluring woman. The desire to do just that overcame whatever warning bells rang in the background.

Thankfully, before his mutinous body could do any damn thing like kiss the stranger he'd just threatened to put out of a job, she stepped back and smiled. "Well, then. Thanks for the advice and I'll talk to *my* team about it, but we won't be keeping you to do it."

He bristled. He'd underestimated this woman, let himself think the panther could be a house cat. And he had the impression he'd live to regret that.

"Excuse me?"

"You want a fight, Dr. Garcia? Well, you've got one. I'll see you back at the complex. Forgive me if I don't offer you a ride."

Mateo watched Olivia storm away and dart into a black town car, the whole time wondering what the hell had just happened. He'd left the filming thinking he'd come out on top, but after his very personal, very intimate argument with her, he had a nagging feeling he'd lost more than just the upper hand.

Hell, he might've cost himself a place in the sport he loved, and this time, there wasn't a backup plan to get him back in the game.

CHAPTER THREE

OLIVIA HUNG UP the phone and dialed again. Anything was better than imagining Mateo's concerned, chocolate brown eyes, eyes she might have wanted to fall into in any other circumstance. Was it those eyes that had unnerved her, taken down her guard? Because she couldn't come up with a rational reason otherwise that she'd have done something so... stupid as to lose her cool on television. It was the one rule of pundit TV: don't give in to emotion.

She was an experienced professional. She knew better. And yet...

When Robert didn't answer for a third time in a row, she left a message.

"He had damn well better be joking, Robert. I'm not working with that man, and don't even get me started on the fact that I had to hear it from *him*, on national television. You made me look like a fool and after everything I've done for this team, I deserve better. Call me back."

That wasn't exactly true, she conceded, recalling the multiple messages Robert had left her. She skimmed through the texts, which were a series of Call me. Now and other similar messages. Robert never put anything in writing he didn't want shared.

His voicemail was more of the same, but with a hint of urgency in his voice.

"I was hoping to catch you before you left for the show.

Some changes are happening around here quicker than we anticipated. Please get back to me as soon as you can so I can talk you through them."

Faster than they anticipated? That was a load of crap. She was well aware of the bureaucracy around a professional sports team. Nothing happened without months of planning and strategic design. And Mateo-freaking-Garcia, a lower-league doctor she recognized from the tabloids' headlines advertising his newest fling each week, knew about it. So how quickly could the news have really come about?

She just likely wasn't included. Besides, why would they talk to the team doc? It's not like a career-altering decision to acquire a lower-division league affected her. Especially when she'd have to work alongside a man like Mateo Garcia, a conservative ex-player with illusions of danger lurking around every corner except in his own love life, apparently. No, scratch that, she'd be *competing* with Mateo for her job, the one she'd worked at tirelessly for the past eight years.

Ugh. This day was turning into a shite sandwich real quick.

She hung up and stormed out of the town car, noting that Frank didn't meet her gaze. He must have been watching the *Wrap-Up* feed on his phone. Dammit. The whole country—the whole football world—was probably watching. She was never doing live television again. Why had she in the first place?

Oh, yeah. Her dad watched every game, every football program on television. The more airtime she got, the greater their connection. At least, that's how she thought of it. Their relationship had been strained since Olivia's mother had passed away and Peter had been thrown into single-fatherhood.

But he never told her why he'd grown distant. Was it because, with her tall stature and blond hair, Olivia was a spitting image of her mother at that age? Because the man was drowning in his own grief and simply couldn't cope? All she knew for certain was that, like clockwork, her father called to check in after each game, each TV slot. So she signed up for all of it, and now she loved her job, what it gave back and taught her about herself and the world of medicine. She was damn good at it, too.

Except now, she was…

A medical expert who's just been debunked in front of six million viewers.

Her phone buzzed in her hands and she glanced down. Her father. Of course.

Want to talk? his text asked.

No, she decidedly didn't. Not to him. The last thing she needed just then was his disappointment on top of her own, her team's and her nation's. Besides that, until she knew the results of his tests, she didn't want to add stress to his life. Better to let him think everything was okay with her.

Can't right now. Heading back into the office. I'll call when I have more information. It'll be fine, though. Little twerp doesn't know what's coming for him.

Is he so little? Or twerp-ish? Olivia swallowed the memory of Mateo towering over as she tore into him, those eyes and lips, and the thick roping of muscle he hadn't let wane since being out of the game. It added a shine to the man she wasn't sure existed beneath the surface. Besides, she had more important things to consider than whether Mateo Garcia was fit or not.

She shook her head, hesitating before adding the next text to her father.

Love you.

She flipped her phone to silent and went in search of the owner of the club, vacillating between wanting to quit the moment she saw him, and using his body as suture practice in a skills lab.

When she rounded the corner of the medical suite at the Manchester training facility, she ran headlong into Robert, whose head had been buried in his phone. Could have fooled her, since he'd been doing a darn good job ignoring her calls.

"So you aren't dead. Which means you've got some explaining to do, Robert."

It probably wasn't the smartest play to threaten her boss when there was another physician in the wings waiting to snatch the career out of Olivia's hands, a career she'd tirelessly strived for. But she was exhausted. She worked hard, took care of her team and volunteered for extra assignments to highlight Manchester's own innovations. All of this to impress a man who barely knew who she was outside of work, and alienate every other man on the planet in the process.

Yeah, a shite week, indeed.

"I left you messages but you didn't return them."

She shot him a glare. "Don't pin this on me. You gave me no heads-up that this was happening, Robert. No meetings about team direction, no 'what do you think about this protocol?', *nothing.*"

"You're not a team manager, Olivia. You're the team physician. It wasn't a priority to keep you in this loop, I'm sorry. But I did hope you'd at least have more information before you made it to *Wrap-Up.*"

"I'm listening."

"Yes, let's talk, but downstairs. I need you to treat Loren. He's torn open his thigh, which is a disaster this close to the opener. I don't trust anyone on your team but you."

"Including Mateo Garcia? Why not ask your new golden boy?" she retorted.

"Olivia," Robert warned.

She threw up her hands as they made their way through

HOW TO RESIST YOUR ENEMY

the Manchester medical suite. Full medical facilities and in-house physicians—in addition to personal trainers—had been the league's original answer to the myriad injuries the players sustained. With club MRI machines and trained medical personnel, they no longer risked the players being met with gawking fans at ER doors, at least not for basic injuries they could take care of in-house.

"You don't need to take this so personally. I have to keep the inner circle tight."

"I could see that making sense if you were offering a contract to a new player, but this is a whole team, with a controversial new doc, that led to the purchase. You didn't think I needed to know I'm going to be competing for my job?"

Her voice had risen to a fever pitch, but she couldn't help the growing feeling of unease that had crept up on her since the taping. Football wasn't her life; it was her father's. But medicine was, and she knew she did good work, and more than that, she cared for her team, for the players she treated. That all of it was suddenly called into question simply because some good-looking guy from a lower division had compiled some scans was jarring.

"This isn't about you, Olivia. It's the protocols we need to highlight and see where we want to put the money for safety. Besides, I think a healthy level of competition is good for you, will keep you fresh."

"Fresh?" she hissed. "Robert, when it comes to training safety, I'm the most innovative in the league. How much more *fresh* can I get?"

"Dr. Garcia is the same when it comes to game-time injuries. Maybe he'll teach you a thing or two you can apply to our match safety since we're getting some heat from the safety commission—"

"Is that what this is about?"

The sinking sensation from earlier was buoyed. Maybe,

if this was just about optics, as it usually was with Robert, she could ride this storm out, while making sure she came out on top of the waves. Mateo wasn't—and couldn't be—her concern.

She wasn't convinced injuries sustained during matches was where the money for team safety should be spent, but Robert was right; why not learn a thing or two while the new doc was around, techniques and protocols she could use when he was gone for good and things went back to normal?

"It's not just the optics, Olivia. You know you have done wonderful things for the team, but sometimes... Well, I'm simply not sure if this is where you want to be. Maybe this will help clear that up for you."

Olivia scoffed, tossed a towel in the bin as they made their way to the triage center. "You know how committed I am to this team and if you're unsure, there are cheaper ways to find out than this. Are you sure this isn't about you and your fear that something shiny and new is out there and you might not be a part of it?"

"Olivia, serious talk now?"

She nodded. What had he thought they'd been doing?

"Reynolds won't be back, and that was an eye-opener."

Her pulse quickened. Had she missed something? Their defensive midfielder was fine the last time she'd seen him.

"Reynolds is off the roster? Why?"

Robert walked her through the physiotherapy room, quiet as the players watched on. None of them met her eye, which meant they'd seen the broadcast as well. She had a lot of work to do to build back her reputation as a doctor her team could trust, and Robert certainly wasn't doing her any favors. That Dr. Garcia was a former player and vying for her gig wasn't, either.

Robert pulled her into her office and shut the door behind

him. "His concussion symptoms worsened. He doesn't want to take the risk."

"We did the scans and he didn't show any lasting, long-term effects. We've altered his training protocol so he'll be protected—"

"I know, and I agree, but I had Dr. Garcia look at the scans, too, and he saw exacerbated trauma after Reynolds was cleared to play. I know these cases are rare, but they're worrisome enough, I've got to make a change. This is it, Olivia."

"How seriously should I take this?" she asked. She hated that her voice trembled. Robert looked away, his gaze on the window that looked out over the physio center. "Am I really in danger of losing my job here?"

"Look, I'm going to use the tournament to see which of the players I'm going to keep for the double roster during the regular season. I can't keep everyone, not if we expect to stay solvent, but I want to see if Dr. Garcia's work has merit. The only way to do that is to see it in action."

"And if it works, I'm gone? Just like that?"

"I can't keep two physicians. It doesn't make sense."

Olivia stared at him, incredulous.

"This isn't easy for me, either. I like working with you, Olivia. But let's be honest. Your connection to football isn't the same as Mateo's. He gets it from both sides of the pitch."

She bit back the reply on the tip of her tongue.

"I'm going to ignore the fact that you've basically told me my lack of professional football experience is getting in the way of my years of medical training. What's your plan here exactly?"

"I'll have Liam pit our guys against Spain's during the tournament to see who performs. It's a great way to see what Dr. Garcia's protocol can do."

Olivia was furious. How did her entire world get upended in a matter of twenty-four hours?

"Walk me through my role, then. I thought this was just a regular tournament, not an interview for a job I already have."

His gaze narrowed. She had to be careful. She could push his buttons, but at the end of the day, he was still her boss.

"It's simple. I want your eyes on our team during training, watching for signs of distress and fatigue. You'll pair with Dr. Garcia to make sure they get checked out after matches. He'll make recommendations, but you're still in charge. For now. We'll play it by ear, Olivia."

She sighed and pinched the bridge of her nose. The warning was clear: *play nice or get cut.*

She ignored it as a hint of excitement bubbled up from the part of her that thrived on challenge. She'd come to Manchester by way of combining the world she loved—medicine—with the one her father did. *Football.*

Maybe this infusion of another team, a project to work on and another doctor with vastly different approaches than her, would be a way for her to shine, like Robert suggested.

If she could disprove Mateo's theories, she'd get her life back—and her father's respect in the process. It was a gamble, but what choice did she have?

"Fine. I'll work with Mateo, but I want you to talk to me, Robert. No more secrets."

"No more secrets. On that note, Garcia is here to shadow you as you stitch up Loren."

She opened her mouth to protest, but before she could, Robert pushed through to the triage center. Olivia's heart fluttered. She'd had an arrhythmia since she was a kid playing on her father's football team for U10s, part of how she'd gotten out of playing the sport her father followed religiously. This wasn't an arrhythmia, at least not in the traditional sense.

It was most definitely a reaction to Mateo, standing perilously close to her intern, a perky, cute blonde from Holland

and probably a decade younger than Mateo. A flash of emotion fired in her abdomen, warming her core. She recognized it.

Jealousy.

That couldn't be the case. She didn't want more with Mateo; hell, she could barely even hear his name without wanting to throttle the guy, which wasn't very "Hippocratic Oath" of her.

So why did that fire thread through her veins when she saw Mateo smile at the intern—handsome and boasting straight white teeth behind full lips?

Maybe because he's poised to take what you really *want? Your career?*

That had to be it. Because she'd seen handsome men like Mateo before, had worked around them her entire career. And sure, the way he talked—so different and serious from his playboy reputation—was interesting. But he was a threat, nothing more.

Maybe there was a way to kill two birds with one text. She sneaked out her phone and wrote her father.

I'd love to see those papers on subdural hematomas on postplay athletes with concussions. Thx. Lemme know if you want to do dinner this week. Miss you. XO

Mateo had come to play, but that didn't mean she wasn't going to be ready to meet him on the pitch with a game plan of her own. And in the meantime, she'd get to work alongside her father, a win-win.

"Dr. Garcia, allow me to welcome you formally to the team, and introduce you to someone you already know. Dr. Ross, meet Dr. Garcia. I'm excited to see the work you two do ahead of this tournament."

Olivia put on her best smile and held out her hand. She wouldn't only do good work—work that stood on its own without help from this man—but she wouldn't let him see how he affected her.

"Nice to meet you, Dr. Garcia. Now, want to see how we do things around here?"

To her surprise, when he took her hand, something shifted in her chest, like it was falling into place. At the same time, energy flowed between her palm and the man she'd deemed as her new number-one enemy.

This wasn't going to be good. Not only was her job at stake, but it seemed her heart might be, too. That was a complete nonstarter. She'd rather be alone forever than answer her body's response to the handsome doctor who'd sliced open her life and left her bleeding on the table.

CHAPTER FOUR

MATEO HAD BEEN part of Manchester's football team for seven days, which meant he'd spent a solid week working alongside Olivia Ross. In that time, two things had occurred to him. First, she was out for blood. Not the players—no, she was a damn good doctor with killer instincts and spot-on timing. And she was right; in his dogged pursuit of game-time injury stats, he'd missed some of what she'd picked up regarding training injuries.

But she wanted him gone. And not just off the team. No, no. That would be too simple. She'd made it clear she wanted to wipe his name off the map.

Second, she was more than he'd first thought she was. She might seem like a fun-loving, gregarious doctor on TV and in the news stories that covered her playful banter with the press. But in person, she was serious, conservative even. Which was the real Olivia? For some inexplicable reason, he found himself dying to know.

"You need to track the equipment you use," she'd told him on day two, pulling out a spreadsheet that rivaled a peds unit's charting.

"I do, but I use MedPlot," he'd countered, showing her the app he found to be more efficient.

"Paper is better. You won't drop paper in the loo and lose your data."

"My data is backed up so if I have a plate of pasta, it won't end up smothering the inventory list." He pointed to what looked like marinara in the corner of her file. "Why don't we do both so we have a backup but also something that can be shared with stakeholders?"

She'd stormed off and he hadn't been sure if he'd won or lost that argument. At least until Robert called them into his office.

"I like this app. Thanks for suggesting it. Olivia, can I expect you two are on the same page with it?"

She'd nodded, but he didn't think for a moment he'd won anything in that exchange.

Also interestingly, Olivia didn't date, although it clearly wasn't due to lack of interested suitors. He'd seen her turn down multiple advances from two members of the Manchester club, enough that he'd considered turning the guys into the human resources team if they hadn't seem properly chastised by Olivia herself.

Never mind the surge of jealousy he felt when Bilken, their striker, brought Olivia fake flowers because she was allergic to the real kind. It was cute, but it invited a thousand ethics considerations.

He'd tried asking Olivia a little about her personal life one night as they walked to the parking lot. Jenna—or was it Emma?—had waited against his Mercedes G-Class, a bored expression on her face while he'd walked Olivia to her car. They'd been the last to leave, and though she'd made it clear she could walk to her car by herself, he felt a growing need to take care of the woman who took care of everyone else.

"Shove off. Just because you can't seem to keep it in your pants doesn't mean the rest of us have the same desire to go crazy after work. Some of us think it's healthy to want a stable, mutually loving relationship."

She'd gotten in the club's town car and driven off without giving him a sideways glance. It left him wondering, not for the first time, why he cared what she thought of him. So what if he took home women who knew what their nights were to him? He was honest, and they were willing. They scratched mutual itches and he got to concentrate on work without complication.

Mateo's pager went off: 999. Damn. Player down on the pitch. He grabbed the medical bag from his locker and jogged off toward the field. What Olivia didn't see was that, to him, it was better to be single and enjoy the pleasures of a woman when he desired them, than to trust another to carry his heart and dreams in their hands. At least, that's what he told himself. For some damn reason, she challenged the idea he'd carried through every decision he'd made, personally *and* professionally.

That only the game mattered.

A game that Olivia, the first woman to pique his interest in years, was trying to kick him out of. The irony would be funny if it wasn't so damn tragic.

"What's going on?" he asked the team's manager, Liam.

"Everett ran into the goalpost. Split his knee open. Might be a fracture."

"I'm on it," Mateo said, running toward the small crowd of players that had gathered by the goalie net.

Except, as he ran up, he realized he wasn't alone. Olivia was already there, her medical bag open, a stretcher behind her. Everett was groaning on the ground, gripping his thigh above the knee, which was split open. And yeah, given the swelling and discoloration, they were probably looking at a displaced fracture at best. A comminuted at worst. Either way, Everett was out for the season.

"They paged you, too? I thought you were on the travel team this week."

The only upside to having two docs on call was that they could take time off the travel schedule as preseason kicked off. The tournament was a couple of weeks away yet and even though they needed time to plan together it was vital they also made sure the team was cared for.

"I was on the field already. If you want to assist, I could use a second pair of hands."

He swallowed his frustration. To the team, it looked like the two physicians were working together to take care of a player.

But he saw it as another in a long line of small grievances designed to keep him from gaining a foothold with Manchester. Like when she'd happened to show up at the CT scan for Trent, reading it first and prescribing a treatment plan without Mateo's input. Or when she'd responded to the manager's request for a physician on call to check out his own ankle that he'd rolled on the pitch even though, like today, she wasn't on duty.

The damn thing of it was, he didn't disagree with her protocol. Just her delivery. In fact, when he'd watched the way she treated a severe case of turf burn the other day, he'd discovered a trick to keep it clean so the player could finish up training, or a match. He was learning from her, even if she refused to see him as anything other than competition.

"Sure. What do you need?" *He* needed this job, needed a chance to prove his protocol worked, but damn if Olivia hadn't given him the chance to show it yet.

"I need Liam to explain why he had our players so close to the goalpost on a wet day without proper PPE."

"I didn't think it was an issue, and in case you forgot, Liv, I'm in charge on the pitch."

Mateo wasn't about to pick sides, but he understood Olivia's dedication to training safety now. At this level of play, most of what the club faced during matches, they faced in practice as well. If she was open to it, he had some game-time strategies he could share with her, but then…

He needed to trust they'd help one another, not throw the other to the wolves. More and more he saw an issue with this arrangement Robert had laid out for them. It was a little too *Hunger Games* for his tastes.

"Let's get him on the stretcher and move him into the bay."

"The bay? What about a transport? This looks complicated."

Olivia only met his gaze for a moment before focusing back on Everett.

"I don't know about you, Mateo, but I can handle complicated."

The verbal blow landed like a thirty-meter-per-second ball to the chest.

"What if this needs surgery?" he whispered. He didn't want to disagree with her care plan in front of the team, but he was supposed to be her equal, not her protégé. To Liam, he whispered, "Can you clear the field? Have the interns bring a stretcher, stat."

If she made the wrong call and Everett paid for it with his career—or worse, his health—Mateo didn't want anything to do with that. They'd need to get on the same page, and quickly.

"Everyone bug out so we can take care of Ev. Head to weights and we'll pick up here tomorrow," Liam, the manager, said.

"Thanks," Mateo said. At least someone was on his side. With a clear field, he and Olivia could assess better what Everett needed. "Are you sure this doesn't need a transport?"

She shook her head. "I don't think so. If you're willing to run an X-ray and help me set this, we should be able to take care of it here. We'll schedule a follow-up with Dr. Conway."

Willing? This was his job. Of course he was willing. He barely contained an eye roll.

Take care of Everett, do your job and keep doing it. That's all you have control over.

"Okay, listen," he said when they were alone. "I know you've been running this show for a while without me. You've been doing this long enough you probably have a way of doing things. But we're on the same team right now and I mean it when I say I want to work with you, not against you."

"You're telling me you wouldn't watch me walk off the pitch and out of a job if Robert offered it to you?" He opened his mouth to reply, but she had him there. "Exactly. As of yet, I can't see a reason to believe that you and your 'protocol' are anything but added expenses. So until you show me a plan that'll keep my guys safer than they already are, I'm not sold. And I'm *definitely* not sold that we're on the same team."

He let her words sink in and nodded. The youngest intern ran the stretcher out onto the pitch and blanched when he got sight of the gaping wound.

It was such a stark contrast to see Olivia in a nice suit and shoes, explaining football medical stats one day, then caring for a fracture and openly bleeding injury the next. She seemed at home in both worlds.

"You're right," he said. She paused in undoing the Velcro straps that they'd put over Everett once he was on the stretcher. She didn't look as if she believed what she was hearing. "I'll start involving you more so we can make this plan together. It's the only way it'll work. It's no secret we're competing for a position, Olivia, but we are both in it for the same reason—to keep our guys safe."

"We agree on that, at least," she said. "For now, let me take the lead. I've worked complicated fractures like this and have the med bay prepped for them." She paused again, this time meeting his gaze. "If you have an idea, though, don't be shy."

He nodded, taking the small win. Nothing happened overnight; he'd learned that much.

"This is gonna hurt until we can numb you up," Mateo said to Everett.

Mateo took Everett's shoulders and Olivia his legs. Carefully, they moved him onto the stretcher. Everett cried out in pain.

"Geezus, mates. You wanna tear da ting off, do ya?" the Irishman said through gritted teeth.

"We're getting you taken care of, mate. You'll be taking the piss out of Jonesie again in no time."

Olivia ran—in heels, no less—alongside the stretcher, opening doors with her key card as they went.

"How you doing, Everett?" she asked.

"Right as Irish rain, Doc." His face had gone pale, though.

"He looks to be in shock," Mateo commented. "Hey Everett, how about we get you dosed and on an IV drip of morphine?"

"No morphine, Doc," Everett muttered. He paused, then looked up at Mateo with deep focus. "I'm part of AA."

Mateo nodded and patted the player on the shoulder. He understood what it cost the player to tell him that. "No worries. How about we'll get you set up with some local anaesthetic, then, but Everett, this is gonna hurt. You sure you're okay with that?"

"I am. This is important," he said through gritted teeth.

"Okay. Squeeze my hand if you need to, but remember I need it to set your knee, so don't kill me, yeah?"

Everett winced and laughed, though his pain response was kicking in. Olivia turned away and motioned for Mateo to follow.

"That was a good call, asking him. He never disclosed his AA meetings with us."

Wait, had he heard right? Did Olivia just agree with him?

"That's what we're here for, to help one another." As he'd

already said, they might be in competition off the pitch, but when it came to their club, they were on the same team.

Olivia nodded and they injected the area around Everett's knee as he winced before Mateo shut the door and wheeled him into radiology.

Ten minutes later, they had their answer. It was a compound fracture that would be better treated with full hospital facilities in case surgery was needed to set the bone. They dressed the wound and called for a medical transport.

"You were right," she said. He didn't nod or comment.

"That's not important. Let's focus on Everett."

He couldn't read the look she sent him. "Okay. I'll call ahead and let them know we've got an inbound," Olivia said.

"Sounds good. Want me to tag along with the ambulance, keep you posted?" he asked, but she held up a finger. She must've gotten ahold of the ER in Manchester.

"Shit. We're both heading in, it seems like. They're short-staffed in surgery and I've got the credentials. They'll give us temporary privileges."

"Shouldn't one of us stay till the end of training?"

"They're ending early at the gym. Liam just texted. Unless you don't want to come?"

Mateo met her gaze. "I'm in. Just wanted to make sure we've covered all angles here."

Her mouth opened as if she wanted to shoot back a reply, but he didn't get the chance to find out what. The ambulance sirens announced its arrival and they wheeled Everett onto the rig.

"I'm out for the season, eh?" he asked. Mateo kept an eye on his blood pressure, as he was in and out of consciousness. Likely it was a response to the incredible pain the player was in, but it was better safe than sorry.

"I think so, mate. But let's not worry about that, okay?" Mateo gave the guy a smile before Everett closed his eyes again. He met Olivia's gaze briefly, a thought shared between them.

Everett might be out for good.

As they made their way through the streets of Manchester, Mateo thought back to his own ride to the hospital, the one that had been the beginning of the end for him. He'd been broken, physically at first, then his heart had shattered when the ER doc had given him the news: a comminuted fracture that would end his time as a professional player. He'd only been on the EFL pitch for two years at that point, had assumed he'd get years to hone his craft and build his relationship with the club.

Without a clue what to do, he'd enrolled in online college classes, realized he had a knack for biology and didn't let up until he'd gotten into medical school. He gave the medics on the pitch that day full credit for saving his leg, giving him at least a chance to walk the sidelines of a football pitch. If he could do the same for other players, maybe his tie to the game and the football family he'd built needn't be in vain.

Somewhere along the way, he'd decided on this path, but more than anything, it was like a pull, dragging him through the darkest time in his life. The light at the end of the dark tunnel? His desire to give back to the community that raised him in football by providing scholarships for young men in untenable living situations.

"Are you okay?" Olivia asked, drawing him back to reality. "You looked like you were somewhere else."

Mateo nodded. He'd overshared with her before and look where it'd gotten him. She might look concerned, like she actually cared about him, but he knew better. She'd find some way to use what he shared against him so she could get the upper hand and look good in front of the manager and owner of the team.

"I'm fine. What's the plan when we get there?"

"I can take this if it's too much—"

"I said I'm fine. Olivia, I might have come from League One, but I graduated top of my medical school class just a year after you. So save me the mentor talk. I know you're just looking for another way to trip me up, or come first, or make yourself look good. But I can handle myself. I have been since I was fifteen and I damn well don't need you to second-guess that. If I mess up with a patient, you can have my hide, but otherwise? Let me do my job. Which, if you recall, is to work *with* you, not against you."

Mateo took a breath and avoided meeting both her gaze and the medical transport's.

He hadn't meant to snap, but damn if he felt the pressure of having to be on guard 24-7 starting to get to him. In his football career, he'd been able to just play and be himself off-season. Ever since he'd stepped onto the pitch as a physician for Leganés, he'd had to be the safety net for others and there was no offseason. It's not like he could let go in his personal life, either. Not when he couldn't trust that the women throwing themselves at him saw even a hint of who he really was. Another reason he kept things simple—no strings meant nothing to trip him down the road.

Of late, he'd taken to wondering who was supposed to catch him if he stumbled on his own, though. Especially since all he seemed to do around Olivia was stumble.

"I'm sorry," she said.

He waited for her to add something, to chastise him for the way he spoke to her, but she just gazed at him as if seeing him for the first time.

"Look, it's fine. Now, what's the plan?"

She smiled, and it caught him more off guard than her usual derision.

"Let's get in there and find a way to save this guy's career."

CHAPTER FIVE

OLIVIA'S STOMACH CHURNED as she scrubbed into the surgery. She wished it was from lunch, but unfortunately, she had a feeling it was the words she'd been forced to eat.

She'd treated Mateo like a second-class addition to her team—their team—and he'd called her on it. Worse, the guy *still* showed up, still did his job, and did it well.

Moreso, he had a relationship with the players she'd tried for and failed at. It was the effortless ease with which he talked to them about the game that had her more than a little jealous. Mostly because they *listened*.

She wasn't so jaded she thought it was because she was a woman in a man's team. Well, not *only* because of that. Mateo spoke with love for the game she'd never really had. Her heart issue had kept her off the pitch after early childhood and the only thing that brought her back to it was the hours her dad spent watching the matches from his couch in his robe just after his wife passed, then later from the stadium when he got to leaving the house again.

He'd take Olivia with him, but she'd never felt anything for the sport other than a connection to a father. Now, with his health in question, she craved that connection more than ever.

"What's the plan?" Mateo asked, glancing at the scans. "Because I think we can save the kneecap."

"Me, too," she agreed. "And listen, about earlier—"

He shook his head. "We can talk about it later, or not at

all. It wasn't appropriate of me to bring it up in the rig with a patient there. Let's just save him and then you can read me the riot act."

She nodded, wincing inwardly at the way he'd automatically assumed the worst about her intentions.

Well, you didn't really give him an alternative, did you? He's only seen that side of you.

Well, so what? She straightened her shoulders. *We're all different in work and outside of it.* Twice that week, Mateo had had a woman waiting for him in the parking lot. He'd walk off with her, arm around her shoulder, laughing and cajoling as if he hadn't just spent the day sullen and serious. And seriously trying to change the protocol of a team that had been going pretty well, if she said so.

Till she glanced out of the scrub room at their star midfielder laid out on a table, his knee sliced open and his career in mortal peril.

"I'd like to go in medially, suture the tear behind the knee, then fuse what we can while we remove any bone fragments."

He nodded. "I'll follow your lead."

They masked up and Olivia took the lead surgeon position.

"Do they do this often, give you medical privileges?" Mateo asked.

"They have been recently, especially when it's a complex fracture. I did my specialty in surgical sports injuries, and Manchester really doesn't have anyone on rotation for anything that niche. Can I get a ten-blade?" she asked.

The nurse handed her the instrument and Mateo, without her even asking, assisted by holding open the access to the torn ligament they'd discovered with further tests. He had good instincts.

"Can I get a titanium suture anchor?"

The nurse handed it to Olivia, who placed it behind the ACL avulsion.

"I can see you care about them. I do, too, you know," Mateo said. He took the suture from her while she tied off the augmentation.

She didn't meet his gaze, but felt it on her. It was more intense than the operating room lights.

"I know," she admitted. "We just approach that differently." She adjusted her angle before tying the second suture. Everett's knee was bad, but she and Mateo could reinforce it with titanium plates and he might have a chance at a career yet. It wouldn't ever be the same, but trauma never left the victims unscathed, did it?

Look at her, at her father. They weren't the ones hurt in the accident that claimed her mother's life, but they still bore the scars.

"I don't know if that's true." She finally met his gaze and instantly regretted it. The past week of working alongside— or against—Mateo, she'd been able to avoid looking at the man. Which was a good thing, because not only had he upended her practice, turned her into someone she wasn't necessarily proud of, but his physicality held a unique power over her that she couldn't figure out.

Just his eyes—the one part of him she could see from underneath the surgical mask, cap, and gown—bore into her and made her feel as transparent as the space between goalposts.

It also exacerbated the squishiness of her stomach.

"I think you and I are more alike than you'd like to admit. I think if you gave my research an honest look, you'd see a lot of what you're already doing in there."

"How so?" she asked. She regretted that just as quickly. Feigning disinterest had been part of her arsenal of keeping the new doc at arm's length, but there, under operating lights and away from the power the football pitch held over her, she found she *was* interested.

In the research, anyway. She still had no desire to get to know the man himself more than she already did. If players were off-limits, surely a doctor who used to be a player—and still was in the womanizing way—was as well.

Besides, he made it perfectly clear in the ambulance how he felt about her.

Her pulse quickened though at the thought of Mateo ever being interested in her. Thank god her vitals weren't hooked up to the machines, or she'd sound like she was in a-fib.

"The research pins the responsibility on overuse injuries and I read the report you gave Liam three years ago asking for players to have more time off so they could rest more complex injuries."

"You read that?" she asked. Was she going to be perpetually surprised by this man?

He nodded and handed her the first titanium plate as it was on her lips to ask for it.

"And I noticed the preventative measures already in place at the MMC," he said. "The stretching protocol, icing and rehab, and even the list of preseason don'ts on the wall. Marty said you did all that."

She had made the Manchester Medical Centre a top-notch facility that could handle pre- and postinjury, including mild to moderate trauma. She'd worked hard to make that happen, and while Mateo wasn't the man she hoped would notice her innovations, on a professional front, she was glad he had.

"But…" she said, alluding to what Mateo had left unsaid. That she'd changed, that three years ago it'd become more important that she show herself as the good-time doc instead of the perpetually serious one thanks to Robert's insistence that the team needed more press. It had the added benefit of giving her and her dad more to talk about, but it felt…cheesy. Manufactured.

It wasn't all Robert's doing, though. She'd thought if she

showed another side to her personality, she might make more friends, maybe even encourage a date or two. She couldn't exactly do that after work, since her job had her on the road or with the team ten months out of the year.

Unfortunately, the only dates she'd drummed up were requests from Bilken and Jonesie.

She was lonely. Yes, she and her dad had seemingly turned a corner, but if he wouldn't talk about real things, like his health, what did they have besides Manchester to unite them? Also, it turned out no one wanted the driven female physician to a top sporting team as a partner.

Mateo held the mangled flap of skin over the knee so Olivia could close the wound now that the plates were affixed.

"But nothing. I know your priorities have changed with the team and I don't need to know why. I just need you to work with me." Their hands brushed as she sutured the top incision. Even through the gloves, the sensation sent a thrill whispering through a long-ignored part of her heart.

Damn, I need to get out more. I can't let just any interaction with a man my age send me into cardiac arrest.

Mateo wasn't just any man, though. He was her competition at worst, her colleague at best—the man who had the power to take everything she'd worked for. And too much was at risk for that to happen.

Maybe it was time she changed tactics. "What are you thinking?"

"I want to work with you. To include you in the conversation as we make the changes Robert wants to see ahead of the tournament. The man seems to get a sick kick out of pitting us against each other, so what if we throw him off his game by teaming up?"

She finished the last suture and looked up, cracking her neck in the process. She needed a whiskey and a shower. A neck rub wouldn't hurt, but two out of three would have to do.

His idea was the first ray of hope she'd had all week. After all, wasn't this Robert's fault? Not Mateo's.

"Okay. I'm in. Under one condition." He met her gaze again and she leaned in. Under these lights, she saw a small gold heart-shaped discoloration in Mateo's right eye.

"My mom says it's my heart on my eye instead of my sleeve," he said.

"Sorry to stare. It's unique." Her own heart fluttered in the wake of knowing something so intimate about the man she was in negotiations with to keep both their jobs.

Olivia walked out and degloved. Mateo followed, holding the scrub room door for her.

"So that condition?" he asked her when they were alone.

"Two actually."

He smiled and she couldn't help her own from blossoming. Damn, this man had crept under her skin in all the wrong ways. He nodded that she continue.

"Okay, first you tell me right away if Robert is going to fire me and I'll do the same. I don't want either of us caught unaware of something so big."

"I can live with that. And the second?"

Olivia swallowed hard, grateful for the mask and dull lighting in this room that would hide the heat creeping up her cheeks.

"You stop flaunting your dating life. The media is latching on and it's pulling focus," she said, not sure if that was true at all. But it was too late to stop now. "Your dating life can't make the headlines over our protocol and the tournament, okay?"

She washed her hands a third time to avoid looking right at Mateo. He was only inches from her, though, and despite a two-hour surgery and long day before that, she still caught the scent of his cologne—something spicy and masculine—

mixed with the ever-present hint of turf. The squishiness came back in her stomach.

"Olivia, look at me."

She turned off the water and shifted her gaze. Her stomach went from soft with nerves to tight with desire as she took in the man in front of her. Tall, professional, yet with an edge she'd only started to see.

"Yes?"

"This about the job? That's it?"

She nodded. It had to be, right? It was what she needed if they were going to agree to be on the same team about this merger. All she knew was that it was important, period. Whether that was to her, or the job, she didn't want to examine too closely.

"Okay," he said, pulling off his surgical cap and tossing it. His hair was adorably tousled. Her hands itched to smooth the wild waves—definitely not part of the protocol. "I can live with those terms. Allies instead of enemies. Shake on it?"

Olivia took Mateo's hand and at the same time held in a gasp. Without the protective layer of latex between their palms, there was no mistaking the electricity buzzing between them.

She searched his gaze for any recognition that he felt the same, but before she could make head or tail of his curious expression, her phone rang. Well, not so much *rang* as sang: "Wildflowers," by Tom Petty. It was the ringtone she'd assigned her father.

"I—" she said, her voice cracking. "I need to take this." She looked down at their still-entwined hands and Mateo chuckled.

"Yeah, sure. Of course. I'll meet you outside."

Olivia stepped out into the hall and answered. "Hey, Dad. Everything okay?"

"Of course, hon. Why wouldn't it be?"

"You never call in a workday. What's up?"

He sighed on the other end and a flash of worry singed Olivia's heart. She hadn't heard that sigh in years—not since she'd lived with him during medical school. He'd make that sound every day he came through the doors, just before dropping into his seat in front of whatever match was on.

"I got some more test results today and had some questions I'd like to get your input on. Mind taking a look?"

The worry turned icy and thick. She hadn't known he'd gone in for another round of tests. She cleared her throat. "Send them over. Of course I'll take a look."

"Already did. They're in your email."

"Anything in particular you want me to check out?" She stopped short of asking what, in particular, his docs had said that made her father, a brilliant surgeon, worried.

"Just a second set of eyes, see if there's something they're missing. Thanks, hon. So, how's the new team looking?"

Olivia pulled up her email while she gave her standard response to the team's performance, the same spiel she gave at press junkets. But her shaking hands belied where her heart and thoughts really were.

If her father wanted to involve her under the guise of medical expertise, it had to be bad.

The labs didn't show much aside from elevated protein and CBC. But coupled with his weight loss and sleeplessness, and the PET and MRI scans…it said all she needed to know.

Cancer. Stage two at least, with what she was looking at. But what kind? Was it treatable? Her father was due at least one more round of more invasive testing before they got answers.

"How long have you known?" she asked. The words were hollow, everything she felt muted beneath fear. Last time she'd been here, she was a child and the pain had been crippling, but what she hadn't known could fill an ocean. Now her medical knowledge worked against her. Her father was older, and sure, he kept fit, but how would he respond to his body being filled with poison?

"So you see what we're all seeing? Nothing magical in your bag of tricks?" He chuckled and part of her longed to tease back, say something like *Not unless you want a shin guard*, but she just didn't have it in her.

"Let's make an appointment with Carl," she suggested instead, giving the first name of the oncologist who'd gone to med school with her father. Neither could speak his diagnosis out loud, but hopefully, they'd have time to build up to that together. "He can get you scheduled for some other tests, and set up a treatment plan. If that's what you want."

She added that as much for her own racing heart as his peace of mind.

She couldn't lose her father, too. Not when they'd barely scratched the surface of their relationship.

"I do. Thanks, hon. I'll message you and let you know when I'm meeting with him."

"I'd like to come," she said. Mateo stepped into the hall, but gave her space. It made sense that they rode back to the compound together, so she wrapped up with her dad. "Is that okay?"

"Sure, sure."

She nodded, even though he couldn't see her. "Love you," she added. Life was too short to hold that in anymore, regardless of how he felt.

"Love you," he said.

She hung up, surprised by her body's reaction to those rare two words from her dad. Tears stung her eyes, but she held them back. A hand on her back, soft but present, alerted her to Mateo's presence.

"Your dad?"

She nodded.

"Is he the one you look up to the stands at each game?"

Olivia met Mateo's gaze. "You've only worked for us a week and we haven't had a match yet this season. How do you know I do that?"

He shrugged, the intensity of his gaze softened by the hint of a smile tugging at his lips. He was handsome. Devilishly so. It wasn't a stretch of the imagination to see how he might pull so many dates with available women. Too bad it reminded her of Henri, the infamous model chaser. That took the shine off, and allowed Olivia to focus beyond Mateo's good looks.

"I've followed Manchester—and your career—since you started."

"Why?" The surprise was as vast as her dad asking for help. She felt unsteady on her feet.

"You're the best in the business. I wanted to learn from you, from how your team operated. Like watching game tape, I guess."

She stared at him, open-mouthed.

Allies. Did he mean that word he'd used to describe them? If he did, maybe there was actual hope they could turn Robert's plan on its head.

Was there no end to the ways this man was going to surprise her? Apparently, her restful night of forgetting about work was off the table.

CHAPTER SIX

MATEO SLID OUT of his silk pyjama bottoms and into bed. He flipped on the bedside light and grabbed a copy of his friend's wife's new book. It was good—a heartwarming story about a ranching family, the Wallaces, in the northwest corner of the United States. He'd read the other four, and *The Cowboy and the Coach* was definitely his favorite. Sure, it was an American football coach, but the feeling of being on the field was real to him.

He settled into the pillow-top king-size mattress and flipped to the final chapter of the romance novel. When his phone buzzed on the nightstand next to him, he reflexively hid the book under his pillow as if to hide it.

No one's here, he reminded himself. Still, he shuddered at the reputation he'd have if the club knew he went home alone most nights after his dates—not to women's beds, as everyone assumed—to read. And read romance novels at that.

He swiped into the text, and sat up straighter. It was from Olivia. He'd nicknamed her "Ally" in his contacts, a joke since a) it was the only woman's name he saved, and a fake name at that, and b) it was an homage to what he'd hoped Olivia would be to him. An ally. He'd meant what he said— he'd been in awe of her career, even if he hadn't understood much of the enigma that was Olivia herself.

He checked his pager before reading it; had he missed a 999 page?

Nope.

Sorry for the late text, it read. I was just curious about the "game tape" you watched before you joined Manchester. Was I doing anything wrong that made you zero in on this team?

Mateo frowned. Olivia usually seemed so confident. Had she not heard the part where he'd told her she was the best in the business and he wanted to learn from her? He certainly had never meant to make her feel like anything she did was wrong. Well, maybe that wasn't totally true in the beginning, after their TV taping. But that was more self-preservation than anything else.

Not at all. I know our approaches differ a little, but yours isn't wrong. There's a lot that happens in training I hadn't realized translates to game day. A lot of overlap, as it were. Sorry if I made you feel any other way.

Three blinking dots appeared then disappeared.
He shot off another text.

I'm not baiting you, BTW. I've got nothing to hide. And a lot to lose. I'm just trying to work with you. Be your ally, like I said.

A new text arrived immediately.

Thanks. I think self-doubt and questioning things comes biologically programmed with me. Thanks for clarifying. And yeah, allies sounds better than "we ride at dawn" enemies. ;)

Mateo stared at his phone, one hand on the reply button. There was no way the self-assured, confident, sexy woman on the other end of the line carried her own doubts and fears.

Or that she'd actually admitted as much to him. Or that she was as funny as that last line made her appear.

He owed her a response, a nod of thanks for taking him seriously enough to trust him.

I have my share of fears and doubts, too. I've probably been projecting those a bit since you intimidate the hell out of me.

An immediate laugh emoji appeared. He chuckled.

Is it because I'm nearly six feet tall and still wear heels? Or the take-no-shit attitude I have to give off at work so I seem half as competent as the men in the club?

He scrawled back a quick response.

I think it's seeing you shamelessly shoot down Bilken and Jonesie, crushing their dreams for the umpteenth time, then suturing someone's leg shut the next minute. You're kind of a badass.

He bit his lip as the three little dots said she was responding. They disappeared like the first time and he cringed. Had he taken the joking too far? The dots reappeared and he couldn't stop staring at them. They went away again, but a text replaced them.

Those guys... I swear my Christmas bonus is just to keep me from going to HR about their relentless flirting. Anyway, they can handle it. I think they just think it's a challenge, like a match against Munich.

He laughed, but she'd raised questions he'd had about her

KRISTINE LYNN   61

and her dating life. Questions he had no right to ask, but felt compelled to, anyway. He threw out a test.

You aren't at all interested in Bilken? He seems nice, if not a little earnest.

Yeah, and not serious enough in his own life that I trust he knows what a state pension even is. Besides, he's not at all in the same place in life I am.

Mateo breathed out a sigh of relief. Was he really jealous of a twenty-year-old footballer? He supposed he was, if for no other reason than the guy could go up to Olivia and ask for what he wanted. Mateo didn't have that luxury. Too bad, too. Because she was intriguing enough he'd like to see where things could go with her. Beyond one dinner or a night together. He could be an ally, yes. Maybe even…a friend? But anything more was impossible given their situation at work.

Where is that? The place you're in? That was something a friend would ask, right?

Honestly? I'd like to be in a serious intimate relationship and I don't think Bilken—or any guy I've dated—has a clue what that looks like. Especially with someone who has so many letters after her name, haha.

Heat pressed against his chest. He wanted to think it was borne of frustration from men who dated below their station to avoid being challenged by a strong woman. Not because he was jealous of men Olivia had dated.

Aren't you one of those men who date unchallenging women? No, he didn't think so. He dated women who he wasn't seriously interested in dating because he didn't want to seriously date. Not because he was intimidated by a woman's strength if she was more successful than him. He liked the challenge of learning from women like Olivia.

But to see her happy with a guy? Why did that thought rub him the wrong way? It wasn't any of his business who Olivia Ross dated.

Put your ego aside, Mat. Be there for her.

Maybe Bilken would surprise you.

Her response was immediate.

Excuse me, didn't we both just agree we were on the SAME TEAM? >:-)

His fingers flew over the keyboard. Romance novels were a relaxing way to end the night, but he had to say, this was preferable by a long shot.

OK, maybe you're right. The other thing to consider, though, is what might happen if you did say yes. They're both what, twenty?

She responded. Going on fifteen.

Exactly. So maybe if you take the chase away, you'd finally get some peace. Not saying that's what it should take! The other option is to kick their asses, I suppose. Someone's got to kick them into touch! He added a guy-shrugging emoji. He'd never so much as used a single emoji in his life, and here he was, shooting them off like penalty kicks in the World Cup.

You may just be a genius. On the other hand, if I end up engaged to a twenty-year-old kid from Germany, you're paying for the wedding.

Mateo coughed out a violent laugh. Olivia was actually *funny*. Who knew?

Yeah, good point. Maybe you should hold out for a guy who can rent a car if you travel together.

A text buzzed against his thigh.

You say that as if the suitors are lining up. Maybe I only half-heartedly reject Bilken and Jonesie so I don't feel like a total loser who goes home every night and reads sappy novels with a pint of ice cream.

Mateo shoved the book in the drawer of his nightstand.

You're kidding, right? A guy would be an idiot not to ask you out. And I read sappy novels, so what's that say?

Was he *flirting* with her? *Damn*. He didn't want her to get the wrong idea, especially since he still wasn't 100 percent sure she wouldn't stab him in the back if it meant saving her job. What did he really know about her, after all?

Sure, if he liked a woman who was gone ten months out of the year and was married to her stethoscope already. Men say they want a driven woman until it comes to supporting one above his own needs. Or at least equal to them.

He swallowed hard. Damn. The truth bomb she'd just dropped left him open and feeling all too seen himself.

Sorry, she added. That particular topic makes me feisty. Didn't mean to unload on you. And you read romance novels?!?! Spill!!

My romance novel habit is a state secret, so as my FRIEND AND ALLY, shhhhhh. ;)

Another emoji. Who was he?

Also, for what it's worth, all I see when I look at you is a strong, independent woman with a damn good job, a cracking sense of humor, and who's beautiful enough to pull interest from professional footballers half her age. Like I said, they'd have to be fools not to line up at your door.

Was he one of those fools?

Well, thanks. I'll put that endorsement on my HeartSync profile. Anyway, sorry for what I said about your dating life. To be honest, it's none of my business. I was probably just grumpy you've found a way to have a social existence outside the stadium.

Mateo thought about the woman he'd taken out to dinner two nights earlier. She'd been stunning, with cascading dark curls and a compact body he thought he wouldn't mind spending some time exploring. But the conversation was dry and so one-sided it was like pitting a professional footballer against a nine-year-old on the pitch.

The truth was, Mateo was bored. He wanted passion, excitement, and challenge. Sure, nights home lying in bed and reading beside someone would be nice, too. Maybe a date in the park kicking around a football. But more than anything, he wanted to feel *alive*.

The last time he had was on the football pitch before a competitive match.

It's not as fulfilling as you'd imagine. Either way, you're right;

I should focus on the team right now and put dating to the backburner. My track record with women sounds as bleak as yours does with men (other than our fan faves, Bilken and Jonesie, haha).

Why don't you date seriously, Mateo, if you don't mind me asking? Since we're "friends" and all.

His heart skipped a beat. She'd used quotation marks, but she'd still called him a friend.

It's pretty simple. Making this life successful isn't just for me; it's to help kids like me get out of their dismal situations. So, I can't afford to be selfish right now, even if yeah, I'd like a family someday.

He did, but hadn't ever admitted it, even to himself.

Is it selfish, though? To want happiness for yourself? Olivia replied. I get it; our jobs don't exactly lend themselves to a happy family life. But we've got to try and shoot for what we really want, haven't we?!

Her question had his mind racing. The women he took out or the rare few he brought home were distractions from the real thing. But was the real thing a possibility when they did what they did for a career?

Yeah, turns out when you combine two of the world's most stressful jobs—professional sports AND medicine—the dating pool shrinks.

Are we...actual allies? Friends? Like, can I ask you something? she asked. Something serious?

He bent over his phone, and typed out a quick Always. I'm all in, Olivia.

66   HOW TO RESIST YOUR ENEMY

Whatever he needed to do to keep her talking to him, he wanted more of it. He'd take this kind of deep conversation over a naked woman in his bed any day of the week. Or most, anyway. Having sex was easy, fun even, but this? He craved this kind of connection. Too bad it had to happen with the one woman who could strip the rest of his life from him. He ignored that and focused on how good this felt.

Do you like what you do? I mean, it's got to be hard watching people play the game you used to all day, right?

Oof. She'd opened a can of worms with that one. But he knew the answer, had known it the moment he'd applied to medical school and not looked back. "Back" was where his life had taken a hard left—and so had his knee.

Yeah. It's painful, but it's better than the alternative, where I'm nowhere near the pitch or the players. At least here, practicing medicine, I can be part of the game.

He was starting to trust her, to a degree, but he hadn't told anyone about the pervasive loneliness he felt when he came home to an empty house after a long day, or walked in after a weekend of travel with the club to no fanfare other than a note from his cleaning person that she'd stocked his fridge with fresh orange juice.

He'd never shared his feelings about the loss of his career, nor the deeper longing for something more.

His phone buzzed, taking him out of his daydream. In this iteration, he'd had a few towheaded toddlers on his lap. It wasn't…awful. It was calm, joy filled. Perfect.

I understand more than you know.

You used to play? he asked.

Kind of. As a kid, and they were the happiest moments with my dad. But I had—have—a heart condition so I couldn't keep going competitively.

Well, damn. He sat with that a minute before responding.

Do you like your job, Olivia? Like, is it your dream career? Would you have kept playing football instead, if you could?

The three dots did their disappearing act a couple times before a text showed up.

I don't know, to be honest. I do know I work as hard as I do because it keeps this connection to my dad. Loving the man who loves the sport has always seemed like enough, and the club is great. But...

The dots played their hide-and-seek game while he held his breath.

In a perfect world? I'd probably take a position where I had a home base and more normal schedule. I love the medicine, but not the life it keeps me from, if that makes sense. Hmm. I've never admitted that to anyone before. Not even myself.

I've had a few of those moments tonight, too, he told her. Thanks for sharing.

She'd done something he'd previously considered impossible before this talk, which was to show more of her hand and allow him to trust her, right now, anyway. He wanted to ask more about her dad—and the conspicuous lack of mention about her mom—but didn't want to push. Before he could think of how to phrase a delicate question, his phone vibrated again.

Well, thanks for this chat, but I should probably get some sleep before I have to be on call tomorrow morning, Olivia wrote.

His heart sank.

Good night. Damn if he wasn't a little sad to be saying goodbye.

Good night, Mateo.

Before he put his phone on Do Not Disturb, he opened HeartSync and started searching. He didn't see a profile for her, and for some reason, that calmed his racing pulse enough he thought he might actually get some sleep tonight.

Maybe he'd read that last chapter of *The Cowboy and the Coach*.

Just in case he needed to replace the image of a sexy blonde woman on a football pitch so his dreams didn't leave him more confused and frustrated in the morning. It was wishful thinking, since all he could see as he opened the book was an image of Olivia's curvy body in only a thin nightshirt, lying in bed. That she was alone, and it sounded like she had been for a while now, didn't help. His pulse kicked up a notch and so did other parts of his anatomy.

Alive, indeed.

Just like that, he knew sleep was off the table.

Damn, he thought. *I didn't see this coming.*

CHAPTER SEVEN

OLIVIA WALKED DOWN the hall, the scent of cleaning supplies still hanging in the air. She liked the quiet of the medical bay when no one else was there yet. It allowed her to focus, to think about her day and her patients from the team in the order she needed to see them.

Checking on Everett was top priority, and Loren's sutures needed to come out. After that, it was more about the preventative protocol for training *and* match day she and Mateo were working on.

Mateo. Just his name in her thoughts had them spiraling and her skin flushed. The other night they'd shared what was the most intimate and personal exchange she'd ever shared with anyone and it had happened over text.

Which was probably why it happened at all. Part of not dating was not having anyone to share her days, her insecurities, her joys with. And she was woefully out of practice, hence the extreme oversharing with the first person who asked any follow-up questions about her life. Had that happened in person, she'd probably be halfway to the Outback with a one-way ticket out of shame alone.

As it was, she'd hidden from him the day after, mortification blossoming on her cheeks every time she thought of what she'd shared with Mateo. How could he possibly take her seriously when she'd told him about her lack of love for the sport she worked for, then info-dumped about her medical issues and washed the whole crap-sandwich down with a swig of *Wanna hear about my lack of a dating life?*

What had she been thinking?

It's true, isn't it? All that stuff you overshared? It was, which was why she'd never really admitted any of it, even to herself, but that didn't matter. Mateo had a way of drawing her out of herself—or the carefully crafted veneer she'd created—and he'd surely treat her differently now. Which meant the beginning of the end with her career.

Until he'd shocked the hell out of her when he walked in her office at lunch, a bag of crisps in hand that just so happened to be her favorite.

"Hey, *friend*," he emphasized. "I thought you might be hungry after a late night at the office," he'd said, tossing the bag on her desk and dropping down into the seat across from her as if everything was *fine*.

She'd devoured the bag while he walked her through the protocol for swapping out athletes he'd prepared for her approval. Of course it looked fine, and she trusted his work, so most of that meeting had been spent replaying her every text the night before, rereading his replies looking for hidden meaning, and wondering why Mateo looked so unfazed about it all.

Because he actually dates. Talking to members of the opposite sex is normal for him, her heart offered.

Or, he's planning on using what he knows against you at some point.

That's just your paranoia talking, the more logical part of her brain chided. But she hadn't stopped thinking about two moments from several nights before.

I'm all in, he'd said. Three words she'd longed to hear from someone she cared about. Then there was his admission that he wanted to help kids like himself.

He'd been just as vulnerable, if not more.

So she'd returned the favor just before their meeting with Robert. The agenda was to cover the lineups for the informal preseason and pretournament game against London United. The meeting was at 5:00 p.m. after they'd both had a 6:00 a.m. meeting with their physio teams and a long day of follow-up medical appointments, so she'd brought Mateo a mug of the green tea he drank each afternoon. She'd even taken to having one herself instead of a second coffee.

The meeting was his chance to throw her under the bus, to claim their work as his own. But he hadn't done that.

"We've come up with a great lineup we feel will maximize the medical benefits of having a double roster, while keeping costs down. Olivia will walk you through it."

She'd nodded and shown Robert their risk assessment and how they planned to avoid injuries in both the tournament and training.

"We?" Robert had asked. Mateo and Olivia had come up with a response to that and she held her breath.

"Yup. It's our medical assessment that equal injuries happen in training and matches. We need a comprehensive approach."

"Hmm. You've given me a lot to think about," he'd said, his gaze shifting between the two. Olivia wanted to ask if that included a way to keep both her and Mateo on staff, but didn't want her question to reek of desperation.

"Thanks for that," she'd said to Mateo. "I worried you'd take me out of the findings."

"Why would I do that? You deserve half the credit for them." He'd nudged her with his hip and that small bit of contact left her wanting more. *Ugh*. She needed to get out and date—or just find someone, anyone, to connect with so she stopped imagining her coworker naked and interested in her.

On one hand, after the "oversharing conversation," as she dubbed it, things with Mateo were less tense. Maybe they were…friends? That created complications as well, but she didn't mind those as much as she'd anticipated.

Olivia's phone buzzed.

On my way in, can I bring you a latte? Vanilla with soy milk, right?

She couldn't contain her grin. He knew her coffee order after only two weeks working alongside him, more than half of that spent avoiding the man at all costs. He also knew she'd already be at the office, even though she wasn't scheduled for another hour.

For this past week, she'd been unable to put her imagination to rest. They'd barely agreed to be allies before he'd somehow sneaked friends into the picture, and now she couldn't help but wonder if *more* was possible. Who was this woman Mateo had unearthed? She wasn't sure, but add it to the pile of things she didn't mind anymore.

Sounds great, thanks. I'll swing by for lunch.

Deal.

"You have a boyfriend, Doc?"

Olivia looked up, the smile still plastered to her lips.

"Bilken. Hi. And, um, no. I don't." He raised his eyebrows as if he didn't believe her. She wasn't sure she believed herself. "What brings you in so early?"

All too late she saw the daisies in his hand. Her smile disappeared.

"They're fake, don't worry, but these ones don't look it, right? I just discovered them. All organic material." He held them out, but she didn't take them. "Olivia, it's been incredible being part of this team—your team. I know you think I'm too young, but I heard you and I can be the kind of man who supports you. I know I can."

They were the right words, words she'd longed to hear… from the wrong man.

"Bilken, I can't accept those."

"Because of him?" He pointed to her phone. She opened her mouth to respond, but…how? "For what it's worth, you never smile like that. Even if he's not a boyfriend, he must be special, no?"

"Hey, there," Mateo said, coming around the corner with two mugs in a drink carrier, a pastry bag on the side. The scent of vanilla and cardamom filled the office.

Olivia willed the smile from her face, but it wouldn't budge. It was so inappropriate to be smiling like an idiot while she rejected one man and another stood there with what looked like breakfast for her. And yet…

Could she have slipped into crush territory?

Dammit. That was *so* much more than inconvenient.

"Sorry to interrupt. I brought some Turkish rolls from the bakery since I figured you probably hadn't eaten yet."

And there was the question: which was more romantic? Flowers, or someone who knew her better than she knew herself?

It was no contest. Her mouth watered and stomach grumbled which it would choose, no question. She agreed, but not as anything other than an ally, or at best, a friend.

You sure? He has *stopped meeting women in the parking lot after work.*

Yeah, because she'd issued an ultimatum. It didn't mean anything more. Nor could it.

Besides, she was still, as far as she knew, competing for her job with Mateo, no matter what plan they hatched to avoid the inevitable.

"Geoff, do you mind if we pick this up later? Dr. Garcia and I have a lot to discuss."

"Sure. Yeah."

Bilken left the room, but the daisies remained. The look on Bilken's face was dejected and Olivia's chest ached. She didn't mean to hurt him but how many times was she expected to say no to a decent thing in the hopes of something *great*?

She picked up the bag of pastries.

"You sure you don't want me to leave?"

"Absolutely not. You had me at Turkish rolls."

"Okay, well, these are hot out of the oven, so I promise they're worth trading out for dinner or whatever else Bilken was offering."

Olivia's chest tightened. Why couldn't she have met a guy like Mateo outside work? Then maybe there wouldn't be this canyon of impossibility between them.

"We didn't get that far," she said.

"Sorry about that." He took one of the rolls out of the bag and ate a bite, groaning with pleasure. Olivia's stomach clenched with desire at the sound.

Knock it off, she admonished her libido.

Still, she smiled in spite of herself.

"I'm not sure if you saved the day or ruined my only chances at a date this century," she teased.

"Hopefully the former," he said and took a seat, snacking on the roll. She snatched the other one and started in on it.

Might as well; he'd brought it for her, after all.

"Mateo, this new friendship is great. Can I call it a friendship?"

He smiled and her heart leaped. She ignored the traitorous organ.

"I thought we already agreed on that."

"Good. Well, in the interest of preserving our friendship,

I want to maybe separate our days a little. You know, not do so many meals together, stop bringing each other food and treats. I don't want people to get the wrong idea."

"You mean like Bilken?"

"Maybe," she said.

His eyes widened. "Wow, so you really might say yes?"

"I mean, no, I don't think I could ever go there, but him coming by reminded me of what I do want. Romance and the whole package. And then there's Robert and what he must think about us working together. I don't think that was in his playbook."

Mateo mimed being shocked, his hand to his chest. "You don't think he had secret intentions for us to use the challenge of being pitted against each other to work together and create a super plan to not only thwart his evil ways, but solve league safety once and for all?"

She laughed, but then remembered what she'd been saying. Her heart kept getting the wrong idea, and she needed to set it straight.

"I don't. He's a snake, and I've always known it. But maybe it's not about him. I mean, I *would* like to date someone, someday, and if they think I'm with someone else, that'll add another complication to my dating life I don't need."

Oh, god. Could she sound any more ridiculous?

His smile remained. He picked up the flowers and turned them over in his hands, as if inspecting them.

"I've been thinking the same thing, actually."

"Oh." The mortification set in. This whole time, he'd been kind to her while trying to find a way to politely send her on her way. "You have?"

"Yep. And I came up with a different solution to the same concern. Wanna hear it?"

She nodded, even though a lump of flour and sugar and shame was lodged in her throat.

"I think we should lean the other way. You know, *convince* other people we are dating."

Her heart—the one that had all but sold her out moments ago—leapt with joy. She did her best to ignore it, but her curiosity was piqued.

"What could you possibly be talking about?"

"Well," he said, polishing off the last of his roll. "I was thinking about Bilken. I mean the guy has consistently brought you flowers and gifts every week for how long? Months?"

"Almost a year."

"Exactly. Without a clear signal to the contrary, he still believes he has a chance, mad optimist that he is. See where I'm going with this?" Against her better judgment, Olivia nodded. "And think of the ancillary benefits. The news will stop focusing on my string of dates and, hey, it's good publicity for men who you want to find you desirable, right? To show them how you can have fun on *and* off the field? And, with our names splashed in the news as football's hottest new couple, it'll convince Robert that he needs to keep both of us. How can he fire one of the Dynamic Duo?"

"Oh, is that our nickname?" she joked.

He pulled up his phone and showed her the latest *Sports Daily* article. Sure enough, their photo—suturing an athlete's leg—was paired with the headline "Dynamic Duo of Manchester's Medical Team Gets to Work."

"I'll bet that gave Robert a headache," she commented. "He *hates* press that reads the situation wrong. Still, he'll can one of us at a moment's notice if it saves him money."

"Maybe. On a personal note, I've got this fake dating thing down. I already bring you coffee and treats—"

"Which my running habits hate *you* for," she added. "And fake dating? You've been reading too many romances, Mateo."

He waved that off. "Or just enough. Anyway, your body is perfect and carbs help you run. C'mon, Doc. You know that."

She couldn't stop thinking about what he'd sandwiched in that sentence. Her body was *perfect*?

"Isn't it enough that we work well together?"

Mateo shrugged and eyed her roll, which she'd barely touched. She handed it over to him.

"Probably for Robert. But I was thinking about this last night—"

"You were?" That he thought of her at all outside work was surprising.

"Yeah." He teased a fabric daisy petal between his thumb and finger. Her stomach got squishy imagining him trying that on her. "And I don't like our odds. He's spending a fortune on the double roster, which we need. Which means he's going to trim where he can, even if the training protocol is necessary, too."

An invasive thought crept in, something that had been in the back of her mind since Mateo came to Manchester and had shown her another way of life, of chasing one's own passions.

Would it be the worst thing in the world if I got cut? She'd have no excuse but to find a career in medicine that let her grow roots. She wasn't convinced anymore that this was it. Instead of fear, that realization filled her with excitement. Hope.

Except…her dad would be so disappointed to lose her box seats, her connection to "his" club. And just when football was the only distraction from a serious diagnosis.

On the other hand, if she did this, the agreeing to fake date Mateo, a former footballer and Young Player of the Year, that might just be the final brick in the bridge she needed to reach her father. He'd love having a guy around to chat about the game. And she'd love having her dad around, period. While she had him. Heat pricked her eyes.

"So what does this fake dating thing look like to you?" When his grin deepened, she shook her head. "Not that I'm agreeing to this ludicrous idea." She snatched the roll back and tossed a bit in her mouth. He chuckled.

"Not *yet*. But here's what I'm thinking. We make appearances together. We mete out interest so it feels belicvable, not like we just dove head first into love with one another."

He laughed, but the term *love* in the same sentence as her and Mateo aggravated her arrhythmia.

"Classic fake dating structure," she said.

"Exactly."

"Okay. I'm with you so far. But I'm going to need something, too."

He sat back, the picture of relaxation. "Name it."

"A dinner a week with my dad. He's a fan and I don't want to get into it now, but I think if we do this, it could…help."

He eyed her as if he wanted to ask something else, but in the end, he nodded.

"Agreed. I'd like to meet the man responsible for this incredible woman I'm working with."

She shoved him playfully. "No one's around, silly. You don't have to pretend in the medical bay."

"I'm not pretending. Olivia, part of what makes this idea palatable is that I enjoy spending time with you. It's not going to be an imposition to put on a little show for the cameras to get what we both want."

"Oh. Thanks."

He tucked a strand of loose hair behind her ear.

"But what are you getting out of this?" she asked because she still hadn't figured out what he stood to gain with this little arrangement.

"The same thing as you. Robert seeing me as vital, and the

world to take me more seriously than they did when I was—what did you once call it? Chain dating?"

She laughed and nodded.

"Anyway, you were right. Hiding from relationships just because I've been burned before isn't smart. Neither is diving right back into the legit dating pool and expecting to be taken seriously. But if the world sees us together, it'll help repair that image. You, my amazing friend and ally, will be the woman who tamed the footballer."

"That even sounds like a fake dating novel's title—*The Woman Who Tamed the Footballer.*"

"See? I knew you spoke the same language I did."

She smiled, but her heart thumped a little out of rhythm. Was that language one of romance, or fooling the public with a classic rom-com trope? The answer mattered. What she'd started to feel the past week for Mateo wasn't more than a crush. But could she keep it at bay so they could pull this off?

If not, the risks would be so much worse than the reward.

"So, you in?" he asked, holding out his hand.

"I'm all in," she replied.

His smile was the brightest thing in the room, which was saying something considering the surgical-grade flood lights over the patient beds.

"Good. Then keep your evening free, Doc. I've got plans for us."

With that, he jumped up, snatched the last bite of her Turkish roll and ate it as he walked out. Just before the door, he stopped and tossed her a wink.

Oh yeah. So much more was at risk than she'd thought. Starting with her heart.

CHAPTER EIGHT

MATEO WASN'T SURE if this was the best idea he'd had, or the single worst one in history. Olivia's hand was wrapped in his and damn if it didn't feel good. *Right*.

"Okay, Garcia, you've got some explaining to do. Starting with why we just drove an hour in midday traffic to get to yet another football stadium."

Mateo glanced from the Liverpool stadium to Olivia, who was in the white blouse and jeans as he'd requested. How could this woman make a simple top and jeans look so effortlessly chic and glamorous?

He'd never tell her, but this fake dating scheme was a double ruse, to him, at least. He'd wondered what Olivia was like out of work, but hadn't felt prepared to do anything about it. Then he'd walked in and seen Bilken with her, and was compelled to act on his idiotic pipe dreams.

Which were to spend time with the enigmatic woman without scaring her off. Because he liked her, and if he was honest with himself, had from the start. Her sass, confidence, even the thin veneer she put up as a protective shell, was inviting to him. And today his half-baked plan was paying dividends, even if the scheme was an act of jealousy akin to something a teenager would pull.

"Didn't I tell you I have a plan?"

"Don't you think the type-A physician you asked on this date would want in on this plan?"

Her scent was different today. Summery and lighter, like citrus and something soft. Maybe vanilla? His mouth was suddenly parched.

"You're a better doc than you are a patient, you know that?"

She nudged him with her hip.

"Are you hoping some reporters will catch wind of this?"

"Believe it or not, I thought this idea up before we agreed to fake date," he whispered, kissing her cheek before she could argue her way out of it. An onlooker on his way into the stadium did a double take, likely recognizing one or both of them. "If anyone happens to see us enjoying time together, then it helps our plan, sure, but this is purely for fun."

Her skin flushed crimson and he longed to feel the heat he'd created. He really needed to keep his head in the game and remember that this wasn't a real relationship, just a ruse to give them both the kind of press they needed and keep them both employed.

But if he was going to set up an elaborate scheme to draw attention in all the right places, why not have it with someone who made him laugh, who was talented and kind in equal measure? Plus it was nice to clean up wounds while they talked about music and the live bands she'd taken herself to after work, or refill cotton swab containers while they chatted about the latest romance novel they were reading. She'd even suggested they read a novel at the same time and text their responses.

Pretending to be more with her was hardly a burden. In fact, it was all too real to him. Which was its own challenge he'd get around to figuring out. For now, though, when she gazed up at him, he had to defibrillate his heart into realizing to her, the date was as fake as Bilken's last bouquet.

"Okay. As long as you know a real boyfriend would buy me a bag of crisps and a fizzy drink."

"Done. And I have a condition, too." He pulled out the small paper bag he'd had tucked in his other arm and brought out a paper sign for Grayson, a Liverpool midfielder. Though they played the same position, Grayson was nothing like Mateo had been—he was clinically precise on the field, a solid midfielder, and stoic. It didn't seem like a game when the Liverpool midfielder chased a defender toward the goal, but a conquest.

Mateo might be serious now—mostly about how the game was played from a bird's-eye, strategic view—but he'd had fun once.

"What's this?" she asked.

"Something fun. I know you used to play, as did I, and our jobs don't really let us take a day off and remember why we used to like this sport."

She opened her mouth to reply.

"Or why I liked it and your dad hoped you would," he continued.

She closed her mouth and nodded. He handed her the sign and took another out for himself that simply said "Go Liv Go".

"Today, we get to just appreciate the game, the smell of the pitch in summer, and the screaming of the other fans. With no stake in the game, I might add, since our plan is to wallop Liverpool and Munich in the regular season."

She laughed and waved the paper in the air, feeling funny in a Manchester kit with a Liverpool sign in her hands. "You're surprising," she said.

He bowed and enjoyed the bubble of laughter that escaped from her. An urge to draw more of that from her bloomed in his chest.

"Do you do this for all your dates?"

Mateo took her hand and spun her around to face him. She

twirled into his arms and to anyone walking by, they likely looked like a couple in love, gazing at one another.

Does she maybe…? his heart started to ask, but Mateo shut it down. He'd barely convinced her to be allies, then thinly made the push to friends, and somehow he'd convinced her to fake date him after a couple of weeks of knowing one another.

"Can I tell you a secret? As my—" he whispered the next word "—*fake* girlfriend?"

She nodded, and a flash of color painted her cheeks.

"I don't actually date as much as others think. I get lonely and call on old friends to join me for dinners. Sometimes I jump on a dating app to find someone like me, someone who likes a little adult company at night." The pink on her cheeks deepened to Liverpool red. "But most of the time I go out for a drink and then head home—*alone*—to read a book. I just don't care what conclusions people I don't know want to draw from that. If they want to think I'm a player off the field, let them."

"A romance book, right?" she asked.

"A *romance* book," he whispered.

She laughed then, and this time, expecting it, he captured the sound in his memory so, if the ruse ended, he'd have it to call back.

"When you shared that the other night, I think I'd have been less surprised if you told me you practice suturing on child's dolls."

"Who says I don't?" He winked and she giggled, tucking into his arm as they resumed their walk to the stadium. He pulled her close, reasoning that they needed to really sell this thing if it was going to work. Or that's what he'd tell her if she asked.

"Thanks for this. I'm not guaranteeing I'll fall in love with football or anything, but it's nice to be out. With you."

"I agree. But keep your mind open. There's something

magical about twenty-two men—or women—fighting for possession of a ball that represents success. Football is graceful in a way American football or rugby can't be. You'll see."

They made their way in the queue, gave his phone to the attendant for tickets to be scanned, and found their seats. Their luck was amazing. It'd been cool that morning when he'd picked up coffee for him and Olivia, with a light cloud cover that seemed to follow the UK around each July. But the clouds had burned off and it was a mild, sunny eighteen degrees. As he'd imagined, a slight tingle washed over his skin as he took in the pitch, inhaled the scent of fresh-cut grass and cold beer.

This place smelled like home. Something he hadn't told Olivia was that not only hadn't he ever taken a date to a match, but also he hadn't been to one since his injury—not one he wasn't required to be at as the team's physician. It was too painful. This didn't hurt, though. It felt like he was on a date with someone he cared about and wanted to show the part of his life he kept hidden from the rest of the world.

"I'll be back," he told her when she was settled. "I owe my date some crisps and a fizzy drink."

An hour and two bags of crisps later, Mateo was the one laughing.

"Refer-eeeee!" Olivia screamed, standing and waving her arms in a crude gesture toward the game, specifically to where the referee stood on the pitch, holding up a yellow card. Turning to Mateo, her cheeks red with exertion, and might he say passion in her eyes, she added, "Did you see that? No wonder Bilken complains about those blokes. They're rubbish at their jobs, aren't they?"

He bristled at Bilken's name, but forced it to roll off his shoulders. Bilken wasn't by her side; Mateo was. He wasn't usually jealous, but for some reason, he couldn't help it around Olivia.

"There are some who really seem to have eyes in the backs of their heads but mostly, yeah, they're rubbish."

Someone tapped him on his shoulder. He turned and was met with wide eyes and a big smile on an older gentleman's face.

"Are you Mateo Garcia?" he asked.

Mateo nodded. "One and the same."

"Well, all right there, son. It's good to see ya round 'ere. I think Liverpool always secretly hoped after your Young Player win, you'd come up to Liverpool and our club could have ya."

Mateo had fielded numerous offers after that. Liverpool had been an appealing one in many ways.

It wasn't hard to imagine himself on the pitch below, finishing out a long, successful career with his team. But then he wouldn't be up in the stands, next to a woman he cared about, in a position where he could influence the direction of a whole league's safety. Maybe things had worked out how they were supposed to.

"Who knows what might've been," he said. "How's the club doing? I've been following a little, but I'm sure you know I moved over to Manchester."

"Team doc, right? With that lady doc?"

"My girlfriend, actually," Mateo said, feeling less and less like that was a lie. He put his arm around Olivia, who yelled at the referee again.

"Sounds like you've got it all sorted there, lad. I'll let ya enjoy the match. Glad to meet ya, like. The boys at the pub won't believe I saw ya here."

"Why don't we snap a selfie so you can prove it and parlay it into some free drinks if you're lucky."

"Ah, you youngsters and your selfies," the man chuckled. "But yeah, if you can work out how to make this camera do that, I'd appreciate it. I wouldn't mind Tom owing me a pint or two for a change."

Mateo managed to pull Olivia's attention from the match and the three of them took a picture with their fan. She laughed with the gentleman about the state of the match and how unfair the ref was being; he must be from Munich, the man offered. It was such an ordinary moment, Mateo's chest tightened.

For a brief second, worry set in.

You're still fighting for the same position, which will get messy if you're actually together.

He didn't disagree with his brain's argument, but how could he stay away when he felt this good with her?

And she wants a man with stability, who isn't traveling all the time, either, said his heart.

Keep her as a friend and let this ride out, both his brain and heart offered in unison.

Mateo tried to focus on the match and do just that, but when Olivia's hand clasped his knee at a particularly tense moment, when a Liverpool player was downed by the Munich keeper sliding into him, Mateo's heart and mind were both silenced by his body's visceral reaction.

"Do we go down there?" she asked. "We can help."

"I think they have their own physicians. We're off duty."

"About that. Who's covering training?"

"The interns have their assessment with the medical board today, so they've asked to have the field." He'd worried at first, since the team was his and Olivia's responsibility, but a day off with her was nice. Needed.

Then she looked over at him, her eyes as bright as her smile.

"Thanks," she said. "This is actually pretty great. I haven't done this—have fun—in long enough I can't remember. I like it." She turned back to the game as it picked up in intensity and added, "If the referees could stop making *shite calls*!"

He laughed, especially when the Liverpool striker shot the ref a crude gesture. She screamed with shared joy.

"That's it, you tell him, Johannes!"

Shit, he realized, sobering up. *I like this woman. Like, really, really like her.*

He'd asked her out to spend time with her, but hadn't expected the feelings to intensify so damn quickly.

It was official. Fake dating Olivia Ross was the single worst idea Mateo had ever had.

CHAPTER NINE

OLIVIA BLEW OUT a sigh of relief. The match had been tight—tense didn't begin to cover it—but in the end, no bad calls from a ref could get in the way of brilliant play from Liverpool. They squeaked by in a 3–2 win at the final whistle.

"I feel like I've been put through a cardiac cath," she said, alluding to the semi-invasive procedure they used to run a series of tests on a patient's heart health. "That was so intense."

"Same here," he said. But something about the way he was looking at her flagged her highly honed medical senses.

"Are you okay?" She put a hand to her chest, recalling the outrageous behavior she'd displayed all match. "Oh shoot. Did I embarrass you on our first date?"

"No, no, nothing like that. I had a fabulous time with you, Olivia. Maybe it's just the crisps."

She linked her arm in his and grinned up at him. "I had a great time, too. It's been a long time since I got swept up in the drama of the game. All I normally see when I'm at a match is the potential for injury and who needs what treatment and care."

They walked toward the car park, and though she was painfully aware of the man on her arm, she'd be lying if she said it felt awkward. It was actually nice, talking to that fan in the stands and watching a match with Mateo instead of inspecting every little thing he did in the medical bay to see if it was better than her protocols.

They actually had more than she thought in common and it was easy to be with him. A little too easy. She felt her heart slipping more than once into real crush territory before she shut that down and reminded herself this was all part of a pact between friends to help each other out.

"It's different as a fan, isn't it?" he asked. She nodded. Whatever shadow had crossed his face just after they left the stands was gone under the bright sun. A soft smile played on his lips.

"Truthfully, I kept picturing a young Mateo Garcia rushing the goal with defenders trailing him. I wish I'd known you when you were playing. But still, it was nice to get a behind-the-scenes look at what makes you tick. We should do it again sometime."

"And soon," he said. She couldn't agree more, not that she'd admit to that just yet.

Once they were buckled, Mateo drove them back. The conversation steered to the match, to plays that stood out and how the Munich fans were likely salty at the Liverpool win. He told her stories about some of the players he knew and she listened with rapt attention. Mateo was fun. Much more so than she'd originally assumed.

At one point, he brushed her thigh at a stoplight and she didn't flinch. She also didn't say what she was thinking—that she wanted him to leave his hand there. He was her *fake* boyfriend and getting too close to him only meant trouble, especially if one of them was cut from the club.

"Want to grab something to eat?" he asked as they passed Beetham Tower.

"I think I should head back and catch up on some reading before we officially start welcoming in the teams next week. Plus, we need to leave *something* for date two, right?"

"Yeah, right." Was it her overactive imagination, or did he seem disappointed?

She bit her tongue from changing her mind. Or telling him what she really wanted. She'd love to get dinner, but that felt too real, too soon for their ruse.

They pulled into the stadium parking lot and she hid her disappointment that the date was over.

The fake date.

"Can I tell you something?" he asked.

She nodded again. Anything to keep him talking and opening up to her. "I'm all in, remember?"

He smiled at that as he turned to look at her. It was fascinating to her how magnetic his gaze focused on her was. Each time it happened, she had to pin herself to her seat so she didn't rush him and plant a kiss on those full lips of his.

That would be awkward.

"That's the first match I've been to since I got hurt."

The breath in her lungs froze. "You never took other dates there?"

"Never."

"But why…?" Olivia couldn't finish her sentence. The weight of what he'd just shared with her—that he'd brought her to his first—was heavy enough to calm her arrhythmia. Unfortunately, it also ratcheted up her breathing.

He shrugged and took her hands. Just like that, her breath evened out as well. The man was a magician. A dangerous magician since his power over her wasn't supposed to be real.

"I've wanted to remember what I loved about the sport, before it became about staying in it at all costs. I like what I do, and think the protocol—even as expensive as it is—will save players' careers in the long run and the cost will even out as teams keep players longer."

She nodded along. She'd stopped disagreeing with him when she'd seen the numbers he produced for their meeting with Robert. He was right; his system worked. Better yet, their systems complemented each other.

"So you're saying we're protocoling ourselves out of a job in the long run," she teased.

"Maybe." The shadow in his eyes was back, turning them a deep brown with a dark black ring. "But being at Liverpool today reminded me, more than ever, what's at stake for the players we're working for. What does it look like on the pitch, not just the medical bay?"

She squeezed his hand. "Thank you for bringing me. I needed that reminder, too."

"Besides, there was no way I was starting our hand-holding in front of Robert. We needed practice," he said, grinning like he had at the start of the date.

"I dunno, I think we nailed it," she disagreed.

"We did, didn't we?"

The silence that filled the car wasn't uncomfortable or ominous, but it *was* laced with tension. The magnetic pull was back, but it didn't seem to only affect her. She'd moved closer to Mateo, but he met her over the center console. Their faces were mere inches apart and this close, she could smell his cologne—spicy and Spanish, like *ñora*—mixed with the sweetness of the espresso and cream he'd had at the match. The blend was intoxicating.

His gaze didn't leave hers, and his hand slipped around the base of her neck, his fingers tangling in her hair.

"Olivia," he said. His voice was thick and he cleared his throat. She licked her lips, her pulse somehow racing despite the slow, thick tension wrapped around them.

Please, she willed him. *Please come just a little closer.*

"I—"

Both their beepers went off, loud and intrusive. The simultaneous buzzing shocked some sense into her and she added some distance between her and Mateo.

She waited a beat before responding, even though the 999 code indicated an emergency with one of their players.

What had they almost done? Kissing in private wasn't part of the plan.

"Shit," they mumbled at the same time. She sat back in her seat and checked her cell, which she'd moved to silent. Sure enough, she had three texts from Robert. Before she opened them, she turned to Mateo.

"Can we talk about what almost happened?" she asked.

He sighed and lifted his gaze to hers. "I'm sorry. That was totally inappropriate."

"It wasn't just you, Mateo. I was locked in that moment, too. But—" She took a steadying breath. "Was this really a fake date, or is there something more here?"

Her heart answered for her, but she ignored it.

His gaze fell to his lap, his shoulders slumped. "I'd like to say the first thing, but I… I'd be lying, Olivia. If I'm being even more honest, which I kinda feel the need to be with that almost-kiss behind us, I asked you to fake date me because I… I wanted real time with you. I'm sorry I lied to you."

"You never meant it?" she asked. "Fake dating me?"

Mateo shook his head. "Not the fake part. How do you feel? Want to give this a try for real, or just go back to being friends?"

She bit the inside of her cheek. What dumb, awful luck to find someone she could laugh and talk medicine with, someone connected to football, someone she was magnetically attracted to…only to have him be the one person she couldn't date.

"I know I'll regret this later, but—" she swallowed hard "—I don't know that I'd ever relax around you if I thought one day you'd have to choose between the job and me. I'm too new to this to think my heart would take that rejection well."

"You act like I'd choose the job in a heartbeat, Olivia. I mean, this might sound crazy after only knowing you a couple of weeks, but at least give me the chance to surprise you, to pick you if that's what it came to."

Her pulse fluttered, and she was hit with the familiar feeling of being breathless when her body experienced an arrhythmia spell. She inhaled deeply, but this wasn't an attack that would abate quickly.

"So, what's the alternative? That you leave the club because you let Manchester choose me instead? Then we're apart either way. I just don't see a way this works, especially, like you said, with us just getting to know each other."

Their beepers went off again.

"I'm gonna chuck this thing into the canal," Mateo grumbled.

"Let's check in with Robert and maybe we can finish this?"

They got out of the car and on the way in, Olivia called the club owner.

"What happened?" she asked when he answered. "We just got back into town."

"Are you close to the stadium?" he asked.

"We're *at* the stadium."

"We?" Robert asked.

She winced, grateful he couldn't see her face at the moment. "Dr. Garcia and I."

There was silence on the other end and finally Robert said, "I'm heading out to meet you, but head toward the med bay."

Olivia hung up and filled Mateo in. They strode down the sterile hall that was eerily quiet for being early evening.

Robert met them at the entrance and led them back to the bay. "You two were out together?" he asked.

"A research trip," Mateo muttered. "To check out the protocol up at Liverpool."

Robert's eyes flitted between them. "And that's why those couple photos cropped up on the *Manchester Evening News*?"

"Photos?" Olivia asked.

Mateo already had his phone out and when his eyes went wide and his face lost its color, she knew. It had to be bad. He flipped the phone to her and she couldn't help the small, audible gasp that escaped.

There was the selfie they'd taken with the fan, but that was to be expected. Heck, it was part of why they'd taken it. Before the kiss had thrown their plan into dangerous territory.

But the kiss…some reporter must have followed them to the Manchester car park because accompanying the selfie was a zoomed in photo of the near-kiss. Olivia's skin warmed as she recalled it. They looked ready to jump one another. The headline was the worst.

"The Dynamic Duo Dating?" it read.

They'd hoped their plan would generate news, but who knew it would be that successful, and just as they'd slammed on the brakes. This was messy and she didn't do messy. She barely did simple and clean.

"We can explain," Mateo said.

Robert shook his head. "Another time. Right now we've got a downed player and the board has asked the interns not to take it for liability reasons. EMTs are tied up at the north end of the city for a riot. It'll be twenty more minutes at least to get help here."

"Good thing we were back," Olivia said. This was what mattered. The job. Anything else was just a distraction, and though Mateo was a delicious distraction in theory, he couldn't be more. That much was obvious. "What can we do?"

Robert pushed through the stainless steel doors they'd installed to separate the triage room from the rest of the med bay and pointed to the body lying supine on the medical bed. A few interns and PTs gathered around him, and one of them held the player's hand.

When she got closer, she blanched.

It was Bilken, and his tibia was sticking out through his skin, which was mottled and white around the injury site.

"What the actual hell happened?" she asked. "Today was supposed to be light training." She pushed everyone aside and used the back of her hand to wipe away the sweat that beaded on Bilken's forehead.

"I was pissed, went too hard."

This was her fault. She'd rejected him and he'd gone and pushed too hard. To top it off, she hadn't been here to help because she was out on a *date*.

He looked so small, so fragile, so young on the table. A surge of maternal affection swelled for her player.

"I need everyone but Robert and Mateo to get out and let me set this before he loses blood flow to his leg."

"You don't want to transport him first?"

Olivia dropped her voice at the same time Bilken's eyes rolled back in his head. "No time. Look at his vitals. Something's pinching off the blood flow. We can reset in surgery if we need to."

Everyone shuffled toward the exit while Olivia gloved up.

"Don't worry, Geoff," she said, using his first name as she filled a syringe with local anaesthetic. "This is going to hurt, but it's to help me save your leg. I need you to focus on that poster over there on the wall and squeeze Dr. Garcia's hand if you need to. Can you do this for me?"

Bilken groaned but gave a subtle nod. They were losing him.

"Mateo, Robert, I need you over here. Robert, hold his hips. I can't have him bucking while I set this. Mateo—"

But Mateo was already gloved up and pinning down the player's shoulders. He had nitrous oxide over Bilken's nose and mouth, not near what he'd need to avoid feeling anything, but enough to override the worst of it. At the least, it would get him calmed enough to get his blood pressure under control. If they didn't set this soon, he'd go into shock and the risk of losing a limb—or his life—increased tenfold.

"Okay, team," she said, the syringe at the injury site, another on the surgical tray beside her at the ready. She injected both into the area around the exposed flesh and bone, knowing even combined with the nitrous oxide, they'd only dampen the pain Bilken was about to experience. "Let's make sure this guy starts the season next year, shall we? On three."

She grabbed a scalpel and pushed it against the knee.

"One...two..." And then she sliced.

CHAPTER TEN

MATEO DIDN'T KNOW what to do with the woman at Bilken's bedside. Olivia had brought him a paper bouquet of flowers for his bedside table, an inside joke between her and the player. Mateo warmed at her thoughtfulness, even if a shadow of jealousy lingered from earlier. She might seem cold or unfeeling at times, but he saw the front for what it really was—she actually cared too much.

"So, you and Doc?" Bilken had asked when he woke up.

"No comment," she said. Robert arrived and called Mateo out into the hall.

"So you two are dating, huh?" Robert asked Mateo when they left the room. Wow. The whole world seemed to know what he and Olivia still hadn't figured out yet.

Mateo shot her a glance, but she was focused on the patient's chart. They'd had a rough time setting the bone enough that Bilken could get transported, but he was stable now, at least. His recovery would be hard, but Olivia was a miracle worker and had managed a complicated surgery that went from a simple bone set to a complex blood loss. Thankfully, by the time Bilken decompensated, medical services had arrived to assist.

"Like I said, boss, it's not like it seems," Mateo started.

That wasn't exactly the truth—what it seemed from the photos was that the couple had actually fallen for one another.

Maybe not *love*, but there was so much actual attraction in the photo, it was palpable.

He still felt her silken hair wrapped around his fingers.

Robert regarded him, and then the barest hint of a smile flicked the corner of his mouth.

"I don't like being surprised," he started. Mateo didn't imagine he did. "But, as long as it doesn't get in the way of your work, this isn't a bad look for the team. I've already had emails in the past hour from *Sports Daily* and *London Times* to do an op-ed on your partnership, which started with the tournament and League One acquisition. It's all positive press so far. But the minute that changes, we're back to the original game plan."

Meaning one of the docs was out of a job.

Mateo considered how to respond. Telling the truth was off the table, as was the result of their fake-ruse-gone-rogue— breaking up and staying colleagues.

Which left only one option. Going along with the ruse a little longer. He could bury his feelings beneath his pervasive need to stay in the game, right? He'd done it before.

"Thanks, sir," Mateo hedged. A visceral need to talk to Olivia alone propelled him forward. It would all go to hell if she betrayed that they'd agreed not to date. "I'm gonna chat with Olivia about a treatment plan for Bilken and we'll update you as necessary. We should chat about another starter, though. None of the League One guys have been part of those plays on the pitch."

"I'll talk to Liam. Thanks." Robert left, his signature frown back in place.

When he'd departed, Mateo touched Olivia's elbow. "We need to talk," he said.

She held up the X-ray she'd taken after she'd set the tibia and closed the wound.

"I'd say. Look at this; we're damn good. He's not only

going to recover, but he'll play again." Her smile was as big as it'd been at the match earlier and his own blossomed.

"You're amazing. But listen, about Robert."

"It's fine. I'll just tell him I'm sorry, we had a weak moment. He'll forget about the photo in a week."

"You can't do that," Mateo said.

She put down the X-ray and raised her eyebrows at him. "Why not?"

"Because he likes the two of us together. He's got press ops lined up and story requests are flooding his inbox. I'd say we keep this going—just small, public appearances—for a little while. Then we can make it look like we broke up amicably over time. By then, he'll see how well we work together and he'll forget to chop off one of our heads."

"What about—" Her cheeks reddened.

"The fact that we almost made out in the car park? Or my attraction to you in jeans and a Liverpool kit?" he teased. She stuck her tongue out at him. He laughed. "We're adults. We can do this. Haven't you ever been attracted to someone you knew wouldn't work?"

She frowned. "No, but I know what it's like to fake loving something for someone else."

"Your dad?" he asked. She nodded.

"How's he doing?" She bit her bottom lip and tears sprang to her eyes. She shook her head. "I'm sorry. We can unpack that later. As for this whole 'pretend we're together' thing, if there was another way, believe me, I'd take it. But Robert took the bait and we have to follow through." He paused and picked up the X-ray, grateful to have something to do with his hands. "Don't we?"

She took the scan back from him. "I need to write up my notes about Bilken and make a treatment plan for him once he's out of the ICU…" She trailed off.

Olivia pinched the bridge of her nose and sighed. If this

were a real relationship, he'd do anything he could to ease the discomfort she so clearly felt. But that wasn't his responsibility. Or was it? Only one thing was absolutely clear after their near-kiss. He liked the woman, whether or not he was supposed to.

The tournament was just a week away, his career was under a spotlight, and he'd gone and fallen for his competitor.

Rookie mistake, indeed.

Mateo's skin itched. His whole life, he'd prided himself on putting his dreams and goals above any other desires he might have had. And he'd achieved most of them. Become a professional footballer? *Check*. Sign with a Premier League team? *Check*.

Even when those dreams had fallen apart, he'd pivoted and made new goals.

Go to medical school. *Check*. Sign on as a physician to a Premier League team. *Check*. Create a protocol for the health and safety of players so no one had to endure what he had? *Check*.

He'd even coached secondary school football to pay for medical school once his football career ended and savings ran out. Nothing had gotten in his way. Until Olivia.

If she didn't agree, everything he'd worked for might disappear as quickly as his career had ended. Worse, he'd have played his one hand with her and lost before he'd even had a real chance to make things work.

"I'll tell you what," he said, taking her hand and squeezing it. "Why don't you meet me on the pitch after our team meeting? We can talk then."

They had a final club discussion before the teams started arriving for the competition Manchester was hosting. Nerves bundled in his stomach the way they used to before a big match.

"Yeah, that sounds good." Her smile was tight, and her

eyes looked tired. It'd been a long day, and a long couple weeks.

"I'm sorry this all happened. I didn't mean to complicate things," he said.

"It's not your fault. To be honest, I thought it would work, too. But if I've learned anything in the first thirty-odd years of my life, it's that the easy way out is usually anything but."

Her words sounded laced with experience and residual hurt. One more thing he understood on a cellular level. In a different world, he and Olivia might actually be good together.

"I agree. Again, sorry. I'll see you tonight?" he asked. She nodded.

The meeting was painful, as Mateo thought it might be. Two hours of going over every meticulous detail of the plan with the whole club—trainers and managers included. Some players would be starting, others would sub in, but since the rules of professional football play dictated that a player couldn't reenter the field of play once they'd been brought off, there was a lot of pushback from the team's first string about being brought off before they were ready.

Robert had watched the whole time from the back, as had Liam. This was where Mateo's plan got dicey. There was no way, really, to see if it worked, except over time if they logged fewer injuries overall. But there were other factors; even a fresh player was susceptible to injury the moment they stepped on the pitch for practice or a match.

Jonesie had asked about that. "How ya gonna notice if it's working?" he asked.

Mateo felt Olivia's body tense as they stood shoulder to shoulder.

"You should suffer fewer injuries overall and your muscles will recover from strenuous play quicker, so along with our other strength training and safety measures, we should see you not only playing injury free for longer, but playing stronger, too."

"So it's like giving the kitchen floor a sweep? If I do it right, me mam won't notice. But if I screw it up, it'll be obvious."

The club laughed, but Mateo nodded. "Yeah. That's exactly it."

"Would this have helped Bilken?" the keeper, Harlow, asked.

A question that reminded Mateo of his own career-ending injury and the what-ifs that still haunted him.

"Maybe," he said. "Listen, there is no magical cure-all pill we can take to prevent injury in professional sports."

"If there was, Maradona would have taken four," a second-stringer called out from the back. The room rumbled with quiet laughter.

"All we can do," Mateo continued, "is look at why we're getting hurt, and how often, and make safe choices that counteract that. This is one of those choices, difficult as it may be for us to adapt our way of thinking."

There had been some subtle nods at that, but there were still so many stoic, angry faces out there.

"Why didn't Doc Ross think of this, then? She's been here forever."

An urge to wrap a protective arm around Olivia surged wild in his chest, but before he could jump in, she spoke.

"A good question. Like Dr. Garcia said, there's no one way of working a medical protocol, especially for a kinetic team in the Premier League—which we intend to be throughout this season, right, lads?"

That had rallied some of the quieter players, but there was still a pervasive heaviness in the room.

She grew serious then. A professional like he'd seen in her from day one in the medical bay. Why did the world only see the fun-loving, trash-talking side when she had so many facets to her? It made good TV, sure, but she was an experienced doctor and a damn good one at that.

"I run my show differently than Dr. Garcia—that's not up for debate. I focused on training, rather than matches. Maybe that worked, maybe it didn't. I operate with what I know at the time, and right now, this new system seems like a good fit for our club, given the number of overuse injuries I've treated. Liam and I have worked on similar systems in the past, so he and I are supportive of Dr. Garcia's protocol. Even if you don't agree with it now, we hope you get on board. It's about keeping you in the game long term, gentlemen."

Olivia gave him a subtle nod, which he returned. He couldn't have said it better himself.

You don't have to. You just have to prove her right.

After that, it was more of the same, until no more hands were raised. The faces looked as concerned as he felt. Robert's included.

He approached Mateo after the rest of the crowd had dissipated, including Olivia, who'd excused herself to grab water. "I trust you, Mateo, but you'll understand that if this doesn't work, we'll have to make some changes pretty quickly to keep our season going smoothly."

It wasn't a question.

"I understand. We've got this." He cringed inwardly at the *we* he'd used.

"I believe you do. Now, get some rest. The first team arrives before dawn and I want you all ready to perform."

Rest. What was that? No way he was getting any tonight. But Olivia could. He pulled out his phone to text her a cancelation for their meetup that evening,

I'm on the field, a text from her read.

Sighing, he made his way to the pitch. The lights were still on, and would be for another half hour.

"What made you say all that?" he called.

Olivia didn't answer. She faced the stands, and he could tell from where he stood, halfway to midfield, that her arms were crossed. Mateo inhaled deep the smell of the turf. It was thick, as was the air. A shiver rolled over him; the last of a British chill lingered. In August, he knew they'd be wishing for the chill to return, but for now, he longed for the heat on his skin.

Nights like this, he missed home. His mother. He inhaled again and could almost smell her *sudado de pollo*.

Olivia turned to face him. The lights shone on the damp streaks tracing her cheekbones and jaw.

He used the pad of his thumb to dry both sides.

"I believe what you told me, what the reports say. I don't know how I missed it, but I did. This will work, Mateo."

"You're Team Mateo?" he asked, referring to how the team had taken sides.

She smiled and sniffled at the same time. The effect was adorable.

"I've got two medical degrees and can extrapolate data. But I'm not pinning on a Mateo button or anything."

"Two?" He whistled. "Now you're just bragging."

"Anyway," she said, laughing, "we're on the same team. We might have to do some shady stuff to make others believe that, but I don't need to fake date you to believe it myself. I'm mature enough to eat crow when I've earned it."

"Can I get that in writing?"

Her laughter rose in pitch. She looked...*happy*. Or at least less miserable. He felt a measure of pride at being responsible for the change.

He glanced to his left and saw one of the footballs hadn't been returned after training. He jogged over and dribbled it back to Olivia.

"Show me your skills, Doc."

Olivia lunged for the ball, but was too slow. He wove around her, then kicked the ball in the air, juggling it.

"Now who's showing off?"

Mateo paused, the ball delicately balanced on the edge of his trainer.

"Oh, this?" he asked. The light danced in her eyes. She bit her bottom lip and he dropped the ball. "You haven't seen anything yet, sweetheart."

"Sweetheart? I haven't agreed to this ruse again yet."

He shrugged, juggling the ball again.

"I don't actually want it to be a ruse. I think we've shown we've got chemistry. Let's see where it goes." This time, he added some tricks his old manager in Colombia taught him. The man had been a football genius. If there were degrees in managing ball play, Torres would have had far more than two.

"Fancy," she said, kicking off her heels and ignoring his suggestion. "Can you keep it from me?"

"Are we doing this?" he asked. "'Cause I don't think you want to take me on the pitch."

"The pitch, the medical bay. I'll challenge you anywhere you want, Garcia."

He smiled, imagining that. *Anywhere?* His libido was shameless.

"Deal," he said, dropping the ball on the damp turf and skirting to Olivia's left. He took off down the pitch at half speed, but that was still enough to stay out of reach. So he slowed just enough for her to catch him. "You've gotta be quicker than that, Doc. You sure you ever played?"

She scoffed.

He passed the ball through her legs and she squealed as he picked her up, moved her out of the way, and deposited her a few yards down the pitch. All while dribbling the ball.

"You're *cheating*."

"I dunno. We didn't set rules, did we?"

He kicked the ball back in the air, but kept his gaze pinned to Olivia's.

"No," she said. She was breathless, her hair wild in the damp air, and her eyes issuing more of a challenge than her words had. "We didn't. Do we need to?" she asked.

They weren't talking about football anymore. Or medicine. Or anything work related.

He let the ball drop. They inhaled together, their breaths evenly matched. Mateo put a tentative hand on her hip, drawing her closer. His brows rose in question. She nodded a response.

"It'll rain tonight," he said. His voice felt as thick as the air.

"No. The forecast didn't predict that."

He'd gotten used to feeling the weather out, literally. It'd helped him make some pretty close calls that had kept his players safe, knowing the weather they'd play in.

"You want to test me on this, too, Doc?"

As if she finally understood, she shook her head and inhaled deeper. She shivered. The arm not wrapped around her rubbed her exposed upper arm in an attempt to warm her. It only served to heat up a different part of his own anatomy.

So much for being a mature adult who could bury his feelings.

"Mmm. It does." He wrapped the other arm around her waist, nestling his hips against hers. "So, what do you say? Wanna actually try this thing?"

"For real?" She gestured with her chin at their embrace.

"I'm going to be straight with you, Olivia. I'm fully aware of the reasons we wouldn't work, but I am also fully attracted to you. Am I completely misreading things thinking you might be attracted to me, too?"

"No. You're not misreading anything."

She shivered again and he tightened his embrace.

"Okay, so can we act on these...*reactions* while keeping our eyes and hearts open?"

Just saying it out loud made him laugh.

She smiled. "If we're honest the whole way through. If it doesn't work, we pull back."

"I like that." He liked all of that except the idea of pulling back. Right now, in her arms, he thought he understood why it'd never worked with anyone else. Olivia was his *equal*.

"So, maybe we at least agree to some rules before things get confusing."

He nodded. Yeah, rules for not letting his feelings spiral out of control while he was sleeping with an attractive, brilliant, sexy, fun woman. What kind of rules were there for that?

"Okay, lay them on me," he said. Maybe Olivia had a better sense of how to do this.

Her grin kicked up on one side, wicked and delicious. She leaned up, barely needing to stand on her toes to reach him, and kissed him.

It was brief, perfunctory, but damn...

He felt lit up from the inside, as if he'd discovered electricity at that moment.

"That's not what I meant," he whispered. Forget thick—his voice was one step above baritone.

"Did you mind it?" she asked. Before she could think for a second he didn't want her with every cell in his body, he took her mouth with his and their lips parted, both eager to taste the other. Her tongue tangled with his before he pulled back.

"I don't mind, but tell me now if this isn't in the rule book."

Olivia smiled at him, and it was as if the ground trembled under the turf.

"Anything goes on the football pitch," she said, echoing six of his first words to her the day they'd met.

Oh, man. He had a feeling, as Olivia's hands slid up the

back of his shirt, raking her nails across his skin, that he'd have to rethink a lot of things now.

"But off the pitch, so to speak, we keep separate from work, right? We don't let this interfere with the team."

"Of course," he said, sliding his own hands between her pencil skirt and her skin. Was she not wearing panties? He was hard in seconds.

He could—would—keep work separate. That would be easy…right? Then Olivia's mouth was on his again and he couldn't remember why it mattered.

CHAPTER ELEVEN

OH, GOD. I'M KISSING Mateo-freaking-Garcia.

Olivia's first thought was what her father would think. Well, not first, but it did flit into her mind before Mateo's tongue teased hers out and his teeth raked along her bottom lip.

Then all she could think about, want, see was the man in front of her. For the first time in her life, she put everything else aside and was fully, wholly in the present.

Which meant she felt each of Mateo's fingers as they pressed against her shoulder blade, tasted the sweet cream of the decaf coffee he'd nursed through the meeting. She could also appreciate the length of his erection pressed against her core. She shivered, but it had nothing to do with the temperature.

When a raindrop landed on her forehead, she pulled away from the kiss.

"You're a magician," she teased.

"Oh, I've been told I have magic hands before," he teased back.

She laughed, her head thrown back. "I'm not sure if you're arrogant or just brimming with earned confidence."

"Care to find out?" He kissed the base of her neck as three more raindrops landed on her skin.

She pushed him away. "Yes, but not here. I meant you're a magician because you called the weather better than Gus on BBC."

Mateo had so many smiles she struggled to catalog them all. There was his thin-lipped one when he was about to contradict someone—usually her. Then there was the soft smile he wore as he worked and thought no one was looking in the medical bay. But this? The positively wicked, full-teeth smile? She hadn't seen it outside the time she spent alone with him and she tucked it away to recall later.

"Let's get this lady to dry land. My place or yours?" he asked.

She met his mischievous smile with her own. "I've got a better idea." If they were going to do this—and she still couldn't believe they were, but that was future Olivia's problem—they might as well have a little fun. "Come with me."

"Oh, that's the plan, but where are we going?" he asked.

Who knew the staunch, serious physician could be such a flirt?

She stopped under the stadium tunnel nearest the exit to the stadium and wheeled on Mateo. Her skin prickled with anticipation.

"*Here?*" he asked. "What about cameras?"

She shook her head. "Not outside the changing rooms."

"Um," Mateo said. "Still…"

"I thought anything goes—"

He tickled her side, eliciting a higher-pitch squeal than she imagined herself capable of.

"I didn't mean hot sex with the doc." He glanced around, then shook his head and pulled her into his chest. "But why not?"

With that, he unleashed on her just as a torrential downpour began on the pitch.

His hands clasped the base of her jaw, his thumb traced her cheekbone and his lips covered hers. When he pinned her against the wall, she moaned.

"Yes," she whispered. "Please."

It was pleasure unlike she'd ever known, just to feel this man, this athlete, against her. She knew anatomy, especially the specific anatomy of a world-class athlete—she'd made it her specialty in school. But Mateo broke all the rules.

He was all hard edges and strength, but with enough give that she melted into him. His chest was a wall of heat she clung to for warmth, though her body's shivers weren't at all from the cool rain making a privacy sheet around them.

She ran her hand under his shirt, sliding across his abdominal muscles. These weren't the young muscles of a twenty-something athlete. No, Mateo was forged man and steel. His muscles had muscles on them.

Testing how functional his physique was, she lifted a leg and wrapped it around his waist. He ground his hips against her and growled. Her stomach flooded with liquid heat that only intensified as he slid his hand over the small of her back. He undid a zipper and tugged, and the skirt fell to her ankles, exposing her hips and butt.

"Let me in," he whispered against her flesh. His breath both warmed her skin, then cooled it as his lips traced a path along her collarbone, her neck and her jawline.

She opened up for him, hooking her other leg around his hip. He rocked against her center, his warm-up suit not leaving much to the imagination. When the time came, he would fill her completely. She clung to him, using the wall behind her for support. He braced himself with one arm, then used the other to slip two fingers between her wet folds.

She moaned, the pleasure so intense it almost sent her over the edge immediately. When his fingers slipped inside her, teased her bud, she cried out.

"Oh, God, yes!"

Okay, the jury was in. His muscles weren't just for show. This man knew how to use each and every one. God, what he must have been like on the football pitch. For a moment,

Olivia felt a pang of regret for the sport that would never know his talents. In a flash, she viscerally understood the importance of his protocol trial.

He was a brilliant physician, a damn good colleague, but that'd been a second calling. He'd been ripped from the sport he loved because of an injury and now only wanted to protect others from the same dismal fate.

"Come here," she said, unhooking herself and standing on her own. She leaned up and kissed him thoroughly, deeply.

"What was that for?" he asked, pulling back. "Not that I'm complaining or anything."

"I just wanted you to know I like this. I like…you." Heat spread across her cheeks. "Not that I'll admit that to Robert, but I'm not as pissed to be working with you anymore."

"High praise," he said, his smile wide. "But I'm glad. I like you, too, Olivia."

Her stomach tightened.

Why couldn't she just give him the praise he deserved? He was a hard worker, had reinvented himself and was devoted to a sport that had tried to ruin him. But saying that, and how much she'd learned in the short time they'd known one another, was too close to real feelings and she couldn't be sure what she'd do with those.

Eyes open, they'd agreed to. And hers were.

Her hands were wrapped around his waist, his lower back as taut as the rest of him.

"You know, you could afford to eat a cookie or two," she teased. Anything to take the pressure off the way the conversation was headed. She tried to pinch his side, but nothing was there except hard flesh. All she got for her efforts was a playful nibble of her earlobe.

He trailed his tongue along the base of her neck and whispered, "What if I eat something else instead?"

Olivia barely had time to gasp with excitement before she

was laid out on the bench along the hallway, Mateo between her knees. He slid hands along her thighs, until he got to her ankles. He pushed them open and dived into her folds. Using his tongue and fingers, he toyed with her sensitive core, teasing it until she writhed with desire.

She could handle this distraction from real feelings. As far as she was concerned, a successful tournament from a medical perspective, and a few well-timed orgasms were all she could ask of this man.

"I want you inside me," she said. Had she ever been so bold with a lover before? She didn't think so, but Mateo's wicked grin as he gazed up from between her legs meant she didn't care. He made her want to say just what she desired because he'd give it to her.

"Oh, that's happening, but not until you're screaming my name." With that, he dipped his tongue until it was pressed against her sensitive spot. What he'd been doing before was half-effort compared to now. He sucked and pulled at her, drawing her closer to sweet release. Her hands were tangled in his hair, which was peppered silver along the sides. God, this man was handsome. And he was talented. And kind, and brilliant, and—

He thrust two fingers inside her and she forgot everything else.

"Mateo," she groaned. He sucked on her core harder, flicked her center in a tempo that rose in climax just as she did. "Mateo," she said, louder this time. He increased his pace, thrust his tongue inside her. "Mateo!" she finally screamed.

Her body tightened and she spasmed, an orgasm rolling through her. Only then did Mateo kiss his way up to her lips.

"I like my name on your lips."

"I like your lips between my legs," she said. Her voice had a far-off, dreamlike quality about it. She'd feel sleepy, sated, if he'd been anyone else she'd shared that with. But for some reason, coming at his hands and mouth only increased her want for the man.

Mateo laughed, but she shook her head.

"Mmm-hmm. No laughing. Only nakedness. Now." She sat up and tugged at his pants until a screech whined through the din and roar of the storm outside, stealing her attention. His, too.

It sounded like twisting metal, then a crash exploded in the night. Everything went eerily silent after that. Only the patter of rain on the roof of the arena let Olivia know she could still hear.

"What was that?" Mateo asked. He stood and she followed, feeling vulnerable in only a blouse. She tugged her skirt up and shook her head.

"I don't know. It sounded like a car crash."

She was already throwing on her shoes when he looked back toward the medical bay.

"That wasn't a car. It sounded like a bus or transport truck."

Olivia's eyes lit up, her body a live wire between the mind blowing sex she'd just had and the realization that followed.

"The Italian team." She glanced at her watch. "Lazio was supposed to arrive around now."

Olivia called 999, alerting them about where to roughly go. Then she and Mateo sprinted through the training room and back to the medical bay. Mateo filled three duffel bags with gauze, bandages and antiseptic, while Olivia filled a cart with blankets and tarps. She threw on a pair of warm-up pants and a sweater. The rain still came down heavily, and the sky was pitch-black, save for the limited streetlamps along the street behind the stadium.

Last minute, she threw some torches in the cart and headed for the door behind Mateo.

"We should call Robert," Mateo called back to her.

"I will once we see what's going on. I don't—" She cut herself off when they rounded the corner. Rain fell in heavy sheets around them, making it hard to see more than a few feet in front of her. But what she could see was horrific.

A bus lay on its side, the front crunched against the parking garage. A long line of asphalt was stained with tire tread, bags, and bodies. The bus must've rolled and slid for twenty meters before it crashed into the garage. The pale blue bags and bus meant she was, unfortunately, right.

The Lazio club had arrived, but not at all how they were supposed to.

Only then did the noises break through the warning bells in her mind. Shouts, other people running out of their apartment buildings to see what had happened and, in the distance, sirens headed their way.

But it wouldn't be enough. Not if five emergency transport vehicles showed up.

"Let's triage, Mateo. But call 999 back and let them know to send reinforcements for more than twenty injured. Tell them to hurry."

Mateo nodded and whipped out his phone, sheltering it from the rain. "I'll fill Robert in, too."

She thanked him and then put the nosy neighbors to work building tent structures for rain protection and bringing extra supplies.

This was going to be a long night and they needed all the help they could get if they were going to save the lives of their visiting team.

As Olivia looked over at Mateo, who was already kneeling in front of his first patient, she couldn't help but breathe a little easier. With him by her side, they could do this. The only question was—had they gotten there in time?

CHAPTER TWELVE

MATEO WIPED THE rain from his eyes. When he brought his hand back, it dripped a muted red. There was so much blood. This was his third patient and each was as bad as the last. The rain looked like it'd caused the bus to tip—likely because it couldn't slow down on the wet asphalt. The players on the left side of the bus were worse, but a few who'd been thrown from the windows were the most critical. Mateo thought they'd all been seen and triaged by him or Olivia, but he couldn't confirm.

A scream tore out as he pressed the gauze to the gaping wound on the patient's abdomen. He didn't know the Italian player except from an article in the sports section of the *Times* from last year. The kid was young, his whole career in front of him, and he'd brought a young wife and newborn child with him from Ghana.

Mateo shivered. The sirens screamed closer, more of them than before.

Thank God.

Mateo called out to the man from the apartment closest to the crash site. He'd run over and offered to help in any way they needed him. Since he hadn't fainted at the sight of the carnage, Mateo had assigned him to grab supplies and clear the field. Two other men were erecting park tents over the two docs.

"Grab me that blue bag."

The man, his unofficial scrub nurse, did as instructed.

"I've taken three medical training courses. I know the name of some of the stuff in there," he told Mateo.

"Good. I need the compression bandages and more gauze. What's your name?"

Mateo's patient was unconscious, but stable. Keeping his right-hand man calm was his next priority after making sure the Italian player wouldn't bleed out on his watch. He wouldn't leave just a career behind; the man had a family. The stakes were so much more dire than just a game.

Mateo glanced over at Olivia, who was loading another player on a stretcher. She'd already attached a neck brace, so there must be reason to think there was spinal damage. She looked calm, composed, and in charge, even as her sweater and body were soaked through. Thank goodness she was his partner in this. They might not always agree on player protocol, but he couldn't ask for a more competent trauma medic in an emergency.

"Mike."

"Nice to meet you, Mike. Listen, can you run over to that woman there—her name is Dr. Olivia Ross. Ask her what she needs. I'm good here for a bit."

Mike nodded and took off.

Mateo wrapped the gauze and compression bandage around the patient's abdomen and checked his pulse. It was weak but steady and hadn't decompensated since he started triage. It was as good an outcome as they could ask for.

Those emergency rigs better hurry the hell up.

Mike came running back over. "Dr. Ross is good. She says she ran the triage and there aren't any fatalities as far as she can tell. But the driver sustained a head injury and needs to be extracted from the site. She said to tell you she's headed there now."

"Thanks, Mike. Are you training to be an AAP?" Mateo

had trained as an associate ambulance practitioner during med school.

"An air ambulance staff."

"You'll be good at it. Find me if you need any recommendations."

Mike smiled, threw his shoulders back.

"Can you sit with this kid and make sure he's stable?" Mateo asked him.

"Of course. I've got this."

Mateo believed he did. "If his pulse gets thready, call me back over." He took off toward the front of the bus, his feet splashing in ankle-deep puddles. This weather wasn't helping anything.

"Olivia?" he called.

"Up here."

He glanced up and saw her head protruding from the window above him. The bus lay on its left side, so the driver's-side window was two and a half meters up. It was also smashed into the concrete garage, leaving broken glass in the path.

"Be careful. Watch for shards of glass."

"I'm fine, but I need you in here. I can't lift him out safely and he's got a bleed I can't easily reach."

"Do you want to wait for the medics?"

Something shifted inside the bus, and a loud crash echoed off the walls of the garage. A couple surprised screams from inside the vehicle sent Mateo's pulse racing.

"Olivia, are you okay?"

"I'm fine. Just a bin that fell. It doesn't look like it hit anyone in here. I need to get this bleed. His pulse is weak and he's unresponsive. Medics can move him, but I have to get him stable."

Mateo came around the side of the bus, and save for the

windshield, which was a horror show of splintered glass and twisted metal, he couldn't see a way into where Olivia was.

"Dammit," Mateo muttered. They needed to get the driver out safely, but they weren't AAP personnel. They didn't have extraction equipment. "Where are those rigs?"

As if they'd sped up at his bequest, three ambulances rounded the corner.

"Olivia, I'm passing you a kit. Try and apply pressure to the wound while I tell the AAPs where we're at with the victims."

"Go. I'll be okay. But Mateo?"

He paused, his own pulse anything but weak at the sound of urgency in her voice.

"Hurry back."

"I will," he promised.

Mateo flagged an ambulance for the driver and passengers still trapped inside the bus. This wreck was horrific. The bus must not have been able to slow much at all coming off the motorway with the torrent of rain that fell out of nowhere.

"Who's lead doc on-site?" one of the AAPs asked Mateo.

"I am, and so is the physician inside the crash site. She and I are the team physicians for Manchester and were working late when we heard the crash. This is the team that's supposed to be arriving for a week-long tournament."

"Damn. Okay. Did you do a field assessment?"

Mateo nodded and told the medic what had occurred, who was in more dire need of transport and care, and anything else he'd observed, including Mike's assistance.

"You guys saved a lot of lives tonight," the medic said. He gestured to the crash site, debris everywhere, victims moaning with pain, others unconscious and in need of the immediate care wouldn't abate.

Mateo let that sink in. He'd not had two seconds to process their impact—or the impact to them. But a flash of pride warmed him in the downpour.

He might've brought joy to fans as a professional footballer, but as a medic, he was exacting real change. He couldn't forget that, not even as he was overwhelmed by thoughts of the beautiful woman he still tasted on his lips.

He'd have to tread carefully there. Speaking of Olivia...

"Do you have everything you need?" Mateo asked the medic. "I have to get back to Dr. Ross. We could use your help, too, if they can spare it."

"You sure you're up for more?" the medic asked.

"Of course. You need the help and these guys are ours. We owe it to them."

"Give me a sec to relay this to the team, and I'll meet you there. Be careful, though. That bus looks stable for the most part, but you don't know what happened to the inside. There could be exposed wires and protruding metal."

Mateo nodded. And Olivia was right in the belly of it.

"You're okay without me here?"

"You did your part. Help her till we get there, but man...?" Mateo turned around. "Thanks," the medic said.

"It's the job." He rounded the corner and heard a muffled cry. "Olivia? How's it going in there? What can I do?"

The rain pounding against the metal made it hard to hear her reply.

"Olivia, I need you to yell. I can't hear you out here."

"I need a light and cauterizing wand. I'm going to need to cauterize this wound or he won't make it out of this bus. I removed the debris, but the bleed isn't setting."

"I've got the wand and light, but what about a second pair of hands?"

"If you can get a torch set up above me, and then be my perioperative from up there, I think I've got it."

Mateo glanced at the toppled vehicle. If his knee could

bend at the angles it needed to climb the underbelly and assist Olivia from up top, it was as good a plan as any. It also left the windshield free for medics and the extraction team to get to Olivia as they were able.

"On my way up. Talk me through what you see in there," he said. He wanted the patient cared for, and he had the best possible physician on his case at the moment. But the protective need to make sure Olivia was okay surged in his chest.

"There's broken glass, a lot of it. The front of the bus is intact, but there's a broken mesh bag of footballs and other gear along the floor, which is the line of windows. It's making it hard to find solid ground to stand on."

Mateo used his forearms to lift himself up onto the wheel well. Propping himself on the chassis, he tried to bend his knee to work around the twisted, slick metal and it wouldn't go. Between the moisture in the air and tightness from showing off on the pitch earlier, he was buggered. Dammit.

"Are you in a safe position?" he asked.

"I am. The patient is, too, but there's no place to lay him down and the seat belt is digging into his side. If I release it, he'll fall and then we're in real trouble."

Mateo pivoted and approached his climb with the other side of his body. It worked and he was able to pull himself over the top of the bus and peer down into the cavern of blackness. The streetlights reflected off the rain-soaked leather steering wheel and off the shards of broken glass, giving the whole scene a macabre feel.

Mateo shone the waterproof torch down.

There, in the middle, Olivia maneuvered around the obstacles in her way to apply pressure to the bus driver's wound. She didn't glance up at him, but shot him a thumbs-up.

"Thank you. Did you bring the bag?"

"Got it. Talk me through your plan."

It was so much easier to hear her up here. He felt a desperate need to slide down into the bay with her, if only so she had an actual second pair of hands and support. But he'd just get in the way. The only good news was the patient being unconscious. If they felt trapped while they were injured, who knew how volatile they could get.

This was the best option to take care of both of them.

"I need a syringe and ten ccs of Dilaudid."

He understood her choice. Toradol—usually what they gave players after a traumatic injury—wouldn't work with a patient who couldn't cauterize.

Mateo filled the syringe and handed it down with a field suture kit and clotting agent.

She glanced up at him, her makeup smudged under her eyes and blood streaked across her forehead and cheeks. She looked as if she'd gone to battle.

"Thanks," she said and he nodded. "This is perfect."

She'd not asked for the kit but he'd assumed that was next. This would save her time. Precious time she'd need.

When Olivia applied the coagulant, the patient's head lifted.

"What—" he started. He looked down at the wound, then at his surroundings, then began to thrash. "What happened? Why am I here? Oh, God. Am I going to die?"

Olivia met Mateo's gaze, her eyes wide with fear. She'd come to the same conclusion he had about the patient. He reached down to pull her out of there but she shook her head.

"Sir? I'm Olivia, a doctor. You're okay, but you need to stay still. You sustained an injury when your bus crashed and I need to make sure I can stop the bleeding. Can you do that for me?"

"I—" the driver said. He choked on a sob. "I can't feel it. Is that bad? Am I dying?"

"No. I gave you a shot to numb the area so you wouldn't feel the pain. What's your name?"

"George. I'm a new grandfather. I haven't even met her yet, my granddaughter. Kept saying I'd come by and kept gettin' too busy. She only lives across town. What if it's too late?"

He sobbed, and the movement shook the seat, loosening a couple shards of glass from the window above. They fell around him and Olivia. Mateo needed to get her out of there and now.

"Olivia—" he called down.

She shook her head again, and put a hand on George's shoulder.

"George, you're going to meet her if I have anything to say about it. But you need to do everything I tell you. Can you do that?"

He nodded. Mateo marveled at Olivia's calm when she was obviously worried for her own safety. She talked the patient through what she was doing and reassured him each step of her procedure. Only once did he cry out in pain, but otherwise, she deescalated the situation with no incidents.

She was incredible. Mateo's chest swelled with pride. That was his colleague. The woman and physician he got to learn from and with.

The AAPs arrived at the bus and though Olivia had the situation under control, Mateo was glad to see them. He wouldn't feel good until she was safely out of the wreck.

They had Olivia shield her eyes and then cleared a path to where she was.

"Okay. We're going to pull you out so we can get in and extract the patient. Ready?"

In one fluid motion, she was out. That was it. He ran over to her without thinking about the perception, the impact or even his own feelings. Only that he needed to hold her after what they'd both been through.

Olivia landed in his arms and he pressed her against him tightly. Her body shook and if they weren't getting pelted from the rain, he had no doubt that his shirt would be soaked with her tears.

"We did it," she whispered into his chest. "We saved them."

"We did. You were incredible."

Mateo kissed her damp hair and then looked over her head at the wreckage behind them. Half a city block was destroyed, not to mention the corner of the parking garage. The pale blue of the Lazio warm-ups and duffels that had been tossed when the bus flipped were not only darkened by mud and rain, but blood and vomit as well. Most of the ambulances had sped away and the neighbors had gone back inside.

It was still a disaster. There probably wouldn't be a tournament now, nor a way for Mateo to test his protocol in the Premier League with Manchester's club.

But Mateo didn't care. How could he care about a sport, a *game*, when people's lives were on the line?

The game is what helped you cope with your own loss.

True. Football had been his escape and his way to grow his own strength so he could leave a lonely, often tragic, life behind in Colombia.

But as Mateo held Olivia, he realized something. Everything was different now: his need to be right about the protocol, to prove his worth as a football physician—all of it. And he'd bet every last cent of his salary that it had to do with the woman in his arms.

Whether or not he could separate his feelings at work wasn't the issue anymore. When the bus had crashed, so had his willpower to stay away from Olivia. Life was too short to pretend he wasn't intrigued when he was—how had he put it?

He was all in.

If she wasn't, he understood. He could hide his feelings and be there for her. Anything to stay close to her, to make sure he never had to see that fear in her gaze again.

She met his gaze, her makeup smeared and eyes red.

"Come home with me tonight?" she asked. "I need to hold you."

"Always," he answered, and as soon as the word was out of his mouth, the crashing in his own chest silenced. So did the rain, easing to a drizzle.

Only Olivia's soft breathing filled the ominous silence.

Mateo shivered. He wasn't leaving the site unscathed, either. The question was—what would life look like in the morning?

And would he survive the changes?

CHAPTER THIRTEEN

OLIVIA'S PHONE RANG shrill and intrusive against the cavernous walls of her master suite. She let it go to voicemail, but it only picked right back up again. Olivia rolled over to where Mateo had held her last night as she'd shivered through the barrage of trauma images. The fallout from the accident would leave a mark forever. She was a physician but most of her work was isolated, related to sport. What they'd done last night had been nothing short of wartime trauma care. At least Mateo had been willing to let her cry out the barrage of feelings without becoming impatient.

The bed was rumpled but empty. Her chest ached but she ignored it. Why would she care if Mateo left once she fell asleep? He'd done what she'd asked and held her.

It isn't enough. Her heart spoke the truth. Just before she'd fallen asleep, she'd had the overwhelming feeling that she'd somehow got it all wrong. That Mateo was the answer, not the question.

But in the light of day, that wasn't possible; he was still her rival, even if they'd allowed friendship to blur the lines.

Yeah, friendship. Is that why his head was buried in your—

She shook her head, willing those images from her mind as well; they were just as likely to ruin her day. Hell, her career. But she couldn't ignore the way Mateo had been there for her. Not just holding her after the rescue, but each step of the way before that. He'd let her run her cases with her patients without being overbearing or assuming his way was best. Bare minimum stuff, sure.

But he'd also supported her, been gentle and patient. And if she was being honest, when his lips had met hers—

She put his pillow over her head and screamed. So much had happened last night, not least of which was her feelings for Mateo overriding their promise to keep things professional.

The Italian team was in shambles. The shouts and screams of pain might not ever fade from her memory, and why should they? Some of the accident victims would wear their own permanent scars, those that lived, that was.

On the fourth call in as many minutes, she snatched up the phone, prepared to yell at whoever wouldn't get the hint. And her stomach dropped out.

Her father.

All three missed calls from earlier were from him.

He never reached out before noon on a weekend. But that was before his diagnosis.

"Dad, hi. Are you okay?" She needed good news.

"Oh, Olivia, thank goodness you answered. I was starting to get anxious over here."

"Anxious? Why? How are you feeling, Dad?"

There was a pause on the other line and she could feel her pulse against the glass of the phone screen.

"I'm fine, just a little nervous about tomorrow. But are you okay?" he asked.

His first chemo appointment. How was her head so wrecked that it had gone clean out of her mind?

"I'm fine. Sleepy, but fine otherwise. I had a rough night—"

"The accident. Yeah, I know. It looked horrific."

Olivia sat up in bed, suddenly alert. "How did you know I was there, Dad?"

"You're the headline, hon. You and Garcia. Are you two doing all right? That kind of trauma, especially if you're not used to seeing it every day—"

"Hey, Dad?" she asked. "I'm fine, and I love you, but can I see you at your appointment tomorrow?"

He assured her he was fine if she was so she hung up and opened up her web browser. Pulling up the *Times*, she gasped.

"How…?" she asked. She hopped out of bed and ran down the stairs, not caring to put on trousers. There, at the front door, was Mateo, holding a big brown take-away bag and three papers with different headlines.

"Have you seen these?" he asked.

"You're here," she said, bringing him inside. Her neighbor, Patrice, peeked out of her drapes.

"Of course I'm here. I just went to get us food. You know all you have are protein shakes and white wine in your ice-box?"

She smiled, in spite of all the drama behind—and in front of—them.

"Well, since I'm hardly here, I only keep the essentials."

He leaned down to kiss her, and the news, the worry about her father, all of it melted away. The gesture was so simple, so ordinary, but at the same time filled with a promise she had no right to expect. The last thing he needed was her to break the one rule they'd set the night before.

But that was before the crash had upended her world as well.

"We're going to talk about what constitutes essentials someday, but for now, we've got pancakes and jam, bacon, sausage, eggs done three ways because your fake boyfriend from before neglected to find out how you take them, and coffee and tea because I know what you drink at work, but I'm not sure just how British you are at home. Oh, and these." He held up three periodicals, all showing her and Mateo in

KRISTINE LYNN 129

front of a mangled heap of metal and glass and debris. "Flowers were off the menu for obvious reasons, but just know I'd have rather brought those since they'd add beauty to your day instead of…"

He waved the papers.

Every paper, both at her door and those littering her inbox, was splashed with photos of the crash. Well, not just the crash, but her in Mateo's arms. On the front pages as well. No wonder her father had been worried.

Mateo and Olivia's embrace in the rain after she'd broken down and he'd held her was private, or at least she'd assumed it was. When her job was over and the world slowed, Mateo had been there to catch her, and he hadn't let her go until the last of her sobs had quieted. She'd felt seen and cared for in a moment of utter despair, wondering if they'd done enough. If they'd saved everyone, or if the night had left a permanent mark on this team.

So who had captured this intimate moment?

More importantly, why? They weren't the story—Lazio's bus crash in the storm was. And yet…

Even the publishers that didn't print in color showed the severity—and therefore tenderness—of the moment, both of them soaked to the bone and their clothes stained crimson. His eyes were closed in the photo, and though Olivia's face was buried in Mateo's chest, she'd been sobbing. One of his hands was protectively wrapped around her waist, while the other cupped her head tenderly.

Behind them, the carnage of the bus wreck painted a gruesome backdrop.

She'd temporarily forgotten that was why she'd gone to the front door in the first place, but the reminder was in her hands, loud and obtrusive.

"Who did this?" she asked, taking one of the papers from him.

The headline above the image read, "Not Just for Show—

Football's Power Couple Saves Busload of Italian Crash Victims."

"I don't know," he said, echoing her thoughts. "It's a tacky ploy, taking photos of us when the real story is the victims. It feels cheap."

Olivia was used to that. It was why she didn't date in the public eye—not till Mateo, anyway. She was under so much scrutiny as a female in a male-dominated sport as it was. The last thing she needed was her love life under a microscope as well. That was why this had seemed like such a good idea with Mateo. It controlled the story with the press and kept the focus on their medical connection.

Or at least that had been the plan. So far, though, both stories the news got ahold of were so far outside Olivia's control, they might as well be in outer space. Olivia scanned her story for news of the victims, but only a few sparse details were shared, details she already knew.

Thirty-eight souls on board the bus, including managers, sports docs, players and other support staff.

Four patients left the crash site in dire condition.

Fourteen critically injured victims were taken to area hospitals for treatment.

Twenty patients were wounded, but received care on-site by the AAP staff who responded, as well as the two doctors who'd been working late.

That last detail had an unexpected effect on Olivia.

Working late...

An image of Mateo bent between her legs flashed in her head, erasing the photo of their more benign embrace on the front pages.

She slapped the paper on the table.

"You know what?" she declared. "I'm hungry. Why don't we eat and then come up with a plan for how to address this? We have to meet with Robert—presumably to chat about the implications for the tournament. He already sent us an email, but I haven't checked it. I hate to say it, but I'm sure he will be looking for a way to capitalize on the drama of it all. I'd like us to be on the same page there, at least."

"Good idea," Mateo said, adding his paper to the pile. "I haven't read it, either, for the same reasons." He divided the food onto plates, with her pointing out what she liked—scrambled eggs and pancakes, bacon over sausage, and coffee. Definitely coffee. "I don't know if you're interested, but I wanted to go see the victims at St. Mary's Hospital. I made some calls while I was getting breakfast and it seems like most of the worst cases were brought there. No offense to Robert, but he can wait."

Olivia's stomach tightened. Who was this man? She'd had the same thought, but worried Mateo would want to ensure his protocol was still part of the discussion going forward. It was his career on the line, too, and so much was up in the air now.

The two ate in silence, and at one point, Mateo put his hand on Olivia's knee. It felt natural, like they'd forever done breakfast together this way. Her chest flushed with desire, the way it always did when he was around. Not exactly a recipe for keeping heavy feelings at bay.

"Can I ask you something?" she said, breaking the silence.

He smiled, chewing still. When he'd swallowed, he said, "Of course. That's a given. You can always ask me anything, Olivia."

"You mentioned leaving Colombia because of the poverty and family trauma, but do you ever go back? I guess I'm curious who's in your corner?"

He raised his brows, but his smile remained.

"Damn. Heavy hitting in the morning."

"You don't have to—"

He waved her off. "I don't mind talking to you at all. I

trust you, Olivia. It's not a good story, though. You sure you want to hear it?"

She needed to know more. She told herself it was because she would be able to make better decisions about working alongside him if she knew his backstory and what biases might drive his medical decisions, but that was a weak argument. And her heart knew it. She didn't actually have any qualms about Mateo's safety measures anymore; she'd seen them in action in Manchester's practices, and in the weeks since the double roster had taken effect, pre-injuries had been down 12 percent from preseason the year before. This, combined with the training safety plans she'd enacted, would change the game for Manchester, and hopefully the league.

You just want to know him. *Because you care.*

She reluctantly agreed with her heart, but her mind added its own take.

And you're worried about what might pull him away from you if you pursue the very real, very deep feelings you're having for him. If he goes home, you've risked your heart for no reason.

Damn her overactive brain.

She swallowed hard and snatched a piece of Mateo's bacon. "I'm sure."

"My dad and uncles were part of a cartel in Colombia. My dad wanted my best interests, but it didn't always align with his lifestyle, right?" Mateo shrugged and his smile faltered. Olivia clasped his hand. "My mom got me into football to ensure I'd stay out of that life."

"Was that really possible?"

"It wasn't easy. Thank goodness I was a bit of a natural at football. We didn't have the money or power outside of the cartel for any other choice."

"We?"

"My mom and dad. He left the cartel, and my mom and

I both lived in fear it would cost him his life. But they died in a car accident on the way home from one of my tournaments. It was my fault they died, not the cartel's like I always worried about."

Olivia heard the regret mixed with anger buried in Mateo's words. He'd been through so much to get here.

She leaned over and pressed her lips to his.

"It's not your fault, Mateo," she whispered.

Olivia could live a hundred more years and not forget the way Mateo's brows pulled in, his jaw set and his eyes instantly watered. It was pain personified. She didn't need a medical degree to suss out that the man in front of her was suffering.

"Maybe not, but football saved my life and took theirs. It's been a complicated relationship, that's for sure."

Olivia's heart ached. How selfish was she to wish he didn't have a family so he'd stay with her? Or that if he couldn't stay with Manchester, she'd know now and could protect her heart from falling all the way when he left her?

Now she'd give anything to know he had a family safe and sound in Colombia. Instead of creating distance, like it should, that knowledge only strengthened her feelings for the man. They were both part of a sorry club of kids who lost parents young.

"Anyway, I'm hoping to give back to a scholarship program in Colombia that will help kids like me—" *orphans*, he must have meant "—pursue football as a way of finding an alternative family."

On top of being handsome, brilliant and forward-thinking in the medical bay and calm when she was spiraling, he was selfless and kinder than she'd given him credit for.

Ugh. Did she have no sense of self-preservation?

"But, Olivia?"

She focused on him. "Hmm?"

"I shared this with you as a—" he paused and looked down at their conjoined hands "—friend. Please don't let it shape your opinion of me if we have to fight for our position with Robert. I'll land on my feet. I always do."

Olivia nodded, afraid the lump in her throat would choke her if she tried to speak.

"Okay," he said. "Speaking of which, what should we do about this email from Robert?"

Glad to focus on something other than the uptick of her arrhythmia each time Mateo squeezed her hands, she sighed, extracting herself from his grasp to check her phone.

She scanned the email and read parts aloud to Mateo.

"He wants to meet us both, but not until after lunch. On our way to visit the Italians let's brainstorm how to pitch him a way for us both to stay regardless of what happens with the tournament."

The idea of anything else—Mateo or her leaving—wasn't anything she'd entertain. Wow, how quickly things could change…

"You want me to fight to stay around?" he asked. She hated that he sounded genuinely surprised.

"Of course. You're good for…for the club. You show them a new way of doing things that complements what we were already doing." Mateo leaned in, his hands on her thighs. Her breath hitched in her chest. "And you help everyone take things seriously when they're supposed to be."

His thumbs pressed into her inner thighs, tracing the inseam of her pants. She gasped.

"And you bring them a sense of calm where things used to be a little frantic." Her voice sounded breathy and high.

"Calm, hmm?" He moved his hands to the top of her thighs where they met her waist. He rubbed the point where they met and she inhaled a sharp breath. "What if I want the *club* to be wild, maybe a little passionate and free?"

Mateo leaned forward and kissed her neck, trailing his tongue along her collarbone. She leaned back in her chair, allowing him access to her neck, her sex, all of her. He moved to her mouth, kissing her tenderly, inquisitively, testing her resolve. He tasted of coffee and maple, and even though she'd eaten her fill of breakfast, she was consumed with hunger.

A different kind of hunger. One that seemed unquenchable around Mateo.

"I want to be wild with you."

The words were heavy, carrying more meaning than simply desire for Mateo's hands and lips on her. Though she wanted that, too. The moisture pooling in her panties was evidence of just how badly she wanted this man.

He took her words as an invitation to ravish her, starting with her mouth. His lips crashed into hers and as his tongue slipped between them at the same time his thumb rubbed the sensitive center of her core, she moaned with pleasure.

"Tell me what you want, Olivia. I'll give it to you." He pulled back, meeting her ravenous gaze with one of his own. "Anything."

She held in a gasp of surprise, wondering if he knew his words sounded as heavy and filled with double meaning as her own had been. Surely he didn't. He had too much at stake to think about risking his own heart in a relationship doomed from the start. Even if she and Mateo got to work together for a season, two even, it wouldn't last forever. Then what?

But as she nodded and spread her knees to bring him closer, she didn't care. The injured football team, the meeting with Robert, the fact that she might be unemployed by that afternoon—it faded to the back of her mind to be dealt with later that day.

Mateo picked Olivia up, cupping her backside as she wrapped her arms tight around his neck. He walked them toward Olivia's bedroom, and she felt good for the first time since the crash. She might be in trouble in a million little ways, but not with this beautiful doctor carrying her to pleasure.

Only this moment mattered.

She'd figure out the consequences to her feelings later, reasoning that one morning of sating physical desires couldn't make things worse than they already were.

After all, they'd already fooled around. How much more intense could their lovemaking be?

CHAPTER FOURTEEN

MATEO WALKED THROUGH the crowd of reporters in front of the hospital, his mind barely registering their questions.

"Do you have any idea how many patients you each worked on last night?"

"How long have you and Dr. Ross been dating? Does your relationship ever get in the way of work?"

"Have you heard anything from Lazio's management expressing their thanks for what you did?"

That last one caught his attention briefly.

"Olivia and I didn't help for recognition or praise. It's our job as doctors to do no harm and assist when we're called upon, and I can assure you we hope never to be glorified for our successes. In fact, we're only in that photograph because one of you breached a private moment between two grieving doctors, devastated by the loss of our fellow team."

Anger surfaced briefly, but was replaced by a gentle squeeze of Olivia's hand in his. He didn't see how his dating life had ever been newsworthy, but especially now, with dozens of injured in beds behind them.

Another reminder surfaced. His parents in beds much less modern, beds they'd died in.

Football was just a game in the end; his relationship with Olivia, though it began that way, was anything but. He cared for her, and each time they held hands or…more…her impact on him grew. He couldn't imagine what he'd do if she was on one of those beds...

All he could see, imagine, were her arms wrapped around his neck as he kissed her earlier that day. As he buried himself in all that she was and offered. She erased his past, or at least its hold on him. And that was the most dangerous part.

Could the paparazzi see through his cultivated calm to how thoroughly, how wonderfully, how completely he'd been screwed? Calling it what it was—lovemaking—was guaranteed to make things worse. Because as he thought of her mouth trailing kisses down his chest, across the swathe of his abdomen, finally taking his length inside her while she kept his gaze—

He shook his head. That was the problem. Hooking up with her in the stadium had been exciting until the tragedy struck, but damn if a morning with her hadn't changed everything again. The soft stirrings of lust, paired with the need to take care of her, had almost overwhelmed him the night before. It was compounded by telling her about his parents that morning. He'd never shared that with anyone, not even his found families in Real Madrid or Leganés. Sharing in that world wasn't necessary, and he'd appreciated that at the time but it hadn't helped Mateo heal.

Not till Olivia had he considered unburdening himself and letting someone else in.

And in addition, he knew each of her curves by heart. The way her neck always fell to the right side when she was happy and sated. He'd always been a quick study, but with Olivia, he didn't have the reflection he needed to see through the desire.

He needed distance to think through his exploding feelings, but as they made their way to the surgical suites, following the head of orthopedic surgery, that wasn't going to happen.

"If you two are comfortable scrubbing in, we need all the help we can get. There are too many patients who need immediate surgeries if we're going to save their careers, some of them their limbs."

Mateo shared a wary glance with Olivia. Her cheeks were still somehow flushed, even though they'd showered and gotten ready after their lovema—*sex* from earlier.

"I think we need to," she said. "And I'm comfortable with the procedures you've outlined."

The ortho doc had listed an array of surgical bone settings, steel plate placements, and two more complicated reconfigurations that required orthopedic expertise paired with a vascular surgeon.

Mateo and Olivia wouldn't be on those surgeries, but even the plate placements were something he rarely did; he'd only done two in medical school. Olivia had far more experience than him. Not for the first time, he bloomed with pride watching her confidently mark an *X* next to patients she knew with certainty she could assist. She worried the corner of her bottom lip like she had the night before when he dipped between her legs again, using his tongue to taste her, flicking her center until she released her lip and his name into the air—

Okay. This was getting out of hand. He could let this go for today. He was a professional, for crying out loud.

He glanced down at the list. He'd only placed three of his own marks, all bone settings that seemed uncomplicated. But he'd added a check mark next to *X*'s where he felt he'd be a valuable second.

The orthopedic surgeon gave them the waivers and surgical schedule, which meant their meeting with Robert had to be postponed to the next day. They'd come to the hospital to visit, never imagining the horror show of injuries that awaited them.

When the hospital team asked if they'd scrub in, Mateo had known their days were going to shift. Time was of the essence, especially since the stakes for professional footballers were higher than for most ortho cases.

If they didn't get help, they wouldn't play again. Some might not anyway, would be lucky to walk on both their own legs, but for those they could save, Mateo *had* to help. It was a more intense version of what he'd signed up to do with Leganés, with Manchester—use his own experience as an injured player to fuel his need to help others escape that same fate.

"I'll be your second on the first two, it seems," he said to Olivia as they dressed out in their scrubs. How did the woman make the baggy green outfit look as appealing as a fitted pantsuit? She was a damn magician.

A magician whose tricks he needed to ignore if he was going to perform well today.

Reminding himself of the stakes he bore on behalf of the Lazio team helped.

"Thank you. I'm glad to have you here. This kind of pressure—"

"It's a lot."

She nodded, placing the surgical cap. "I knew you'd understand. If you feel like you need a break today, please take one. This must bring up memories of your own career."

They scrubbed in and masked up before walking into the surgical theater.

"It does, but not any more than each time I have a player on my table. That fear is always there, or it was until last night."

"What happened last night?"

He chuckled, but it didn't come with any humor. "Besides the decimation of another team in a freak rainstorm-caused bus crash?"

Her eyes crinkled, belying a smile behind the mask. "Besides that."

The anesthesiologist had the patient sedated and he was ready for the dual bone setting and screws that would be a permanent fixture in his hips. Hopefully, with time and rehab, he'd play again, but never the same.

"It's all a game, isn't it?" he asked. She took a scalpel and met his gaze before concentrating on the leg in front of them. "I mean, it's a game that allows us to take care of families and build futures, but it doesn't fix political systems or broken families or even international relations. It's a diversion and it can be taken away in a heartbeat. You know?"

She nodded, but kept her focus on the patient. He held the skin flap open and applied a retractor.

The room fell silent. He couldn't help the way the words just fell out of his mouth around Olivia, like he physically couldn't restrain himself from laying his joys, his goals, even his deepest fears, at her feet. Even those about her.

Somehow he knew she'd carry them well, regardless of whether it was a bad idea to keep sharing them before he could make sense of his emotions.

"Thanks," she finally said. "I do understand. Football, as you know, isn't my favorite pastime. It doesn't even make the top five, if I'm being honest. Or at least it didn't until you reminded me what started me down this path."

"Your father?" he asked.

"Mmm-hmm."

Olivia held her hand out and he placed a bone saw in it. This was messy, awful work, but watching her deftly make cuts and repairs filled him with wonder. He'd already learned three new techniques that would help him in the med bay.

"My dad closed up when my mom died. I don't think he knew what to say to me and I was too young to figure out how to bridge that gap. So I'd watch games with him on weekends and evenings until I grew up and had to go to uni and get a job and—"

"Start your own life?"

"Yeah."

142 HOW TO RESIST YOUR ENEMY

"And the game was your connection."

She nodded. "First pins, please." He handed the screws to her, and moved the retractor so she had better access. The femoral neck fracture of the hip wasn't the worst he'd seen, but permanent screws weren't great for a professional athlete regardless. "That and medicine. I always knew this was my path, even before my mom died. I loved the stories my dad would share when he got home from work and would practice operating on my dolls to save their lives."

They both laughed.

"I'll bet that went over well."

Olivia asked for another screw. "They stopped buying Rainbow Brites after two of them lost limbs to my poor suture skills."

Mateo smiled, imagining young Olivia practicing medicine in her room, dreaming of days like today.

"I'm sure your dad was proud to think of you following in his footsteps."

Olivia shrugged sadly. "I sort of wish that wasn't the only way to get his attention. Since he got sick—"

"Doctors, the patient's BP is dropping steadily," the anesthesiologist interrupted.

They both looked at the screen and Olivia shook her head.

"Intraoperative hypotension," she said. "We need to increase the arterial pressure and get out of here quickly. Are you comfortable setting the left femur while I work on the last two screws?"

Mateo nodded. "I'll stay out of your way, but let me know if you need an assist."

They worked in silence, both handing instruments to one another and the surgical assistants. While they closed, Mateo thought about Olivia's father.

He was sick? How so? If it was serious, how could he keep

this amazing woman at arm's length? Goodness knew Mateo had tried and failed.

It's not your concern. No, it wasn't, but that's what bothered him. He wanted it to be. He wanted the fun and laughter, the damn good sex, but also to dig into the serious parts of what made this woman who she was.

Whether it was a good idea or not, or if the stakes were so high that he'd impale himself if he took even a slight misstep, he liked Olivia Ross.

Like, a lot.

"Can I meet him?" Mateo asked.

"My dad?" she asked. She made her last suture and set down her instruments. To the anesthesiologist she said, "I'm ready for you to take him off. Go slower so I can keep an eye on his hypotension. I'll order a watch for the first twenty-four hours and make sure it doesn't swing the other way to postoperative hypertension."

She gestured for Mateo to follow her to the scrub room. When they were behind the sterile field, they pulled down their masks.

"You want to meet my dad?" she asked. She bit her bottom lip, but her head tilted to the right. She wanted it, too.

"I do. I don't want to make you uncomfortable, but yes, I'd like that very much."

Her pause said maybe she was feeling the same way he was—that they'd slipped from fake dating friends into something more, something *real*.

"In the beginning, that's all I wanted, but now it's—"

"Different?" he offered. She nodded. "I know." He glanced at the door, aware of the possibility of someone walking in on them. The nurses and anesthesiologist were busy transferring the patient to the recovery room. "But it's in a good way, at least to me."

"What do you mean?"

It was all or nothing now. If he came clean and she rejected him, that would be it; he'd put it to rest. But he had to believe the way she gazed up at him with bright eyes, biting her bottom lip, that she felt more for him, too.

"We only have a couple minutes before we have to get down the hall, so feel free to think on this. But I promised I'd talk to you as things shifted, and they have. I like you. I think, if we're speaking in the language of the books we both love, I 'caught feelings' for you somewhere along the way. Actual ones. If I'm not mistaken, you feel something, too."

"I feel…something." Her cheeks echoed that.

"And I want to take the bumpers off this, Olivia. I think we can keep our work life professional, if not separate, while we explore that *something*. What do you think?"

She smiled, but then fought it back. He could see the struggle warring on her delicate features. Her pursed lips said the argument in his favor was winning. He mentally crossed his fingers.

"I just don't know. With work, with Robert…it's just so complicated. And I don't want my dad to get too invested if things don't… He might not—" Her voice broke, and so did his heart.

"Olivia, you bring me so much joy. I care about you and would never ask to meet him if I wasn't serious."

Her face was a blank canvas, betraying nothing. A full thirty seconds later, she wrapped her arms around his waist.

Hope buoyed him.

"Okay. What does that look like? Dinner with my dad, I mean. The rest we should talk about when we don't have a full day of surgeries ahead of us." He laughed. "But I'm… open to it."

"Maybe we could all do dinner at my house one night?"

Holy shit. Was this what optimism felt like? He'd spent so long just keeping his head afloat and trying to survive, he didn't know what it was like to dream. To *want*. Now that he did, he wasn't sure he could go back to the alternative. She'd changed so much about him in such a short amount of time. What would his life look like a year from now?

"I've never been to your house," she said. He closed the space between their lips, kissing her softly.

"I know we've got to get going, but I'd like to rectify that this evening. Come over for an adult sleepover and we can talk about your dad. I'd like to hear what's going on with him if that's okay."

"Can we have a pillow fight?"

He laughed, the sound both out of place, given their surroundings, and oddly in sync.

"I don't see why not. Be careful what you wish for, Ross. I've got a few tricks up my sleeve and I'm not above cheating to win in the bedroom."

She deepened their kiss, opening for him before pulling away and leaving him half hard with desire.

"Oh, I'm counting on it, Garcia." At the door, she stopped and turned back to him. "But I'm bringing my own tricks."

Mateo smiled. This woman was either going to be the thing that saved him from drowning in responsibility and worry, or the anchor that dragged him under.

For the first time in his life, he didn't care, because sinking to the depths with Olivia Ross didn't sound like a bad way to go.

CHAPTER FIFTEEN

A WEEK LATER, Olivia was exhausted. Her father's numbers had improved although the chemo was already taking a lot out of him. Still that fear that she was running out of time—the same fear that had nipped at her ankles since she'd lost her mom—remained. She took every available chance to spend time with her father, no longer caring that all he seemed to want to talk about was football. She'd sit with him in pure silence if it meant more time with him.

It was the same at work. If she wasn't with her father, she was working alongside Mateo to help keep the tournament afloat. Their meeting with Robert had gone incredibly well, all things considered. He'd kept the tournament, citing the rise in ticket sales and support for the Italian team as his reasons for going ahead with it, which she wasn't sure about at first.

Until she saw how drastically those were both understated. In fact, Manchester had sold out of tickets each day of the week-long tournament, for each match, far surpassing their original expectations. It was good news, but also came with a challenge Robert had issued.

With the world's eyes on them now, things needed to go perfectly.

Meaning, if there wasn't a measurable change in the club's safety, Robert wouldn't keep Mateo's protocol, especially not the more costly double roster. That included doctors.

As for the support for the Lazio club, that was under-represented by Robert as well. As Olivia walked the halls of the stadium on the first game day, she didn't see one arm not wearing a pale blue band in solidarity for the injured team. Half the crowd wore the kits of the first teams to play—Manchester vs Liverpool—while the rest of the fans showed up in the same blue as the armbands.

Olivia choked up every time she walked by someone and they pointed to their arm, giving her a smile she wasn't sure she'd earned.

She'd helped at the accident site and in the hospital, and she and Mateo had made headway in the postaccident operative care of the most egregious cases from the crash. That felt good.

But the crash, followed by the tournament—and in fact, every day she'd spent with Mateo since she'd met him on the show all those weeks ago—had changed something fundamental about her. He'd worn down her walls with respect to love in her life, and in doing so, illuminated her true feelings about her role as team physician. She loved the way the sport rallied people together, gave young athletes a place to call home.

She might've come to football, and sports medicine, because of her father. But she did love the medicine, especially since she'd been able to branch out and work at the hospital from time to time. Her passion inside the surgery room had proved she thrived with a blend of community service and working closely with an organization.

But was it with *this* organization? The long hours, the lack of trust she had in the owner... She had to consider that it might not be the best fit, especially given the fact that she and Mateo were still actively in competition for one position. And she wasn't the front-runner, not in Robert's eyes.

But her father... How could she think of moving teams

when he was in the middle of fighting for his life? She needed to stay in Manchester at least to see him through his treatment.

And then there was Mateo...

They were still so new as a couple, but she also couldn't imagine *not* sharing such a life-changing decision with him. Before she asked him, though, she needed to be crystal clear about what she wanted, and with her father as sick as he was, that might be a while.

What would her life look like if she pursued another team and let Mateo stay where he was valued? Her career, her relationship with her father, and her new intimate partnership would all change, if not vanish.

Or you could both get everything you want, including each other.

She didn't know if there was truth to her heart's gentle nudge, but time would tell, and hopefully she and Mateo could work together until she'd gotten her dad to more steady ground and could consider all angles honestly.

She turned the corner toward the medical bay and smiled. *Mateo.* It was an auto-response each time they crossed paths.

"Hey there, beautiful," he said. He kissed her on the lips and the heat spread from her core south. Another auto-response by her body. Her questions could wait. This was all she needed, for now.

"Hiya, handsome. Where are you headed?"

He gestured behind her. "A meeting with Robert and Tomás Grazio."

"The new Lazio club owner? He's here?"

Tomás Grazio, a former professional footballer turned business mogul, had been in negotiations with the Italian team to purchase the club. After the accident the former owner, Antonio Bellario, had flown down to support the club, but let the administrative staff know he couldn't afford to keep the team while floating the medical costs and added insurance.

He sold at a steep discount to Grazio, a move that shocked the football world.

The former player had made a big show of leaving the sport when he'd retired at twenty-seven after a string of bad press about his bad-boy attitude on and off the pitch.

"Yeah, he flew in to meet with Bellario and the manager to find out how he can help."

Olivia scoffed. "Nice. How about not purchasing a team in crisis?"

Mateo shrugged. "It's not ideal, but at least this way, the team stays in play. It would have dissolved entirely if Bellario had kept it. I admire the guy, actually."

"If you say so. Did he ask to see you?"

A shadow passed over Mateo's face, but quick enough she couldn't say it'd been there at all.

"No, I did. I just have some questions I'd like his thoughts on. Figured another player's insight into some things wouldn't hurt."

An alarm bell rang in her head, but she pushed it aside. Mateo had always been honest with her, even when it wasn't information she wanted to hear. She owed him her trust; he'd tell her when he was ready.

Olivia inched closer to Mateo, cognizant of the steady stream of people bustling around them. She craved proximity to the man, even though he practically lived at her house. After they'd spent the night at his house—a simple, but tasteful apartment in the center of downtown—Mateo had brought over a change of clothes each night and only left to go to work, arguing her place was closer to work. Not that she minded him sleeping over one bit.

They made love—spectacular, mind-changing, toe-curling love—each evening and she fell asleep in his arms each night. She couldn't stop the magnetic pull of him. In two steps, she was in his arms in broad daylight.

At work. So much for taking it slow. It made everything

so much more complicated, but at the same time, it was the clarity she needed. This feeling, this certainty that there was more to life than on the pitch, was what mattered. The rest would fall into place.

"You're very pragmatic, Dr. Garcia," she teased. He bent down and kissed her, overwhelming her senses with the taste of espresso and vanilla. Blended with the Spanish-spiced cologne he wore, the effect was a powerful aphrodisiac.

"I've been told that, Dr. Ross." He kissed her again, his lips trailing her jaw until they reached her ear. He whispered, "But I've also been told I can abandon all logic and kneel before a powerful woman. Can I kneel between your legs tonight?"

Heat flashed from her stomach to her sex and her knees almost buckled.

"Mmm-hmm," she managed.

Someone cleared their throat and Olivia stepped back, the real world crashing into her as Tomás Grazio smiled warmly from the doorway.

"I need this man for a minute, if you don't mind. I'll have him back before the match."

"Of course. I'm Olivia Ross, by the way." He shook her hand and met her gaze, professional and brief.

Not exactly the womanizer she'd envisioned.

"I know who you are, and I'm pleased to meet you. Your work is impressive in the field. I'd love to catch up at some point, pick your brain."

"Sure. Anytime."

"Shall we?" Mateo said, gesturing toward his office.

Why did she get the feeling Mateo was leading this meeting and it was about more than he'd let on?

Mateo kissed her goodbye. "See you later, sweetheart."

He strode off, chatting with Tomás about someone from their pasts—a player they'd both known during their time as professional footballers.

Now that she had room to breathe without Mateo's cologne choking her good sense, she found it odd that she wasn't invited if he'd only wanted medical advice.

Unless…

Was he looking for another job?

Surely not. But why else would he seek out Grazio and not include her, or at a minimum tell her what he was up to? As far as anyone knew, she was still a contender for the physician job, so even if he was applying to other teams, she shouldn't care. Heck, she'd been considering the same thing just moments earlier.

Her hands trembled. *So why does this feel different? Am I jealous?*

She didn't think so. She didn't begrudge Mateo any success, another drastic change since they'd met. In fact, she championed anything that would get him closer to his dream of building life-changing scholarships for kids.

That was it, though. Sure, anything outside staying in Manchester to make that happen meant he'd be pulled away from her. But she'd planned on involving him in her decision to leave or not so they could make an honest go of a relationship where they weren't working for the same club. And it seemed as if he didn't trust her enough to do the same.

The worry turned to fear. For the first time, Olivia had something to lose outside her father's influence in her life.

It didn't feel good.

She slammed a drawer of bandages shut and cried out in pain when her finger caught between the metal and its wooden frame.

"Dammit," she hissed, tears springing to her eyes.

Her phone rang and she answered it without looking at who it was.

"This is Olivia," she said, nursing her finger under a

stream of cold water. Damn, this hurt. A small trickle of blood pooled along her nail bed.

"This is Olivia's father."

She smiled, sniffing back tears that were unwarranted from such a small injury.

"Hey, Dad. Are you doing okay?"

"Yep. Just checking in on the tourney. I'll be by after my appointment to see the match today if that's still okay."

She forced a smile even though her father couldn't see it.

"Of course it is. I can't wait to see you." That was the truth. Her father's illness was both a nudge pushing her toward a life she wanted for herself and an anchor keeping her tied to Manchester. There wasn't any guarantee how much time they'd be given.

Her phone chimed and she swiped it open. A text from an unknown number. She almost ignored it until she saw the first line of the preview.

Hey, Ollie. Just wanted to say I saw your photo in the paper and it's taken me—

Olivia's heart thumped wildly in her chest. She knew that nickname, knew the man who'd called her that, without her permission, either.

"Hey, Dad? I've got to sort something out. I'll see you later?"

"You bet, hon. Go Manchester!"

She didn't echo the sentiment before hanging up and swiping open the message, anticipating the angry reply she'd send back. Until she read.

—a while to work up the courage to write to you. I know I more or less ghosted you after our last date, but I was an idiot who was threatened by a powerful woman. Does it help at all to know I've been chastising myself ever since?

Either way, I've done some deep work to examine why and would love to tell you about it. Over dinner, perhaps? I'm not traveling anymore, so any night works for me... Anxiously awaiting your reply, Knox XO

A sense of injustice washed over her as she finished packing the med bags they'd bring to the pitch for smaller injuries during the tournament. The text was, on one hand, exactly what she'd hoped for—a chance to be with someone who would appreciate her drive and need to be independent, while still offering her a safe place to land. Someone who wouldn't consider her to be "too much" because of all she wanted out of life. Someone who wasn't emasculated by the passion she carried in all she did, and would be supportive of both her work and home life, where she craved a family and stability.

On the other hand, it was too late. Or at least, she hoped it was. If Mateo really was leaving for Italy—the only reason she could see him being pulled into a private meeting with Grazio—then maybe it was in her best interest to keep the lines of possibility open for someone who would be there.

She spotted Bilken with a beautiful young nurse she recognized from the hospital. Their arms were wrapped around one another, despite his use of a crutch to walk. Olivia smiled, but it felt weak. Forced. Everyone, it seemed, was figuring out what they wanted and getting it. Why did it still seem so out of reach for her?

Give it time. Let Mateo come to you and explain.

She whipped out her phone again and wrote Knox back.

Thanks for reaching out. Things are insane right now with the tournament. Touch base next week sometime? Be well. Olivia

It was succinct, vague, but still open-ended. She couldn't imagine saying goodbye to Mateo, or being with anyone else, but if he left, she really needed to think about how to build a life she'd be happy in either way.

As she thought it, though, she realized it would only be half possible without Mateo. He'd been the one to ignite her passion—for both work and love. It was his influence that showed her the secret love for the game she held tucked in her chest. Sharing that with anyone else seemed unconscionable.

Olivia looked out over the pitch, her home for a decade now. Her heart wasn't in this place, maybe never had been, but it craved this sort of work, something Mateo had helped show her. Unfortunately, if he left, she'd be right back to who she'd been before she met him—a doctor for a Premier League team. With two discernible changes: a new relationship with her father and perhaps options to finally date as well.

All thanks to Mateo, the one thing she hadn't seen coming and wanted more than all of it. The irony didn't escape her notice.

Do you have to stay if he leaves?

She supposed she didn't, but moving to the other club in Manchester would only solve one of her challenges.

Somehow this day, this month, this life, had taken a turn.

She'd inadvertently been handed everything she'd sought out when she and Mateo decided to fake date their way to success. So why didn't that make her as happy as she thought it would?

CHAPTER SIXTEEN

THE CROWD SCREAMED with a fever pitch as the striker for Manchester sent a volley kick soaring over two Liverpool defenders and…the goalie. Mateo, ostensibly neutral at this moment, cheered. His stomach did the same thing it used to do before a game, tightening with the thrill of a good match. It didn't seem to get the memo that he wasn't about to take to the pitch.

He got out his phone, ignoring the missive from Lazio's owner. That had been a helluva meeting. He'd come up with the pitch for joining Grazio's team once it became clear that Robert was going to fire Olivia after the tournament. Mateo couldn't say anything to her until he'd gotten the official word that his backup plan would allow her to stay in Manchester, but keeping it from her had damn near taken him under.

So would leaving her behind, but that was better than stealing what she'd worked so hard to achieve. He loved her—of that he was certain—and that meant making her happy, even if it cost him his own happiness. There was still a chance they could give this thing a go, though.

Grazio had not only accepted Mateo's offer, but also he hadn't negotiated Olivia out of it, which was a key part of Mateo's pitch—Olivia as part of his team. In fact, Grazio had upped the ante, making the offer impossible to refuse. Excitement blended with nerves, making him nauseated.

Because his own happiness rested in the hope she'd want to go with him.

He shot her a text.

Great goal. Makes me want to trade kits and go play around for a bit. Hope you're cosy up there. Wish I could have my arms around you while we watch Liverpool lose. ;)

His phone buzzed. She'd given his comment a thumbs-up but then the little three dots saying she was responding disappeared. *Hmm.* He gave another glance up to the skybox. She didn't seem to be talking to anyone else. Her gaze was focused on the field.

I hope she's okay. If Robert broke his promise and told her before I could...

Robert was a jerk, but not an idiot; he had to know he needed to keep Olivia happy now. Robert was the only one Mateo told that he was leaving Manchester, namely so Robert wouldn't fire Olivia. If he did, he'd face the wrath of the safety commission, who he was just starting to appease with the double roster and work from Mateo and Olivia.

Liverpool rushed the field but were stopped by the Manchester midfielders, who stole the ball back and began a slow push back down toward their adversary's goal. The crowd hadn't simmered since their last goal, and screamed with fury or pride, depending on the kit they wore.

Manchester scored again, a nice half volley that hit the inside corner of the net, yielding the team a nice 3–1 lead.

Mateo's skin prickled with anticipation, which had nothing to do with the outcome of the game. In the email on his phone, he had everything he'd asked for before coming to Manchester: stability, security, and safety.

He'd be in charge of building the Italian team back from rehab, while creating a comprehensive training regimen and medical protocol like he'd sold to Manchester. He'd have a dedicated team, almost unlimited funding and access to whatever other resources he needed. Including a scholarship that would offer orphaned footballers a chance to train with the best. In Grazio's mind, it acted as a feeder program to bring those players up through the ranks, while giving them a family to rely on along the way.

Grazio had even included a stipend for Olivia to join if she ever wanted to leave Manchester. Mateo wouldn't push her, though, not when she'd made it clear she needed to be with her father as he healed.

The new Lazio club owner, Tomás Grazio, was either crazy or stupid for offering such a golden contract, but after just two hours with him, Mateo was convinced he was just crazy enough to help the Italian team make a comeback like no one had ever seen before.

Mateo raked his hands down the stubble of his chin.

It was, in short, a dream come true.

Except...

Leaving Olivia was impossible to imagine. At least, if he posed the offer, she'd have a choice and he wouldn't be the one responsible for tearing her from a job she loved.

The dream burned a hole in his pocket as his heart struggled to meet that excitement. Because she'd gone from warm and pliable in his hands earlier in the week to chilly enough he felt the cold from where she stood above him in the press box.

Mateo glanced up. Olivia's face was stoic, and Peter looked tired.

He was desperate to talk to Olivia about the offer, but the timing hadn't been right. The woman had been so damn busy these past couple of days, he'd barely seen her. The last time he had, she'd been upset after her father fainted from weak-

ness after chemo. At the very least, her job here was safe…
Maybe it would take a load off her to know that.

Mateo thumbed the phone in his pocket as Liverpool made
another meagre attempt at moving the ball down the pitch.
He could hardly concentrate, he was so in his own head.

The crowd jumped out of their seats as the buzzer went
off and Manchester stormed the pitch to celebrate their easy
win. Mateo clapped the manager on the back and left, sure
now that his medical services wouldn't be needed.

His afternoon was now free since the win, giving them a
break until the next day.

That meant he could join Olivia and her father at dinner,
something he'd been excited about until she'd pulled away
the past couple days. He figured it was because she was with
her dad until she'd gone radio silent during the match. Now
he couldn't shake the feeling something was off.

You're projecting since you're the one with a secret.

Maybe, but Mateo didn't consider it a secret. It was something he needed to share with the woman he was falling for
since he'd done it for her. But it was also more nuanced than
simply a selfless act of love.

Because what if he asked her to come, and she said no? Or
worse, she said she didn't want to date him long-distance?
He'd be crushed.

Either way, dinner was sure to be interesting.

Mateo was two glasses of wine in and Olivia had barely spoken to him.

A thousand questions bubbled up in his throat, desperate
for answers.

Do you still want to be with me? If not, why meet your father?
Did Robert tell you about me taking the job in Italy?

He needed food, stat, or he ran the risk of blurting out everything he was feeling. He also needed this dinner to be over so he could talk to her in private. She hadn't given him any indication she wanted heavy commitment right now. So why did he still want to lay the choices in front of her and hope with every cell in his body she wanted to come with him?

Because I love her, and that doesn't change if she doesn't feel the same.

"So, Mateo, tell me more about your double-roster plan. Where did it come from?"

He smiled. Talking about his work was as good a distraction as any. Especially when it involved the only other thing besides football and Olivia that brought him joy.

"My mom, actually."

Olivia's head shot up from the piece of bread she was moving around her plate.

"She was a big believer in safety, especially in competitive programs like the Premier League and even more in prominent youth feeder systems. She used to talk to me about it when we'd take day-long bus rides to other cities in Colombia for me to play. How if she was in charge, she'd have a double roster, upgrade equipment, and a dozen other ideas."

"She sounds like an intelligent lady."

"She was. Both ahead of her time and place—England might be okay with female coaches and physicians, but that wasn't ever going to be a possibility for her. So when I had to…make a career shift, I never forgot what she said about player safety. It's because of her I'm here, for so many reasons. And I have your daughter to thank for a lot of what I've learned since."

Olivia's dad smiled but if Mateo was reading her right, Olivia herself only frowned as if she were puzzling him over. It was how she looked at him when they first met.

He thought they'd moved past that. Didn't she know if she was confused, she could just ask him? He'd tell her anything she wanted to know.

Peter smiled. "A father likes to hear that. Especially given my recent diagnosis. Speaking of, Ollie, before you got here, Mateo and I were talking about your position at Manchester. He seems to think it was because of me, and I'm inclined to agree with him. But would you do something different if you had a choice?"

Olivia choked on her wine, her cheeks red. "You talked about me?"

Mateo hadn't known Olivia that long, but he recognized the barely tamed fury in her set jaw, her wide eyes. He'd just wanted to test the waters on if Olivia would want to stay in Manchester or if she was open to more.

"We were talking about your career arc and how you pursued sports medicine because of how it connected you two."

Peter just kept smiling as if nothing was amiss. "I wish I'd known that, hon. But really, if you want to get out of sports medicine because it's not for you, I understand." Olivia's brows shot up as if she was torn between a laugh and scream. Mateo shot Peter a look, but the man continued, seemingly oblivious. "I'm sorry football is all I talk about. That can change, too. That guy you dated, Knox, called to reach out about the diagnosis and instead filled me in on what cryptocurrency was. If I can listen to him talk to me about banking for thirty minutes, I can talk to you about anything. I promise I'll do better."

"Knox?" Mateo asked. Apparently, he had more to worry about than whether Olivia wanted to go with him to Italy.

"An old friend," she said to Mateo, while managing not to look at him. "I'm sorry he reached out to you, Dad. He texted me and I told him about your diagnosis, and he took it too far. I'll talk to him."

Olivia's leg trembled beneath his hand. Why did he feel as nervous as she appeared?

KRISTINE LYNN

161

"Do I need to worry?" Mateo asked. His chest itched with anxiety.

"No, he's just a guy I went out with a couple times. Listen, Dad," she said. "Maybe in the beginning I didn't love my job, but I loved *you*. And I found my passion through that, so I don't have any regrets, if that's what you're asking." She took a breath, and Mateo's heart still wondered about the other man she'd mentioned. How had so much shifted in less than a week? "Can I ask why you're just noticing this? I mean, you never seemed to care about other aspects of my life beyond what I did on the pitch before. I also didn't expect you two to start talking behind my back about it..." She glared at Mateo.

"We weren't, hon." Her dad at least had the good sense to appear confused.

"It seems that way to me. As for Manchester, I'm not sure if they're the right club for me, but what I want isn't possible. I want a life of stability, where my father isn't sick and the only thing we talk about isn't football. I want a boyfriend who talks to me instead of my father when he's concerned, and I want the same opportunities that he is offered because I do the same good work."

To Peter's credit, he didn't shrink away. A few rogue tears fell on his cheeks that he didn't bother to wipe away.

"I wish I wasn't sick and that I wasn't a coward. Football is the only safe thing I could think to bring up. Everything else was something you and your mom talked about. What could I possibly add?"

"You could have asked me questions. Sure, it might have been awkward, but that's better than avoiding the rest of life because it's hard."

She shook and all Mateo wanted was to hold her tight to his chest, to take away this grief. All he'd ever wanted was for her to be happy. That he might be contributing to her feeling the opposite nearly broke him.

"You're right. I wanted a full life for you and felt supremely guilty that the wrong parent died."

"And you never thought to *become* the right parent?"

Mateo winced at the accusations she threw.

"To take me to lunch, sit me down and ask if your only child, your only family, was happy? Because Dad, that would have changed *everything*."

"It's not like that," he tried. "I—"

She held up a hand, silencing him.

"No. I've given you grace because you're going through something unimaginable, but I am, too, Dad. And I need you. Not to talk to someone else about me, but to listen when I talk to you. Because if Mateo could have figured out that I did everything I did for you, then you should have, too."

Silence blanketed the table. It wasn't comfortable as it was when he and Olivia sat in silence at the office, both working alongside one another. No, this was filled with tension. Mateo grew more and more uneasy.

"Olivia," Mateo said. "Can we talk privately?"

"About what? The meeting you took with Grazio?"

He wished he could channel his facial expressions into something resembling calm, but he was so damn tired.

"Olivia—" Mateo started.

"Actually, I think I need to leave," she said. Her voice quavered, breaking him in half. "You two have somehow found a way to make tonight about you when it was supposed to be the three of us spending time together and celebrating the team that at least one of us still works for."

"Olivia, I didn't mean to hurt you."

"It doesn't mean you didn't. Both of you."

"Hon, it looks like you need some time. I'll reach out tomorrow when we've all calmed down."

Peter walked out of the restaurant, but not before leaving the bill paid.

Olivia met Mateo's gaze, her eyes wet and sad.

"I'm going to grab a taxi," she stated. "I need some time to think."

CHAPTER SEVENTEEN

As Olivia flicked the light on in her living room, a deep sense of loss enveloped her, making her heart's arrhythmia act up again. She shed her shoes, her socks, and her jacket as she walked up the stairs.

The doorbell rang and she considered ignoring it. Her neighbors could wait. It rang again and she sighed. This day just needed to end already.

"Mateo," she whispered, opening the door to a tearstained face she knew as well as her own.

"Can I come in?"

"I asked for time," she said. Even as she said it, though, her body revolted, longing for the man filling all the empty spaces inside her. And there were a lot of empty spaces.

"I know. But you need to know everything first, then I'll walk away if that's still what you want."

"You got offered a job, didn't you?" she said. Finally, she met his gaze. His eyes were wide and this close, she heard the soft exhale of his breath, felt it on her cheek. It was proof before his confirmation.

"More or less. I asked for the meeting and the job with Italy, but not for the reasons you think."

"It doesn't really matter, does it? You're leaving."

"I am, but that means you can stay. Robert wasn't—" His chin hit his chest and he sighed. "He wasn't going to keep both of us, so I made a call. How did you know?"

"It's the only thing that made sense with you being pulled into that meeting with the new club owner alone, without me. Why didn't you tell me, though? I know we're new, but this decision involved me, and my career, too."

"You weren't exactly in a headspace to hear me, were you? I mean, you've been so distant the past couple days."

She nodded. She had, hadn't she? Because this was what she'd feared. Sure, it sounded selfless on one hand, but then why hadn't he let her in? He clearly didn't know her as well as she'd assumed he had. Because if he did, he'd know making a unilateral decision like this without talking to her was as egregious as leaving her because he couldn't handle her success. Both were unconscionable in a partner.

"What—" She steeled herself to ask a question she wasn't sure she wanted the answer to. "What does the offer include?"

"I'd be in charge of the Italians' safety for their club, and I guess their feeder programs, too. They want a med station like ours here, but open to the youth leagues who are underfunded, including my scholarship program. It'd be a lot of work, but it sounds rewarding. And they said I could bring a team, Olivia. That means you, if you want."

His words were hedges, but like it or not, Olivia knew him by now. The light in his eyes said he was excited about this. Even though she felt a surge of jealousy at his ability to make medical change in a substantive way—and more than that, the way he'd found his own calling—she couldn't imagine a person more fit for the job. She'd never get in the way of that. His offer to take her was likely a bandage to cover up any bleeding from breaking her heart with this decision. It wasn't real.

Her need to be there for her dad was clear, and so was Mateo's need to follow this path.

Maybe…maybe things had turned out just how they were supposed to. Until she found her own calling and her dad was healthy, she'd only be an anchor, dragging him down. If she loved him, which she had an overwhelming feeling she did, this was the only way.

It didn't take much effort to put on an honest smile for him. Even if it hurt.

"It's amazing, Mateo. It seems perfect for you. Congratulations."

He took her hand. "Would you come with me?"

"I can't," she whispered. Her heart revolted again, her body in a push-pull with her mind, which was resolute. "I need to see my dad through his treatment and find my own way to make a difference. Going with you would only hold you back."

"Can we still find a way to make this work?" Mateo asked. "I want to be here for you."

Olivia's pulse sped up. She leaned back, giving herself space from his scent—musk and spice. Those would only keep her from doing what she needed to protect them from a mistake that would damn them both to a half-life neither actually wanted.

"I don't think that's fair to either of us, Mateo. Let's just appreciate what we were to one another while we were able."

He gathered her into a tight embrace where she wasn't safe from his physical pull on her, nor his captivating scent. He was going to make leaving as difficult as possible, wasn't he?

"What are you talking about, Olivia? We can't just give up. We'll help your dad and then we'll see where we're at."

"Mateo, it's not the same outcome we imagined, but this job will allow you to bring money to programs and kids like you, kids who need you. You can't be focused on me and my dad while you do that."

That quieted him. He opened his mouth, shutting it again.

"This is about more than the job, Olivia. We fell for one another."

"We did. But just because there's chemistry here doesn't mean we're compatible."

Olivia bit her lip. Why couldn't she just see into the future, to a life with Mateo in Italy, happily sharing a cappuccino with him at a café, telling him about her new career? Because it wasn't in her cards.

"How so?" he challenged. "You've felt like home to me pretty much since you yelled at me on national television."

"That's not what I mean. The job in Italy was a good idea. It's years of practicing medicine and building a program for underserved individuals like you used to be, Mateo. And for more money than Robert could pay you, even if he intended to keep us both. Keeping part of your—" she almost said *heart* "—thoughts here won't keep your head in the game. And you'll need that, won't you? This just won't work, not without a healthy amount of resentment at some point from one of us."

"Why do you want me gone so badly? Have you…?" He dipped his chin until it rested on her shoulder. "Is there someone else? Who is this Knox guy, really?"

It would be too easy to tell a small lie, to say she had met someone so it would be easier to say goodbye to the best man she'd ever met.

"There's no one. You set the bar too high for anyone else."

"Then *why*?"

Her heart had already broken when she made the decision to end this…this thing between them. This was just stepping on the shattered pieces.

"Because you have the chance at a dream job. If I get out of your way, you can chase that. Please stop trying to convince me otherwise. I can't make you take the job but I can tell you we won't stay together if you don't."

She trailed off, and when he brushed her cheek with the pad of his thumb, she was surprised to find he wiped tears away. When had she started crying?

"Okay," he whispered. "I'll walk away. But I'm not done

with you, Olivia. And I don't think you're done with me, either. We've both got a lot on our minds and hearts right now, and—" He crooked her chin until their gazes met. Her stomach fluttered with anticipation and her breath hitched in her chest.

He continued, "And maybe you're right. Maybe we can only happen in a place where the conditions are perfect. But I think our imperfections are what made us real all along. Someday I hope you see that."

Mateo gave her a sad smile before opening the door and stepping out of it.

"Olivia?"

She glanced up.

"I hope you never stop trying to find what you're looking for. Because you deserve it."

Olivia was breathless as the most beautiful man she'd ever met shot her one last smile, one she was certain she'd never forget as long as she lived, before he walked out the door.

The words he'd told her—words she'd waited a lifetime to hear—floated around her, bathing her in a mist of her own mistakes.

There was so much she wanted to say, to take back, but the bottom line remained. She'd met Mateo as one version of herself, a version that was steeped in someone else's dreams. If there was a perfect place for them, she knew it included figuring out who she was first, and giving him a chance to do the same. It might hurt like hell, but Olivia Ross would discover who she was and not stop becoming that woman no matter the cost.

She used Mateo's words as her lifeline, her new mantra.

Never stop trying to find what you're looking for. Because you deserve it.

With that in mind, Olivia got to work. Before she built a new life, a few more walls had to come down.

CHAPTER EIGHTEEN

MATEO HELD THE box of mementos he couldn't see bringing with him to Italy. Nor could he imagine throwing them away. They were tokens of his time working with—and loving—Olivia. He still couldn't quite believe that time had come to an end. But somehow, after the final match of the tournament that afternoon, he was on a plane to his new home, his new life.

Damn if he wasn't leaving behind something incredibly important to him, though. And there was no way he was leaving without seeing her again. He'd endure a thousand excruciating moments if he got to look into Olivia's eyes and catch a glimpse of what they'd meant to one another. What he wouldn't give to see his future in her gaze as well.

Wow, how the tides have shifted. A little over a month earlier, Mateo had been happy with the occasional thread of companionship to warm lonely nights, but the thought of anything more had been a nonstarter.

With his own storied past mired in love and loss, giving in to a relationship just hadn't seemed worth it. Now it felt like he couldn't breathe without Olivia. How could she really be ready to let that go? He understood that he'd messed up by not involving her in his decision to chase a job with Grazio's team, but to give up on them entirely? At least she'd be here in Manchester, and he could hope their teams would meet up on the pitch. Any chance of being near her he had to cling tight to, or he'd fall off the precipice of grief he'd created for himself.

Mateo stared at the offensive cardboard box, the newspaper articles and drafts of Manchester's safety protocol on one side, more personal items like the sports romance Olivia had loaned him on the other.

"What am I supposed to do with you?" he mumbled.

"What are you supposed to do with whom?"

Mateo pivoted around. He'd thought he was alone, but Tomás Grazio was there, hands on his hips, a gentle smile on his face. Here was a guy Mateo understood. He, too, had a reputation he was trying to outrun, a futility in a world of elite sports where fans and clubs had the collective memory of centuries behind them.

"Hey there, boss. You got my text?" Mateo asked, picking up the stack of papers closest to him.

"I did." His gaze lingered on one framed photo Mateo had sneaked into the box. "Are you going to tell me you're reconsidering? Because I wouldn't blame you." Tomás picked up the frame. "You seem to have really made…connections in this place."

He had, which was why he had to go, to protect her job. Still, they'd helped one another through personal and professional sticking points by fake dating, sure. But in the end, what they'd had together had been more real than anything else he'd ever felt.

The sorry thing was, he was damn near certain she felt the same way, but the timing of Robert's impending firing, leading to his job offer and move, and her father's cancer diagnosis was piss poor at best.

"I know it's what's best. What's ahead of me is everything I've ever wanted and I'm beyond grateful for the opportunity."

Tomás waved him off. "It's earned. And you're helping me more than you know with my own rehabilitation project."

Mateo wasn't sure if his new boss meant Lazio's club or himself. Maybe both. He had a lot to learn about his new position—that was for certain.

"Speaking of earned, you should have the signing bonus in your bank account as of last night."

"Thank you. I saw it and it's more than generous."

"Great, so then what can I help with?"

"You've given so much to me already, but I need one more thing."

Mateo couldn't read the mogul's face, but he crossed his arms over his chest and leaned against the med table. Mateo had stayed up late the night before thinking through this, wondering how he'd missed it in the first place.

"I'm listening."

"You're giving me the resources to bring on a team of people to help build this program," he started.

"Of course. You'll need people you can trust. Not just physicians with sports medicine backgrounds, though that would be helpful. But who want to work with the community at large. My plans are big and I'm hoping my work with you will just be the beginning."

"That's my thought exactly. I'm glad we're on the same team."

"Not everyone you hoped will be making the move, though?"

Mateo nodded. He didn't miss when Tomás glanced at the photo again. His skin tingled with anticipation.

"Not yet. But that might change. I need your permission to hire someone who is undergoing cancer treatment and will only be able to work once he's better. He's brilliant, though."

"Mateo, I picked you because I trust you. If that's what you want, go for it."

Mateo smiled. "Thanks for understanding how important this is to me."

"I've compiled a list of apartments for rent in my area of town. They're safe, most of them gated and with a phone call to the owners there, they'll be cheaper than other options in Positano. Shall I put two on hold?"

Mateo's head was spinning. "Yes, please. I'll let you know if that changes. May I ask why you're being so accommodating, though? I'm grateful, but I've never had a boss like you before."

Tomás shrugged and smiled. "I didn't do things right for a long time in my life and now I have the chance to do better, so I'm going to do just that. Plus, something about you reminds me of…me. We both know what it means to leave the sport before we're ready, and we're both doing anything we can to stay in it. Besides, when I saw the way you went above and beyond for the club during—and after—the crash, I knew I wanted you on this project. Your pitch was timed perfectly."

Hmm. He'd thought the opposite, but maybe Tomás was right.

"But now I need a favor from you."

"Anything."

"Make sure you both don't let anything distract you from this if you choose to make a go of it." Again, Mateo wasn't sure whether Tomás meant the game or the job. "Life and football are both too difficult to take on half-heartedly."

Mateo couldn't agree more.

"I understand, and thanks. I'm going to make this work for all of us." Just not unilaterally this time. This time, he'd let her choose. Mateo held out his hand and Tomás shook it.

With that, he was gone, and Mateo was where he'd been fifteen minutes earlier, alone with his box of memories. Except somehow, everything was different.

He had the final piece of the puzzle but this was still Olivia's call.

He ran to her office, but the shades were drawn and the lights off. *Weird.*

He tore off down the hallway toward Robert's building.

"Sorry," he called out to the two interns he almost ran into. "Hey, do you know if Olivia is around?"

They looked at one another, then at him. "Um, no. Not anymore."

"Olivia Ross," he said. "Dr. Olivia Ross?"

They both stared at him strangely.

"Yeah, she's like, gone. Not here anymore. Like, forever."

The two ladies walked away, tittering to one another, no doubt about what a colossal prick he was to not know or realize that his supposed girlfriend had what, quit?

Well, they wouldn't be wrong.

He slowed his pace, his pulse not getting the message. It skyrocketed like he had sprinted across the pitch and back for ninety minutes.

Gone. Forever.

His mind replayed those words on a loop, sending his nervous system into a panic. In the length of time it took him to make his way to Robert's on the top floor of the complex, he'd gone through fight, flight and freeze.

She was gone.

Forever.

Still, he didn't believe it. Couldn't. He'd been expecting another chance to see her, maybe even hold her. To share with her the plan he'd exacted to make all their dreams come true. He felt the removal of her from his life as if she'd been surgically excised.

Alone.

Forever.

He shook his head and knocked on Robert's door.

"Yeah." The word was more command, less question. "Door's open."

Mateo made his way into the shrine to all things Manchester, from framed photos of players to mounted kits to trophies and medals from matches and tourneys. The man loved the game; that was for certain.

"Ah, if it isn't the man of the hour."

"Hey, Robert. You ready for the match later?"

"We're gonna wipe the field with Real Madrid," Robert said.

Mateo had to give it to the guy. Whether he agreed with Robert's way of managing, the guy was all in.

"Care to make a friendly wager? Say twenty pounds?" Robert offered.

"You're on."

"Anyway, what brings you by? You'll be at the match, right?"

"Of course. I'm the doctor on rotation. I'm just here to check in on Olivia. She wasn't in her office—" Mateo didn't need to finish his sentence. Robert's smile fell the moment he mentioned Olivia's name.

"She really didn't tell you, huh?"

"Tell me what?"

"Olivia left, Mateo. She told me she'd give notice, but to be honest, with the look on her face—like someone volley-kicked her puppy into the stratosphere—I didn't have the heart to enforce it. Poor woman looked miserable."

Mateo sat down on the edge of the plush armchair beside Robert's desk. But she'd said she loved working for a club. Maybe not Manchester, but she'd known he quit so she could stay and take care of her dad and set herself up for a move—hopefully to Italy.

Robert didn't say anything at first.

"You actually cared about her, didn't you?" he asked after a pause.

Mateo nodded. "More than almost anything. She's special, amazing. Perfect." For him, anyway.

"You know, I wondered when you two first started dating how long it would last. I didn't know you well, but I know Olivia. You're right—she's special. But you two seemed different enough I figured it'd be a challenge, that you'd break up and I'd be left with one of you." Robert chuckled. "I've got to say, I didn't see being without either of you on staff. Figures Grazio was able to tempt you with his offer. Anyway, I wish you the best, and am sorry things shook out the way they did with you two."

Mateo smiled sadly.

"Oh," Robert added. "She did leave you these documents."

Mateo perked up as Robert handed him a manila envelope, a book and an outline of what looked like a safety protocol.

"Thanks," he said, getting up to leave. "And I'm gonna hold you to that bet. Madrid might just take this whole thing."

Mateo wanted to know what was in the letter, but not before laying out his heart—and plan—out to her. He'd read her last words once he'd tried everything to let her see what she meant to him. Until then, he couldn't read her goodbye. The protocol he'd dive into while he waited for the match to start. He couldn't leave the club in a lurch, but he knew where he was headed the second the whistle blew.

He looked over the novel.

It was a dog-eared romance with a worn spine. The idea that Olivia might've been reading this and thinking of him warmed his skin. But why give it to him now? He'd ask after he talked to her. The last thing he needed right now was to read a book with a grand gesture and reunion that might not be possible for him.

Once he was in the tunnel, he looked over the protocol.

HOW TO RESIST YOUR ENEMY

She'd come up with what seemed to be some brilliant medical approaches to a team coming back from injury, which Lazio's club definitely qualified as. Many had life-long disabilities that may end up costing them careers, but with Olivia's ideas, there was renewed hope.

Of course there was. But if she was staying in football, why give him a protocol like this? Had he been wrong about what she might be looking for? That made his intervention even more prescient. She had to know what he was offering—all of it—before she made a decision that could cost her the career she loved.

Mateo didn't have much time to kill before the final match. He hustled back to his office, made himself a pot of coffee and ordered a car to pick him up immediately after the match.

Hopefully, he wouldn't be too late.

CHAPTER NINETEEN

MATEO PACED ALONG the sideline. Real Madrid was up by a goal, but aside from his friendly bet with Robert, he didn't really care. It wasn't the World Cup.

So why couldn't he settle into the match and just enjoy his last one on these British sidelines?

Because she's not here.

The crowd went wild as Manchester tore down the field, beating all the defenders to the goal, scoring with a volley kick that made Mateo's stomach flutter with excitement.

When the whistle came from the pitch, announcing a stoppage in play with two minutes remaining, Mateo tore up the stairs to the normal fan level. He could leave the rest to the interns.

He made his way around people queuing up for drinks, the loo and even merchandise. At least the Lazio kits were still doing well, all the proceeds going to the families of the injured.

As he turned a corner, he ran headlong into a blonde with her hair tucked into a Man-U cap. It was the scent he noticed first—floral and expensive. He looked down at her face. Mild surprise tickled his skin as his gaze connected with eyes he'd peered into so many nights and mornings, feeling happier than he ever had in his life.

Hope and desire mingled in his blood, making him warm.

"Olivia," he whispered. He reached in to hug her, and

though she stiffened at first, she softened around him at last. "What are you doing here?"

"Um, I came to grab the last of my things, but I couldn't leave without seeing your two teams compete. I'm a little embarrassed to say—"

"You're an actual fan of football?"

She bit her lip and chuckled, showing her kit. It was a Real Madrid keeper shirt and he laughed.

"You're probably confusing the hell out of the other fans with the hat and kit combination." The sea of people around them faded, everyone finding their way to their respective queues or seats.

"I'm rooting for both. What are you doing up here? I mean, I wasn't hiding from you, but—"

"I love you," he whispered. He cleared his throat. Now wasn't the time for soft declarations.

Her skin flushed. "You read my letter?"

"No, I couldn't. Not until I talked to you."

"The book—"

"I didn't get to, either."

"And you still—"

"Love you? Yes. Very much."

"Oh, Mateo—"

"Just," he said, holding out a hand, "hear me out. If you don't like my offer, I'm gone on the next flight out of here and you don't have to ever see me again. But if you do…"

A young girl ran between them, a Manchester kit on. Her blond curls reminded him of a young Olivia and he smiled. What he would have given to know this woman all his life. As it was, he felt robbed of precious time with her. He didn't want to think about how he'd feel if she left forever.

"Okay." She accepted his hand as he ran through his pitch one more time. "Go ahead."

Mateo steeled himself with a deep, fortifying breath.

"When I asked you to come with me to Italy, I'm not sure you understood. I asked for the job not only for me, but for you as well. I wanted you to have options when your dad was better, but before that, I didn't want Robert to fire you. Which, I tried to keep from you, was inevitable."

"I found that out when I went to quit. Again, why didn't you say anything? It's not that what you did wasn't selfless or that I wasn't appreciative of the gesture, but having my life decided for me was an awful feeling."

Mateo squeezed her hand. "I know. And I'm sorry. Of all the regrets in my life, that's up there, Olivia. I tried to save you when I should have realized you could damn well save yourself."

She gazed up at him, and the hint of a smile on her lips buoyed him. "Keep talking, Garcia."

"Well, you know I get to pick my team in Italy. And the contract for both of us is amazing, Olivia. Half of what we're doing is going to be working with the public, building a sports medicine complex for youth teams and sports facilities in Positano that retirees can use. I'll need someone who doesn't mind a Premier League team physician job that won't involve travel, but pays a fortune, and is situated on the Amalfi coast. We'll have a lot of fun but also do so much good for the community…"

"*We?* Who else would be on your team? Assuming I've agreed, which I haven't, for the record."

Mateo reached in his blazer pocket. "Obviously, I'm hoping you agree, but your father is the only other one on my list. After he's healed, of course. If he comes, I reached out to the hospital down there and they've already saved a spot for him in their oncological treatment center."

Olivia's hands trembled as she took the sheet of paper he extended. She eyed him warily, but read over it, her mouth opening wider as she continued. She put a finger to her lips and a small gasp escaped. She must have gotten to the end.

Finally, her hand fell and she met his gaze. She didn't throw the contract at him, so that had to count for something, right?

"You already have this prepared?"

"Well, you were part of the contract since I pitched it to Tomás. Then I got your envelope with your ideas and was even more certain you'd be a perfect fit for his vision. I'm sorry I didn't think of bringing your dad sooner, but when I figured it out, I came straight to tell you. To ask you," he said, wincing at his slipup. "From now on, I come to you, first, Olivia. For everything."

"Tomás agreed to this?"

"He did. He wants you there, too. We can negotiate the job and benefits, but I meant what I said—this will keep you in one place, for work at least. It's not just football injuries you'd be working with, either. You'll be in charge of planning and implementing a comprehensive community medical program and it's the same length of time for your contract as mine. I want you as a *partner*, Olivia. Please, just give me a chance."

"Mateo…"

He stopped, breathless. He was pushing her too far, like he had when they were first paired in the medical bay. But if he didn't lay it all on the table and she walked away, he'd always wonder if he did enough to let her know how he felt.

"There's no pressure here, Olivia. I just wanted you to know how valuable you are, how sorry I am that I screwed it up by using external factors to convince you to fake date me when we first met instead of just being brave enough to ask you out for real. I was scared about how much I cared about your opinion, how quickly you were opening my eyes and changing my mind. I'm also sorry I didn't involve you when things got tough. I tried to fix it myself, but that's not love."

She bit her bottom lip and his stomach roared with desire.

"The thing is, if I've learned one thing in this amazing life I've led, it's that there's so much beauty, so much love and adventure, but there doesn't ever seem to be enough time. And I want to spend what's left of mine loving you and building a life both of us have been dreaming of. I think—even though I'll never speak *for* you again—that you might agree we found this in one another."

She inhaled and closed her eyes. "Mateo, please."

His chin sank to his chest. "Go ahead. I'll shut up now."

She squeezed his hand and when he glanced back up, tears lined her bottom lids.

"I said too much, didn't I?"

Olivia shook her head. "No, it's perfect. But my dad—" She glanced behind her, her brows furrowed. Was she looking for him?

"He's invited. Did you see the contract?"

"I did, and I'm grateful, but I can't speak for him any more than you could speak for me."

He braced himself.

"You have to ask him yourself," she continued.

"That's all I was hoping to do." His chest heaved with hope and he pulled her into his embrace. Kissing the top of her head, he whispered, "If he says yes, would you come?"

She nodded, then glanced up at him, her cheeks stained where tears had fallen.

"Of course. It's perfect."

"Where is he right now?" Mateo asked.

"Now?" She laughed, a sob escaping. "Last time I saw him, he was in line for one of those new churro hot dogs that American company brought over." She gestured behind them and Mateo felt that impending sense of time chasing him slip away. Her hand still grasping his, he took off.

"Show me where."

They walked ten booths over before they found Peter.

"Mateo! What a pleasant surprise," Peter said. He paid for what looked like a meter-long churro and joined them. "I wondered if you were still around. Olivia told me about your new position and I have to say, I'm a jealous man. I don't know what I'd give to start over a medical practice in the sun on the coast."

Mateo grinned as he took the remaining sheet of paper from his breast pocket.

"I was hoping you'd say that, sir. Now, there's no pressure, but you should know I made the same offer to your daughter. I love her and want to be with her, but I understand how selfish it is to ask you both to follow me to my dream position to make that happen. Still, if there's any chance..."

Peter's response to the job offer was similar to his daughter's, except he laughed heartily at the end of his read through.

"Son, this better not be a prank or I'll take what I've learned from watching donkey kicks for the past five decades and boot you into next week. I might be a little weak from chemo, but I can still pack a punch."

Olivia and Peter shared a glance. Something unspoken passed between them, but Mateo couldn't translate it.

"I believe you could, sir. But it's not a joke. I want both of you to join me in Italy. And Olivia, you don't need to decide today. Take some time and think about it, because for me, it's more than just a job. I'll respect you if you turn me down completely, or just want to come to Italy and work and never see me personally again. But know if you give me even a hint of the go-ahead, I'm going to work every day to let you know how damn much I love you and want you to be loved in the open. I don't have a problem being with a strong woman and I sure as hell won't have a problem telling anyone who listens that you're the best thing to ever happen to me. But—"

"Yes," she said.

Mateo was pretty sure the whole stadium quieted so he could hear that one word. But what—

"Yes," she repeated. "We want to join you. Right, Dad?"

Peter nodded, his own eyes watery now. Heat built in the back of Mateo's throat as well.

"I'll, uh, give you two some privacy as you hash out the details," Peter said.

When they were alone again, Mateo took Olivia's hands in his.

"Are you saying yes as my medical partner, or—"

"I'm saying yes as your partner, period."

Mateo couldn't keep the grin from blossoming on his lips.

"I'm sorry if I ever made you feel I was unsure about you, but I couldn't let a new relationship get in the way of the good you can do for others, no matter how much I love you."

"Say that again."

She smiled and playfully thwacked his shoulder. "I love you, Mateo. More now than ever. How did you figure it out, though? Exactly what I would need to say yes to this job?"

He shrugged and kissed her. Man, this woman turned him on, inspired him and made him feel safe, all at the same time. It was remarkable, actually.

"I realized I had been hearing you every minute since we met, even if it took a moment to register."

She leaned up and planted a kiss on his lips that held the promise of a lifetime in its gentle touch.

"Every minute?" she teased.

He laughed, his head thrown back in joy. "Okay. Maybe not from the first second. But it didn't take long, Ross."

"Not for me, either."

He kissed her again, this time deepening the connection so she might feel the love and hope and commitment he was giving her in exchange for her love and trust.

He couldn't wait for all the moments they had in front of

them, moments he'd get to witness more of her happiness and hopefully make more of them happen for her. Gratitude washed over him for all she'd given him and for what they would give one another.

Because for the first time in Mateo's life, he had time on his side, a family in his corner and the love of a helluva good woman.

What more could he ever ask for?

EPILOGUE

OLIVIA CHASED PENELOPE down the pitch, the toddler's blond curls waving in the sea breeze.

Pen giggled, somehow able to dribble the youth football despite barely being able to climb a set of stairs by herself.

"Mama take?" she asked.

Olivia laughed. "I don't think I can, hon," she said. And that wasn't a lie. Her daughter—the best thing to happen to her with the exception of Mateo, her loving, amazing husband—was too good already.

Mateo ran up alongside them and pretended like he was going to steal the ball.

Pen squealed and deftly moved around him.

"The girl's a prodigy," he commented. The awe in his eyes as he watched their daughter avoid Peter and put the ball in the goal was one of the sexiest things about him. Whatever joy and support he brought Olivia, it was compounded when he became a father. Little did he know, she was about to let him know some more good news in that department.

"She's your child through and through," Olivia laughed.

"I dunno, love. She told me she thought I was being *testarudo*. I think she got that from you."

Olivia giggled and nodded. "My husband being stubborn? No, I don't believe it." She leaned up and wrapped her arms around her husband. "Have I told you how happy you make me?" she asked.

"Once or twice," he said. She nudged him with her hip. His eyes were light and playful. It was one of her favorite looks of his. Next to sultry and filled with desire for her, or serious and concentrating when Pen tried to tell him something in her toddler speak, or professional when he was at work… It was safe to say she loved each side of her husband. "I hope it's obvious how much I love you and our family, Olivia."

"It is. In fact, it's about to get a whole lot more obvious how much you love me in eight months or so."

There were some pretty great moments she and Mateo had shared since they all moved to Italy four years ago. Her father's call that he was in remission was one. Seeing Lazio get added to the Premier League not two years after the horrific crash had taken out most of their team was another. Finding out she and Mateo were pregnant with Pen was definitely a big one. Her doctor sharing that her heart was strong enough to bear children with minimal complications had to be added to the list.

But this moment was rising to the top. Surrounded by the rest of their family, seeing Mateo's eyes and smile widen as he figured out her clue was nothing short of beautiful.

"We're having another baby?"

"We are. Like it or not, Pen will be a big sister soon."

Mateo picked Olivia up and twirled her like her dad was doing to Pen.

"I love you, Olivia. Thank you for these gifts. I don't know how I can ever repay you."

Olivia gestured around them, at the sun setting over the Tyrrhenian Sea, bathing everyone she loved in a warm orange glow.

"You already have, love. You're my real-life romance novel."

She'd been given everything a woman could want. Her happily-ever-after was in each day, each sunrise and sunset, each patient she saved.

It was in her family and heart, both which were full.

Olivia Ross, physician and wife and daughter and mother, was in love with her future and she had the stubborn doctor holding her to thank for all of it.

* * * * *

PARISIAN SURGEON'S SECRET CHILD

SUE MacKAY

MILLS & BOON

PROLOGUE

IN THE SURGICAL ward at Paris Central Hospital Nurse Camille Beauregard looked around while she waited as general surgeon Etienne Laval filled in another nurse on a patient he'd operated on that afternoon. Something didn't feel quite right.

On the opposite side of the four-bed room they stood outside, a post-op patient lay overly still, her chest barely rising or falling. Her hands were spread wide and tight on her abdomen.

Camille raced across. 'Hello?'

'Camille? What's up?' Etienne called after her.

'Something's wrong.' The woman's face was grey and glistened with sweat. 'Hello, can you hear me?' Reaching for the patient's wrist, Camille found a weak, slow pulse. She slammed the emergency buzzer at the same time calling to the nurse Etienne had been talking to. 'Amelie, get the defib. Now.'

'Cardiac arrest?' asked Etienne, already at the other side of the bed with his interlaced hands close to the woman's chest, ready to do compressions as he checked over what he could see.

'Not yet. I'm being prepared because I believe it's going to happen.' *Please keep beating, heart*, she pleaded in her head.

Then they were surrounded with nurses and a trolley of emergency equipment.

She reached for the defibrillator, still certain the situation was about to deteriorate.

'Prepare the defibrillator,' Etienne commanded as he tore open the hospital gown covering the woman's chest.

'Onto it.' Camille had the defib pads in hand and immediately put them in place. 'Get the machine up to speed, Amelie. We might not need it but time is of the essence if we do.' Deep down she knew what was coming.

'Yes, it's happening. Now,' Etienne cut in. 'Stand back,' he continued when the defib beeped. It was ready.

Camille held her breath as the current lifted the woman partially off the mattress. As she fell back the line on the defib screen rose, fell, rose and fell. 'Phew, that was close.' *Thank you, heart.* Her own heart was beating wildly. Sometimes this work could be too much.

'Agreed.' The relief was also obvious in Etienne's voice. 'Whose patient is she?' he asked, his gaze totally focused on the heart monitor where the green line moved up and down.

'Beau's,' the head nurse, Karina, told him. 'She came up from Theatre about an hour ago. Amelie's her nurse.'

'There were no signs of anything wrong with her heart. I checked often.' Amelie sounded defensive. 'It's all there in the notes.'

Camille gave her a quick smile. 'It's all right. These things happen sometimes, Amelie.'

As the head nurse took over monitoring the woman Etienne stepped back. 'I'll call Beau to let him know what's happened.'

'Thanks, Etienne,' Karina replied. 'Pass the phone over when you're done. I need to ask him a few things.'

SUE MACKAY 9

With nothing else for her to do, Camille went to check on one of her patients in another room along the corridor. Her hands shook as she thought about what might've happened if she hadn't sensed something was wrong. Sometimes instinct was a game changer, but that was the first time hers had kicked in quite like that, something to be grateful for. Odd how shaken she felt. It wasn't as though emergencies didn't arise with post-op patients. Thankfully there were less than two hours to go before she was off duty and out of here on three months' leave. It was hard to believe how uptight she was. But then emotionally she was all over the place what with heading away to Montreal in two days' time, and another, bigger issue to contend with.

'Camille. Wait.'

Her heart sank. The very man she was going to talk to later and change his world for ever, along with hers, stood beside her and she hadn't even seen him coming. Hadn't sensed his presence. For her telling him her news was going to be as drastic as saving that woman's life. Difficult was another word for what had to be said. Lifting her head slowly, she faced Etienne. 'Yes?' Why did he have to look so hot? To fill her head with memories of getting as close as humanly possible to that amazing body? Reminding her of a need for more of the pleasure he'd induced in her?

'You were brilliant. How did you know she was in trouble?' Wonder shone in his eyes.

For a brief moment she felt all tender inside. 'Instinct, I guess.' She shrugged. What else could she say when she didn't fully understand what had gone down either? 'I sensed there was a problem.'

'And leapt in to deal with it. Well done.' He touched her shoulder lightly.

Highly out of order on the ward, but no one was around

10 PARISIAN SURGEON'S SECRET CHILD

to see. And right now, with what she had to tell him later, she wasn't about to make a fuss. Unfortunately there was no denying the heat that casual touch created within her. A heat that had already led to a one-night stand after a staff party where she'd seen a different, sexier side to surgeon Laval and been instantly attracted to him. The one night together hadn't been enough and they'd continued to indulge their passion for more incredible nights over the following weeks until she'd begun to think she might be getting too involved and called a halt to the fling. *If only it were that simple.* 'Thank you.'

Turning, she headed down the ward, checking her watch and ignoring the thumping under her ribs. *She* wasn't having a cardiac arrest, merely stressing about how to deal with the conversation yet to come. Etienne would not take her news lightly. More than likely he wouldn't believe it, but that was no excuse not to tell him. She'd put it off until now because she had to work alongside him on the ward until she left for Montreal. Having him give her the cold shoulder because he might not accept her news would be hell. He'd been ultra careful about using protection. She'd been sceptical when she'd first realised she'd missed a period, but blood tests didn't lie.

Etienne had the right to know she was pregnant. She wanted him to know. Her child was not going to grow up as she had, always wondering who his father was, where he was, why he didn't love him when he hadn't even met him. Her hand touched her tummy. Twelve weeks. She was certain it was a boy in there. There was no reason behind that, just a feeling she was right. And look how well her instincts had played out for the woman recovering from abdominal surgery minutes ago.

The fling with Etienne had been amazing, unlike any

she'd had before. So good that he'd begun sneaking into her head when she wasn't looking, even tapping on her heart, which was why she'd pulled the plug—much to his amazement. Apparently women didn't ever do that to Etienne Laval. His reputation went before him. He was open to short flings, nothing else, and he decided when they were over. By all accounts the women he slept with usually hung around for all they could get. He was single, wealthy beyond comprehension, and incredibly handsome. No doubt a great catch in some people's books. He would be in hers too if love were possible, but it wasn't. She wasn't seeking financial help from him, and, frankly, that was about all he could offer because she doubted that, with the way his emotions remained untouchable except in bed, he was available for love any more than she was.

Her heart had been smashed once when she'd trusted the wrong man. She wasn't falling for Etienne when he wasn't into anything deep and meaningful. But she would tell him the truth and hope they could work together amicably over raising their child when she returned to Paris. She instinctively crossed her fingers, knowing what a long shot that was. Telling Etienne tonight would give him time to accept the situation and think about how they managed parenthood when they weren't in a relationship. She would raise her child, but also wanted Etienne to be a part of his upbringing, just not a part of her personal life.

She'd be back from Montreal before the birth and then they could sit down and work out everything in a way that suited all three of them.

Two hours later Camille drew a deep breath and stepped purposefully up to the partially open door of Etienne's office, then stopped.

12 PARISIAN SURGEON'S SECRET CHILD

She could see through the gap that he was sitting in his chair with his feet on the desk, a phone to his ear, looking good enough to eat and reminding her how wonderful making love with him had been. She should call what they'd got up to sex, not lovemaking, and keep it in line with not wanting to get too involved, but it wasn't easy. There'd been something about Etienne that ignored her need to remain as protective of her heart as she usually was.

'No, Mum, I will not take Beatrice to the ball. She's completely focused on marrying me when we aren't even in a relationship and that's the last thing I ever intend doing.'

Silence ensued as he listened to his mother.

Camille knew she should knock on the door to let him know she was here. It wouldn't help her case if he caught her eavesdropping on a personal conversation. Or ogling that tight, sexy body of his, which should be the last thing on her mind. Etienne could be a big distraction when she didn't have her sensible hat on. Raising her hand, she paused as he continued talking.

'She's already tried the "she loves me" approach.' The fingers of one hand flicked in the air as he spoke. 'I'm so over what women come up with to try and move in with me, or get a marriage proposal. The only lie I haven't encountered in a while is the fake pregnancy one, and I bet it's not far away again. Yes, I am a cynic, and you know why. I expect women to lie to me, not be honest. I will not take Beatrice to the ball.'

Camille's shoulders sagged. She immediately straightened up. She was tempted to get out of here. Etienne had just given her the best possible reason to keep her mouth shut, except she didn't want to do that. She couldn't. It wouldn't be right for any of them. If only there were a chance he wouldn't automatically disbelieve that she was pregnant, and thereby refuse to accept he was the father. Her own father had left before she came into the world, not to be seen until he wanted something from her.

Basically Etienne had just proved her suspicions right about how he'd react to her news. However, he *was* her baby's father and therefore deserved to know just as her child deserved to have a father in his life. She wasn't about to demand she move in with him, she only wanted him aware of his parenthood, but his barriers were already up and she hadn't even uttered a word. No surprise there. He was always friendly but never once, even when he appeared completely relaxed, had she been able to see past that to what lay behind his handsome face.

Time to face the music. Her heart was heavy. She knew what it was like to grow up without meeting her father until she was twenty and then ruing the years she'd wasted wondering who he might be and longing to know him, along with cursing her mother for not telling Grandma and Grandpa who he was before she died. At least *her* child had a decent man for a father despite his issues about what women expected from him.

Etienne was still talking. 'You also know why I never intend becoming a parent.'

He didn't even want children? Didn't want to be a father? That was altogether different. She *was* out of here. Etienne was not going to know he was already on the way to becoming a parent. Not now, probably never. Make that definitely never. Her blood was suddenly boiling. Her child wasn't going to know the same pain she had because of her father. She turned away.

'Camille, what are you doing here?'

She swore under her breath. He'd spotted her. What

14 PARISIAN SURGEON'S SECRET CHILD

could she say to that? Especially since his mother would no doubt hear whatever came out of her mouth? Their brief fling had ended abruptly because she'd known she was starting to fall for Etienne. Hoping to get into a serious relationship with this man was like believing her phone never needed its battery charged up. If she'd even been looking for a long-term connection he wasn't her type, which didn't help her to understand why she'd begun falling for him in the first place. Like her, he didn't do serious relationships, or so he'd told her the very first time they'd slept together. Not that there'd been any sleeping going on. She pushed the door open fully. 'Nothing important.' Only the most important thing in her life at the moment.

'Just a minute, Mum. I have an idea. Camille, would you go as my partner to a charity ball my mother's organising?'

'No, thank you. I'm busy that week.'

His face froze. Of course he wasn't used to being turned down. He gave a deliberate shrug as if to say he didn't care what she said. 'I haven't told you when it's being held.'

'I don't do balls.' Not true. She loved dancing but he wasn't to know that.

'Really?' He was looking at her as if she'd lost her mind.

She probably had, but there was a bigger problem between them. Even if she weren't heading to Canada, going anywhere with him was off the cards until he knew about her pregnancy and then he'd no longer ask her to accompany him to a coffee break on the ward if she was still working there. He'd been away at a conference until today and obviously hadn't heard this was her last day for a while. Anyway, she was not prepared to go through the

SUE MACKAY

pain of being made to look like a selfish, lying woman who had obviously schemed and connived to get what she wanted from him. Coming here was turning out to be a huge mistake. She managed a shrug of her own. 'Really. I'm off home now, so carry on talking to your mother.' She turned to leave.

'Wait. Why *did* you drop by?'

The only lie I haven't encountered in a while is the fake pregnancy one.

'It's all right. I made a mistake.' One she did not want to accept. For all the wrong reasons in this case, Etienne expected someone to tell him that he'd unwittingly fathered a child because he'd been lied to about it before. He deserved to know it was true in her case, and then make some decisions, but not right now, when she was so angry and upset. She'd be back in Paris well before her baby arrived. She might talk to him then. It could be easier to do once she'd spent a few months thinking through what she'd heard and how to make it work for everyone. But right now she couldn't see herself ever telling him.

A sudden sense of loss took over from all the other emotions simmering through her, forcing her to turn and look at him one last time. It might've been a fling, but there'd been something warm and special about their short time together, despite how Etienne hid behind a façade he thought no one saw—more reason why she'd walked away with her heart intact while she still could. And now she was carrying *their* baby. 'Goodbye, Etienne,' she said softly.

Going to Montreal with her grandmother was a trip that had been a long time coming. Her grandfather grew up there and moved to Paris when he met Grandma, who was Parisian through and through. He wanted his ashes

16 PARISIAN SURGEON'S SECRET CHILD

taken to Montreal when he died to be buried alongside his parents. She couldn't pull out without letting Grandma down, and that wasn't happening no matter what else was going on in her life. Not after everything her grandparents had done for her from the day she was born.

Inexplicably her eyes blurred with tears as she made her way to the elevator. Deep down she mightn't believe Etienne was really her type but there was no denying he was a wonderful man and that she did have strong feelings for him. She'd got herself into a right mess getting pregnant. So much for taking every precaution available. Something had failed. Now she had a number of serious problems to sort and whichever way she went someone was going to get hurt. If only Etienne were easier to approach, other than when going to bed with him, but he wasn't. Unfortunately she would never trust any man, wonderful or not, with her heart after the one she had loved and believed she'd spend her life with, Benoit, had forgotten to mention the wife and two daughters he lived with. Never again would she give her heart away. It was too painful when everything went belly up.

Etienne wondered what he'd done wrong for Camille to react as though he'd asked her to go to a hanging. It was refreshing on one level, he had to admit. Also rare. It also sucked. He actually liked more about her than just the awesome sex they'd shared during their fling. Their first time together had come about because she'd looked so sexy in a short skirt and tight top accentuating her perfect figure, something he'd only guessed at before as she was always in scrubs at work. To his surprise she hadn't tried everything possible to get more than a few nights between the sheets.

She'd snuck under his radar when he'd thought he was invincible. Worse, it had been Camille who'd finished their time together, not him. A totally new experience for him. 'When was I last turned down for any invitation?'

'Seems to me she could be a keeper.'

Etienne groaned. He'd forgotten about his mother being on the other end of the phone. Camille was a distraction when he wasn't being careful. 'Come on, that's excessive.' In his book there was no such thing as a woman being a keeper. Yes, he was a cynic, but after being hurt once, twice wasn't happening. 'I'll go on my own to the ball. It's not as though I won't get to dance with women who aren't already hooked up with a man.'

There were always females attending without partners for various reasons. Besides, while he was happy to take to the dance floor, it wasn't essential. He'd do his bit at the auction to raise funds for a children's charity, catch up with people he knew, and then maybe get an early night for a change. Life had become boring, he decided. Safer but dull as cold fries. Which did not mean he was going to step beyond the firm barriers he kept around his heart. Nor was he going to have a family. Not after going through the agony of losing his brother and watching his parents struggle to deal with their pain while supporting his sister and him. It had been so hard for all of them.

'Who is this woman? Did you call her Camille?' Of course, she knew the answer to that. His mother had a habit of stirring when it came to his lack of a love life. She refused to accept that because his first and only serious girlfriend had wrecked his belief in true love, he wasn't interested in finding another woman to try again. She probably had a point. He did get lonely at times, but not enough to go through pain like Melina had caused him.

18   PARISIAN SURGEON'S SECRET CHILD

Melina had opened his eyes completely, never to be closed again. Only weeks before they were due to marry he'd overheard her talking to a friend about how relieved she'd be for all the fuss to be over so she could get back to focusing on her own plans for the future. She'd said she'd do everything required to help Etienne and his family with their many business and charity commitments so no one thought she was there only for the lifestyle, even if that was why she was marrying him.

When he'd questioned if she'd loved him at all Melina had said love wasn't all it was cracked up to be and that working together on projects was more important. Basically she was all about herself, and not a lot for him. It had shocked him to the core to hear her say that love wasn't important. Hence he'd cancelled the wedding only for her to tell him he couldn't because she was pregnant with his child. That had been a desperate lie. There was no baby. He hadn't spoken to her since. What he'd struggled with most was that deep down he'd regretted there not being a baby despite believing he didn't want to be a parent. He'd begun to accept he was going to be a father and then it was torn away from him; a reminder of why he wanted to avoid parenthood.

'Etienne? You're not answering me,' said his mother.

'Camille's a nurse on the surgical ward.' A very caring, firm but sympathetic nurse whom patients adored, and doctors appreciated. A nurse whose instincts were off the planet after what he'd witnessed today. Camille calling off their fling had been a novelty, one he hadn't quite managed to put behind him. Something he admired and that kept him aware of her far too much.

'Sounding better by the minute,' chuckled his mother.

'Time I checked up on a patient. Talk during the weekend.' He hung up before Mum could add any more point-less comments to the conversation. Camille had turned him down so he'd go alone to the function. Say no more.

It never failed to amaze him how women believed they only had to be exceptional in bed to get a free ride into his life full-time. No wonder he wouldn't be rushing to the altar any time soon. More likely never. To think he'd loved Melina like no one else. When they'd first met he'd fallen hard and fast, and had never wanted to be without her at his side.

He hadn't trusted another woman with his heart since, and doubted he ever would. Just because Camille Beau-regard didn't swoon at his feet didn't mean she wouldn't be out to get what she wanted from him either. Yep, he was definitely a cynic, but that was what kept him safe. Wasn't it?

CHAPTER ONE

AS THE WHEELS touched down on the runway at Charles de Gaulle Airport Camille grinned with excitement and relief. She was finally home after fifteen months in Montreal. A tumultuous and heartbreaking period of her life along with some of the most wonderful moments to lift her spirits. She was ready to do the decent thing and introduce her wee daughter to her father no matter what he said or thought. She'd been wrong about having a boy, and couldn't care less. Elyna was her adorable girl.

She was as ready as she'd ever be considering that Etienne wouldn't be easy to confront, would be looking for reasons not to believe her because apparently every woman wanted something from him and would go to any length to get it. But it had to be done for her daughter's sake if not Etienne's, and she wouldn't put it off any longer.

She'd let Etienne down by not stepping up and telling him before she left for Canada. The fact she'd heard him saying he'd never believe a woman who told him she was having his baby was irrelevant. That he didn't intend being a parent was different, but she owed him the opportunity to rethink that. Guilt had weighed heavily on her from the day she'd held Elyna in her arms for the first time. It had been a very brief moment before the doctors had taken her daughter away to Paediatric Intensive Care where she'd spent weeks in an incubator. Being born eight weeks premature hadn't given her the best start but she'd made up for it ever since, growing fast and being so cheerful and alert to everything going on around her. Elyna was amazing.

As she turned to her sleeping daughter tucked firmly in a child seat with a pink blanket wrapped around her, Camille's grin slowly faded. Etienne might want nothing to do with his child, or he might demand more than his share of time with her, and want to have all the say in how and where she was raised. He wouldn't. Would he? It just showed how little she really knew the man. Their fling had been amazing but it had been all about the wonderful sex, not spending time getting to know each other on a deeper level.

After the way Benoit had treated her when she'd loved him so much, getting too involved with a man was something she had no intention of doing again. The day a woman had knocked on her door five years ago and introduced herself as Benoit's wife and the mother of his two children Camille had closed herself off to ever being that vulnerable again. Not only had Benoit broken her heart but he'd shown her she was far too trustful and should never have readily accepted the things he'd told her about himself. But wasn't that what a person did when they loved and trusted someone? Believed them. To check out everything Benoit had said would've undermined their relationship and her feelings for him—and exposed the truth before she got too invested in him.

She fully expected Etienne to refuse to accept Elyna was his daughter because he was already waiting for someone to try that trick again, but it'd still hurt if he

PARISIAN SURGEON'S SECRET CHILD

thought she could be so selfish and conniving. At least it'd be less likely he'd want to take charge of Elyna's life, but if he did that'd be the worst outcome. They'd be forever fighting over Elyna's parenting and how to raise her, because no matter what ideas Etienne came up with she would always stick by her daughter. Elyna was more important than anyone else in her life.

There lay her biggest fear, because she'd never be able to afford the ongoing legal costs if Etienne did get down and dirty over who raised their child. With his extreme wealth she hadn't a chance. She sighed. She still owed her daughter the chance to know her father, even one who'd said he didn't want children. Elyna needed him in her life so they had to work through this. It wasn't in her to keep Etienne a secret from Elyna. Her own mother had never told anyone who her daughter's father was even when, two days after she gave birth, she knew she was dying from severe septicaemia. Camille didn't want Elyna to know that pain. It had undermined her ability to believe her mother had been a loving person, even when her grandparents had said she was and that she'd adored Camille for the short time she was with her.

But having finally met the man when she was twenty, Camille had finally understood why her mother had kept her father's identity a secret. She hadn't liked him from the moment he'd turned up at her apartment to introduce himself in a smarmy manner, trying to ingratiate himself in her life because he'd missed out on so much due to her mother being a lying bitch. He'd turned out to be only about himself and was a useless piece of work, relying on others to pay his way through life. Why her mother had ever got together with him was beyond Camille's comprehension except for wondering if maybe love really was blind.

At least Elyna didn't have a father like that. He was upright and kind, and could be fun when he wasn't wondering what someone wanted from him, which appeared to be most of the time he wasn't concentrating on patients. But he also wasn't going to immediately believe her when she said Elyna was his.

Camille unclipped her seat belt and glanced around at the disembarking passengers. She'd wait until they'd finished getting their bags down from the overhead lockers and made their way to the front before getting her own gear.

'Do you want a hand with Elyna?' a stewardess asked when the plane was nearly empty. The woman had been a treasure throughout the flight, taking Elyna for a walk up and down the aisle when she got grizzly and feeding her so Camille could enjoy her own meal.

'Thanks, but I'll be fine.' Her little girl was still sound asleep and hopefully would remain so for a while longer, though collecting luggage and going through Immigration would probably wake her. With a bit of luck she wouldn't be too unsettled, but the chances were slim. As good a reason as any for spending money she shouldn't on a taxi instead of catching the train to her apartment where her friend, Liza, had kindly got in supplies for the next couple of days.

Liza had visited her in Montreal when Elyna was two weeks old and had happily accepted the role of surrogate aunt, since Camille had had no close family other than her grandmother who was counting down the time she had left in this world. 'Come on, baby girl. We have a

24 PARISIAN SURGEON'S SECRET CHILD

special place to go.' Home. Her home, left to her by her grandparents. Her safe haven.

Important as it was to go and see Etienne to inform him he had a daughter, she wasn't doing that today. If only she'd had his number she'd have talked to him months ago when she'd realised she wouldn't be returning to Paris for a lot longer than first planned but she'd deleted it after overhearing him say he didn't want to be a father. And she'd had no luck with his secretary at the hospital, either.

Before her grandmother had died, she'd talked about Etienne with her and how what he'd said had closed her off to giving him a chance to rethink his stance on fatherhood. Her grandmother's gentle persuasion had made her see he deserved to know regardless, and that there had to be more behind his statement than the fact women lied to him regularly. That wasn't a strong enough reason to never have a family, surely? Finally, Camille had accepted Grandma was right and there was only one way to find out where Etienne stood. For that she had to face him.

Thirty minutes after exiting the plane Camille piloted a trolley laden with bags and Elyna sitting in the carrier space towards the taxi rank. People were pushing and shoving, talking and laughing, shouting and cursing. She was back in Paris. It felt so good to be home.

'Camille? Is that you?'

What? Only Liza knew she was arriving today and she didn't have a deep, husky male voice. Looking around, she tried to find someone she knew.

'Camille, it *is* you.' Etienne Laval appeared in front of her, looking as stunning as she recalled. 'Thought I recognised that mass of blonde hair.' He leaned in and brushed a light kiss over her cheek that set her skin afire. 'Where have you been?'

Etienne. No. Please no. Anyone but Etienne. Not when she had Elyna with her. Her heart sank. So much for getting time to settle in before talking to him. She wasn't ready. Would she ever be? Probably not. But now? At the airport? No way. Elyna came first and any minute now she'd let rip with grizzles, which would not go down well with Etienne or anyone within hearing distance. So far she'd been interested in what was going on around them but that couldn't last much longer.

'I've just flown in from Montreal and am really tired so I need to grab a taxi, if you don't mind.' She was being abrupt but she so wasn't ready to confront him. Already her mind was tossing up the many questions he would ask. Worse, rubbing it in that there was no way he'd ever believe he was Elyna's father. Then again, she had no idea how he'd react if he did believe her and that was harder to cope with, as there were lots of questions she needed answers for. About his role, her role, what he'd want. On and on they went.

His face fell and he took a step back. 'Fine.' Then his gaze dropped to the trolley. More specifically to Elyna. His eyes widened. Then his mouth flattened. 'I see congratulations are in order.'

If only you knew. 'Thank you.'

He looked around, then back at her. 'Did you travel without help?'

'Yes.' As if she had a nanny on hand.

'Then shouldn't someone be picking up you and your precious cargo?'

Ironic to say the least. Her smile was weak. 'I'm on my own.'

26   PARISIAN SURGEON'S SECRET CHILD

'No partner?'

'No.'

His face became devoid of emotion. 'Really?'

'Yes, really.' Suddenly she felt lonely. There was a battle looming and she had to face it on her own. Even Liza wasn't around, having gone off yesterday to Marseilles on her first holiday in over three years.

'Where're you headed? Your daughter will be exhausted too.' Talk about persistent. Something to remember. Though she did know that much about him, she recalled.

'Rue Roy. In the 8th arrondissement. I have an apartment there.'

'I know where it is.' Of course he did. He'd dropped her off there once during their fling. 'Come on. My driver will give you a lift on the way to my house.' He was looking at Elyna with studied indifference. 'She's cute,' he muttered.

Her lungs went on hold. Would he figure it out? Did he remember the time that she'd dropped into his office and then left without saying why she'd been there? Probably not. She hadn't been that important in his busy life. 'I think so.'

Now Etienne was studying her closely.

A cold shiver ran down her back. He suspected something wasn't right, and when he let that settle in his head there really was only one way to come out the other end. That was not something she was prepared to talk about here. 'Thanks for the offer of a ride but I'll grab a taxi.' The queue was shrinking quickly. She wouldn't have long to wait.

Ignoring her, Etienne pressed an icon on his phone. 'Alain, I'm ready. We've also got two passengers.' The phone returned to his pocket. 'Sorted.' He stepped nearer and took the trolley from her lifeless hands. 'This way.'

This was definitely not the man she'd known. Too abrupt, but then again he was only thinking about what he wanted. *Stop, Camille. That's unfair. Give him a chance to think everything through.* He'd always been considerate as long as she didn't want anything personal from him, and today she'd be giving him the biggest shock possible. Would he believe her? What would he want to do about it if he did? 'Etienne, give me back the trolley. I am not going with you.' She needed to get Elyna to the apartment where she could crawl around letting off steam. 'I mean it.' Getting away from Etienne was a priority.

He started walking along the pavement. 'So do I.'

To think he'd tried to find Camille when she'd first left the hospital. He'd told himself he just wanted to know why she'd come by his office at the end of that day, which he did, but even more he'd realised he longed to catch up with her and pass the time of day. Just as well he hadn't or he'd have looked silly since it seemed she'd moved on with her life pretty fast after their fling. Strange how that was what *he* usually did. Said goodbye to one woman and quickly found the next one willing to keep his sheets warm for a few weeks. Cynic to the fore. Selfish, perhaps. He might be driven to protect himself from falling in love, but surely the time had to come when he might let go a little and try to find someone who mattered more to him than a few rounds of sex?

He instantly glanced sideways. Why did that particular thought arise out of the blue? Camille might have tweaked his interest, but she was a mother now, and she

PARISIAN SURGEON'S SECRET CHILD

hadn't done that by herself. But she had said she was on her own.

Another glance to take in the beautiful sight dragging her feet beside him. The shadows beneath her eyes didn't detract from the classic features that made Camille look so lovely. Her tangled, long blonde hair still had the power to make his fingers itch with the need to run through the waves that cascaded over her shoulders. Her clothes were casual, no doubt practical when flying long haul with a toddler, but his memory could still picture what the clothing covered, and raise his temperature above normal. No denying Camille had got to him more than any other woman since Melina. Also, no denying he was not open to another fling with Camille, or to getting to know her better in more ways than sexually. Especially now she had a child. And now he was on edge. Something didn't feel right.

Deep down he'd suspected she'd come to tell him something important the night she'd turned up in his office doorway and then walked away again without saying a word. She'd even turned down the chance to go to the ball with him. So unlike other women. She hadn't been one for cornering him and suggesting anything she thought might get attention from him. It had been the thing about her he'd most admired other than her nursing skills and concern for others. For Camille to do that said there had to have been something she'd needed to discuss with him. Then again, he might've been looking for what was usually never there—a genuine friendliness towards him.

He looked at the little tot before him. She was lovely. Not intending to be a father, he wasn't one for getting all soft over babies, but this little girl unexpectedly stirred

SUE MACKAY 29

him. The child was a girl, right? Camille likely wouldn't dress a boy in bright pink. Not the Camille he thought he knew. But how well had he known her? Not very, other than as a nurse and a sensual lover. Then she'd gone and had a baby within a time frame that caught at him, had him wondering the impossible. Surely, he had to be wrong. The child was tiny so the timing didn't fit. Did it? 'How old is your daughter?'

Camille's head shot around and she stared at him. 'Eleven months.'

Then she wasn't his. Relief should be pouring through him, but instead the tension growing since he'd first seen Camille kept increasing. 'She's tiny.'

'She was eight weeks premature.'

Kick him in the guts, why didn't she? But she still hadn't said the girl was his.

A car pulled up at the kerb. Alain. Relief filled Etienne. Though why he should be relieved he had no clue, other than this was a familiar thing to do. He wanted to talk with Camille so he could put his mind at rest about her child, but not here on the pavement at the airport. Nor in the back of his car where Alain might overhear. It had to be a private conversation in a place where no one could interrupt. 'Camille, this is my ride. Please get in. Alain can drop you off at your apartment.' Had he sounded concerned for her in a positive way? He hoped so, because so far he'd been abrupt, and that wouldn't get him anywhere when what he wanted was to find out the truth—though he suspected he might already have an idea about that. But he was getting ahead of himself. He needed to hear it from Camille, first.

Her smile was tight. 'All right. I guess the sooner I get to my apartment, the better. My girl's exhausted and has

30   PARISIAN SURGEON'S SECRET CHILD

had enough of sitting in one spot for so long, no doubt thinking I'm a terrible mother for not letting her crawl up and down the aisles in the plane.'

'I can't imagine you're a terrible mother at all.' It was true. She'd be firm but kind and caring. Or so he believed.

Startled eyes met his. 'Thank you again.'

He liked that he'd surprised her. He wasn't the only one feeling out of sorts here, which added to the feeling he might be right about the child being his. 'Do you need supplies for the kitchen?' They could stop at a super-market on the way. He'd be helpful, if nothing else.

That messy hair that entranced him swung across her shoulders as she replied. 'No, thanks. My friend's organ-ised everything I need for the next few days so I don't have to go anywhere.' Turning away, she placed the por-table seat in the back of the car before lifting the toddler from the trolley and brushing a light kiss over her little face, tightening his heart in the process. Then she leaned inside and settled her daughter into the portable seat be-fore attaching the seat belt.

Heat instantly blasted through him. Camille's figure appeared to have filled out slightly, probably due to the pregnancy, and she looked even lovelier. As she reached further to adjust the seat belt, her trousers stretched across her sexy backside, further outlining the curved shape and reminding him of how he'd held her against him, arous-ing him. Spinning away, he strode to the driver's door. 'Alain, we're going to Rue Roy.'

Whether he'd stay and talk to Camille about these strange thoughts regarding the little girl whose presence was tipping his world sideways was a decision suddenly beyond him. Remembering Camille's sensational body wrapped around him as he slid inside her had brought him

SUE MACKAY   31

out in a sweat and was messing with his mind. Worse, those memories made him want to touch her, feel her satiny skin under his fingertips. That was an absolute no-no. He was not getting intimate with Camille—now or ever again. Especially when he had no idea what was going on. He could not be this child's father. He couldn't. Could he? His heart shifted, making him wonder how he'd feel if he was.

The back door clicked shut as Camille settled herself beside her daughter. He made to go around to the front passenger seat, then stopped. The last thing he was, was a coward. He might be worried about how much seeing Camille again had rattled him, but he was strong. Melina had not taken that away from him, only his ability to fall in love or trust again.

Opening the back door on the other side to Camille, he slid in beside the little girl, who was again staring at him with enormous blue eyes, her thumb in her mouth. She didn't get those eyes from him. They were all Camille. Something like love flickered under his sternum. It couldn't be love. He didn't know this child who probably had nothing to do with him. He hadn't even known she existed until a few minutes ago. But something was pulling at his heart, saying 'look at me', and it wasn't only those eyes. It went deeper—down to the part of himself he never shared. His heart and the longing for love and family, if he could get past his fear of losing a child as his parents had.

Damn it. His hands clenched on his thighs. *Camille, you might just have upturned my life. I don't know what's going on and I don't know if I want to find out.* He might be in real trouble here. He glanced across to Camille, his heart stuttering again, this time at the worry filling

32 PARISIAN SURGEON'S SECRET CHILD

her face. He owned some of that for taking charge about giving her a lift to Rue Roy. He had been blindsided, but that didn't mean he had to be an arrogant sod about it. 'Camille, please relax.'

She blinked in surprise but said nothing. Nor did the tension tightening her body diminish.

Sinking back into the leather seat, he stared sightlessly out of the window.

'Where did you fly in from?' Camille eventually asked in a stilted manner.

Turning back, he told her, 'New York. I've been to a general surgeons' conference for discussions on new technology regarding bowel surgeries.'

'Was it useful?'

'Yes, but I think it'll take time to come into full use around the world.'

Etienne couldn't help himself. He looked down at the tot sitting between them. She was still staring at him and now her mouth was puckered up, looking cute. Again there was a lightness in his chest. Could she really be his? Nothing about her seemed familiar. No Laval features, but neither could he see Camille in her face other than those beautiful eyes. 'Who does she look like?'

'My grandmother.'

'Not your own mother?' He knew nothing about Camille's family, in fact knew next to nothing about her at all.

'From photos I've seen I'd say she's a bit like her, *oui*.'

'You don't remember what your mother looked like?'

'I was only two days old when she died.'

Etienne slumped back in his seat. It was time to shut up and stop asking questions if he was only going to get appalling answers. He might want to learn more about her but nothing so dreadful. 'Camille, I don't know what to say. Sorry seems inadequate.'

'And irrelevant,' she replied briefly. 'It's the only life I've known and I was very happy growing up with my grandparents. Also very lucky. They were wonderful.'

She hadn't gone for the sympathy vote in an attempt to get him onside. He appreciated that, and felt a softening towards her. But then it could be exactly what she'd set out to do. Yes, once more he was being cynical, but he'd had enough lessons from grasping women to last him for ever so it was hard to put those aside with Camille, however briefly. It was also very tempting to do just that. There was something special about her that used to catch at him at times when he wasn't being too cautious. Something he had to remain aware of so he didn't get caught out and lose his heart once more. Yet he couldn't keep quiet, feeling compelled to learn more about her.

'What about your father? Where was he when you were growing up?'

'My mother never saw him again after she told him she was pregnant.'

There was a chill in her voice that had him sitting back and looking at her. He suspected he wasn't the only one with trust issues. Did this explain anything about the little girl sitting in between them?

Damn, why had he called out to Camille the moment he saw her at the airport? Feeling pleased to see her meant nothing compared to the confusion and fear building up inside him now. The sooner they reached Rue Roy, the better; he'd be able to go home and get back on track.

Except he already knew that wasn't happening any time soon, if at all.

CHAPTER TWO

SUDDENLY ELYNA BEGAN to cry. She'd had enough of being restrained. Throw in exhaustion and it was no surprise. Camille was only grateful her girl hadn't had a complete meltdown while on the plane. There'd have been daggers in her back from annoyed passengers.

'Hey, sweetheart, we're nearly there.' She rubbed her daughter's head softly as they drove through the familiar streets of home, taking it all in and trying to ignore the tension rippling off Etienne. Whatever his reaction when he learned he was Elyna's father, Camille was thrilled to be here. She'd missed home, especially in the weeks after her grandmother died, and couldn't wait to return to Paris where she belonged.

Unfortunately it hadn't been a matter of packing her bags and getting on a plane. She'd had a funeral to organise, lawyers to talk to, then the interment of Grandma's ashes in the same plot where they'd put her grandfather's nearly fifteen months earlier. There was no way Grandma was going to be interred anywhere but with him. It had taken a few weeks to sort it all out, but she'd got there.

Now here she was, back in Paris. Weird how she and Etienne had bumped into each other at the airport, as if forces outside her control were playing games with her. She'd intended going to see Etienne as soon as she'd settled in to tell him the truth, but the time had arrived sooner than expected and now she had to get on with it. She felt relieved he was about to find out his role in Elyna's life, but equally nervous. He'd think she was lying because she wanted money or a gracious lifestyle from him. Looking at Elyna, she mentally crossed her fingers, hoping he'd at least listen to her. All she asked for was his acknowledgement that he was Elyna's father.

'It's been a long day for you, hasn't it, little one?'

Elyna cried harder.

Delving into her bag, Camille found the milk bottle and slipped the teat into Elyna's mouth. 'There you go.' Chances were she'd shove it aside as the formula was cold, but not a lot could be done to fix that until they reached the apartment. Any minute now, she sighed. So much for going away for three months. It had taken a long time to get home, many months of pain and sadness over her grandmother's illness and inevitable death, but all along Elyna had added sunshine and love to their days, making things a little less heavy despite being so premature.

Elyna. So far she'd managed not to say her daughter's name out loud because when she did all hell would break loose, and she didn't want that happening in the car with Alain in the front. Elyna was Etienne's grandmother's name. It had been a connection to his family, and also one she really liked.

'It must've seemed like for ever for her,' Etienne commented in that reserved manner he used when not wanting to get too involved with someone. Most of the time.

The voice he used with patients, and with her whenever they'd enjoyed an evening together and it was time for him to head home alone.

36   PARISIAN SURGEON'S SECRET CHILD

'It seems like days since we left Canada but I have to say I'm really proud of her for not getting too upset during the flight.'

'Have you been in Montreal ever since you left Central Hospital?'

'Yes. I went with my grandmother for three months as she wanted to spend time with Grandpa's family, but everything went wrong.' She paused, wondering how much to say. 'Anyway, I've finally made it home.'

He studied her intently. Looking for problems that didn't exist? 'You've had a rough time since leaving Paris, haven't you?'

It sounded as though there were other questions behind that one, but she ignored those and went with, 'I was busy with Grandma and my daughter.' *Our daughter, Etienne.*

Relief filled her as Alain pulled up right outside her apartment block.

Staring up at the building, Camille fought not to give in to the sudden threat of tears. It seemed like for ever since she'd left and she'd been waiting to return for so long she'd started to think it might never happen. When her grandmother had become ill there was no way she'd ever have let her suffer without being there to look after her, even though she also had two nephews living there. Bringing her grandmother back to Paris hadn't been feasible either. Medically Grandma had been diagnosed with heart failure but Camille knew it was more likely a broken heart that took her. She'd missed Grandpa so much over the three years since he'd died that she'd never again been the vibrant lady Camille had known all her life.

'Are you all right?' Etienne asked from outside the

car where he stood holding the door open, looking expectantly at her.

What *was* he thinking? He kept looking at Elyna as if he suspected the truth, but that could be her own wishful thinking. 'I'm fine.' She concentrated on extricating Elyna from the car seat. The last thing she wanted was Etienne noticing how upset she was. He might take advantage when she was dreading the discussion they were about to have. 'Hey, baby girl, we're home. You don't have to be buckled in for much longer.' Holding Elyna close, she clambered out of the car.

'Alain, can you give me a hand with Camille's bags? Want to use the pram, Camille?'

'Please.' At the moment when her body ached with exhaustion the thought of carrying Elyna even the small distance to the elevator and up to the apartment seemed too much. 'I'll open it.'

'I do know how to use a pram,' Etienne informed her. 'I have two young nephews whom I've spent plenty of time with.'

So Elyna had cousins. That could be good going forward. 'How old are they?'

'Jacques is five, and Michel is three,' he told her as he set the pram in front of her. 'Here you go.'

Placing Elyna into it, Camille shivered at the cry of annoyance her daughter made. 'Nearly there, sweetheart. Just a few more minutes and you'll be free to explore your new home.' *I promise we're not going anywhere for the next couple of days if it means you have to be restricted.* Though it would be wonderful to stroll along the streets and breathe in Paris, she couldn't buckle Elyna into the pram or a seat anywhere for a while after the long flight they'd endured.

38   PARISIAN SURGEON'S SECRET CHILD

'Lead on,' Etienne called over Elyna's grizzles.

Not bothering to reply, she headed to the main entrance and tapped in the access code for the building. Liza had given her the up-to-date code in her last email. It might be an old building but it had the modern features that made keys a thing of the past and life a little easier.

The elevator rose to the third floor and the doors whooshed open. For a moment Camille didn't move, simply stood fixed to the floor. She was home, about to start a new chapter of her life, and she wasn't certain how that was going to unfold, which it would start doing the moment she stepped into the apartment she'd grown up in and inherited from her grandparents.

Etienne peered at her. 'Camille?'

Lifting her head high, she stepped out, pushing the pram as she strode along to open the door and go inside, followed by the men with her bags. On the oak sideboard was a vase filled with roses and a card saying 'Welcome Home' leaning against it, no doubt from Liza. Her heart expanded as she walked through to the lounge with the kitchen and dining area to one side.

Stopping in the middle of the large room, she slowly pivoted, taking in the family photos on the walls and on top of an oak cabinet, the rows of well-read books on the shelves, the couch she'd often lain on while watching TV, the view out of the windows of familiar buildings on the opposite side of Rue Roy. She could see and hear, smell and feel her grandparents. They were here. This was a part of them, where they'd raised her, loved her, given her a wonderful life. The tasty family meals eaten at that table, the discussions they'd had in this room about her career, schoolwork, boyfriends. The arguments about wearing make-up when she was only twelve, and what she was wearing to go to the movies with her girlfriends.

'Camille, what's up? Are you all right?' Etienne was looking up at her from where he'd crouched to release the strap holding Elyna in the pram.

No, she wasn't all right. She was overwhelmed. She hadn't expected these emotions to blindside her. It had been over six years since she'd moved out to share a pokey apartment with Liza but she'd thought she was coming back to the one place she loved most to get on with life, not to have so many memories flood her and make her sadder than she'd been at her grandmother's funeral.

Etienne stood in front of her, his hands on her shoulders. 'Camille, don't cry.'

She hadn't known she was. Using her forearm to wipe her face, she was surprised how wet her cheeks were. 'It just struck me how much I've missed home and now my only family isn't here any more.' Never would be again.

His hands were surprisingly gentle given how well he kept his emotions locked down. 'You have your daughter.'

Looking up at him, she nodded. 'True. I do. But now I'm the adult.'

His smile was the most genuine he'd given her. 'You'll manage. Very well, I think.'

The smile stabbed at her vulnerability. Etienne was the last person she should be exposing her emotions to, and yet she hadn't given it a thought, hadn't been aware how much she had shown him her true self. 'You're right, I will do better than manage. Elyna comes first.'

Etienne's head jerked up. 'Elyna?' He studied her once again with that intense look he did so well.

'Etienne, I need to tell you something.' She could

barely hear herself speak over the thumping in her chest. She hadn't meant to say Elyna's name, but now it was out there the moment she'd been equally dreading and wanting was here.

'I'll be waiting in the car,' Alain said from somewhere behind them and moments later the door closed with a soft click.

'Elyna. My grandmother's name.' Etienne stared at her, disappointment filling his eyes, his face. Because he believed she'd used the name to try and manipulate him?

'Yes.'

The air whooshed out of Etienne's mouth. He stared at this apparition who was changing his world as she spoke. His heart pounded. How dared she? 'You've called her by my grandmother's name,' he snapped, fury whipping through him so fast he nearly lost his balance. Those strange feelings of intrigue and softness when he'd first laid eyes on the little girl now had an explanation—if he believed what Camille was hinting at. Did he? Not likely. How could he when his ex-fiancée had already tried to win him over with the same dubious methods? But this was Camille, the one woman he'd thought was better than that.

'Yes.'

'Why?' he snapped. She was using the child to get to him. What made him think she was different from any other woman who'd tried to trick him into a relationship? Camille was smarter, that was all. She'd gone deeper with her selfishness. Stupid, stupid, stupid man. He took a long breath in an attempt to calm down. Losing his temper would work in her favour, not his.

Camille leant down to place her daughter—not his—

on the carpet. 'I think you've worked it out already.' Her mouth was grim, her blue eyes dark as storm clouds as she dropped the final bomb. 'Elyna is your daughter,' she said quietly, but firmly. No doubting she meant it.

Did that mean he had to accept this without question? No damned way. 'I'm supposed to believe you? Just like that?' What about that sense he'd had of being her father? It had to be wrong. 'You've got to be crazy to think I'll accept this based on your word.'

Camille's shoulders drooped. 'I never thought you would. You have issues around believing women when you think they might want something from you.'

'Low blow.' But true, he conceded to himself. 'So you used my grandmother's name to get to me?' Feeling blindsided again, he looked around and found himself gazing down at the little girl who sat on the floor staring up at him with those wide eyes. She was gorgeous. But his? Born eight weeks premature and eleven months old meant she could have been conceived eighteen months ago during their fling, if they'd been exclusive, which he suspected they were. Camille wasn't like that. Another sucker punch. His head whirled. This was insane.

'I would never do that.' Camille sank down onto a chair, her arms tight around her body. At least the tears had stopped, making it easier to watch her without softening towards her. 'While I was pregnant I believed I was having a boy. When I had a scan I didn't even ask for verification. I had a name picked out, and bought blue clothes. When the baby was born I was stunned. I know it sounds stupid, but it's how I felt. I had to choose another name and went with your grandmother's. I found it online.'

He started to speak but Camille talked right over him.

'Give me a moment to explain. I love the name Elyna.

But I also wanted her to have some connection with your f-family.' She spluttered to a stop.

His heart heaved. If Camille was telling the truth, then he was indeed a father. Father to that lovely little girl watching him, her face filled with innocence, as if begging him to accept her. Strange how his usual reaction to a woman trying to pull a trick on him wasn't rushing to the fore as heavily as usual. Did he actually believe Camille? Or did he simply want to and just didn't know where to go from here? Not likely.

'Were you ever going to tell me? If we hadn't bumped into each other at the airport, would you have come to see me?'

'That was my first priority on returning home.'

'Oh, really?' Sarcasm dripped off his tongue. He wasn't doing very well, being snippy, but this was frightening. Being told by a woman she was carrying his child when she hadn't been was bad enough, but he'd held Elyna in his arms, which made things so much harder to push aside. He drew a breath to apologise for his rudeness but Camille cut him off.

'Really. Etienne...' She paused, seemed to gather strength from deep inside. Locking worried eyes on him, she continued. 'Do you remember that time I turned up at your office when you were on the phone talking to your mother?' She didn't wait for an answer. 'I'd come to tell you then.'

He remembered as clearly as if it had been yesterday because he'd often wondered if Camille had overheard him being so cynical. He'd been ashamed that she might've. 'You overheard me saying that no one had played the pregnancy card on me for a while.' That wasn't an excuse though. If, and it was still a big if, he was Elyna's father she still owed it to him to have told him.

'Would you have believed me? Be honest, Etienne.'

She had him there. He wouldn't have. Instead he'd have dragged up every reason not to after Melina trying the same trick.

Camille nodded. 'Exactly. Believe me, I wanted you to know. Yet I walked away without a word because you obviously wouldn't have accepted the truth. That's when I decided to go it alone and never tell you.'

'You just said it was a priority to tell me.' Nothing added up, which was too much like how conversations with Melina had generally gone.

'It is.' Her hands were clenched together so tight they were white. 'I was wrong to think I'd never tell you. When we were in Montreal, my grandmother pointed out you deserved to know. What you do about it is another issue.' She shivered. 'Elyna also deserves to know you're her father. Growing up, I didn't know mine and it was hard. I don't want that for Elyna.'

He wasn't getting sidetracked by that. 'So you believe you were wrong not to tell me before she was born?'

Camille straightened her back and locked a formidable look on him. 'I do but nothing I say can change what's happened. I am truly sorry but I was only protecting myself and Elyna.'

'You think that little of me?' That was new.

'Remember what I overheard? You were expecting another woman to try to fool you about a pregnancy. That made me realise you trusted no one. I wasn't going to listen to you tell me as much. I'm not perfect by any means but I am honest, especially when it's important.'

44 PARISIAN SURGEON'S SECRET CHILD

If words could burn he'd be seared. 'And me knowing about Elyna's important now?'

'Yes. For all of us.'

'You left the hospital on leave, but you could've come to see me there later on, or phoned me to arrange a meeting.'

She straightened her back further and lifted her chin, but her hands were shaking. 'I left for Canada two days later. Grandma was taking my grandfather's ashes over to be buried in his family plot and I went with her as she'd been there for me my whole life. I'd never have let her go on her own even when she had Grandpa's brothers to stay with. She was frail and unwell, but we meant to return home within three months and once I decided to tell you I fully intended seeing you before Elyna was born. Except Grandma became very ill with heart failure and couldn't fly home. I stayed out there with her until the end.'

Despite all the emotions filling him, the strongest was sorrow for Camille. Her obvious pain at her loss was unavoidable. 'Hell, Camille.' No wonder she'd broken down in tears when she walked in here. It took all his self-control not to go and haul her into his arms and hold her tight.

Damn it, he was letting her win him over already. What was wrong with him? He never trusted women when it came to getting close. He and Camille weren't that close, or even heading that way, but her putting it into words that he was Elyna's father had floored him. He might actually want it to be true, but it wasn't easy to let go of the past and move on. Time to get back to the red flag hanging between them.

'There are phones in Canada.' Sarcasm was the lowest form of wit, but right now his head was all over the place and he didn't know where he was going with this other than listening to the deep-seated need to protect himself. The fact he hadn't walked out already was another warning sign. He might believe Camille and that was so outrageous he couldn't breathe properly.

Camille winced. 'I deleted your number when our fling finished. When I tried to get it from your secretary at the hospital, she refused to give it to me, and on my third attempt she made some very rude comments and hung up.'

'I left Paris to do a nine-month contract in Nice about two months after you went away.'

'So your secretary lied to me when she said you'd told her to tell me to get lost.'

'She did.' He had no idea what that was about.

Elyna gave a frustrated cry.

Camille scooped her up in her arms. 'Sorry, sweetheart. I promised you warm food and then forgot.' She kissed her girl's forehead. 'Come on. Let's see what Liza's put in the fridge for you.'

Again Etienne felt his heart do some crazy thumps. Camille and Elyna together made a lovely, heart-wrenching picture. But he couldn't just accept he had a role in this little family's lives without going through all the questions threatening to stymy him. Could he? No damned way. Melina had told him she was carrying his child when she hadn't even been pregnant. What was to say Camille wasn't using another trick to get him to fall into her trap?

Watching her holding Elyna while removing a container of food from the fridge he saw nothing to say she was lying to him. She was comfortable with Elyna, and didn't keep peeking at him to see how he was reacting. She wasn't nagging him to accept her news. Instead she

46 PARISIAN SURGEON'S SECRET CHILD

was giving him space. Unheard of in his experience. There came the cynic again. Time to put it away? Could be. He crossed to the kitchen area and took the plastic container out of Camille's hand. 'Let me do that.'

She stepped out of his way, looking a little shocked. 'Are you sure?'

'Right now I'm not sure about anything, but I can do this while you comfort your daughter.' *My daughter, too?*

Elyna was still unsettled and her tiny fists were punching the air between her and her mother's breasts.

'Only warm it to a point you can still dip your finger in without it getting too hot.' Camille was watching him as he found a dish and spoon, wariness filling her face.

He liked that she was prepared to tell him what to do despite what hung between them. 'I've done this for my nephews.'

She shrugged as if to say, So what? 'I get a bit paranoid when it comes to Elyna.'

'Fair enough.' He had no doubts about her being a fiercely protective mother. He'd seen her looking out for patients when something went wrong and that came nowhere near what she'd do for her child. 'Who's Liza?' It wasn't important but he needed a moment or ten to catch up with everything. Not that it was working. He couldn't get past the fact Camille had confessed he was Elyna's father. Despite his earlier suspicions it was as if the ground had been taken out from beneath him and he were standing on air. He was a father. Truly? He focused on preparing to heat the mushy food. Easier than working out where his emotions were with this.

Camille's mouth was tight. 'Liza's my best friend. We shared an apartment in our twenties. She's Elyna's surrogate aunt and would have her if anything happens to me.'

His stomach plummeted. If he was the father then that was something he should've had a say in, like the little girl's name, though he couldn't argue with the one Camille had chosen—other than he had initially thought it had been used as another way of sucking him in. Go carefully, he warned himself. It still could be. 'Why did you think you needed someone to step up to that role?'

'I don't have any family to be there for Elyna if something happens to me.'

'If what you say is true then she'd have me, and my extended family,' he snapped. This hurt. Badly. Because he *was* already accepting Camille mightn't be lying about his role in this little girl's life. Father. Parent. He swore under his breath. This was the last thing he'd expected when he'd boarded the plane in New York many hours ago. But why would it have occurred to him he had a child? Camille hadn't rushed to tell him about her pregnancy or make demands of him. *She came to see me at the hospital before she went away.*

'I did mess up, I admit that, but I deserved better, to be a part of the pregnancy, and the birth if possible, especially since she came so early,' he said quietly.

'So you do believe she's your daughter?' Was that hope in her face?

'It's too soon to say. There's a lot I still don't know.' He drew a steadying breath. If he wasn't truthful, how could he get annoyed if Camille wasn't? Except so far she appeared to be only honest. 'What you overheard that night didn't encourage you to talk to me but you didn't try again.'

'You'd have changed your mind about my pregnancy just like that?'

She had him there. It was seeing Elyna in the flesh

48   PARISIAN SURGEON'S SECRET CHILD

that snagged at him and brought questions about her parentage to the fore. 'That's not the point. You should've tried,' he repeated stubbornly.

'I'd been dreading telling you since you always made it clear relationships weren't for you. I wasn't looking for one either, but once I heard you say something about not ever wanting children, I couldn't stay.' She certainly didn't hold back.

He drew a shaky breath. 'Fine. I'm prepared to hear what you have to say and go from there.'

Camille slumped against the bench. Again tears filled those eyes that had unexpectedly followed him into sleep some nights when he'd been feeling lonely for company with a woman who'd want him for himself and not the family fortunes. That was definitely something he was not mentioning to her. Not now and maybe never. She slapped her hand across her eyes to clear away the moisture. 'Etienne, I am truly sorry.'

Once more she'd taken the wind out of him. It wasn't her words. No, all too often he'd heard those before. But never had he so keenly felt the sorrow, believed the genuine feeling behind the apology.

'I should've stayed that night and told you the truth, but it wasn't easy after hearing what you said. It hadn't been easy before that. Nor was it any easier when Elyna arrived.'

'I shouldn't have said what I did to my mother.' If he wasn't back-pedalling then what was he doing?

'You weren't to know what I'd come to tell you. You weren't even aware I was there.'

'True.' But he realised he would've reacted exactly as she'd expected if he'd known. He really had become a less than decent man over the years. Melina had stolen his trust, but he couldn't blame her for how he'd regarded other women. There were plenty who'd done all they could to win him over, but there had to be many more decent women if he'd only stopped to take a long hard look.

The microwave pinged. Relieved to have something mundane to do, he opened the door and removed the bowl to stir the mush. Mundane? If Elyna really was his daughter then there was nothing humdrum about preparing her food. Was she his? 'She doesn't look anything like me.' Or her relatives on his side. Ouch. Was that acceptance of the fact she was his? No. Too soon to be certain. But then how to go about finding out? A DNA test would give him the answer he needed but he wasn't keen. Too clinical. He wanted to know more about everything else, like what Camille expected from him regarding shared parenting and where she'd live. His head was telling him one thing and his heart another, and until they were on the same page nothing would be clear.

Was Camille like everyone else and just trying to get what she wanted from him? Or was she honest when she said she was looking out for her daughter? How was he supposed to know the answer to that or all the other frightening doubts roiling in his brain? Creating doubts that suggested he might be looking at Camille differently from how he normally approached women. Face it, he liked her a lot. Enough to have tried to find out where she'd gone after leaving her job at the hospital. He hadn't got far, wary of being seen to be too interested in her. No one he'd asked at the hospital had known where she'd gone, other than her being on extended leave, and when he'd gone around to her old apartment, he'd been told she no longer lived there.

50   PARISIAN SURGEON'S SECRET CHILD

Camille reached for the bowl, dipped her finger into the pumpkin-coloured mush. 'Perfect.'

He presumed she was referring to Elyna's meal. 'We have a long way to go yet.'

'Absolutely.' Camille settled Elyna into the high chair Liza had provided, still amazed that Etienne hadn't left by now. He'd been shocked, even snippy at times, but altogether he was a lot calmer than she'd expected. 'I'm ready to talk about anything when it comes to Elyna, whenever you want.'

'I appreciate that. So Elyna's Canadian?'

Going for formal now? It could've been worse, though it did make her feel oddly out of place. 'With Elyna being born in Canada I applied for her French citizenship.'

'So she has dual citizenship?'

'Yes.' Was that so bad? 'I intend raising her here so it made sense to do that straight away.'

He was still staring at her, but she could see her words sinking in. 'I understand what you're saying, Camille. I wouldn't have expected any less of you. It just occurred to me that she was Canadian by birth, that's all.'

So he was more shocked than he'd shown. 'Thank you.' Those darned tears were back. She rubbed her face. 'You must be wishing you hadn't seen me at the airport.'

He gave a tight smile. 'It's been an interesting couple of hours I hadn't predicted.' Then he asked, 'Can I make you coffee? Or get you something else to drink?'

He'd do that for her when he was still so rattled by her news? He wasn't an unkind man but he had surprised her as she'd thought he'd want to keep aloof while they got down to business. Yet somehow he'd understood her distress, which was more than she did right now. She was all over the place with her feelings about Etienne, Elyna, coming home, everything. The tension holding her tight backed off a notch. 'Coffee would be lovely, thanks.'

'Mind if I have one too?'

'Of course not.' She was hardly going to say no when he was being polite. *Relax, Etienne. It's been a shock, yes, but I'm not going to spring any demands on you. Unless you decide you want to take my daughter away from me, that is, and then you'll have a battle like none you've ever known.*

'I think a certain little girl wants to go down.' There was a glint of amusement in his grey eyes. Eyes she'd never forgotten since she'd left his bed for the last time.

Elyna had gobbled down her food and was now trying to push out of the high chair. Thankfully the strap prevented her winning that battle. 'Come on, little one. Let's set you free to rush around and use up some of that energy fizzing through you.'

On the floor Elyna headed off, crawling to the chairs and then the coffee table. Looking at her phone, Camille gasped. 'Where's the time gone?' Hours had passed since the plane had landed.

'Time flies when you're having fun,' Etienne quipped, surprising her yet again.

Fun? Right. Though it was a relief he wasn't sticking to the hard-nosed man whose life had just been tipped upside down, she conceded. 'Do you really want coffee? Or would you prefer wine?' It might help lighten the mood between them and she'd seen a bottle of Chenin Blanc in the fridge, thanks to Liza.

Etienne stepped back from the coffee machine. 'You've got me.' He removed his phone from his jacket pocket. 'I'll tell Alain to go home. I'll grab a taxi home later.'

52 PARISIAN SURGEON'S SECRET CHILD

Damn. She'd walked into that one. Coffee would've been drunk quicker and he might've been on his way sooner. Not a lot she could say though. Looking around, she spied her girl trying to climb up one of the bookcases and rushed across. 'No, Elyna, get off there.' If the bookcase tipped she'd get hurt with a lot of bruises to colour her pale skin. Snatching her daughter up in her arms, she kissed both cheeks and took her over to the sofa to put her down. 'I see I'm going to have to keep a sharp eye on you.'

'You need to get someone to put some screws through the back of the bookcase to fix it to the wall if she's going to become a little monkey.' Etienne was gazing at Elyna as he poured wine into the glasses he'd found. There was a look of need in his eyes, as though he really wanted Elyna to be his daughter.

He was as vulnerable as she was, Camille realised with a shock. Throughout their fling she'd only known him to wear a kind yet aloof face. Even more so at work with his patients and their families. The staff were also kept at bay with that look. Everyone thought the world of Dr Etienne Laval, but no one ever got behind his barriers. Not even her when they were between the sheets, naked as the day they were born, being physically intimate and yet mentally separate. 'I'll get onto it tomorrow, find a handyman online.'

Etienne said tightly, 'I'll do it after I finish work one evening this coming week.' He seemed to be taking over already.

Not likely. 'That won't be necessary. I'll be here all day. I resigned when I was in Montreal longer than expected, and I still haven't got a new job yet. The two interviews I've set up are three days away.'

SUE MACKAY 53

'I said I'd do it, Camille. Why are you looking for work when you've got Elyna to take care of?'

She turned to stare at him. *Here we go, getting to the crux of his deep concerns over being used.* Fair enough. He had every right to find out as much as possible about how she was raising their daughter, and what she didn't expect from him. 'I need to work, though not full-time. Liza runs a crèche nearby.' At Central Hospital. 'Elyna will go to her when I can't be here.' *Don't try and argue with me.* 'We've got it sorted.'

'I expect to partake in decisions about Elyna's life if I accept she's mine.'

Did that mean he *was* accepting her as his daughter? Or was he looking for other ways she might be trying to get something from him? 'We will talk about everything and I'm happy to work things out together, but I wasn't here when I applied for the positions, and I had to get things organised for Elyna as soon as possible.'

'Where have you applied for positions?'

She named the hospitals. 'I've talked online to the head nurses at both places and now need to meet up and take a look around.'

'You don't sound overly enthusiastic about either of them.'

He was too observant. She shouldn't be surprised. He'd always been so. 'You're right. But it's hard to suss out things online. I like to get the feel of where I might work before making up my mind.' If only she could go back to the surgical ward at Central Hospital. She'd considered ringing the head nurse, Karina, to see if there might be a position open but that would mean working alongside Etienne, which wasn't a good idea until they'd sorted out where they were going with Elyna, and then only if

PARISIAN SURGEON'S SECRET CHILD

it was going well between them. That was if he'd even returned there after working in Nice. 'Where are you working now?'

Etienne didn't answer, instead asking her a question. 'What about your old job?' He was watching her closely as he handed over a glass. 'I don't doubt you'd be taken on in a flash if there's a position available.'

He was putting that out there despite the bomb she'd dropped on him? Because he was accepting of her or wanted to keep a close eye on everything she did regarding Elyna? Locking eyes with him, she said, 'Do you think that's wise? I mean, we have a lot to sort out and, if you're still at Central, working side by side might crank up the tension, not defuse it.'

'I do still work there and I get where you're coming from, but I reckon we're both better than that. We worked well together during and after our fling. Sure, this is deeper and there're a lot more issues to get through, but I believe neither of us would make it difficult at work.'

She was completely perplexed as to where she stood. Etienne was being genuinely positive about Elyna so she needed to reciprocate for all their sakes. She'd also far prefer to take a position at Central than anywhere else. It'd been the best job ever and though she couldn't expect to walk back into the same role it would be fabulous working in a familiar environment when she had so much else to deal with. 'I'll think about it.'

He flicked her a small smile. 'Good. Do you still have the same phone number?'

He hadn't wiped her number when they'd finished? She nodded. 'I have. This is weird.'

Etienne sat down at the table opposite her, wine in hand. 'You're absolutely certain I'm Elyna's father, aren't you?'

SUE MACKAY 55

What? The man could change subjects faster than a blink. 'Yes.'

No comment came her way.

She tried again. 'Look, I know you're going to have lots of questions about Elyna and I have no problem answering them.'

'You bet I do.'

Despite her knowing that'd been coming, his abrupt reply still hurt. 'I did not sleep with anyone else prior to or during our fling.' There hadn't been anyone since either but that wasn't something he needed to know as it did not affect his paternity. She didn't want him feeling sorry for her because she hadn't had anyone else in her life recently. He wouldn't know how wary of getting involved with men she was, and that even a short fling like theirs had been rare for her. He'd no doubt have had his share of women since she'd walked away from him. She hadn't known she was pregnant at the time. That news had come later, knocking her to her knees, and making working with him those last days difficult. If only she'd told him the night she'd gone to his office then this would all be over and the decisions made—or they'd currently be doing battle in the courts.

Etienne sipped his wine while he studied her, a raft of emotions flitting across his face, the strongest of which appeared to be embarrassment and that was something she'd never expected.

When the silence went on too long she couldn't take it any more. 'Any comment?'

His eyes darkened to a deep steely grey. 'I'm sorry you heard what I said to my mother.'

'Even if I'd still had your number I wanted to tell you

56 PARISIAN SURGEON'S SECRET CHILD

face to face so you could see I was being truthful. I also wanted to see your initial reactions.'

'I think I understand that.'

What? Etienne wasn't trying to make her feel bad? Long-held caution kept her wary. She did not accept he wouldn't have more to say. No doubt he needed time to think about everything so it was possible he was waiting for another day to lay out his true feelings about what she'd done, then follow up with what the cost to her heart was going to be in terms of Elyna. 'Everything changed when Grandma became so ill. She was my priority after caring for Elyna.' The guilt over letting down Etienne rose once more, threatening to choke her. This wasn't getting any easier.

The sound of little knees and hands slapping the carpet coming towards him made Etienne smile despite the turmoil going on in his head. So he had a daughter. That was if he could believe Camille when she said he was the father. For one, she hadn't rushed to let him know with a list of demands in her hand. Secondly, he really couldn't find it in him to believe she'd lie to him. That was foolish because enough other women had worked hard at trying to convince him of one falsehood or another, but if in doubt, he only had to think about how Camille had been the one to call off their fling, not him, to realise she was different. *If* he was truly honest, he'd been disappointed when she had. They'd got on so well, and there hadn't been any problems with their relationship. It was a fling and Camille accepted that, hadn't looked for anything else.

Yet when she'd left he'd realised he'd been coming to want more from her. Which had scared the pants off him and made him determined to protect himself. But it had backfired. Instead he had become restless, especially after Camille had quit nursing on the ward where he'd worked. So restless that he'd taken up the nine-month contract in Nice that his friend, Fillip, had offered him.

Yet the restlessness had continued and he'd begun to feel a little lonely, as though he was missing out on something important. Spending time with Fillip and his wife, Torrie, and their kids didn't help, only made him finally see what he was missing out on and accept the deep-seated need to have a family of his own that he'd been denying himself. But letting go the restraints he'd placed around his heart didn't come easy. Now it appeared he might have to—if he truly believed Elyna was his.

'Up.' Elyna was staring at Etienne. 'Up.'

'Persistent, aren't you?' Persistent and cute. Even knowing lifting Elyna into his arms was going to undermine his determination to keep her at a distance until he was absolutely certain he was her father, Etienne couldn't resist.

'Very,' Camille agreed. 'Apparently it's normal.'

Turning away from Camille's all-seeing eyes, he drew a ragged breath. She was the last person he wanted to notice his vulnerability. This had turned into one hell of a day, one of the worst he'd known in a long time. And maybe one of the best, too.

After a drawn-out moment that chilled him he turned back. 'Camille...' He paused. Was he about to go too far, to make her believe he was an easy target? Or was he actually moving forward, accepting her for who she really was? Would it be wonderful if he could do that?

'Yes, Etienne?'

'This isn't easy for either of us. I am trying to work my

58   PARISIAN SURGEON'S SECRET CHILD

way through it all because it's so important,' he added, and immediately hoped he'd never regret saying that.

'Thank you.'

He got his smile. It hit him hard in the solar plexus. She was beautiful—add in that smile and there were no words to describe her. Other than beautiful, and caring, and just what he wanted in his for-ever woman if he could finally let go of the shackles holding him back.

'Would you like another glass of wine before you head away?' she suddenly asked.

He should call a taxi, get home and have that shower he'd been promising himself from the moment he'd walked off the plane, but he couldn't find it in him to turn Camille down. He needed more time with her. He wasn't entirely certain why but he truly did want to be with Camille at the moment. Scary maybe, but for once he couldn't find it in himself to haul up the usual barriers and act like the arrogant man he was often called. He did behave arrogantly at times to hide the despair he felt at not being able to trust a woman and therefore most likely never going to have his happy ever-after that, until Melina had lied about her pregnancy, he'd always believed was a natural part of adulthood.

'Yes, I'd like that.' Sitting drinking wine with a woman he wasn't close to was rare, and made him feel light-headed in a strangely happy kind of way. No matter what Camille had done regarding Elyna, and the jury was slowly coming round to her side, he wanted to un-wind from a massive day. Long-haul flights were always tiring, but this exhaustion was all to do with the other problems thrown at him in the last few hours. 'Would there be a red available?'

'Do you like Merlot?'

He nodded, exhaustion taking over. Which was why he should leave. 'Definitely.'

'Then it's your lucky day. Liza left a bottle in the cupboard.' Camille grimaced. 'Sorry, I meant—'

He held his hand up. 'It's fine. I know what you meant.'

Her smile returned, and he found himself relaxing some more. So easy to do, which was odd when he'd usually be thinking of the reason behind every single word she uttered, every one of those smiles she gave him, every move she made. Seemed that the cynic was taking a back seat for once. He knew it wouldn't remain there, but it felt good, almost exhilarating, to be free of his other persona for a while.

'Good,' Camille said as she got out fresh glasses.

Elyna tapped his chin with her tiny fist. She was such a cutey. His heart did a flip. This was really his daughter? Who'd have believed he was a father? Certainly not him. Did that mean he did now? he wondered yet again. He wasn't quite one hundred per cent there yet, but yes, he could admit to himself he was well on the way. Elyna was already moving into his heart, making him soften towards her as she stared up at him with her mother's stunning eyes.

'Hello, little one. You've got food all over your face.' Looking over to the kitchen, he saw a cloth on the counter. 'I'll wipe it clean.' He made to stand up, but didn't really want to lose that soft touch where her hand lay.

'Here, use this.' Camille was already there, curiosity filling her face.

Of course she was on edge about his reactions and what he thought, and this was another step, although she wouldn't know in which direction. *Join the club, Camille.* 'Hey, Elyna, let me wipe away that sticky stuff for you.'

60 PARISIAN SURGEON'S SECRET CHILD

Elyna tipped her head sideways, eyes shut tight, as was her mouth.

Laughter bubbled up through his chest. 'She's not afraid of me one little bit.'

'Why should she be? You're not a monster.' Camille returned to pouring the wine. 'I have tried to warn her about those, though she hasn't a clue what I'm talking about.'

'She's very young for that, surely?' The goo came off Elyna's face and she opened her eyes again. Snatching the cloth, she held it to her chest as though she'd won a prize as she wriggled down to the floor again.

'Like I said, I'm ultra cautious when it comes to my girl.' She handed him a glass.

'Thanks.' Raising it in a salute: 'To sorting this out without too many difficulties.'

She nodded and took a sip of her wine before saying, 'I'd prefer none of those but that's being naïve.'

'Naïve is the last thing you are.' The Merlot was good. Not one from his family's estate but nearly as good. He was biased but that was what good families were all about. Leaning back in the seat, he closed his eyes for a long moment. Easier than looking at Camille and remembering the fantastic body her clothes covered. Safer than remembering kissing his way from her mouth down to her core, or recalling sliding inside her to be surrounded by glorious heat.

Enough. He sat up in a hurry and red wine sloshed over his trousers. Clamping his mouth shut over the oath that sprang to his tongue, he glared at Camille as though she was at fault. Of course she was. If he hadn't been thinking about her the wine would still be in the glass.

'You'd better take those pants off so I can run cold water over the wine.'

SUE MACKAY 61

Take my trousers off? Here, in front of you? No, thanks. There'd be no stopping him reacting to her in a completely wrong way. 'I'll be fine. I'd better get a move on.' He was suddenly in a hurry to get away and put some space between them so he could think more clearly. Standing up, he said, 'I'll be in touch.'

'What's your number?' Stress darkened her eyes as she nibbled her bottom lip. Far more worried than she'd let on?

He couldn't stop looking at her. His heart was pounding with similar worry. He wanted to hold her and say everything would be all right. But first he had to believe it himself. 'I'll send you a text so you have it.' His feet didn't move. Instead his arms lifted of their own volition and he placed his hands on her shoulders. She was shaking. 'Camille.' What could he say to make everything better? His hands tightened as her warmth stole into his palms. Leaning nearer, he drank in the sight of her lips, recalled the feeling of them on his skin, teasing him, tormenting him. An overwhelming need to kiss her tore through him.

Camille stared at him, her mouth slightly open as though waiting for his kiss.

Torment. This was ridiculous. She'd dealt him a body blow like no other. There were huge problems hovering between them and he wanted to kiss her? That would be the worst thing he could do. Spinning around, he strode out of the apartment without a backward glance. Camille was not getting to him. Not at all.

Tell that to someone who'd believe him.

CHAPTER THREE

'Who's ringing at this hour?' Camille groaned as she rolled over in bed two mornings later, still worn out from the flight home and how her mind never stopped thinking about Etienne and what he intended to do about Elyna.

Nine-thirty.

What? It couldn't be. Elyna would've woken her by now demanding food and cuddles.

The phone was still playing her favourite tune. She didn't recognise the number. 'Hello, Camille Beauregard speaking.'

'Camille, this is Karina Prout. Welcome home. How are you? You've been gone for ever.'

What was this about? She hadn't applied for a position back at Central Hospital. 'Hello, Karina. I'm good, glad to be home at last.'

'I heard you're looking for a job and want you back here. We've missed you.'

She hadn't expected that. Seemed Etienne had talked to Karina so he obviously still had no qualms about working together. 'Did Etienne mention I can't work a full week, that I require part-time hours?'

'Yes, he did.'

Did she want to work on his ward? It'd be all right

when things were going well, but what about the days when they might be at a stand-off?

'He also told me why. Congratulations on becoming a mum. It's awesome news.'

She didn't know the half of it. 'I don't know, Karina. I loved working there but things have changed.'

"Come and have a chat. No pressure,' Karina laughed.

She had nothing to lose. 'All right. I'll be there today at one if that suits you.' Liza's crèche was at the hospital so leaving Elyna there for a little while shouldn't be a problem. If only Liza were here. But she had amazing staff covering for her while she was in Marseilles.

'Something for you to think about is do you want to do five half-day shifts per week or three full days? We can accommodate you either way since you've got a wee child to consider.'

It sounded as if she already had the job. There was a shortage of nurses at the moment, but this was happening fast. 'I think I'd prefer five half-days. That way Elyna isn't at a crèche all day.' And she'd get fun time with her every day.

'Sounds good to me. I wouldn't have wanted my daughter spending long days in a childcare facility at that age either. You've got the half-days.' Karina laughed again. 'That sounds like I've sent your name forward to have you signed on already, but I'm sure you know where I'm coming from.'

Camille found herself laughing too. It felt good to hear Karina agree with her choice. Solo parenting meant every decision was up to her, and sometimes she liked to know she was on the right track, even over something like work hours. 'I'm looking forward to catching up with you.'

64   PARISIAN SURGEON'S SECRET CHILD

'Hopefully the job's what you're looking for. Oh, got to go. See you later.' Click. The phone went silent.

Camille stared at it. Had that really happened or was she dreaming? No, that was Karina. Etienne must have told the head nurse she was looking for work. So he intended keeping her close, for whatever reason, adding to her confusion and wariness. She leapt off the bed and grabbed her robe. Because she'd thought he worked there all the time she was away she'd never checked to see if there was a position available. They did work well together, but that had been before Elyna.

Would they be able to get along just as well when it came to raising Elyna? She had her own ideas on being a parent and the last thing she wanted was Etienne taking over completely. Would he though? She had no idea. He hadn't contacted her since he left on Sunday night, which surprised her. Guess he'd been assimilating everything and making some decisions about what he was going to do about it. All she could do was wait to hear from him and deal with each problem as it arose. She'd been relieved to have some time to get used to the fact he now knew about Elyna. She no longer had to face that worry, but there were a lot more things hanging in the air regarding what happened next. Waiting to talk about everything wasn't her style now the main issue was out there, but she knew she had to give him time or everything would explode faster than a hand grenade.

Suddenly rare excitement tripped through Camille. She really was back home. She still couldn't believe she'd slept in after finally falling asleep well after midnight. She hadn't the night before, worrying about his reaction to her news. Like on Sunday night when she'd first gone to bed he'd been on her mind, first as a problem over their

SUE MACKAY

daughter, but then it was the memory of his long, well-built body wrapped around her as he made love to her so tenderly taking over her thoughts until she finally fell asleep. Now he was back, foremost in her mind again.

'Mama. Mama, up.'

Swinging around, she lifted Elyna from the cot and into her arms. 'Hello, my girl, you've had a big sleep.' Not a peep all night. Showed how tired she'd been too. Bringing the cot into her bedroom might've helped. She hadn't wanted Elyna waking and thinking she was in a strange place and Mummy not there. She'd leave it in here for a couple more days before putting it in the bedroom that had been hers growing up. 'Oh, Grandma, Grandpa, I miss you both so much,' she sniffed.

'Down.' Wriggle, wriggle.

Back to reality. Icky nappies and grumpy child. 'Let's change your nappy first.'

'No.'

After a few minutes' debate Camille finally had the nappy changed and Elyna's face washed and now her daughter was charging around the apartment on her hands and knees as if she was on an adventure, happy not to be constrained.

Her favourite tune played again. This time, Etienne's name lit up the screen.

She wasn't ready to talk to him. He might spoil her good mood, but avoidance wasn't her style. Except when she'd overheard how he was waiting to be lied to about a pregnancy. 'Morning.'

'Morning, Camille. Thought I'd better warn you I told Karina you were back and looking for work.'

Shouldn't he be operating at this time of the day? He always used to have a heavy schedule and nothing should've changed in the time she'd been away. He was nothing if not predictable about his work routine. He said it made for easier days and less stress for patients. 'Too late. She's already called and I'm going in to see her today. She's given me a choice of which hours like she's already arranged the contract.'

'Good. Anyway, I'm between ops so talk later.'

Was that a promise? She started to reply then realised he'd gone. Great. He'd just pricked her happy bubble by reminding her that he had no problem with coming and going in her life as he saw fit. Time for a shower, food and getting outside for a walk in the park, she decided.

'Ready,' the anaesthetist told Etienne. 'Obs are good.'

Picking up the scalpel, Etienne shoved everything else out of his mind. His patient did not need him reflecting on Camille and how she affected him just by being herself. 'This should be straightforward but the growth is large so complications could arise,' he told the team at the operating table. Colleen Willows had a massive lump on her colon, which appeared cancerous on the X-ray.

'That's a biggie,' the junior doctor commented a while later when Etienne removed the fibroid.

One of the nurses shuddered. 'Why didn't she notice something wasn't right? It's not like she wouldn't have had some indicators, surely?'

Behind his mask, Etienne grimaced. 'Her husband said that, despite a family history of bowel cancer, she ignored his pleas to see her doctor. It's like she's been in denial.' Which he'd never understand. He'd dealt with similar situations before, and knew there was no understanding some people, but that didn't make it any easier

SUE MACKAY 67

for him to deal with the situation. There were downsides to being a doctor.

'It still doesn't make any sense,' the nurse muttered.

'I agree.' Etienne concentrated on tying off blood vessels before suturing the incisions he'd made earlier. The growth he'd removed had been placed in sterile bags to be sent to the laboratory to be studied under a microscope. The X-ray showed signs of the disease but only when a pathologist examined the sample could it be signed off as positive or negative. As with all his patients, he fervently hoped Colleen would come through the treatment that lay ahead in good shape.

A little over two hours after making the first incision into Colleen's abdomen, Etienne stepped back from the table and straightened his back. 'Done.' He'd check on her later in the day when she was settled into the surgical ward.

The ward where very possibly Camille would soon be nursing. Camille. The moment he didn't have a patient to focus on she slammed back into his mind. He'd never forgotten her after their fling. Hard to do when they'd continued to work alongside each other, but even when she'd left the ward he hadn't been able to put her in the past. Something about her seemed to like hanging around, keeping him aware of her in ways he hadn't experienced in a long time. Since Melina he'd become very self-protective in matters of the heart. Possibly too protective, but how else was he supposed to remain safe? Now that seemed to have blown up in his face with the arrival of Camille and her daughter back in town.

After she'd left the hospital she'd seemed to have cut contact with those she'd worked with. Hearing what she'd had to cope with in Montreal, he understood. He hadn't

68 PARISIAN SURGEON'S SECRET CHILD

tried too hard to find her either, because that would have shown he was interested in what she was up to and it was bad enough admitting it to himself, let alone anyone else figuring it out. He was known to only have flings and nothing deeper. Not that most women took any notice, often persisting with the *'I'm the one'* thing he never fell for.

Except Camille. She hadn't hung around, hadn't asked anything more of him than some fun time together in bed. Of course she'd piqued his interest by being different, but not enough for him to think she could be special. Yet he had missed her. A lot more than he would've believed.

Now Camille was back and had told him he was the father of her daughter, and while his instincts were in denial, his heart was sending different messages that had him in a right state wondering what to do next. In the early stage of her pregnancy she hadn't hung around expecting to be financially supported and taken into his family as his wife. Instead she'd gone away to support her grandmother at a difficult time. Neither had she rushed to let him know he had a daughter once Elyna was born. She certainly hadn't made any demands on Sunday, either, although that had been a hectic and emotional day as it was. Learning he was supposedly Elyna's father had rocked him to his roots. Plus woken him up to all sorts of possibilities. Good ones—and not so wonderful ones.

As he scrubbed his hands he kept picturing Camille smiling at Elyna. She'd even smiled at him occasionally, though warily. She'd poured *him* a glass of wine when he was too exhausted to head away. After a long-haul flight with a toddler, coming across him at the airport and then telling him her child was also his, she must've been more shattered than he had, yet she'd been nothing but open and caring.

Ahh, not always open, he reminded himself. She hadn't discussed much about Elyna and what she expected of him if he accepted his role in her daughter's life. While he was accepting it far more quickly than he'd have believed possible, he wasn't quite ready to tell Camille yet. The barriers were still firmly in place when it came to protecting himself. He needed time to think about everything. For him the first question was, if he did step up, where would Camille and Elyna live?

Camille had a nice apartment in a good part of the city, but he wouldn't be moving in with her. It was too small. They'd be stepping around each other all the time. Anyway, he had a perfect house, which he had no intention of moving out of. Why would he when he had five bedrooms and bathrooms, two lounges, a modern kitchen and a gym? If anyone was moving it should be Camille.

How would she take to that idea? Something made him think she wasn't going to rush in gleefully and make the most of his comfort and wealth. Of course, he could be making a huge mistake and really she was cleverer than he'd thought in getting everything she wanted. Except he didn't quite believe it. Camille had a heart of gold when it came to looking out for others, and the same would be true for Elyna, only many times stronger. Her love for Elyna was fierce, and so obvious a blind man could see it. And he wasn't blind. Except in the love department.

His head spun. There was no way of knowing what was going to happen until he'd spent more time with Camille. Something he'd get on with sooner rather than later. In the meantime he'd go up to the ward to check two patients he'd operated on earlier.

70   PARISIAN SURGEON'S SECRET CHILD

As he stepped out of the elevator his senses were immediately on high alert. A light laugh coming from the nurses' hub sent shivers of longing down his back. He'd know that gut-wrenching sound anywhere. Camille was here. Her interview should be over by now, surely? Did this mean she was keen to take the job before she'd even had the other interviews she'd lined up? He hoped so.

Not because he'd be able to keep an eye on her, but because she was one of the best nurses he'd worked with. Not to mention how much she intrigued him. She had him thinking outside the box when it came to his usual reactions to single women. Forget looking stunning and sexy, forget she was claiming he was the father of her daughter. What really rocked him was how she could look him in the eye and speak her mind without trying to be coy or cute or needy. Camille came across as real. Simple as that. Also as complex, because for him it was a rarity. His cynical side coming to the fore once again? Absolutely, but then that was what usually saved him from trouble. Was Camille trouble? Or a genuine woman who wanted nothing more than for him to be a good father to their daughter?

'Hey, Etienne, good news,' Karina called from the hub. 'Camille's agreed to come on board, starting next Monday.'

Camille turned to face him as he crossed to join them, surprise registering on her face. 'Etienne? What are you doing here?'

'I work here, remember?' he teased.

'You set me up.'

'I did.'

Camille stared at him for a moment longer before turning back to Karina, pure determination taking over. 'The job's perfect for where I'm at right now.' She looked back at him. 'I'm going to do five hours a day, five days a week.' *Don't even think about arguing with me*, said her steadfast gaze. 'I am not going to put Elyna in the crèche for full days. It'd be too much for her.'

Totally agreeing, he nodded once. 'Fair enough. Welcome back.'

For a brief instant Camille looked stunned. Hadn't she expected him to agree so readily when he'd told Karina she was back in town? The thing was, he agreed wholeheartedly with her decision. If she had to work, then shorter days were better for her too. 'Mornings or afternoons?'

'Both, depending on who else is working. Either way I'll be covering the middle of the day.'

So she'd be with his patients when they came up from Theatre. He found himself smiling far too easily. Whether for his patients or himself he wasn't sure, and he wasn't delving deeper to figure it out. Instead he'd enjoy the moment. 'Great.'

Camille's eyes widened briefly.

His smile grew. It was fun surprising her. 'I'm glad you've got this sorted.'

Karina cut through his thoughts. 'We're going for a coffee unless there's something you need me for. We've got lots to discuss.'

'I'll leave you to it, then.' But his feet were glued to the floor as he watched Camille. 'How's Elyna? Got over her long day flying home?'

Camille appeared surprised he'd ask in front of Karina. 'She's all right, still a bit scratchy at times. Right now she's at Liza's crèche downstairs.'

The hospital crèche? Very convenient, and, yes, close

to Camille's apartment. 'It was hard on her.' As it had been for him, though not because of the hours in the plane. Camille still looked tired around the edges too. Time to get back on track, and stop letting her distract him. 'Go and have that coffee, you two. There's nothing you need to hang around for regarding my patients, Karina. I presume the two women who came into the ward earlier are doing well?'

'They're both awake and comfortable. No problems.'

'Good to hear. I'll still check on them. There's another woman coming up shortly. I'll fill you in later.' He needed to stop talking and move away, but it wasn't easy. He liked being with Camille. Scary, right?

'Come on, Camille. Let's make the most of the quiet,' Karina said.

Camille watched her walk away before turning to him. 'Will I be seeing you this week?'

'Yes, tonight.'

Her eyebrows flew up. 'O-kay.'

Again he'd surprised her. Point to him. 'See you later.' He was being childish, but he wasn't used to dealing with a woman who could rattle him so easily. It might be good for him.

The emergency bell rang through the ward. Loud and demanding.

'Room five. I'll grab the gear.' Karina was already racing to get the emergency trolley.

Etienne nodded. 'I'm heading there.' He rushed down the corridor to room five.

Camille was right behind him, no doubt instincts of old kicking in. 'I'm here if needed.'

'Good.' Since she was about to start work here again

SUE MACKAY

73

there'd be no questions asked if she did get involved with helping the patient. 'Hopefully you're not required.'

Through the door of room five, he looked around, saw a man sprawled upside down half out of bed. 'Luca, what's happened?' He'd operated on him yesterday for liver cancer and he'd struggled with pain and mild after-effects of the anaesthetics. 'Luca?' Etienne reached the bed. 'Can you hear me?'

'I pressed the button,' a man in the next bed told him. 'He was lying back against his pillow like he was asleep but then the next thing he jerked about and slumped over the edge.'

Etienne had his hand around Luca's wrist trying to find a pulse. 'Nothing.'

Camille was at the other side of the bed, her fingers on the carotid artery. Unreal. The last time they'd worked on a patient together on this ward they'd dealt with a cardiac arrest. She shook her head. 'No pulse.'

With help from Camille on the opposite side pulling the man towards her, Etienne lifted Luca back onto the bed. 'Where's Karina with the trolley?' he demanded. There was a lot of phlegm dribbling from Luca's mouth. Had inflammation started in the liver where he'd operated?

'Right here. What do you need?' Karina said.

'Defibrillator.' The hospital gown covering Luca's upper body posed no problem as Etienne tore it down the front. He wasn't wasting a moment getting scissors from the trolley. This man was dying before their eyes. He immediately began compressions, not waiting for Karina to get the defib set up. This was *his* patient who'd come through a serious operation. He'd been reluctant to increase the analgesics any further as Luca was already on

74 PARISIAN SURGEON'S SECRET CHILD

strong medications. At the time the heart indicators had been normal for post op with nothing to suggest there were any clots in his arteries, or inflammation around the wound site.

Camille was poised, ready to give Luca two breaths the moment he stopped the compressions. Thank goodness for her. No other nurse had responded to the emergency.

'Where is everyone?' he asked on an intake of air.

'At lunch or seeing to patients coming up from Theatre,' Karina told him as she placed electrical pads on the exposed chest before them. 'We're short-staffed, remember?'

Another reason to be glad Camille was coming back to work here, he thought. No matter what lay between them, he was pleased about that. 'I repeat, welcome aboard, Camille. A bit sooner than you'd expected though.'

Her reply was a soft smile.

'Your turn,' he said with a return smile as he reached the thirtieth compression.

After giving Luca two breaths she stood back to let Karina finish setting up to send an electric current through him.

'Stand back, Etienne,' Karina warned before he could start more compressions.

He stepped away and watched Luca, digging deep for positivity that all would go well for his patient. It was entirely out of his hands now. All he could do was watch the green line running along the bottom of the defib screen and wait for it to lift up and down continuously.

It didn't.

Etienne clenched his hands together and began compressing down on Luca's heart once more while Karina got the defibrillator up to speed once more, all the while muttering, 'Come on, man. Don't let this happen. You can start breathing again. Now.'

The room was eerily quiet. No one else was talking, the other patients focused on what was going on.

'Stand back.'

He and Camille stepped away, watching the screen as the current struck.

Please, please, please, come back, Luca.

Luca's body jerked. The line lifted, dropped. Lifted again, and dropped, lifted once more, and then again and again.

In his chest, Etienne's heart thumped hard. 'Thank goodness for defibs and switched-on nurses.'

'And excellent doctors,' Camille said quietly beside him and squeezed his hand, this time surprising *him*.

She understood him so well. It brought a lump to his throat. He needed someone on his side right now. Not just anybody, but someone who knew him even a little. Camille.

Dressed in pyjamas, Elyna had been fed and bathed, and was charging around on her knees playing with her teddy bear. She squealed the ceiling down when the doorbell rang.

'This should be fun,' Camille said to herself. 'Parenting isn't all wine and roses.'

'Someone's excited,' Etienne commented with a small smile as he followed her into the apartment, and spotted the lively Elyna.

'I've tried putting her in my bed only to have her climb out and crawl out here, screaming as though I'd deprived her of everything she could possibly want. I'm surprised the neighbours haven't banged on the door to complain.'

76 PARISIAN SURGEON'S SECRET CHILD

She doubted Mrs Auclair would do that, being a grand-mother of three boisterous young boys, but sometimes when a person had had a bad day there was no accounting for what they'd say.

Elyna raced at Etienne and slammed into his legs, wrapping her little arms tight around his calves.

Etienne bent down to lift her up in his arms. 'Hello, Elyna. Did you tell Mummy I came to see you in the crèche today?'

Elyna stopped shrieking to stare at him, her eyes wide.

'You did? That's good, kiddo. Now, what's your problem? You can't still be overtired from your big day on the plane.'

Camille laughed. As if Elyna had a clue what he was saying, but he was being friendly and kind. Camille sighed. Why wouldn't he be? He wasn't an ogre. Unless he fought her for custody of their daughter. *Stop it. Give the man a chance to show where he's at first.* No doubt he'd still be coming to terms with her news and, despite indicating he might believe her on Sunday, with time to reflect he might've changed his mind. For now she'd accept how intrigued Elyna was with him and let everything else go. It seemed the only way to deal with the large pit in her stomach that had been growing bigger over the last hour as she'd waited for Etienne to turn up.

'I was told you'd dropped in.' She was taking it as an indicator he was beginning to accept the truth. 'I took Elyna to a park by the Seine on the way home and she went crazy crawling around with a little boy there with his mother. Once we got back here she crashed and slept on and off for the remainder of the afternoon, either in the pram or on the couch. I didn't put her to bed in the hope she'd fall asleep quickly after dinner. Seems I got that wrong.'

'From what my sister's said over the years she's been raising her little boys, there's no such thing as getting it right all the time when it comes to parenting.' Etienne was still looking at Elyna and his smile had grown.

Camille felt her heart skip a beat. Could this work out? He was a wonderful man when he wasn't wary of being taken for a ride, which unfortunately was a lot of the time. 'Yes, and she's not quite one. I can't imagine what the teenage years are going to be like.' She chuckled. 'Every day's exciting though.'

'I can see how much you love being a mother.' Now his steady gaze was on her, no hint of anything but respect coming her way.

'I do.' When she'd first learned she was pregnant she'd worried that she might not be any good at being a mother as she'd never had one, but she'd always known she'd give it her best shot. She had great role models in her grandparents to fall back on.

'Elyna, you're one lucky little girl.' Etienne leaned down to stand her on her feet, holding her until she had her balance. Elyna instantly plonked down on her bottom.

'Would you like some wine?' Camille asked. 'There's more of the Merlot and the Chenin Blanc we had on Sunday.'

'Thank you, I would.' He rubbed his lower back as he tried to stifle a yawn. 'Merlot, please.'

She headed for the glass cabinet. 'I've got cold chicken and salad for dinner.' Nothing fancy but easy to prepare.

Etienne straightened and stared at her. 'That's not necessary. I only came to have a talk,' he growled.

It didn't take much to get his back up. His ingrained

78 PARISIAN SURGEON'S SECRET CHILD

caution was showing itself again. 'Don't worry, I'm not trying to ingratiate myself with you by making you dinner. You've been at work and will no doubt be hungry. As I need to eat I figured we might as well have a meal together. That's all.' It might also help keep things on an even keel.

He continued to watch her as she poured the wine and handed him a glass, making her wonder what was coming next. But he drew a breath, as though trying to relax, and said, 'I apologise for being rude. Dinner would be lovely, thank you.'

Phew. 'Good.' Hopefully it was another step in the right direction. Sinking onto a chair, she sipped her wine and waited. He'd come to talk, he said. Where was he going to start? Should she get things under way? Or would it be better to wait until Elyna was finally tucked up in bed? *What am I doing, waffling along in my head like this? I'm usually a lot tougher.* Yes, but she didn't want to get on the wrong side of Etienne unless she had to. He deserved better than that, and so did she. So did Elyna, for that matter. 'You are her father.'

Etienne returned to watching Elyna with the softest smile. 'She's adorable. She appears happy and healthy for being born so early. She didn't have any serious health problems?'

'There were a lot of minor infections in her lungs and mouth during the first three months. Feeding was difficult, and she had to be fed intravenously for a long while. Otherwise everything went well. Now she's so energetic it's crazy. Though she does sleep a lot,' Camille added.

He frowned. 'No long-term health problems at all?'

'The paediatricians didn't think so. I admit I'm scared to get too ecstatic in case they're wrong. I lost a lot of sleep in the first weeks of her life thinking about everything that could go wrong.'

'Were the doctors good? Knew what they were doing?'

Camille smiled. He sounded like any father she'd known. 'Relax, Etienne. They were superb. I have no complaints about how they treated Elyna. None whatsoever.'

'Just checking.' He took a big sip of his Merlot, and turned back to her. 'It's been a huge shock, but I'm sure you know that. You were right. My instant reaction was to disbelieve you. It still is. I have more questions to ask, but...' Another mouthful of wine. 'The moment I first saw Elyna I sensed something about her that I can't explain.'

Camille felt her mouth drop open. Had she heard right? This was Etienne Laval, a man who did not share personal feelings with anyone as far as she knew. That probably didn't include his own family, but still. Grappling to get her head around what he'd said, she closed her mouth and swallowed hard. Then she waited because she had no idea what to say. It would be too easy to say the wrong thing and lose ground fast.

He smiled tightly. 'If only you could see your face. Obviously it's my turn to shock you.'

He could say that again. But she wasn't asking him to. 'Can you explain more?'

'Not really. I looked at your daughter and thought she was gorgeous, and I didn't want to let you go without finding out more.'

'So that's why you insisted on giving us a ride.' Disappointment rose. She'd been silly enough to think he'd actually been pleased to see her.

'Not entirely. I offered...' He winced. 'Okay, I insisted,

because I'd sometimes wondered where you'd gone, and what you'd been doing.'

He'd thought about her after she'd left the hospital? Was that a good sign? She'd thought about Etienne a lot, but then she had been carrying his baby. Truth was she'd missed him and hadn't got over him as she'd hoped. 'Now you know.'

He stood up and reached for her glass. 'Want another one?'

'I didn't realise I'd finished that one.'

'It was very small. Because you're thinking about Elyna, I take it?'

'Yes.'

'Another small one won't hurt, though maybe you could make it last a bit longer.' He gave her a light but genuine smile. 'I'm not lecturing you, Camille. I'm sure you'd never do anything to endanger your daughter.'

The way he said 'your daughter' was deliberate and firm. Still not acknowledging that Elyna was his daughter, too. Small steps, Camille thought as she rose to put the meal together, and was grateful they were getting along all right at the moment.

'So you've got a sister. Any other siblings?' Camille asked.

His face closed up.

Was there anything they could talk about without him getting upset? 'I'm sorry if I've said the wrong thing.'

'It's all right. We had a brother, Hugo. He was a year older than me. Hugo the second. Dad's the first.'

Camille's stomach scrunched in regret. She heard where this was going. 'Etienne, stop. You don't have to tell me.'

'You know what? I never talk about this and yet I find I want to tell you.'

She reached for the Merlot and topped up his glass, stunned at what he'd said. 'That means a lot.'

Etienne sipped the wine and stared at his hand. When he spoke it was so quietly she strained to hear. 'Hugo was fourteen when he had an accident on a quadbike at the vineyard. Going too fast, but he was a teenager. It's natural to think you're infallible.'

She glanced at Elyna and shivered. Who knew what lay ahead? Not that she wanted to know.

'He broke both femurs and pierced his bowel. It was an infection in his abdomen that took his life. During the operations he underwent no one noticed a second perforation of the bowel.'

'What? That's terrible.'

'Appalling.' Etienne took a deep breath and continued. 'Hugo always intended to go into the family wine business and eventually take over from Dad running the vineyards. I was meant to pick up the line after Hugo died.'

'Instead you chose medicine because of what happened to your brother?' It made perfect sense.

He nodded. 'Dad was very disappointed with me. My sister was thrilled because, like Hugo, she'd always wanted to be a viticulturist. It took some persuading to make Dad accept she was the ideal choice but they got there and now he wouldn't have it any other way. Cariole married a winemaker from Marlborough, New Zealand, and it's a perfect match in the vineyard and off it.'

'Hence your two nephews.'

'Yes.' Finally he smiled, albeit sadly. 'That's my family. We're close and there for each other during the difficult times. And the good ones,' he added more determinedly.

PARISIAN SURGEON'S SECRET CHILD

Family. It was all she really wanted. Camille sighed. She was a mother, but to have the other half of the picture at her side would be wonderful. It would never be Etienne. He had too much baggage to let go of before he'd ever fall in love with anyone. As for her, she still had trust issues, and even though Etienne had got to her in ways she'd never have believed, she wasn't really in love with him. She might think he was wonderful and sexy but she couldn't hand over her heart to him. He'd only give it straight back.

Placing plates and food on the table, she sat down. 'Eat and enjoy.' They didn't need any more gloomy conversation. But she would love to know what he was thinking regarding their daughter. Ask him? Or give him the space he seemed to need?

'I'm glad you took the position at Central Hospital,' he commented as he forked up chicken. 'I think you'll enjoy being back in familiar surroundings. It's one less hassle for you.'

'I hope so.' It had been too easy to give in and ignore her concerns regarding Etienne. So far she hadn't regretted her decision but then she hadn't started work properly yet. She was ready to settle down and this was another step forward. Hopefully there'd be more of those to come.

CHAPTER FOUR

'TELL ME MORE about your family,' Etienne said on Wednesday night. Once more he was sitting at Camille's table eating a delicious meal. She certainly knew her way around a kitchen. This time he'd provided the wine, bringing one from his cellar that came from the family estate. Elyna was tucked up in bed sound asleep after he'd read her a bedtime story. Something he'd thoroughly enjoyed doing. He enjoyed being around children but under the circumstances he hadn't expected to already be quite as relaxed with Elyna as he was.

Last night he and Camille hadn't done much talking about the issue hanging between them. He'd been more intent on hearing about Elyna's birth and follow-up. There was so much he'd missed out on that a burning need to catch up took over everything else, leading to the fact he had to accept he was Elyna's father. At least they seemed to be getting on all right, but the ingrained doubt he carried remained. There was a lot to talk about before he was one hundred per cent certain where he was going with raising Elyna. Together or separately? Hence his question about her background. There were clearly some trust issues there for her as well.

She sipped her wine. 'Like I said, my grandparents raised me as my mother died two days after I was born.

My mother was their only child and there was no other family to take me in.' She toyed with the glass. 'It must've been hard at times as they weren't young, but I couldn't have asked for a better upbringing.'

Unless it had been with her mother. Every child wanted to be with their parents. 'What about your father? Didn't he ever come to meet you?'

'Oh, he stepped up all right.' Bitterness tightened her face and soured her words. 'At my twentieth birthday party.'

'That was the first time you'd seen him?' This was not the story he'd expected. Camille was so balanced in her approach to life this was a shock.

'The first, not quite the last.' The level in her glass dropped as she took a large mouthful. 'It took a bit to convince him I wasn't going to hand over money every time he demanded it. He thought I owed him.'

'For what?'

'For existing.'

Etienne banged his glass down and stood to go around the table and lift Camille up into his arms for the biggest hug he had in him to give. 'Camille, you are the most amazing woman I know.' She hadn't let the low-life drag her down. She had to be strong to have managed that after waiting so long to meet him. Bet her grandparents had a lot to do with her strength.

The tension gripping her since he'd mentioned her father began to ease, her body softening in his arms. 'Thank you.'

Slowly lowering his arms, he reluctantly stepped back. Holding Camille was special. But not wise when he had no intention of getting close to her. 'I mean it.' It was the first time he'd ever said anything like that to a woman not from his family since he'd broken up with Melina.

Sinking back onto her chair, Camille lifted her glass again, then put it back down. 'I'd better go easy.'

'You've hardly touched it.' Other than that large gulp she'd taken a moment ago. 'Sit back and enjoy. Even have a refill if you'd like.' He made an instant decision, and hoped he didn't come to regret it. 'I can sleep on the couch for the night if you're worried about Elyna.'

Her reply was to blink, then take another small mouthful. Her lips lifted in a self-deprecating manner. 'I don't usually over-indulge, but thinking about that man makes me seethe.'

Returning to his seat, Etienne picked up his knife and fork and continued to enjoy the delicious casserole she'd made while listening to Camille tell him more about the man who'd fathered her. He didn't want to stop her as he sensed she didn't talk about the subject to anyone and it might be good to get it out there for once. It was interesting that, by confiding in him like this, she made him feel closer to her in a way he hadn't expected.

'My mother met him while in Montreal visiting her uncles. From the little I've learned he was raised there. He came from a poor background but wasn't doing anything to help himself get ahead except relying on others.'

'How did you learn that?'

'I went on the Internet.'

'Of course.'

Camille placed her fork on her empty dish. 'Grandma told me that my mother refused to say anything about him even when they were dating other than to say he was a great guy.'

His mouth dried. He wished he hadn't asked about her

86 PARISIAN SURGEON'S SECRET CHILD

family. It must be painful for Camille to talk about her father. He did appreciate her openness and honesty, and again he felt grateful.

'I wonder how he tracked you down.'

'No idea. He didn't say. I presume he went online too. Somehow he learned my name. I was probably vulnerable as I'd grown up wanting to know who my father was so I was open to hearing what he had to say.'

'I'm glad you had the nous to tell him where to go.' Etienne lifted the bottle. 'Sure I can't top up your glass?'

Pushing it towards him, she gave a crooked smile. 'A very small one. Might as well add that to the list of things I'm doing tonight that I never do.'

Warmth stole through him. He was meant to be keeping his wits about him and judging how genuine she was about not demanding to be taken in along with Elyna and given a comfortable life from here on, but she undermined his determination far too easily. If he didn't overthink it, it felt wonderful she wasn't using Elyna to get something from him. He groaned internally. He was already accepting that Camille was becoming important to him, and that had nothing to do with the little girl sound asleep down the hall. Though Elyna did add to the wonderful picture of the future he was beginning to imagine. 'Does that include allowing me to sleep on the couch?'

A hint of pink touched her cheeks. 'There's a bed in the third room.'

Why did I say that? Camille asked herself silently. I mean, seriously? She wouldn't sleep a wink knowing he was just down the hall. Offering Etienne a bed meant he would stay. If he didn't stay she'd still probably lie awake all night anyway thinking about the times he'd shared a bed with her during their fling. That was one hot body under his expensive suit. A body she'd never forgotten despite everything else going on in her life. Nor had she forgotten the man behind the aloof smile. A good man with a big heart, though he didn't like to share that any more than she did hers.

'Sounds more comfortable than the couch,' he admitted, then laughed. 'I don't think I need to stay the night, though. You haven't had too much wine and Elyna's perfectly safe.'

Her heart sank with disappointment. Had she wanted him to stay? When there was so much between them that needed sorting and most likely wasn't going to be straightforward? Unfortunately she did. 'Your call.' *This is the man you started falling for, remember?* It didn't matter. She was long over that, had put him firmly aside. All that mattered now was he was Elyna's dad and they needed to work out how to go forward in a way that suited them all. Except that was a lie. Whenever he was around she got a warm sensation of something like love deep inside her heart. It made her wonder if she'd found what she'd believed she'd never want again after her disastrous relationship with Benoit.

Etienne's eyebrows rose slightly. 'I'll head home but I'd like to spend time with Elyna when possible.'

Camille felt her mouth fall open. 'Are you saying—?'

'That I believe she's my daughter?' He hesitated, as though afraid to answer. Once he put it out there, if he thought she was, then there wasn't any going back. 'I am coming to think so. Though there are things I'd like to know sooner than later. You're asking a lot of me to simply accept her as mine, yet I can't find it in me to think it's not true.'

88 PARISIAN SURGEON'S SECRET CHILD

Her head spun. She didn't begrudge him for his comment about asking a lot. But to say he believed her—because that *was* what he was saying, wasn't it?—was not what she'd been expecting so soon. He knew how to surprise her, which normally she'd find thrilling, but not when it came to Elyna's parentage. 'I'll answer your questions, but remember I've got some myself.'

His mouth tightened, but all he said was, 'I'm sure you do.'

She didn't know how to interpret that so she waited for him to go ahead.

Finally, he continued. 'Why did you break off our fling?'

She gaped at him. That was the last thing she'd expected him to ask. It had absolutely nothing to do with Elyna, and she wasn't keen to share how she'd been feeling about him at the time. Lying wasn't an option. He'd see right through her. Nor was it something she liked to do. She went for the middle road. 'It was time. I don't let any fling I'm involved in carry on for too long.'

'Why?'

'Because then it's no longer a fling but something like a relationship and I don't do those.' Damn. She'd just set herself up to be asked why not, and she wasn't exposing her gremlins over having her heart broken by the one man she had loved.

Etienne opened his mouth, closed it again. Then he nodded as though he understood where she was coming from. Which was quite possible given the way he'd spoken about past relationships to his mother that night she'd gone to tell him she was pregnant. 'You didn't want anything else from me.'

Dead right. Especially once she'd started worrying she

might be falling a little in love with him. 'We got together for sex with meals often thrown in at lovely restaurants. I had a wonderful time but it couldn't go on for ever. It's not how I do these things. Not that I've had many flings.' Shut up, Camille. He didn't need to know that.

He leaned back in his chair and drained his glass. 'Let's move on before we get into a mess we can't undo.'

'Why did you go to Nice? You always said you had your dream position here in Paris.'

'I'll have another wine before I go into that one.' Etienne was off the chair and in the kitchen before he'd finished the sentence.

Camille wondered what she'd said. It had seemed like a straightforward question but she should know better. 'It's okay. Forget I asked.'

'No, it's all right.' He sat down again and added a small amount to her glass before emptying the last of the bottle into his. 'I became restless. Everyone around me seemed to be getting their lives in order, marrying, having kids.' He shrugged too eloquently. 'I don't know. I missed you. The fact that you'd dropped by my office that night when you'd never done so before also kept nagging at me.'

She couldn't believe what she was hearing. Etienne admitted he'd missed her? No way. He couldn't have. He didn't ever get close to a woman.

He was still talking. 'I took a break and went to Nice where my friend's a partner in a surgical clinic. They needed someone to cover for another surgeon on maternity leave. Once there I thought I'd get over the restlessness, but it never wavered so at the end of my contract I returned home.'

She waited for more but it wasn't forthcoming. Etienne had said all he was going to. He'd wound her up with half a story but she wasn't letting him know that. 'Are you happy working at Central again?' she asked.

'Mostly.'

Camille stood up and collected the dishes to take to the kitchen. End of that conversation, apparently. Though it was more than she'd expected.

Etienne stood up. 'I think it's time I went. Yes, I am going home. Thank you for a delicious meal.'

'You're welcome.' Most of the time. Camille banged the plates into the dishwasher. She was being abrupt but she was suddenly impatient to know what he intended for the future. Their future regarding Elyna. His hints that he was getting there suddenly weren't enough. She needed to know. Now. But she wasn't going to beg. 'Goodnight.'

'I'm on call for the next couple of days so I might not have as much time to pop in.'

'You have my number. Any time you have something to discuss you know how to get hold of me.'

'I do.'

Suddenly Etienne was in front of her, reaching for her. His eyes were fixed on hers, watching her closely as his head lowered slowly until his lips just brushed hers. 'Camille,' he sighed as he pulled back swiftly.

Leaving her chilled and hyped all in one. 'Yes?' Had he been going to kiss her? As in a deep, heart-twisting kiss?

'Damn you, Camille. You do my head in.' His mouth suddenly covered hers, his tongue delving into her mouth, kissing her as if there were no tomorrow.

She was responding, pouring everything into their kiss, tasting him, feeling his hands on her waist, smelling his spicy scent. This was Etienne, the man breaking through her resilience, causing her to rethink not trusting her heart to anyone again. Then just as suddenly she was being put aside.

'Goodnight, Camille.' He walked away, and the main door closed quietly behind him.

All her energy drained away and she sank onto the nearest chair. 'Damn you, Etienne Laval. There are two of us trying to figure out what to do and you're not playing fair.' Not that she'd expected him to be on board straight away. In fact he was further ahead than she'd thought he'd be at this point, but it was so hard waiting for him to front up and be straightforward with her. But to kiss her as he used to? To wake her up in such a hurry she'd struggled to keep up, only to have him walk away? Goodnight, he'd said. Where did that leave her? Apart from in a right pickle of heat and longing, that was.

Tightening her arms around her upper body, she held on as if she were about to fall apart. She did care for Etienne—a little. Or a lot. She wasn't sure which. But whichever, it was enough to tip her world upside down and have her wondering if she'd made a mistake coming home and telling him about Elyna.

No, that wasn't right. Elyna would benefit from knowing her father. Her mother mightn't, but that wasn't Elyna's problem.

On Friday morning Camille swung Elyna up in her arms and kissed her cheeks. 'Guess what, little one? You're off to play with your new friends while Mummy goes to work.' Where she'd probably bump into Etienne at some point when he came to check up on his patients, which was the last thing she needed after that kiss. But then they had to make this work so she'd straighten her back and deal with whatever came along.

92 PARISIAN SURGEON'S SECRET CHILD

Here he comes, Camille thought as she read Bella's tympanic temperature monitor two hours later. She'd sensed his presence almost before he appeared in the doorway. Her skin had tightened and her head felt light. Toughen up, she reminded herself.

Etienne was striding towards his patient but his eyes were on her, looking surprised. 'I didn't think you were starting until Monday of next week.'

'Karina asked if I'd cover for a few hours as they're really short-staffed this morning.'

'Where's Elyna?'

'In the crèche downstairs,' she ground out. Did he think she'd left her small daughter at home alone? Of course not, but he had to know she'd make sure Elyna was sorted before she agreed to come in. 'Bella's temperature is thirty-nine point six.' He needed reminding that this wasn't the place to be discussing their daughter. Or anything personal.

He looked at her for another moment, then nodded. 'It was much the same when she was in recovery. It's not uncommon post op but keep an eye out for infection at the wound sites.' Etienne grimaced. 'Sorry, you know that.' He turned to his patient. 'The surgery went well, Bella. We removed all the lymph nodes from your left side where the cancer was, and took out the first one on the other side. The lab checked it and it's clear of cancer.'

'That's got to be good news, thank you, Doctor. I'm just glad it's all done. I don't regret having both breasts removed. It was scary waiting to get rid of the cancer. I'd hate to go through this a second time.'

As she listened, Camille slipped the pulse oximeter on Bella's finger to get a blood oxygen saturation level. 'Normal,' she told Etienne a moment later.

'Good. Have you given Bella anything for the pain since she came up from recovery?'

'That was next on my list. Though Bella's hesitant about having analgesics. She's worried she'll get too used to them.'

He turned back to his patient. 'I understand but, as I warned you before we did the procedure, you'll have some severe pain as the effects of the morphine wear off. It's better to maintain a level of painkiller that keeps the pain at bay and then wean you off.'

Bella nodded slowly. 'I have a thing about taking drugs of any kind. I'm reasonably young and fit. I can get through it all right.'

From the notes Camille knew she was thirty-three and a gym addict. 'I know what you mean about taking analgesics. The side-effects can be annoying, but it will help your recovery if you don't have too much pain over the first few days at least.' Etienne was probably about to cut her off for taking over but sometimes a nurse could get through to a patient more easily than a doctor. 'It's hard enough dealing with losing your breasts without adding severe pain to the situation.'

Bella blinked, rubbed her face. 'You're right. This is horrible. But I had to do it for my husband and kids. And me.'

Where was her husband? Camille took her hand and held it lightly. 'You'll get through this with their support.'

'I know. All right, I'll take the painkillers for now.' Suddenly Bella straightened up and plastered a smile on her tense face. 'Willem, you're here.'

A man of a similar age was crossing the room to Bella's bed, worry filling his face. 'Bella, darling, how are you?' He made to hug her, then must've realised he shouldn't and carefully sat on the edge of the bed instead.

94 PARISIAN SURGEON'S SECRET CHILD

Camille stepped away and glanced at Etienne, who was watching her, not his patient.

He nodded. Thank you, he mouthed.

A thrill ran through her. They were on track with working with patients if nothing else, and that made her hopeful they could move on from that decimating kiss. Except she already craved another one. *Stop it, Camille. Be sensible for once.* 'I'll get the tablets for Bella. I'm presuming you've signed for them.'

'You know I have.' It was said with a small smile.

This was Etienne when they'd been having a fling, warm smiles and so sexy he had her constantly wanting to get close to him. But— No, forget the buts. Let everything go. Move on. 'Just checking.' She nodded and headed away to the drugs cupboard before realising she didn't yet have access to it. It had been mayhem when she'd arrived so Karina had suggested they worry about it later when everything calmed down. 'I need someone to open the cupboard.'

'I'll do it,' Etienne said. 'But first I want to check on another patient I operated on this morning.'

'Pierre Cabot?' The sixty-four-year-old had had two hernias repaired. 'He was sleeping when I checked on him twenty minutes ago.'

'Let's hope he's awake now. The last thing I like doing is waking patients post surgery. They often tend to be grumpy.'

'That's because you're probably poking around their wound site.'

'I know. Weird, isn't it? Who'd be a doctor?' He *was* light-hearted today.

She wondered what he'd had for breakfast because she'd get in a box of it for her bleaker mornings when she worried about how they were going to manage dual parenting if—when—he came on board. *But I'm not thinking about that now.* It'd spoil the good atmosphere.

'Hey, Etienne.' Karina appeared in a doorway. 'You were right. We do need Camille back here.'

Camille turned to stare at him. 'You said that?'

'Relax. I merely reminded Karina you're an exceptional nurse.'

Whack. Her heart slammed her ribs. He'd said that? Despite their problems? Camille felt happier. 'Let's go see Pierre, and then I can give Bella some drugs before she changes her mind again.'

'Hopefully her husband will help us there,' Etienne said as they walked down the ward.

'I doubt anyone can if Bella's determined not to take them, but for now we're winning.' Taking painkillers certainly helped people through the post-surgery time when their bodies were protesting about having been cut and stitched.

Karina caught up with them. 'When you've done that take a short break, Camille. We've got more patients coming up from Theatre in about forty-five minutes.'

'Will do.'

'There's tea and coffee in the staffroom off the office,' Karina added.

'I'll just pop down and see how Elyna's doing,' Camille said.

'Fine.'

'I'll come with you,' Etienne said when Karina was out of earshot.

'Great.' Despite not giving her a definite answer he was stepping up to the father role all too easily. It was

96   PARISIAN SURGEON'S SECRET CHILD

definite progress, and made her relax about everything a little more.

'It's handy having the crèche your friend manages right here in the hospital.'

'It makes life easier not having to stop off elsewhere on the way.'

'You'll be able to see her in your breaks. So will I,' he added quietly.

She further softened towards him. 'She'll like that.'

'If you need help with the fees please let me know.' When she glanced at him in surprise, he shrugged. 'I know. That's not how I usually am. But I'm getting my head around the fact that you'll probably never ask me for anything and I'd really like to share more with you than just hugging Elyna.'

Camille stopped abruptly. The man was being so open she was struggling to take it all in. 'Etienne, if you're totally on board about being her father then I'm not going to stop you being a major part of her life.'

'Except asking me for help financially.'

True. 'I am who I am.'

'Tough, independent, determined. To name a few of your better characteristics.' The smile that came with that told her he wasn't about to complain about those features.

It was a lot to take in. 'Come on. We're meant to be seeing a patient, not patting each other on the back.'

Etienne laughed, a deep, warm sound that lightened her step as she headed into the room where the patient lay sleeping. After all the tension and doubts since bumping into Etienne at Charles de Gaulle she couldn't believe how good she was feeling. And happy, because he seemed to care about her and how she was coping. No wonder those feelings of tenderness she'd felt for him during their fling were rushing back into her heart. This time she wasn't going to walk away so fast, if at all. She had to see where it led and if they didn't make it then she'd have to toughen up some more and move on. Whatever happened in the future Etienne was always going to be in her life because of their daughter.

Friday evening. It had been one of the longest weeks of his life, Etienne thought as he rang Camille's bell. Finding out he might be a father, trying to see Elyna and Camille whenever possible, a busy operating list, then being on call. He was exhausted.

'Come up,' she said when he spoke into the voice box. 'Door's open.'

She was playing with Elyna when he stepped inside the apartment. His heart expanded as he watched them, heads together, creating a structure of some sort with building blocks. Mothering came naturally to Camille. Nor had she been impatient with him as she'd waited for him to accept he was Elyna's father. How she was going to react to the invitation he was about to offer her he had no idea. It might make her pause, or she might see it as an opportunity to get closer to his family.

'Hi there, Etienne. Look who's here, Elyna.' Camille turned their girl around so she could see him.

'Hello, Elyna.' He couldn't take his eyes off the two females sneaking into his heart far quicker than he'd have believed possible. Was this why he'd mostly stayed away from flings since returning from Nice? Because Camille had already got to him in an unexpected way? Face it, even in Nice he hadn't gone looking for a bed companion more than a couple of times and those had been one-night stands. Again, he had to wonder if Camille was the reason for his abstinence. He might be accepting he was Elyna's father but to accept he was falling in love with her mother was a whole different story. One he was beginning to consider exploring. Which was huge. He'd take it slowly, because that was the only way to go and still feel in control.

'You want to hold her?' Camille asked.

Of course he did. Reaching down, he swung Elyna up into his arms and spun her around. 'Hey, little one.' Brushing a kiss on her brow, he felt his heart lift. This was what it was like to be a dad. Very damned wonderful. Glancing at Camille, he found her watching him with something like relief in those blue eyes. 'Do you still worry I might walk away from her? Because, rest assured, I will never do that.'

'I believe you, believe in you.'

Sucker-punch him, why didn't she? 'I don't know what to say to that.'

'Don't say anything, just accept it.' She looked around the room, before returning her gaze to him.

'I'll do my best.' Etienne huffed out a tight laugh. Lately his life hadn't been as devoid of excitement as usual. He'd been happy spending time at the vineyards helping his sister and brother-in-law, plus spending time with the little guys, and hadn't missed the casual affairs that had used to take up a lot of his spare time. That was when the restlessness had finally subsided. He wasn't quite where he wanted to be but at least he wasn't wasting time worrying about it any more. 'There's a lot for me to get used to. Like spending time with you both.'

Camille was gaping at him, slightly stunned.

He chuckled. 'It is possible for me to lead a quiet life, you know.'

Her mouth tipped up into one of those bright smiles that twisted his heart. 'No, I didn't know you could manage that.'

Nor had he, until this particular woman got under his skin and harassed him with images of her smiling and laughing and groaning with sexual pleasure when they'd made love. It had been more than just sex towards the end, and one reason he'd been somewhat relieved she'd pulled away. Then there'd been all the reasons he'd wished she hadn't. 'Guess there's a lot for you to learn about me, going forward.' He had a plan for getting that under way very soon that he'd put to her shortly.

'Down,' Elyna cried, wriggling in his arms.

'Sure thing, little one.' He set her on her feet, holding her until she had her balance, which lasted all of five seconds. 'You certainly know what you want, don't you?'

'She was born like that,' Camille commented in a loving voice.

If only she could speak to him in the same way. Another thing he'd have to work on if he wanted more than a platonic relationship with her. Did he? Or didn't he? A huge question and one he wasn't prepared to answer yet, maybe never. 'But she was premature.'

'It was obvious from the get-go that she had a determined nature. No giving up even on the less than easy days.'

'How did that make you feel?' He'd bet his career that Camille would've been as determined as her daughter.

'Hopeful, and in sync with her.'

'I wish I'd been there for you both.' It was true. He struggled with what he'd missed because he hadn't known Camille was having his child. 'I'm not looking for trouble and trying to blame you,' he added hurriedly.

'If it's any comfort, I'd have liked having you there. There were days in the first weeks that I despaired of

Elyna making it through the horror of being wired to every machine imaginable that did everything for her.'

He stepped close to place an arm around her shoulders. There was a light quiver going on under his hand. 'For what it's worth, Elyna doesn't look any the worse for her early start in life.' His hand tightened around her before he remembered what he was going to ask later and dropped his arm to put some space between them. 'Can I ask what you've got planned for the weekend?' Hopefully nothing important. He wanted time with Elyna to start making up on what he'd already missed out on.

'Topping up the pantry, taking Elyna for walks in the park, not much else.'

'Then how about you join me for lunch tomorrow? At my house,' he added so she understood that he was opening up more of his life to her. But that was only the beginning. His chest rose as he drew a breath. 'My parents will be there. They are dying to meet you and Elyna.'

Camille's mouth fell open. 'What?'

'I've told them about Elyna. It had to happen and I figured the sooner they knew, the sooner we could make some plans for the future. Besides, why shouldn't they know they've got a granddaughter?'

'Of course it's the right thing to do. Because you haven't straight out said you accept Elyna's your daughter, I hadn't expected you to have talked to them already. But then, why wouldn't you have? Are they all right with the news?'

'Beyond all right. Mum can't wait to hold Elyna and hug her. I warn you, she can be a bit OTT when it comes to her grandchildren.'

Doubt was settling over Camille's face.

'You'll be fine, Camille. They want to get to know you

too. They won't put you through the mill with a million questions. I'd stop them if they did but it won't happen.'

Her face didn't clear. Instead she shrugged. 'I've known this day would come, but it's going to be hard.'

'So you'll come to lunch?'

'Yes.'

'I'll pick you up at eleven.'

'We'll be ready. How about a glass of wine?' she asked.

'I'll get it.'

Camille watched Etienne walk through to the kitchen as though he didn't have a care in the world. If only she felt half as confident. She was meeting his parents. Tomorrow. They'd know that she hadn't told Etienne she was pregnant before leaving Paris to go to Montreal.

'This day was always going to come,' she muttered. But she was no more prepared for it now that Etienne accepted Elyna was his than she'd been at any time since seeing her positive HCG result. 'Time to suck it up and get on with reality.'

If only tomorrow were a few weeks away. More time to allow her to get used to the idea of fronting up to Etienne's parents might help. Or not. It wasn't as though this were happening within days of Elyna being born. She'd spent many hours thinking about Etienne's parents and how they'd react to the news they had a granddaughter. Anyway, since when had she become a coward? Etienne had surprised her in more ways than one. His acceptance of Elyna had been easier than she'd thought possible. The fact he was taking her to his house tomorrow was unexpected. She didn't think they were that far into this parenting relationship for that.

This time tomorrow she'd know a bit more about Eti-

102 PARISIAN SURGEON'S SECRET CHILD

enne's family, which had to be good. Fingers crossed. Etienne seemed to have a solid relationship with them so it would be strange if they didn't reach out to their grandchildren. She wanted Elyna to have wonderful grandparents willing to be there for her whenever needed as hers had been for her. It was hideous imagining how her life might've turned out if not for them. At least Elyna had a father who wasn't denying his role, just taking time to accept it completely, which was way more than she'd had.

'Up, Mama. Up.' Elyna stood before her, stretching her arms up. 'Up.'

Swinging her into her arms and hugging her against her chest, Camille blinked as sudden tears appeared at the corners of her eyes. 'I'm so lucky to have you, sweetheart. So is your daddy.' He just had to learn how lucky. Or did he already know?

Etienne brought the wine through, suddenly looking tense. Camille watched him close the curtains in the lounge. He'd been relaxed only moments before. 'Everything all right?'

'Why wouldn't it be?' He pulled a chair around to face her and sank down, his elbows on his knees.

She wasn't going there. Instead she'd wait him out because in the end he would speak his mind. He wasn't one to hold back when it was important.

As the silence grew deafening she began to squirm. Should she say something? Ask what was bothering him? Then it hit her. He wanted Elyna. Inviting her to his place was the first step to upping the ante. He was going to make it difficult for her to keep her daughter. 'Etienne.' She stopped. What to say without sounding desperate? And doing that wouldn't help her side of the story.

'Relax, Camille. We need to find a way for both of us

to be with Elyna as much as possible. I don't want to only be a drop-in dad. I want to be fully involved in her life.'

'I agree.'

He went quiet again. Where was this going? 'I have something to ask you.' He paused, staring at the floor between his legs before he then lifted his head and fixed a steady gaze on her. 'Will you marry me?'

He could have knocked her down with a feather! That was the last thing she'd expected. 'Did you just say what I think you did?'

'I asked you to marry me, Camille. That way we can raise Elyna together, share a home, be a family.'

What about love? What about more children? What about sharing their lives completely? No, this wasn't about them. It was only about their daughter. She couldn't, wouldn't, do it. Not even for Elyna because, in the end, without love it wouldn't work for any of them. She stood up, unable to sit still a moment longer. 'I hear where you're coming from, Etienne.' She paused. Took a deep breath. 'But my answer is no, I will not marry you.'

His head jerked back. His eyes were wide with shock. He'd really believed she'd say yes!

That hurt. Big time. She was not like the other women he'd had in his life. This might be about Elyna but he'd still believed she'd grab the opportunity and say yes so all her problems would be solved. 'I won't marry you because to me marriage is purely about love. Without that it's hollow. I won't do it.'

He stood up slowly and came to take her hands in his. For once, they didn't feel soft and warm, but chilly and rigid. 'I think you're wrong. No, we're not in love, but we get along well, and I believe we would grow together over time.'

104   PARISIAN SURGEON'S SECRET CHILD

Pulling away from him, she gazed into his lovely grey eyes and tried to keep her head on straight. It wasn't easy because he already meant so much to her. Enough that she suspected she might already be on the way to loving him. She accepted that, but it didn't make saying yes to his proposal right. She hadn't completely lost her head over him yet. Anyway there was no suggestion he might feel the same about her. 'That isn't how I perceive a successful marriage to be. I don't believe you do either. You're trying to do the right thing by your child, but, Etienne, it won't work.'

'The one thing I've always said about you from the first time we got together is that you can be brutally honest.'

'I'm not going to change.'

'I wouldn't expect you to. Or want you to.' He moved away. 'I'm sorry you don't see my proposal as being the best solution for us all.'

So was she. More than sorry. How ironic that Etienne wanted her to accept his offer for all the wrong reasons. 'I'm sorry, Etienne, but I won't change my mind.'

He came over and placed a light kiss on her cheek. 'We'll see about that. See you tomorrow.' Then he was gone, leaving a challenge hanging in the air.

We'll see about that.

Etienne had asked her to marry him. But he didn't love her. She shivered. What could be worse than a loveless marriage? Or one where she loved him and he didn't reciprocate her feelings?

A tear snuck down her cheek where he'd kissed her. She'd thought a proposal was the ultimate dream but not in this case. So close yet so far.

CHAPTER FIVE

'I HAVEN'T ASKED where you live,' Camille said as Etienne manoeuvred through the Saturday traffic on the way to his house.

'Rambouilet,' he told her, surprised she hadn't looked it up. But then Camille didn't seem to spend all her time finding out everything possible about him or his family. 'Near the Versailles Palace,' he added in case she didn't know. He was still trying to accept she'd turned his proposal down.

'I had a friend who boarded in that area while doing her nursing training. It's lovely.'

He glanced sideways to see if her face had lit up in anticipation, but no, she looked the same as she had since he'd picked her up. Tense and worried, even a little angry. 'Camille, everything's going to be all right.' With his parents anyway. 'I haven't mentioned to them that I asked you to marry me.' He was determined not to get into an argument with her about Elyna either. They'd done pretty well so far, and long may that continue for everyone's sakes.

She softened a little. 'Thanks.'

'But?'

She huffed out a breath. 'I do feel guilty about not telling you earlier, no matter what the reasons, which means your parents also missed out on Elyna's first year.'

He could agree with her, but in the end what'd happened couldn't be undone so he might as well let it go once and for ever. He wanted to get on well with Camille, not become awkward and guarded around her, and maybe one day she'd change her mind about marrying him so they could co-parent their child better. For that to happen he needed to stop kissing her as he had the other night. That kiss had messed with his mind ever since. He wanted more but was going to resist.

'I've explained to my family what went down and why and no one's raised any doubts so you can put it behind you. We might be coming at this from different perspectives but we're in it together, Camille.' He meant it. Making a happy life and home for Elyna was important, and so was co-operating with Camille. If she'd let him in, that was, and hopefully his plans would see to that despite the kiss. It had been a mistake he couldn't afford to repeat.

She turned in her seat to regard him thoughtfully. 'Until last night you've been good about everything. I know there've been times when you wanted to spit out what you really thought of me.'

His chest tightened. Only Camille would say that. Just as only Camille got to him in an unprecedented manner. 'Have you always been so honest when it comes to saying how you feel?'

'Probably not always, but most of the time, sure. My grandparents never hid anything from me about my mother and that helped me growing up. Right from the first time I asked about my father they told me they knew nothing about him. While that was hard to take I learned to be as honest as them. It doesn't always win me any favours,' she said with a small smile.

'Don't change on my account. It's refreshing.'

'I'll do my best,' she agreed, relaxing further.

'That's all I expect.' Damn, he needed to relax too or lunch would be a failure, something he didn't want, though, knowing his mother, it would go well no matter what. She was excited about meeting Camille and Elyna. 'Did I tell you Mum's thrilled you've given Elyna her mother-in-law's name?'

'I'm pleased she's okay with it. Apart from being a family name, it's pretty.'

Etienne smiled internally. He had to agree. Not only the name but the wee girl who had been given it was also pretty, just like her mother. When was he going to stop thinking about Camille in that way? She was his daughter's mother, not his lover. Or the love of his life.

Turning into his driveway, he pulled up beside his father's vehicle and sighed. Home sweet home. He enjoyed living here, even though it did get lonely at times. Hopefully that would change in some ways. He was about to let Camille and Elyna into his home, and maybe fully into his heart, though that could take a lot longer. Not so much with Elyna. She was there already. It was harder with Camille. Old fears were difficult to ignore.

She was staring around at his home and the beautiful gardens surrounding it. Amazement filled her eyes as she turned to him. 'This is spectacular.'

He nodded. 'I was very lucky to have inherited the property from my grandfather. His gardener's grandson is my gardener, which is a real bonus otherwise you'd be looking at a shambles of long grass with no flowers and shrubs.'

108 PARISIAN SURGEON'S SECRET CHILD

'I doubt that very much,' Camille retorted around a smile. 'You'd never let that happen.'

She was right. He wouldn't. But he appreciated that she believed it of him. Suddenly he was nervous, an unusual sensation. This was going to be all right, wasn't it? Camille wouldn't walk out in a huff if someone said the wrong thing? She was struggling but surely she wouldn't become difficult with his parents and deny them access to Elyna? No, that was one thing he could be certain about: she wanted Elyna to know her only grandparents because of how close she'd been to hers.

He'd have to wait and see how any other concerns played out. No point in second-guessing. His stomach was tight. Camille had knocked at his certainties and made him wonder where he was at—like how often the thought of love crossed his mind and heart when he was with her. That had nothing to do with Elyna. She was a separate matter. Her mother was his biggest concern at the moment.

'Come on, let's go inside.' He needed to get the introductions out of the way. Then hopefully everyone would relax a little. His mother was worried Camille mightn't take to the family in an open, caring way. His father was more concerned about what she might be after, as he'd been for a while, but now believed he'd been wrong to think that.

Going around to the other side of the car, he opened the back door and unclipped Elyna's safety belts before lifting her into his arms. 'Hey, little one. You're about to meet your grandparents.'

Camille stared at him. 'You do totally believe me.'

His stomach dropped. He hadn't actually put it into

words for her yet. 'Yes, Camille, I do, otherwise we wouldn't be doing this.'

'Thank you. I wanted to believe that was why you suggested this, and the reason behind your proposal, but a part of me struggles with you accepting the truth after whatever's happened to you in the past, which I still know nothing about.'

He closed the door, and started walking towards the main entrance. 'My ex-fiancée told me she was pregnant when I broke up with her. I'd overheard some rather brutal comments from her to a friend, about her plans for our future. The pregnancy was a lie, designed to get me to reconsider calling off our marriage.'

'No wonder you made that comment the night I came to see you.' A warm hand touched his back. 'There are some selfish people out there.' Her tight voice suggested she'd also had her share of being mistreated by someone special. He wondered who it might have been.

'Come inside and meet two people who're nothing like that.' His steps were lighter as he walked beside Camille. She hadn't said he was an idiot to believe other women would do what Melina had, and that she'd never do something like that. She'd just accepted what he'd told her and understood his pain. With his hand on the door, he hesitated. 'Camille, are you all right with this? I know it's not easy for you, but I've got your back. Not that you'll need me, but I understand if you're nervous.' If he was nervous then she was probably falling off the edge even though she was one strong lady.

She blinked at him. 'I'll be fine.' Strong words, but not quite the strongest he'd ever heard her speak.

Placing his hand on her elbow, he led her inside and through to the cosy family room where the fire was blaz-

110 PARISIAN SURGEON'S SECRET CHILD

ing, emitting warmth they both needed right now. 'Mum, Dad, I'd like you to meet Camille Beauregard.' He meant it. Not only did he want them to meet her, he longed for them to like her—a lot.

'Camille, I've been watching the clock constantly from the moment Etienne left to collect you both.' His mother rushed at Camille and wrapped her in a hug. 'I'm Louise, by the way.' She pulled back a little. 'And this gorgeous man is Etienne's father, Hugo.'

Camille looked a bit stunned at being held so tight by the woman she'd been worried about meeting.

Etienne smiled. That was his mother to a T.

Camille looked across to his father. 'Hello, Hugo. It is good to meet you both. I've been looking forward to this day for a while.'

Dad nodded. 'I'm glad you're here, Camille. We both are.'

In Etienne's arms, Elyna began wriggling to be let down. 'Hang on, little one, not so fast. There are some people longing to meet you.'

Camille stepped back from Etienne's mother and drew a breath. She hadn't expected to be hugged, and she felt a lot better about introducing Elyna to her grandparents now. She reached for Elyna, taking her from her father and holding her out to Louise, her heart thumping so loudly everyone must've heard it. 'Louise, Hugo, this is your granddaughter, Elyna.'

Tears competed with a huge smile on Louise's face as she tentatively took Elyna in her arms. 'Hello, sweetheart. You're gorgeous, aren't you?'

Stepping back, Camille bumped up against Etienne and felt his arm go around her waist. His strength supported her, gave her more confidence. So far everything was going well, but that didn't stop her knees knocking. Meeting Etienne's parents and introducing Elyna to them was huge. She couldn't believe they were here doing this. She needed to relax and go with the flow. Leaning her head against Etienne's shoulder, she watched Elyna studying her grandmother with a smile growing larger by the minute. 'At least she's not screaming the house down,' Camille murmured.

'She readily accepts strangers, doesn't she? She didn't back off from me the first time we met either.'

Camille shuddered. 'As I said before, I'll have to focus on teaching her not to talk to strangers.'

Etienne laughed softly. 'Can you wait for a year or two? I know what you mean though. It's scary even thinking about it.' Father to the fore.

She liked that. He was good with Elyna but that had never been one of her concerns. They'd resolved the biggest one. He'd finally fully accepted he was her father. His parents certainly had. The joy on their faces was heart-warming. It made her happy. So far so good. Too good? Cynic. Ouch. Wasn't that what Etienne called himself that night at his office? Were they more alike than she'd realised? 'I imagine there'll be lots of things to worry about over the next fifty years,' she murmured.

Another laugh. 'Only fifty?'

'Once a parent, always a parent,' Louise said as she passed Elyna to Hugo.

So much for thinking she and Etienne were talking between themselves. Of course they were in a small area and everything could be heard. 'When did you last tell Etienne not to talk to strangers?'

Hugo answered before Louise could say a word. 'When

112 PARISIAN SURGEON'S SECRET CHILD

he told me I didn't know what I was talking about. He was about nineteen at the time,' Hugo added with a grin.

A laugh bubbled out of Camille's throat. 'That old?'

'I know. You'd have thought he was only three.'

'Here's hoping his daughter's more cautious. So far I'm not sure who she takes after the most. She does like wearing pink, which I doubt has ever been Etienne's preference,' Camille teased.

'There was one time...' Hugo stopped and laughed. 'You want to get down, don't you, missy?' Placing Elyna on her bottom, he watched her start to charge around the room inspecting everything she came across.

Glancing at Etienne, Camille saw him grinning as though he was happy to see her getting along with his father. It wasn't hard to do. Both Hugo and Louise hadn't made her feel out of place at all.

Louise followed Elyna as though she didn't want to leave her. She looked smitten.

'I think we should have a glass of wine before lunch,' Etienne announced. 'Nothing unusual about that in this family, Camille.'

So she'd gathered over the past week with Etienne's regular, albeit brief, visits, due to him being on call. 'As long as you don't intend starting Elyna on wine tasting yet I'm happy.'

'What would you like? There's quite a variety to choose from. All made on the family estate, of course.' The pride in his face made her understand how this family stuck together through everything.

'I'd like a white, but I'll let you select which one.' She wasn't going to be presumptuous and make a choice when her wine-tasting skills came down to either liking it or not.

'While you're pouring the wine I'll check on lunch,' Louise said. 'I hope you like duck à l'orange, Camille.'

'It's one of my favourite meals.'

'Come and chat while I attend to the duck.' She sounded friendly but Camille found herself wondering if this was when the questions began.

It had to happen and the sooner they were out of the way, the better. 'Sure. Anything I can do to help?'

'Not a thing. I know what it's like when you've got a little one to take care of. Never a spare moment.'

'True, but I love it. I never quite expected raising a child to be so hard and yet so much fun. I must've been in la-la land.'

'And you're doing it on your own.'

Was that a question in disguise? 'So far, yes, but I have absolutely no regrets.' Wrong, there had been. 'What I meant was that I don't regret being on my own. I do regret not telling Etienne before I left for Montreal.'

Turning to face her, Louise leant back against the high-end bench top and locked a formidable gaze on her. 'What happened can't be undone, Camille. There were two of you there that night and after Etienne told me what had happened I think he has to own some of it too. I've told him so.'

Wow. Really? 'Thank you. Etienne has told me he does feel that way.'

'Then there's nothing to worry about, is there?'

Only what happens next. 'It was good to clear the air.'

'You two have a lot of decisions to make. Don't rush. A mistake now could take its toll on Elyna in the future.'

'I agree.' Camille sighed. If Louise weren't Etienne's mother she might want to have an in-depth conversation about what to do going forward. Louise didn't appear

114 PARISIAN SURGEON'S SECRET CHILD

to be pushy or demanding, and only wanted what was best for her granddaughter, and no doubt her son when it came down to it.

Etienne appeared, carrying two glasses of wine. 'Here you go. Try this one, Camille. It's our Chardonnay.' He knew it was her favourite choice.

'Thanks.' She sipped it and blinked. 'That's beautiful.' She tried another sip. 'But then I am an amateur when it comes to varietals.' She'd drunk enough in her time but had never got invested in the subtleties of wines. Maybe it was time to start. 'Explain the flavours to me.'

Louise rolled her eyes. 'Not if we're going to eat lunch on time.'

Etienne laughed. 'We'll save it for another day.'

'Good. Then I won't reveal my lack of knowledge to everyone.' So there would be more days together. She'd known that was going to happen but wasn't sure how close they'd get after last night. It was meant to be all about Elyna and nothing to do with the increasing sense of longing for Etienne in her heart. To think she'd walked away from him when she'd been in the midst of an amazing fling. Now she'd turned down his proposal. But saving her heart came first. So would she put as much distance between them again? Not possible when Elyna was the reason for seeing so much of him. That would not be right. Elyna came first. But her heart was a close second.

'The duck's ready, Camille. What about Elyna? I take it you brought food for her?'

'Yes, it's in the chilly bag. I'll get a plate to put it on, if that's all right?'

'Camille.' Etienne sounded stern. 'You don't have to ask permission to use anything around here. Just do whatever you want.' He took a step towards the bag she'd mentioned, and paused to look at her. Then he picked it up, looking perplexed, before opening it.

Was that because he wasn't used to having to say that to the women he brought here? More likely others made the most of being in his territory and not holding back when they wanted something. *Well, Etienne, I'm not going to charge around as though I have every right to be here.* Because she didn't. He might be her daughter's father but that didn't give her leeway to make herself at home. 'Elyna's lunch is in that pink container. It's an assortment of fruit and snacks.'

'It looks good,' Etienne said as he headed to a floor-to-ceiling cupboard and got a plate. 'I've put a high chair in the dining room. It's the one I used when my nephews were Elyna's age.'

'You're right at home with little ones,' Camille noted. He'd been on the ball from the moment he first met Elyna. 'Are you going to supervise her meal?'

'You bet.' Then he looked around. 'Unless you want to, Mum?'

There was longing in Louise's eyes but she shook her head. 'No, that's your job, Etienne. What's Hugo up to?' She disappeared out of the kitchen in a rush.

Etienne looked gobsmacked. 'She's trying to stir things up.'

'She's supporting you,' Camille said around the lump forming in her throat. It'd been a while since she'd had her grandmother to do that for her and suddenly she missed her and Grandpa so much that pain crashed into her chest. They'd supported her throughout her life, and when she'd told Grandma she was pregnant her news had been welcomed, not turned into something negative.

116 PARISIAN SURGEON'S SECRET CHILD

Most of all she missed the easy love that had always come her way from her small family. The love she'd believed Benoit had felt for her had turned out to be false and the experience had put her on alert when it came to sharing her heart again. But more and more she wanted to try, to take a risk and possibly find true happiness. Her eyes went to Etienne placing his daughter in the high chair. Could he be the one? She'd certainly never felt so light and hopeful with any other man since Benoit. She believed she could trust Etienne, that if he gave his word he'd stick to it. He wouldn't lie about important things, or indeed anything at all. But, she warned herself, she'd believed that once before.

Pulling out a stool from the island in the centre of the kitchen, she sat to watch Etienne and Elyna, and her heart swooped like a bird on a breeze. They were perfect together. Right from the first time she saw him, Elyna had accepted her father as if he'd always been in her life. Etienne hadn't really backed off all that much either. He'd been shocked, wary and angry but he hadn't out and out accused her of lying to him, which was huge after the way he'd been treated in the past.

'They look good together,' Louise said quietly from behind her.

Spinning around, Camille nearly fell off the stool. 'You're right. They do.'

'I've got something to show you,' Louise told her as she dug into her enormous handbag. 'This is Hugo's mother when she was about Elyna's age.' She handed over a photograph of a little girl in a white dress sitting on a high-backed chair.

Camille stared at the photo. 'I thought Elyna looked like my grandmother, but they could be the same girl, they're so alike.' If ever proof of paternity was needed, this was it, but she wasn't about to say so. That would be tacky. Reaching for her wine, she took a mouth-watering sip, without tasting anything. 'Unreal.'

'You know Elyna was my mother's name, not Louise's, don't you?' Hugo stood beside Louise watching her. He obviously hadn't heard what Louise had just said.

'Yes, I did.' Was that a problem for Hugo?

He stared at her for a moment, then smiled. 'Thank you. I'm pleased you chose it. It's good to keep the name in the family, and it's beautiful.'

All the air gushed out of her lungs. Hugo had just said he approved of her.

Then she felt Etienne's hand on her shoulder, giving her a small squeeze. 'There you go. Elyna has grand-parents.'

Camille's eyes closed as she tried to take everything in. She'd come here today expecting a grilling, and instead had been accepted for her role in this family. The words slipped out without thought. 'Thank you all so much.'

Etienne couldn't stop the banging going on in his chest. Even removing his hand from Camille's warm shoul-der didn't calm his heart. She was turning out to be one amazing woman. As if he didn't already know. Yes, well, maybe he did.

He returned to the other delightful female in his life. 'Hey, little one. You've finished all that food already?' Obviously making up for a slow start to life. It was hard to picture her at birth, weighing only two kilos, attached to every imaginable tube and monitor, fighting to sur-vive. Now she wore a perpetual smile and giggled a lot, sneaking into his heart far too easily. As her mother had

118   PARISIAN SURGEON'S SECRET CHILD

a way of doing. Lifting Elyna out of the high chair, he placed her on the floor, where she immediately headed for the boys' toybox he'd brought out last night.

'Lunch smells delicious,' Camille remarked, walking past carrying a platter with the duck à l'orange.

'It'll taste even better.' His mother knew how to put a great meal together. He was lucky with his parents. They had been there for him and his sister growing up, and when they'd lost his brother they'd suffered deeply but had still managed to help him and Cariole cope with their grief. Camille had missed out on having parents. Though her grandparents had been wonderful she'd admitted to feeling a loss by not having her mother around. She didn't say that about her father.

He pulled out a chair for her, then went to get the wine to replenish everyone's glasses before sitting down beside her. 'You feeling comfortable?'

'Yes, I am. More than I'd thought I would.'

'Would you like to stay the night? You'd have your own room.' *Unfortunately*, his mind threw back at him, along with images of her stunning body curled around him as they got their breath back after another round of amazing sex. 'There's a cot for Elyna. We could spend more time getting to know each other better, which is important if we're going to make life easy for her.' Forget sex. As wonderful as it had been, it would get in the way of sensible decisions about where to go from here with Elyna.

Her eyes widened, and she looked thoughtful. 'I didn't come prepared for that.'

'Most things you require are here, except for clothes, which I guess is probably the most important,' he said with a grin. 'There are shops a couple of streets away if necessary.'

Her hair swung side to side as she shook her head. 'No,

SUE MACKAY

119

I can't.' She paused and stared at her fingers as though the answer to his invitation was there. Then she looked up and he knew he wouldn't be having house guests that night. 'Can I take a rain check? I haven't come prepared with food and clothes for Elyna either.'

'It can be sorted easily enough.' It stung that she hadn't leapt for joy at his invitation, but again, this was Camille. When was he going to learn to accept her independent ways?

'Etienne, I'm not saying no for ever, only tonight. It's already been a big day for me, and Elyna. I didn't sleep much last night for worrying about how your family would react to me. I'd like to be at home tonight where I feel comfortable.'

He had to go along with that even if it seemed as though she was looking for an excuse not to stay. 'No problem. How about I show you around my home later when Elyna's taking a nap?' Then she'd understand how spacious the place was and see that they could live here in the future without bumping into each other at every turn.

Relief filled her face. 'I'd like that. From what I've seen so far it's a beautiful home.'

'It is.' At least he'd won that one. Camille would do just about anything to make sure Elyna knew her family and that they had a part in her life but she would also take care of herself so that Elyna didn't suffer from any mistakes they might make on this strange journey. 'Good. Now let's enjoy lunch. Mum, do you need a hand with something?' She and Dad were taking their time in the kitchen.

'No, thanks. We're coming. Hugo's just opening a bottle of champagne.'

He'd bet they were deliberately giving him and Camille some space. 'My family use any occasion to have champagne. Hope you like it?'

120 PARISIAN SURGEON'S SECRET CHILD

Her tongue did a lap of her lips. 'I love it. That's one wine I'm picky about and I know I'm about to have one I'll really enjoy.'

'So much for the Chardonnay.' He hadn't filled the glasses yet, so no loss.

'Here we go.' Dad placed glasses of champagne at each setting.

Etienne waited till his parents were seated then raised his glass. 'To a great lunch.'

Camille nodded as she lifted her glass. The smile she gave him turned his head and put his heart further out of whack. He was so not ready for this. If he kept telling himself that, then finally he'd have to believe it. Wouldn't he? What if he didn't want to? What if he truly was falling for Camille and wanted the whole caboodle?

And now he was supposed to eat lunch with that question banging around in his skull?

CHAPTER SIX

ETIENNE SLIPPED THE taxi driver more than enough for the fare, before brushing a kiss on Elyna's cheek. 'Goodnight, sweetheart.' If only he could do the same to Camille, but he didn't need a slap across the face. It'd be a verbal one, but still. If only she'd agreed to stay over they could've gone down the road for breakfast, then taken Elyna to the park, doing the things families did on a Sunday morning. Being turned down—again—had hurt. Again. Considering he always expected to be used, it surprised him when Camille didn't.

'Goodnight, Etienne,' the woman toying with his sanity called quietly as she slid into the back of the taxi beside Elyna. At least it was goodnight, not goodbye.

He strode around and grabbed her door before it closed. Leaning in, he said, 'Sleep tight.' He wasn't going to. Images of that sexy body had been hassling him, knocking him off centre ever since he'd picked her up that morning. They weren't likely to disappear just because he needed some sleep. Not when those figure-hugging jeans and the aqua-coloured merino polo-neck jersey that accentuated her full breasts and narrow waist kept reminding him of the feel of her warm, satin skin as he'd made love to her. It wasn't as if that had happened yesterday, yet he still had clear, vivid memories of their nights together!

122   PARISIAN SURGEON'S SECRET CHILD

'Absolutely.' She made to pull the door closed and this time he let it go.

'See you soon,' he called as the taxi pulled away. 'Because we have an issue to resolve and it isn't Elyna.' It did include their daughter, but right now all his heart was concerned about was getting closer to the woman who'd borne him a child and gave him a fierce hope that he might find a happy life in the not too distant future.

Back inside, he poured a brandy and downed a mouthful before going to his office where a firebox gave out welcoming heat. Settling into his leather lounge chair, he stretched his legs out in front of him and leaned his head back.

'What a week. And to top it off, Camille turned my proposal down.' It still rattled him. He couldn't recall a woman who'd have done that. He'd spent his whole life aware of people who wanted to be his friend, his lover, his wife all because of his wealth. Fortunately he did have genuine friends who liked him for himself. Those he treasured. Then along came Camille and tipped his thinking upside down. She'd said no. She didn't want to marry him. As plain as it could get. Thinking about it, her answer hadn't been totally out of the blue. He should be grateful she wasn't out to grab all she could, yet he was privately peeved that she hadn't said yes.

His ego had been bruised and he wasn't used to it. *Get over yourself, man. Stop feeling sorry for yourself.* Was that what this feeling was? Had he expected Camille to drop to her knees with gratitude over his proposal? And when she hadn't, had he not been able to believe her reaction because no one else would have refused him?

He got up to pace the room. He wasn't liking what he

SUE MACKAY

123

was seeing about himself almost more than he didn't like Camille's rejection.

Did her refusal to marry him mean she didn't have any feelings for him at all? Other than as a colleague and possibly a friend sharing their daughter's upbringing? There'd been moments when he'd caught her looking at him with what he'd thought was longing. But he'd often been wrong when it came to reading Camille so what was to say he was right about that?

Camille wanted love. Believed in love when it came to a permanent relationship and marriage. She wanted to love her husband and be loved in return. She'd get no argument from him. That was the golden dream. A loving, happy, sharing marriage with two people raising their children together. The problem being he couldn't give her that. No damned way. No one was getting the opportunity to undermine his love if he got that far. No one. His heart was tough now, stronger for the ugly lessons it had learned. There'd be no stepping away from that and trying again however much he wanted to.

Pausing to pick up his glass, he took another mouthful of brandy and then twirled the glass in his fingers. Was his shock and disappointment over Camille saying no really only because his pride had taken a hit? Or did it have something to do with the whirling emotions that filled him whenever he was with her? Did he actually love her or mainly feel comfortable around her because she made no demands on him?

Time to be ruthlessly honest. He did have feelings for Camille. Feelings that grew stronger by the day but that he didn't want to be feeling at all. Every time he saw her his heart lit up, his steps were lighter. She snagged his attention without trying. So what was next? Staying safe was his only option. Which meant not getting too close. Already he knew keeping his distance would be difficult, but a lot less likely to decimate him than it would be if he pursued her. He'd never do that. But he had to accept they'd spend a fair amount of time together because of Elyna. The sooner he got onto sorting out sharing the raising of her, the better, then he'd see less of Camille and be able to get firmly back on track with his life of family and medicine, and now Elyna. He didn't need anything more to keep his feet firmly on the ground. Certainly not a beautiful, caring, understanding woman who'd never take the easy way out of a conundrum.

'It's barely gone six o'clock,' Camille groaned the next morning as she clambered out of bed after a sleepless night to pick Elyna up out of her cot. Her head was full of fog and her body ached in every place imaginable. 'Damn you, Etienne Laval. I need my sleep now I've got Elyna to take care of. Lots of it.'

'Mama, up. Up,' Elyna squealed. 'Up.'

Lifting her up, Camille said, 'You're so lucky to have your daddy.'

Guilt raised its head once more. She hadn't known her father but Elyna had already spent time with hers. She'd missed out on the first eleven months of her life with him but going forward the future looked good. It would not be the same as sharing a home with him, or having a proper family where eating meals around the table at the end of a busy day talking about what they'd done was the norm. She couldn't help that. She was not marrying Etienne. He didn't love her and that was the bottom line as far as she was concerned. She'd known a caring, loving childhood with her grandparents and Elyna wasn't getting any less, only in a different way.

'Mama,' Elyna squealed. 'Hungry.' Her little face was red with effort.

Or was it something else? The nurse inside her kicked in. 'Elyna? Are you all right? Not sick?' Laying her hand on Elyna's forehead, she sighed with relief. No excessive heat there. But what about her stomach? Gently pressing Elyna's abdomen got her a whack on the shoulder with a tiny fist but no cries of pain.

'Brekfa. Now.'

Brekfa? A new word. Woohoo! Spinning Elyna around, she kissed her cheek. 'You're amazing. I'm guessing brekfa means breakfast.' Time for coffee too, now she was out of bed. There wouldn't be a chance to sneak back under the covers for a few more minutes of peace and quiet. Besides, with Etienne appearing in her head almost nonstop last night, she knew there was no chance of any peaceful moments even if Elyna managed to entertain herself.

Opening the blinds in the kitchen, she noted the clear sky. Winter put on some great days. She made an instant decision. 'Come on, we'll have a shower and go for a nice Sunday breakfast down the road at the café by the supermarket.' Then they'd go for a walk along the Seine. The thought of fresh air and not wondering if Etienne was about to ring her doorbell lifted her spirits a little. As if he would. He wouldn't come begging. Truth was she really had no idea what he'd do.

He'd asked her to marry him out of the blue.

Her heart had dropped then and was doing so now as the memory ran through her mind. In other circumstances she might've said yes. Those circumstances being that

126   PARISIAN SURGEON'S SECRET CHILD

he loved her and couldn't imagine living without her. But he didn't. He'd proposed for Elyna's sake, not hers. Not theirs.

Her phone played a tune.

Etienne? If so, she'd ignore it. Right now he was the last person she wanted to talk to. She'd spent half the night having one-sided conversations with him. She didn't need any more.

Liza's name was on the screen. Early for her.

'Hi, Liza. What's up?'

'I'm in town for the day. Problems with my staff. Feel like catching up?'

Perfect. That'd be a reason not to talk to Etienne. 'Definitely.'

'Great. What time and whereabouts?'

'I was planning on going for breakfast along the road shortly but can put it off for an hour or two if you want to join us.'

'Give me an hour and I'll meet you wherever you intend going.'

After giving Liza the name of the café, Camille made her first coffee of the day and heated up some oatmeal for Elyna to get through the next hour or so. So much for Liza having a break for the first time in years. It must be a big problem for her to come back from Marseilles for a day.

Ninety minutes later she had Elyna in a high chair and was pulling out a seat at the table she'd selected away from too many people.

'Hi there.' Liza rushed up and wrapped her arms around Camille.

They held on tight for a long moment before Liza turned to lift Elyna into her arms. 'Hello, beautiful. You've grown so much.' Liza sank onto a chair still holding Elyna. 'I can't wait to chat about everything and hear how it's going with Etienne.'

The downside to catching up was Liza would want to know more than Camille was prepared to tell. Then again, what were best friends for if she couldn't download on Liza? Her chest felt full of liquid this morning. She couldn't believe how much she wanted Etienne's proposal to have been because he loved her and wanted to share his life with her. The realisation had dropped into her head with an almighty thud. It was true. She had fallen in love with him. Totally. If only he could do the same with her, but it was unlikely given his complete distrust of women.

She had her own trust issues, and they hadn't disappeared overnight, but more and more she was coming to think that if Etienne committed to someone—her—then he'd stay by her side for ever.

'Hello, Camille. Where have you gone?' Liza was watching her closely. 'I mention Etienne and you go blank on me.'

'Let's order coffee and breakfast before we talk about him. And your niece is wanting attention from Auntie Liza.'

Liza didn't stop looking at her for another long moment, then she kissed the top of Elyna's head. 'I've been longing to see you, sweetheart. You look pretty. Just like your mummy.'

'I'm not going to talk about Etienne no matter what you say.'

Liza was watching her closely. 'You look terrible, and since Elyna looks fine I can only think of one thing that could cause that. One person.'

It might be good to share her worries with her friend. 'I'm having croissants. You?'

128   PARISIAN SURGEON'S SECRET CHILD

'Same,' Liza said through a smile.

As the waitress placed plates of croissants on the table, Camille's phone pinged. An unknown number appeared on the screen. 'Hello?'

'Camille, it's Louise. I wanted to thank you for bringing Elyna to meet us yesterday. She's absolutely lovely and I hope we'll get to spend more time with her.' Etienne's mother sounded worried.

'Of course you will. You're her grandparents. I'd never get in the way of her being with you.'

'I'm sorry. I know that. You're so kind, but I'm prone to worrying about anything and everything. Ask Etienne.'

As if she was about to talk to him about his mother. She'd be lucky to hear from him at all today. That might be for the best with the state her mind was in. 'If you have any concerns call me and we'll talk about them.' As long as the family didn't want to take Elyna away from her and there'd been no suggestion of that so far.

'I should've said I rang Etienne for your number. I hope you don't mind. He sounded tired. Did you keep him up late?' Louise laughed.

'Um, no, I took Elyna home when she started getting scratchy.' She was allowed to tell little fibs, wasn't she? Better than telling Louise what she was struggling with. But it worried her that Louise might be thinking she was having another affair with her son. Not something she'd raise now, if at all. Etienne could sort that one out.

'You should've stayed and made Etienne take care of her, given yourself a break.'

He would've done that if necessary. But it hadn't been. 'I'll think about that next time.'

Coffee arrived.

'Thanks,' Camille said to the waitress.

'Sounds like you're busy. I'll let you go,' Louise said. 'Camille, please stay in touch and let me know what Elyna's up to.' Louise's wistfulness touched Camille. The woman wanted to be a part of her granddaughter's life and there was no way she'd prevent that. Elyna deserved to know all her family.

'I promise.' She hung up before the conversation continued and got deep.

'You've met Etienne's parents?' Liza asked with a sly smile. 'This gets more interesting by the day.'

'Yesterday. We had lunch with them at Etienne's.'

'So you've been to his house too. What's it like?'

Sometimes it didn't pay to tell her friend what was going on. Liza had no boundaries about what she asked or said. 'It's an old but well-cared-for mansion with lots of rooms and wonderful grounds. Stunning, really. It was stylish while keeping its history in the décor, and at the same time felt comfortable so that a person could do whatever they liked without ruining the atmosphere. A little girl could run around and not get in trouble for touching things.'

'So it's big enough for you and Elyna to live there and not be in Etienne's face all the time, then.'

As in not be married but in a family situation. No, thanks. It would play havoc with her heart. 'I suppose it is, but that's not happening. I've got my apartment, he's got his home, and we'll share raising Elyna accordingly.' She wouldn't mention the proposal to Liza, who'd pressure her to change her mind.

When Liza opened her mouth to say something else, Camille raised her hand. 'No, Liza. Leave this to me to work my way through.'

130   PARISIAN SURGEON'S SECRET CHILD

'So you only want my shoulder to cry on when things go bad?' Liza sounded annoyed.

Now she'd gone and upset her friend. Getting up, she went around the table to hug her. 'I'm sorry. I do need you on my side. It's just that things are going well at the moment and I don't want to jeopardise it by overthinking or talking about what-ifs and maybes.' Not completely true, but best put that way for now.

'That's better.' Liza sniffed and grinned. 'It's all right. I think I understand. But don't let your past dictate how you unravel the future.'

Staring at her, Camille shook her head. 'Do you think that's what I'm doing? Letting my run of terrible men, including my birth father, get in the way of how I deal with Etienne?'

'Yes, I do. From the little you've told me he sounds like a decent guy who'd never let you or Elyna down.'

'He's a decent man, and he'll be a great dad, but I'm not living down the hallway from him.' It hadn't been suggested by Etienne but she felt it was coming as a second option to marriage. 'That would get in the way of me living my life how I want.' She'd love to live it with Etienne if he loved her, but that wasn't happening by the look of it. She certainly wasn't holding her breath, anyway.

Monday came around again and with it the first full week of her new job. Camille smiled as she walked onto the ward and looked around, excitement fizzing through her. She hadn't worked—not counting last week's few hours—since Elyna was born. She'd missed it. Nursing was in her blood. Caring for people came naturally and she always got a sense of withdrawal if she took too long away from it.

SUE MACKAY

131

'Morning, Camille,' Karina called as she approached the nurses' station. 'Ready for a full-on week?'

'You bet.' Apart from dealing with Etienne's presence, she truly was. 'I've missed nursing.'

'We'll have you back up to speed before you know it. Take a seat and I'll run through some staff requisites that I should've done last week but didn't have time for.'

'That'll have to wait a while. I need one of you with George Spik. His abdominal wound has a serious infection.' Etienne stood in the doorway.

'Camille, can you take this one? I'm waiting for a call from Dr Elang in ED.'

'No problem.' Other than getting along as though nothing were wrong between them. Grabbing the thermometer, she followed Etienne, ignoring the thudding in her chest. 'Does the wound need redressing, or has it been done?'

Etienne spoke over his shoulder as he headed down the ward. 'George pulled off the previous one. He's also pulled out his drip. He's running a fever and is very restless. I'm going to put in a new drip with increased antibiotics and analgesics, along with fluids.'

'When did you operate on him?'

'Friday afternoon. I dropped in first thing on Saturday on my way to pick you up and nothing was wrong then. According to the notes George started showing signs of infection late last night. Another specialist has been dealing with him, but I think the infection's getting worse.'

Etienne was treating her as he'd always done at work. One less thing to worry about. But then she'd have been surprised if he'd been aloof around here. Too many people would notice and question it. 'Are you taking him back to Theatre?'

132   PARISIAN SURGEON'S SECRET CHILD

'Most likely. I did bowel surgery for cancer on him but a major infection is unusual.' The worry in his voice caught at Camille.

'Don't start blaming yourself. It might be unusual, but it does happen.'

He stopped and stared at her for a long moment. Then he dipped his head and carried on as though nothing had happened.

But it had. A flicker of gratitude had flashed across his face. Didn't he expect her to say what she believed because of what had happened between them? If so, he didn't know her very well, which he didn't, really. She'd thought she was getting to know Etienne, but she never would have seen his proposal coming. Or his shock when she turned him down.

Following Etienne into the room and across to his patient, she focused entirely on George and what Etienne wanted her to do. 'You want a new dressing, obs and a sponge down.' The man was bathed in sweat.

'Yes.' He leaned down. 'George, can you hear me?'

George opened his eyes. 'Doctor.'

'Good. George, this is Nurse Camille. She's going to be looking after you. I've looked at the wound, and we need to go back into Theatre.'

'Why?'

'I need to find out why you've got an infection.'

'Did you have breakfast, George?' Camille asked. Fingers crossed he hadn't.

'No. Too sick.'

'That's a plus,' Etienne said. 'I don't want to hang about on this.'

Camille placed the thermometer in George's ear. 'Thirty nine point nine.'

SUE MACKAY

133

Etienne nodded, unsurprised. 'Keep a running tally and let me know if it goes up at all.'

'Absolutely. I'll get the gear to put a dressing on in the meantime.' Plus cloths to give George a good wipe down.

'I'll stay with him until you return,' Etienne told her.

She headed quickly for the storeroom where everything used for patient care was kept. Etienne was in doctor mode, not a hint of how he felt about her showing on his face. Hopefully she appeared just as calm. Though she wasn't known for being able to hide her feelings very well so chances were he knew how wound up she was.

Returning to George, she drank in the sight of the gorgeous man standing at the bedside who was doing her head in. If only he didn't have hang-ups about laying his heart on the line. But even if he didn't that didn't mean he'd fall for her. She wasn't his type. What was his type? Confident, poised, used to a very different lifestyle from hers. Not forgetting he was kind, gentle and caring, and not only with patients. He'd been marvellous with Elyna and the same with his parents. Be honest, he was like that with her too. Ka-thump went her heart.

'I've arranged time in Theatre at midday,' Etienne informed her.

'You want me at his side until then, don't you?'

'Yes, I do. Call me if anything changes. Even if it's only point one on his temperature reading.'

'I will.'

He turned to head away, then hesitated and came back to her. 'Thank you, Camille.'

What for? She was only doing her job.

'For not making this any more difficult than it already is.' Then he was gone.

Leaving her stunned yet again. He really could sur-

134 PARISIAN SURGEON'S SECRET CHILD

prise her with his openness at times. 'George, I'm going to clean the wound and then put a new dressing on to protect it until Dr Laval sees you in Theatre.' Etienne intrigued her. A lot. Was there a possibility he might want to get closer to her? To become more than joint parents? It didn't seem likely considering their very different backgrounds, but, as Grandma would've said, anything was possible given half a chance.

'Whatever,' the man on the bed croaked.

Lifting the bedcover away from George's midriff, she began cleaning the red, swollen septic area with antibiotic fluid, careful not to press too hard and cause more distress. Next she placed a wide dressing over the area, keeping the tape away from the wound. 'I'm going to give you a good wipe down all over, and make you feel a little more comfortable.'

'I c-can't stop s-sweating.'

'The infection's doing that. Have you had any rigors? Severe shaking,' she added in case he didn't know what she meant.

'Once. I told D-Dr L-Laval.'

'Good. Remember to tell me if there's anything else that feels abnormal. The more we know, the easier it is for Dr Laval to get on top of the infection and its consequences.'

'He said the s-same.'

'Do you feel hot or cold?'

'Both at d-different times. Cold now.'

Hence his stutter. 'I'll get another cover for you once I've finished cleaning you up.'

On her way to the linen room for the cover she stopped at the desk to call Etienne. 'George is having more rig-

SUE MACKAY 135

ors. I'm about to put another bedcover over him. He's stuttering quite a bit.'

'What about his temperature?'

'That's remained the same as when you were up here.' It hadn't been very long since she'd taken the temperature with Etienne watching but it was something she'd keep doing regularly until he said to stop.

'Arrange for an orderly to bring him down to Theatre three in thirty minutes. There's been a cancellation and I've grabbed the spot.' The line went dead.

'On it,' Camille said into the air. He was getting on with his job, and she with hers despite the image of his handsome face loitering in the back of her head to be looked at whenever she had a moment to spare. He was something else. A man of his word. To be trusted? She believed so, but that didn't mean she was ready to risk taking a chance. Anyway, she'd already turned down his offer of marriage and there was no other relationship she wanted long term.

Two hours later George was brought back up to the ward and Camille returned to his bed to check his obs after reading the notes to see what Etienne had found when he'd gone into the infected site. Three internal sutures had been pulled free so that blood had leaked into the bowel, and infection had set in.

'He must've jerked hard or tripped badly to have caused that,' Etienne said over her shoulder. 'He says he slipped in the shower the morning after I operated but that it was nothing serious. I wonder if he downplayed it because he'd ignored the nurse who'd told him to remain in bed until she was available to oversee his shower.'

136 PARISIAN SURGEON'S SECRET CHILD

'Very likely. It's not the first time I've known a patient to do that. Especially men when their nurse is female.'

'What time are you knocking off?' Etienne asked.

'I've got nearly an hour to go.' Working alongside Etienne had always made her feel good. He appreciated the nurses and never acted superior. More than that, he was happy to discuss cases as though nurses understood everything he talked about. Nothing had changed despite the elephant looming between them.

'Can I call in later to see Elyna?'

'Of course you can. I'm not going anywhere.' Sounded pathetic, but she could justify it because Elyna would be tired after spending half the day in the crèche. 'Maybe you could take her for a walk in the park if she's up to it.'

'I won't be away from here before dark.'

Of course he wouldn't. 'I need to put my thinking cap on. I'll take her for a walk. Might go past the Eiffel Tower. I'm catching up with my city and hoping to instill in Elyna a sense of where she belongs.'

'How about I bring dinner with me?'

She thought he was coming to see Elyna, not her. Did she want him staying past Elyna's bedtime? She had no idea what she wanted. There was only one way to find out. 'That'd be great.'

'Anything you don't eat?'

'Not really. Just don't go overboard with something whacky.' She dredged up a smile to show she wasn't being too serious.

'I'll behave.' His grin looked more honest than her smile felt, plus it was reassuring, which surprised her. He was trying to move on while she kept going over and over his proposal and all it meant.

'Good.' In some ways he was a different man from the

lover she'd known. He'd been kind and fun then, not deep and personal. Though personal was still a fair way off, when she thought about it. Which she did far too much.

'See you later.' He hadn't looked around to make sure no one was within hearing. Was he prepared to let others know there was more to them than a doctor-nurse relationship?

She shrugged the idea away. It was ridiculous when he'd always been very careful about what people knew about his private life. 'Okay.' She started checking George's obs. Work would keep the mind busy and errant thoughts about Etienne at bay. Or so she hoped.

CHAPTER SEVEN

'ELYNA, DADDY'S HERE.' Etienne swooped his girl up with his free arm and lightly kissed her scrunched-up face. His heart expanded with love, such a new emotion for him, and showed him he really, truly did accept she was his daughter. Glancing around, he found Camille staring at him with wonder in those beautiful eyes, from which a stray tear fell. 'Yes, I'm Daddy.' Stepping across the gap between them, he brushed a kiss over Camille's lips. 'Thank you for sharing her with me. Imagine if you'd never told me? But then I suppose I'd never have known what I was missing out on.'

She blanched. 'Elyna deserves better than that. So do we.'

'I know. I might not know you as well as I'd like to yet, but I know that you are a straight shooter when it comes to the truth.'

She shook her head as if she didn't quite know where to go from here.

He had a few ideas but had learned to go cautiously. 'Elyna's my daughter.' It was the absolute truth.

Tears poured out of Camille's eyes. 'Th-that is th-the b-best thing you could ever have said.'

Putting down the bag he was carrying, he put his free arm around her shoulders and tucked her in against him.

He liked making Camille happy. It made him feel happy right down to his toes and back again. With Camille in one arm, Elyna in the other, it couldn't get much better than this. Nodding at the bag, he said, 'I've brought wine from home. Let's have a toast to parenthood.'

Pulling away, Camille said, 'I seem to always be drinking wine, but yes, let's celebrate. I've waited a long time for this.'

'I've ordered chicken fricassee from the restaurant along the road to be delivered at seven-thirty. I've been assured they know what they're doing.'

Finally a small smile lightened her face. 'Five stars do kind of indicate that.' She took the bag and headed to the kitchen, saying over her shoulder, 'It's lovely of you to do this.'

'Any time.' Strange, but he meant it. He'd be happy to turn up every night with a meal to share with her along with wine and light-hearted chatter about their day.

Elyna wriggled in his arm, obviously impatient for some attention. 'Yes, I've got something for you too.' He dug into his jacket pocket and tugged out a small woollen toy. 'Here you go, little one. It's a dog.' He held it out to her. 'Can you say dog?'

Elyna grabbed the toy, a large smile on her face.

'Say dog, Elyna.' Camille was back, watching her daughter as she stared at her gift.

'Og.' Elyna kissed it. 'Mama, og.'

'Say thanks to Daddy.'

Elyna cuddled the soft toy close and stared at him.

'Any time.' He placed her carefully on the floor. 'There you go.' Looking at Camille, he could feel his heart expanding further. They really were a family. A disjointed one for now, yes, but making inroads into sorting it out.

140 PARISIAN SURGEON'S SECRET CHILD

If Camille had accepted his proposal they'd be further on with doing that, but he hadn't given up. Next time he asked her to marry him it would be with all his heart, or not at all.

'I've talked to your mother twice since we saw her on Saturday. She'd like to have Elyna for the day on Friday. It'll be good for Elyna to get to know her plus not to have to be at the crèche every day of the week.'

'Mum's going to ask to have her one day every week.' His mother was giddy with excitement over her granddaughter.

'That'd be wonderful. I do feel bad about leaving her in the crèche so often.'

'Do you work because you need the income or because you enjoy nursing so much?' He had no idea how Camille was situated financially, and it wasn't an easy discussion to have when she was so fiercely independent.

'Both.' Sinking onto the arm of a lounge chair, she looked up at him. 'I'm fortunate to be able to support us as long as I'm careful. It was a toss-up about whether to get a job or not, but in the end I do need to add to my savings and also being a solo parent is hard enough without having some time with other people every day. In Montreal I spent all my time caring for Grandma and looking after Elyna so became a little lonely.' She paused, her fingers flexing on her thighs. 'I also think it's good for Elyna to be with other children.'

'Camille, I'm not going to criticise your decisions. I'm sure it's not easy doing this on your own. I'm here to help and be a part of her life no matter what.' He'd never dodge his responsibilities. It wasn't in his DNA. 'I'd like to set up a bank account for her, under your name, of course.'

'That's not necessary.'

'But it is part of being her father. I'm not undermining what you do, Camille, merely contributing to her financial needs going forward.'

Silence.

Finally Camille nodded abruptly. 'Fair enough.'

She could sound more enthusiastic, but this was Camille. Her strength beguiled him. Add in her sexiness and he was a goner long before he'd realised how much he'd missed her when she'd walked away. 'We'll talk more about it later.' He wasn't changing his mind, just giving her time to fully accept his offer.

She stood up and rubbed her lower back, drawing his eyes there and then lower to her curvy bottom. 'I'll get the wine.'

Definitely sexy. Which added to the things that needed sorting out between them because spending as much time with her as he intended so he'd see enough of Elyna was going to keep him continuously hard and aching with need. Need for Camille. Not a need that could be met by any other woman. 'I'd like a glass of Merlot. It's one of the best from the family winery. My brother-in-law's a great winemaker.'

A laugh escaped those tempting lips as she unscrewed the bottle. 'I'm no expert when it comes to wine but I know what I like and where some of it comes from.'

'Would you like to visit the family vineyards some time?'

Her head shot up, her eyes wide with enthusiasm. 'I'd love to. I've never been on a vineyard. Haven't spent a lot of time out of cities at all.'

Happiness at offering Camille something that seemed to delight her glowed in his chest. All was going well. Careful, don't spoil things by tempting fate. They still had a lot to work through. 'I'll arrange a trip soon. You need to meet my sister and her husband and my nephews.'

'I presume they've heard about Elyna.'

'You don't think my mum or dad could keep quiet about her, do you? Anyway, I've talked to Cariole so she knows what's going on.'

Worry filtered through Camille's eyes. 'How did she take it?'

'She's thrilled. She's always nagging me to find a woman and settle down to raise a brood. Hopefully she'll shut up now.' Not until he was married, but best to keep that to himself.

'That's a relief. My biggest fear, after telling you, was what the rest of your family would say. I came up with a hundred scenarios and most of them weren't good.'

He couldn't help himself. He stepped close to wrap his arms around her, pulling her against his chest. And breathed in her floral scent. 'You worry too much.'

'Hard not to when I knew I was tossing a hand grenade into your life.' Tension rippled through her, making him realise again how difficult all this had been for her.

'We're surviving.'

Camille moved away to finish pouring the wine and handed him a glass. 'Take a seat and relax. Watch Elyna playing with her new toy and enjoy your time with her. She'll be going to bed soon.'

He wanted to say Elyna could stay up a bit later tonight, but he wasn't the one who'd have to put up with a cranky child in the morning. Besides, Camille was right not to change their routine for him. He was the one who had to fit in with them. 'Hey, Elyna, what are you going to call the dog?'

'Og.' She beamed at him as she hugged the small toy to her chest. 'Og!'

'Guess that's going to stick.' Camille chuckled as she sat opposite him. 'Until her speech improves anyway.'

At least she liked the toy, he thought. He hadn't had a clue what to buy when he'd decided to bring her a present. There didn't appear to be a lot of toys around the apartment, but that could be because Camille's possessions were still en route by sea. 'When do your boxes arrive from Montreal?'

She swung Elyna up into her arms. 'Hopefully at the end of next week. Both of us could do with some more clothes now we've settled in and I'm working.'

About to offer to take her shopping, he stopped. That was wrong in all aspects. Camille would turn him down but the fact he'd thought to offer at all was a total turn-around on protecting his heart. But then he was already losing ground there. And enjoying it. More than he'd ever have believed. 'Is it bedtime for Elyna?'

'Story time and then fingers crossed she'll fall asleep.' Camille sent him a cheeky smile. 'You up to reading about turtles?'

'I can hardly wait.' He used to read to his nephews at bedtime but this was different. Elyna was *his daughter*. So yes, he truly couldn't wait.

Within minutes Elyna was tucked up in bed, the cuddly toy held tight against her tiny chest and her eyes filled with expectation. 'Story.'

Sitting on the edge of the bed, Etienne opened the large book filled with pictures that Camille had handed him and began reading the story, altering his voice for each character and making Elyna laugh. Which was so wonderful he became almost tearful. Sucking in his chest, he toughened up and got on with entertaining Elyna.

If only it were as easy to captivate her mother.

After watching Elyna grinning as her father read to her last night, Camille knew her relationship with Etienne had changed for ever. It didn't matter what lay ahead, he was smitten and would be a big part of Elyna's life. Where that left *her* was anyone's guess. Only time would tell, unless she confronted Etienne to start making some decisions about caring for their daughter. It was complicated with both of them working and therefore not always there for her. Living in different areas of the city didn't help either.

Despite everything she didn't regret turning down his proposal. She believed in love, and not even for her daughter was she going into a one-sided marriage. Etienne might have captured her heart, but if he didn't return those feelings then she couldn't bear the thought of sharing his house, and no doubt the marital bed. Oh, she wanted sex with him. Absolutely. The memories of their previous times together remained with her for a reason— he was incredibly hot. And his lovemaking skills were beyond belief. But she was not getting married for great sex alone. What if another woman came into his life who he fell in love with? Where would that leave Elyna? It would break *her* heart, but what would it do to his daughter's?

'Morning, Camille.' The man raising these questions stood at the nurses' station.

Her stomach rolled as her eyes roamed over his sensational body dressed in a perfectly fitted grey suit and white shirt, looking good enough to eat despite her concerns. How had she ever managed to turn him down?

'Morning, Etienne. I see we're getting two of your patients from Theatre later.' Keep everything focused on work, not sexy bodies. Body. Etienne's was the only one she was interested in.

His smile dimmed a little. 'Yes. Carlos Bruffin has a serious prostate infection that hasn't improved since he was admitted thirty-six hours ago for fluids and antibiotics. I'm going to open him up and see what's causing the problem. There's a lump that may be the reason.'

She winced. 'The poor man.'

'Agreed. He's not happy about the procedure but it's that or the infection could turn to septicaemia.' Etienne shrugged those wide shoulders. 'I don't have any alternative.'

He'd hate it but he also wouldn't hesitate if it meant saving the man's life. 'No, you don't. I read Mrs Gossim's file.' The thirty-five-year-old woman had had breast cancer five years ago, and was now dealing with multiple tumours in her bowel. Camille shuddered. Horrific to be facing that at any age, but she was far too young.

Etienne's face turned grim. 'It's not looking good, but if anything's on Sophie's side, it's that she's very positive and upbeat.'

'I've worked with patients like that, and the bad days when they run out of steam are dreadful.'

Looking steadily at her, Etienne nodded. 'You're so understanding. No wonder I like working with you.'

The steel protecting her heart softened. He got to her far too easily. Face it, she liked that he saw behind her determination to be strong and not depend on anyone else to get through life's battles. He'd made her think she could let go of her past hurts and move forward to

146 PARISIAN SURGEON'S SECRET CHILD

a place where she felt safe to give her heart away completely. 'Thank you,' she whispered.

A phone rang.

Etienne pulled his from his pocket. 'Hello?' He watched her while listening to whoever was on the other end of the call. 'I'm on my way.' He slid the phone back in his pocket. 'A patient in emergency needs urgent abdominal surgery after falling onto a metal stake in the garden. I'll see you later if you're still on duty when my other patients are brought up.'

Chances were slight as she had less than three hours to go and he'd likely be tied up for all that. Warring with the disappointment that had no right to raise its head here at work, she nodded. 'Sure.'

His long legs ate up the distance to the elevators, filling her with a longing that had no place in her heart. Except it was already there. What a man. She sighed and picked up the hospital phone to find out if the emergency patient Etienne was about to operate on would be coming up to this ward.

The woman certainly knew how to tip him sideways, Etienne admitted as he rode the elevator down three floors to Theatre. What was worse was that she didn't even try to get him onside. Probably why knocking him off balance worked so easily.

Camille would laugh her head off if she knew how much sleep he'd missed out on since she'd come back into his life. Every time he put his head on the pillow and closed his eyes there she was: smiling, growling, talking, attending to a patient, cuddling Elyna. Looking soft and kind, hot and sexy, angry and determined. Then he'd get up in the morning and go to work only to bump into the real-life version—which wasn't any different from the one in his mind. There was no getting away from her.

He needed to grin and bear it. They were always going to be a part of each other's lives because of Elyna. If she agreed to his next suggestion he'd be seeing even more of her. Yes, he had another idea to put to her.

His phone rang. The head of the surgical department's name appeared on the screen. A timely reminder to get back to thinking about patients and not Camille. 'Louis, what's up?'

'I need you on call for the rest of the week. Jason has had to take time off to go to Tours. His son's been in a serious accident and it's not known if he'll make it through surgery.'

His stomach tightened. The poor guy. No parent would ever want to go through that. Of course, now he was a parent himself it had become a lot more real to think that. 'Of course I'll take over. No problem.'

'Thanks, Etienne. Knew you wouldn't mind stepping up. I'll see you in Theatre shortly.' Louis was gone, no doubt busy sorting the roster before going in to operate on someone.

'Guess I won't be spending much time with Camille and Elyna this week.' Etienne sighed as the door slid open and he stepped out onto his floor. That might be a good thing, giving him more time to think about Camille turning down his proposal and try to see it from her point of view so he got it right with his next idea. She might also understand his suggestion and see he wasn't always going to be available to drop by her place to spend time with his daughter. Yes, this could actually play into his hands.

It sounded as though he was scheming to have his own way. Guess he was a little, but wasn't it also in Camille

148 PARISIAN SURGEON'S SECRET CHILD

and Elyna's best interests to live with him? Or near him, at least?

Later that night when he'd finished up in Theatre after an appendectomy on a young boy, he called Camille. 'Hi, I'd hoped to get to see Elyna tonight but I've been rostered on call and have just finished an urgent surgery.'

'It can't be helped. She's already tucked up in bed sound asleep.'

'I figured she would be.' It was well after her bedtime. 'I'll try again tomorrow night.'

'There's always the spare room here if at any time you don't want to go all the way to your place.'

Seriously? Did Camille just offer him a bed? A solo one, of course. Which would make sleep impossible with her only a door away. 'Thanks. I might take you up on that some time, but not tonight. I haven't got spare clothes with me.' When he knew he was on call he usually stayed in the doctors' quarters to save himself the tedious drive from his house, and now he had another option. He'd have to think about that. It could be great spending even more time with Camille in her home, but it might also add to his concerns over getting too close to her. What if she found a man she loved and moved in with him? They wouldn't be sharing homes then. Life would become tricky when it came to visiting Elyna. He wanted to slam the phone down and head to her place right this minute to make her see they had to work something out to everyone's benefit.

'I'll see you on the ward tomorrow.' She didn't sound too disappointed that he wasn't about to turn up at her apartment, but he'd have been more surprised if she was.

'Goodnight, Camille.' He hung up before he could change his mind and make an idiot of himself.

SUE MACKAY

* * *

Friday night and Etienne was at Camille's for dinner after another busy day. Since the roster changed on Fridays he was no longer on call so there was no chance of being called away before he got down to business. She'd suggested he come to see Elyna and stay for a meal so they could have some time together. He wasn't quite sure what time together meant but was more than willing to go along with it as he'd already intended dropping in to put forward his suggestion regarding where she might like to live.

'Would you like more casserole?' Camille asked.

'That was delicious but I couldn't eat another mouthful. You certainly know how to cook.' It had been a simple but tasty meal he'd eat any day of the week.

'Cooking is my go to when I want to clear my head of other things.' She actually blushed. A rare sight. The dark pink hue suited her. 'I have a lot of great memories of spending time in the kitchen with Grandma.'

'There's always so much affection in your voice when you talk of your grandparents. They were good to you, weren't they?'

'Absolutely. They gave up their dream of travelling the world when I was born. Then when I was old enough to get on with my life and they could go away for long periods, Grandpa was too sick, but not once did I feel I was to blame for them missing out on their dream. I couldn't have been luckier having them raise me.' She paused, looked around the dining room, then continued. 'Naturally I always wondered what my life might've been like if my mother had lived and brought me up, and what I might've missed out on. But in the end, there's nothing I could've changed, and I'm not sure I'd want to.'

'Pragmatic, aren't you?'

'Too much time can be wasted trying to alter the unchangeable. I wasted a lot as a kid wishing for my mother not to be dead and for my father to come get me. Then when he did turn up I knew I'd been lucky without him in my day-to-day life.'

'You make me even more grateful for my family. They've been my rocks.' Always there when he needed support, to celebrate when he achieved a goal, to love him without qualification. 'Like your grandparents, I suppose.'

'Yes, and how I intend being for Elyna.'

His heart swelled yet again. 'Me, too.' Time to put it out there. 'Which is why I'd like to suggest you both move into my house. That way we can share looking after Elyna more easily.'

Camille turned thoughtful, giving him no clue to what she was thinking. 'Do you think that'd work? Sharing a house when we're not in a relationship?'

'As you've seen, it's not a small place. You'd have your own rooms. We'd have to share the kitchen, although your cooking is so good I'm happy to leave the kitchen to you,' he said in an attempt to lighten her mood.

She flicked him a half-hearted smile. 'Knew I shouldn't have made dinner again. Seriously, I understand where you're coming from.'

Here comes the 'but'. He still wasn't used to hearing it. It stung. He was trying to do what was right by all of them and yet Camille was persistent in turning him down.

'I've only just got back home and I need time here to feel properly settled. I got such a bang on the heart when I walked in here the day I returned and I don't know that I'm ready to move away from this apartment quite yet.'

A picture of those tears streaking down her face

crossed his mind, tapping his own heart. 'I understand. You want more time. That's fine.' He could be patient. But they did have to make some serious decisions about how they lived so they could raise Elyna between them. On the other hand, time might help him overcome the need to be with her more often. 'I don't want you regretting a decision further down the track.' There was no avoiding his disappointment though. It would be awesome having Camille in his home, and Elyna racing around in her crazy little girl way.

Camille locked those lovely eyes on him and this time her smile was soft. 'None of this is easy for you, I know that. I've had longer to get used to being a parent, and to think about how to sort out the future. You're just getting started.'

'It's been quite a ride so far but I don't regret any of it.'

One eyebrow rose. 'Truly?'

'Truly.' Enough. Next he'd be admitting how he'd tried to find her after she'd left Paris. Now was not the time for that. The right moment might never arrive. Standing up, he took their plates to the sink to rinse them off before placing them in the dishwasher. 'I'll look in on Elyna, then I'd better head home. The week's catching up with me. I got called in every night.'

'That's rough. I admit to feeling tired after going to work every day this week. I'm out of practice and they're only short shifts.'

'Mum said you looked a little worn out when you collected Elyna earlier.'

Camille nodded. 'From the way she was hugging Louise when I got there to pick her up, Elyna had a great time. I doubt there'll be any problems with her going there regularly.'

152 PARISIAN SURGEON'S SECRET CHILD

'Good. That makes everyone happy.' Another box ticked. This was going well except when it came to the big issues, like his proposal and where Camille and Elyna should live.

Camille said, 'We'll see you over the weekend.'

It wasn't a question. She knew he'd be here at some point. Unless... 'How about we go to the vineyard tomorrow? You can meet the rest of the family. Pack an overnight bag and we'll stay the night.' His mouth had got away on him. Didn't he realise he was not looking to fall in love with Camille? Except he suspected he was already partway there.

She hesitated, then gulped. 'All right. I'll say yes to tomorrow and see how Elyna goes before agreeing to stay longer.'

'Fair enough.' Was she using Elyna to get out of spending too long with his family?

'If she throws a tantrum I won't use that as an excuse to leave, I promise,' she added.

'And if you throw one?' he asked with a forced laugh.

'Then your family will be lining up to toss me out.' Her return smile loosened the knots that had risen in his gut. 'I know this is all part of getting to know each other. I get nervous, that's all.'

'You've already won over my parents so I doubt there'll be any problems with the rest of the tribe.' Time to say goodnight to his daughter and get out of here before he said anything he might regret.

Elyna looked so sweet tucked under her bedcover with Og clutched in her arms that he actually had to brush a tear away before returning to the kitchen to say bye to Camille.

Except she was standing in the bedroom doorway watching him as he made to leave the room and his heart clenched. 'Camille,' he whispered around the lump in his throat.

She reached over to wipe a second tear from his cheek with her finger. 'It's all going to work out, I promise.'

He didn't realise his arms were going around her, pulling her in close. He couldn't have said how long he gazed into those mesmerising eyes before he lowered his head to kiss her full lips. Not a light brush over them but his mouth covering hers, feeling their warmth and fullness. His tongue slipped inside her mouth and tasted her. His arms tightened their hold on the gorgeous body pressed up against his.

Her mouth opened under his, accepting him further. Her hands cradled his head as she pressed against him.

'Oh, Camille,' he whispered.

She jerked her head back, staring at him in consternation before stepping out of his arms. 'This has to stop now,' she muttered.

She was right, it did. But for the life of him he did not want to walk away from her. He wanted her. He was hard for her. He spun around and headed for the main door. 'Goodnight.'

She didn't answer.

Camille's fingers traced her lips. Etienne had kissed her again. She'd bet her pay packet he hadn't intended to. He'd looked surprised when she'd pulled back. She'd been surprised when he'd leaned into the kiss that had turned her on so fast she was still trying to quieten her body. The kiss that took all reason from her mind. Thankfully she'd come to her senses before they'd gone too far.

Tell that to your body.

She was trying. Gazing down at her daughter, she

154 PARISIAN SURGEON'S SECRET CHILD

swallowed the need clawing at her. 'Your father's the most wonderful man I've ever known.' She had to remain strong in the face of his attractiveness. They were not becoming a couple when he didn't love her. She was still coming to terms with the fact that she loved Etienne. She could admit it to herself anyway. She didn't need to mess things up by agreeing to marry him. What about moving into his house? That would be no easier when every time she saw him he took her breath away.

Living together was a good idea as far as Elyna was concerned, but not so much for her. She and Etienne would be forever bumping into each other. Different from working together where there were staff and patients to keep their feet on the ground. In the house there'd be no getting away from him for long periods, and that would not help with getting over him. If that was even possible now.

She'd got over Benoit fairly quickly because he'd been so dishonest about his marriage and family that her heart had rejected him, leaving her with a weight of distrust when it came to loving again. Etienne wouldn't lie to her, wouldn't go behind her back, but she still wasn't prepared to be at his side when he didn't love her.

CHAPTER EIGHT

'THE WEATHER'S DIABOLICAL at the vineyards,' Etienne told Camille over the phone the next morning. 'I think it's better if we give going up there a miss. I don't want the weather interfering with driving home again as I'm flying down to Nice first thing Monday morning for a two-day get-together with other specialists.'

First she'd heard of it but they didn't share everything. Camille looked out of the lounge window as a gust of wind rattled the glass. 'The rain's not far off here either.' Over the road at the hotel tourists were dressed in jackets and boots. This was why most people visited the city in summer, she thought, shaking her head.

'How about you come here for the day? There's plenty of room for Elyna to charge around and you can have another look around the house in case you do decide to live here.'

His offer wasn't going away. It would hang between them like a wrecking ball, though, to be fair, at the moment it was still only a suggestion. Could she spend the day in his house without getting too uptight about the decision she had to make? He understood she wasn't ready to leave her own home. The time away in Montreal had been too long and not getting back to life as she used to know and like it had affected her. She'd never have in-

156 PARISIAN SURGEON'S SECRET CHILD

sisted her grandmother return to Paris when she became so ill, and she'd never regret staying to look after her, but now that she was back she was soaking up her history and starting to get into the life of motherhood as she'd believed it should be. Etienne was wanting to change everything too soon.

'Hello? Are you still there?' He cut through her thoughts, his deep voice reminding her of his lips on hers, his tongue exploring her mouth. So much for forgetting the kiss. She could feel his hands on her waist, his chest against her breasts. And he was only talking to her—over the darned phone, at that!

'Yes. We'll come out to your house,' she snapped in an effort to put that kiss behind her. 'I'll take the train, save you coming here.'

'No, Camille. I have to get a few things at the supermarket and can do that on the way, unless you need anything.'

She wasn't going to win about the train, and as she did need some food items for Elyna she might as well go with his offer. It would keep her onside. Something that was necessary if this was going to be a pleasant weekend not filled with disagreements and constantly being on edge. 'Actually, I do. All right, I'll get organised so we're ready when you get here.' The large last-century clock on the lounge wall had barely ticked past eight, but she doubted he'd take all morning to turn up.

'That should be some time after ten. I'll go to the market first to get fresh fruit and vegetables, and some cheeses.'

Her mouth watered. Nothing like a good cheese for a snack. 'See you later.' She hung up before he heard her stomach growling at the thought of cheese. Her favourite food, along with chicken, beef, vegetables, everything.

Smacking her forehead lightly, she grinned. She felt good, very good, despite spending the day with Etienne. Or because of that? Most likely. 'Elyna, we're going to Daddy's for the day.' Maybe longer. She'd pack enough gear for two days, just in case.

Her phone rang again. Etienne. 'Did you forget you had to be in London for the weekend?' she laughed.

'Pack something to wear in case we go out for dinner.' He hung up.

As if they'd go out when Elyna was there. Unless Louise and Hugo were going to be there too? Surely he'd have told her if that was so? He didn't hide things like that from her. He was more inclined to keep her up-to-date so that she couldn't say he was being sneaky.

Standing in front of her sparse wardrobe, she shook her head in dismay. The clothes hanging there were more than two years old and had fitted her well before Elyna came along. Her curves were a little more accentuated these days. The outfits she'd bought since then were somewhere at sea in a container along with everything else she'd collected while in Montreal. Glancing hopefully at the time, she groaned in despair. There wasn't time to catch a train to the nearest clothing outlet and get back before Etienne arrived. Was there?

'Elyna, come on, we're going out.'

By the time they returned to her apartment with two bags of clothes she was in a panic. She still had to pack clothes and toys for Elyna, plus other essentials, and Etienne's car was parked on the other side of the road.

He got out as she reached the main entrance to the apartment building.

158 PARISIAN SURGEON'S SECRET CHILD

'You're early,' she puffed before he could comment on her being late.

'I must be on a different timeframe from you.' He grinned as he took the pram from her. 'Hello, little one. I see Mummy's been shopping.'

Of course, it was obvious by the logos on the bags she carried where she'd been. Then he eyeballed her. 'You didn't have to go shopping for something to wear tonight.'

Oh, yes, she did. She wasn't going out with Etienne looking like something dragged out of the recycle bin. This was the man of her dreams and even if he was only taking her out to be friendly she wasn't going to look a mess. 'I'm short on decent clothes at the moment.' There wasn't that much extra clothing coming from Canada. She'd been careful with her money over there, not wanting to delve too often into her bank accounts where her inheritance was invested.

'Then I'd better make sure my parents do come to babysit. I'd hate for you to have wasted your morning shopping.' He was grinning so hard her head spun.

She'd never seen Etienne like this before. She liked it. It was as though he was ready to show her more of who he really was. 'No such thing as wasting time when it comes to shopping. Not that I do a lot of it.'

He was still grinning as he retorted, 'You're a female. You expect me to believe that?'

'Naturally.'

'Let's get upstairs so you can pack whatever Elyna needs and then we'll hit the road.' He swung the pram towards the entrance and keyed in the code number she'd given him at the outset.

'I won't be long.' Yeah, right. She hadn't packed a thing before rushing out to go to the shops.

'Don't panic. We've got all day.' He was still grinning. Whatever he'd had for breakfast she wanted some. It made him relaxed and happy.

Etienne wished he could take those words back after he heard someone pounding on Camille's door and a woman calling out, 'Camille, are you there? I need you.'

Camille was in Elyna's bedroom putting a bag of things together.

'There's someone at your door. It sounds urgent,' he told her. 'Want me to see what's up?'

'I'm coming with you.' She brushed past him as she strode to the door. Pulling it open, she said quietly, 'Hello, Maree. What's up?'

'It's Jules. He's fallen and can't speak. I don't know what's going on.'

'We'll come and see him. Maree, this is a friend, Etienne. He's a doctor. You take him to Jules while I put Elyna in her pram with some toys. We'll join you in a moment.'

So, he was only a friend? I'm more than that, Camille, he thought to himself as he followed the distressed woman down to the next apartment. 'Maree, did Jules complain about pain, or a headache before he fell?'

'Earlier he said his head felt funny, but then he seemed to come right.'

A stroke perhaps. 'Has he a history of headaches or feeling funny?'

'*Non*. He's always been healthy. I'm the one who gets sick. In here.'

He followed Maree inside the apartment, thinking how often stroke sufferers had been healthy beforehand. On

160   PARISIAN SURGEON'S SECRET CHILD

the floor in the hallway lay a large man, sprawled awkwardly. 'You haven't tried to move him at all?'

'No, I ran to get Camille. I didn't want to make anything worse for Jules.'

'So you haven't called an ambulance?' Etienne asked as he knelt down beside Jules and felt for a pulse. It was there, weak but steady.

'Should I?'

'Jules, can you hear me?'

One eye opened slowly.

Etienne nodded. 'That's a yes. Maree, call SAMU now.' He didn't want to frighten the woman any further, but an ambulance was required urgently. 'When you get through hand me the phone so I can explain what's going on.' Pressing his fingers on Jules' arms, then abdomen, legs, and getting no reaction confirmed his suspicions.

Camille knelt down on the opposite side of the man. 'What have we got?'

He glanced around to see where Maree was, and, not seeing her, nodded to Camille. 'I think he's had a stroke.'

'Jules, it's Camille.' She was taking his pulse as she talked. 'I'm sorry I haven't had time to catch up with you since returning home. You haven't met my daughter either. Maree did when we shared the elevator the other day.' She carried on chatting quietly as though nothing were wrong. 'Pulse normal but unsteady,' she said in an aside to him.

'We need to roll him onto his side.'

'No problem.' Together they straightened Jules enough to get him onto his side and his head tipped back a little to ease his breathing.

Maree approached, worry filling her face. 'They want

to talk to you.' She handed him her phone. 'The ambulance is coming.'

He stood up and walked a few steps away. 'This is Etienne Laval, a general surgeon at Central Hospital. I believe the man's had a stroke.'

'A serious one?'

'Yes. He does respond to questions by lifting one eyelid very slowly. Other than that, there's no reaction to touches or moving his limbs.'

'I'll inform the paramedic heading your way.'

He pressed off and returned to Jules, where Camille was taking a blanket from Maree and tucking it around the man. 'Can you get a pillow?' he asked.

Maree rushed away.

'On their way?' Camille asked him.

'Yes. I wonder if Maree might go down to let them in when they arrive?'

'I want to stay with Jules,' Maree said as she handed Camille the pillow.

'Of course you do. Will you go in the ambulance with him?'

'Yes.'

'You'll need to take your phone and card with you,' he told Maree, watching Camille ever so gently place the pillow under her neighbour's neck. 'Where's Elyna?' he asked.

'Buckled in her pram in Maree's dining room with Og and a teddy to keep her entertained. Unless she drops them.'

'I reckon we'd hear her if that happened.' His little girl was not known for being quiet when something went wrong.

162   PARISIAN SURGEON'S SECRET CHILD

Camille flicked him a smile that went straight to his gut. 'True.'

One smile and he was thinking of Camille naked in his arms as they made love. It was sex. No, lovemaking. Whichever, he just remembered those nights far too graphically.

'If you like I'll go down and wait for the ambulance. I'll take Elyna with me. She's bundled up warm.'

That'd give him breathing space. Which he didn't really want, but it would be quicker if one of them was there to meet the medics. 'All right. Hopefully you won't have to wait long.'

'Jules, I'm going downstairs to wait for the ambulance. Etienne will stay with you and make sure you're all right until the medics arrive.' Camille stood up, and looked at him. Sadness filled her face. 'I've known him most of my life,' she said quietly.

Stepping around Jules, he wrapped his arms gently around her for a moment. 'Deep breaths.' He wasn't going to say something like Jules would be all right because they had no idea what lay ahead and Camille wouldn't appreciate him trying to gloss over the seriousness of the situation. He never made inane comments like that with patients and their loved ones, or with his friends and family. It wasn't right to raise unguaranteed hope. Backing away, he returned to looking after Jules.

Camille walked away and quickly returned with Elyna in her arms. 'See you shortly.'

'Hope so.' Then he'd hand over to the paramedics and get on with spending time with Camille and Elyna.

At the end of the day with Elyna tucked up in bed at Etienne's and Louise reading her a story, Camille and

SUE MACKAY

Etienne left the house and headed to a restaurant in Versailles with Alain driving. Camille was excited as the restaurant Etienne had chosen had a very good reputation, though she did feel a little underdressed. The dress and jacket she'd bought weren't top of the range. Close, but she hadn't been prepared to spend a few weeks' pay on one outfit. Nor was she used to wearing chic clothes and had surprised herself by feeling she'd like something more special for tonight. Something to do with the way her heart felt about Etienne, perhaps? There was no denying she adored him. It didn't mean she should go OTT in an effort to look appealing though. He'd probably think she was trying to suck up to him even though she had turned down most of his serious offers so far. How much longer could she hold out about moving in with him? It got harder all the time.

Etienne picked up her hand and rubbed his thumb across her palm. 'You look beautiful, Camille. That shade of blue goes perfectly with your blonde hair and blue eyes.'

Did she look unsure of herself? She wasn't used to going on dates recently, and especially to a place like the restaurant Etienne had chosen. 'You're a right charmer,' she said over a dry tongue. She wanted to believe him and yet struggled. From what she'd heard, he'd been out with plenty of stunning women and, while she might scrub up okay, she was not stunning.

'I mean it. Before you ask, I'm not looking to get anything from you.' There was a tightness in his voice that suggested he was annoyed with her response.

She squeezed his hand since he was still holding hers. 'I'm not used to compliments.' Except all the ones she'd received from Benoit. Although she now knew they'd

164 PARISIAN SURGEON'S SECRET CHILD

been about getting his own way and making her believe he was one hundred per cent there for her. She should've realised that was a warning sign. Instead she'd been a fool and fallen for everything he'd said. 'I was letting my past get in the way for a moment.'

'That's something I fully understand.' Etienne set her hand back on her thigh. 'Let's relax and enjoy our evening. Put aside the things we both worry about and need to discuss and make the most of wonderful food, wine and company.'

As she said, he was a charmer, but this she would accept. 'Sounds perfect.'

And it was. Much later she placed her fork on the empty plate. 'That meal was beyond anything I've ever eaten. Seriously amazing.'

'Glad you like it. This is one of my favourite restaurants.'

'One of them?' asked a passing waiter. 'We thought it was your only one considering how often we see you.' He grinned.

Etienne laughed. 'You're right, Gabriel. I was downplaying how often I come here. I can't have Camille thinking I don't do any cooking.'

'As I've seen your spotless kitchen, it's hardly a surprise,' she retorted through a smile. 'Plus the fact the staff here seem to know you well.' She was a little surprised the waiter had made a comment as he passed them. She'd thought that would be a complete no-no in such an upmarket restaurant. But this was Etienne and being friendly was his mark.

'Would you like dessert?' he asked. 'Or coffee?'

'Coffee, thanks.' They'd taken a while over the meal and suddenly she felt tiredness creeping in, which wasn't right considering she was out with the man of her dreams. Dreams that weren't going to come true, she reminded herself.

Etienne was watching her as he beckoned Gabriel back and ordered coffees. 'What's up? You suddenly look sad.'

Sad? Yes, that was one word for the heaviness settling in her chest. She had to get over this love for Etienne and focus on just being Elyna's mother whenever she was with him. Except they were on a dinner date. Or had he invited her out just to give her a break from her routine? She needed to put her happy face on or he'd think she wasn't enjoying herself. 'Just a wave of tiredness. Elyna woke me quite often last night. She was very restless.'

'Nothing wrong with her?' he asked instantly.

'No health issues. She's sometimes belligerent when it's bedtime and on those occasions she can continue throughout the night.'

'How do you stay sane and calm at work when that happens?'

With difficulty at times. 'Who says I do? I focus on why I'm there and do my best to keep Elyna out of my mind.'

'That can't be easy.'

'It's not.'

'Do you have to work as much as you do? I know I've asked before, but if I can help out so you have more time off then please say so.'

Everything came back to what he had and she didn't. Maybe not everything, but enough to suddenly undermine her belief that she was doing a reasonable job as a parent. Wealth didn't answer all life's problems, did it? 'I need to work for my own sake,' she growled, and ignored the twinge of guilt that brought on. Here she was

166   PARISIAN SURGEON'S SECRET CHILD

in a top-rated restaurant snapping at Etienne! 'I did mention before how I can't cope being at home all the time, that I also need stimulus through work.'

He reached for her hands. 'Hey, I'm not trying to provoke you. I understand why you want to work. What I was offering was to help by taking away some of the financial burden so that if you want to cut back your hours you can. Not stop work completely.' His thumbs were brushing the backs of her hands, making it impossible to concentrate on anything else.

She had to try. 'I guess I overreact sometimes. But I don't want you thinking I'm out to get whatever I can.' His thumbs were warm and gentle, cranking up her libido too easily. *Pull your hands away.* She remained as she was, soaking up the moment and all the heat and her longing for him swelling inside her.

'Your coffee, Mademoiselle, Monsieur.'

A small cup appeared before her, cutting through the heat filling her and reminding her where she was. It was hard to shift her hands because Etienne was so warm but she managed. 'Thank you.' Was she thanking the waiter or Etienne? What a mess she was making of her life and possibly Elyna's, too. She needed to sort herself out. Now. Pushing the coffee aside, she picked up her purse. 'I've changed my mind. I don't want coffee after all.' She stood up from the table to head for the ladies' room.

'Camille? Are you all right?' Etienne quietly called after her.

Without turning around, she shook her head. Not at all. In the thankfully empty bathroom she stood staring at her image in the mirror. A pale, worried expression came back at her. She looked hollowed out.

She was an idiot. She loved Etienne more than she'd

ever have believed possible. There was no getting over it, nor was there anything she could do about it. The love was there, filling her heart, her life. She was not going to tell him. Nor would she give in to his request to move into his house. That would make day-to-day life impossible; she'd lose her sanity having to see him every single day. It was one thing to work with him, but totally different to be in the same home, sharing their daughter's mealtimes and play time. She couldn't do it. Not when he didn't love her. She wasn't angry about that. He'd never indicated he might, nor used love as a reason to get her to marry him or move into his home.

She'd called off their fling when she'd been worried he was coming to mean more to her than she could handle when he had made it plain from the outset that he was only there temporarily, for a good time. Seemed that she hadn't ever stopped falling for him, that her feelings had intensified and now she was lost. Totally in love with Etienne, and unable to follow up if she didn't want her heart broken all over again. This time she knew it would be a whole lot worse, because he was such a genuine, honest man and the father of her daughter.

A waitress appeared at the door. 'Excuse me. Monsieur Laval sent me to find out if you're all right.'

Closing her eyes, Camille drew a breath. Opening them again, she nodded. 'Please tell him I'm fine and I'll be out in a minute.'

Of course he'd be worried that she'd suddenly walked away from their cosy dinner. But if she hadn't left when she did she might've said what was on her mind and that could not happen. Sloshing cold water on her cheeks, she patted them dry with a towel and, drawing herself straight, headed back out to join him.

168   PARISIAN SURGEON'S SECRET CHILD

* * *

Etienne watched Camille cross the restaurant. Her body was rigid, her face tight. What was going on? One moment they were sitting there happy and chatting, enjoying the evening, and then suddenly she left him without a word. Now look at her. It was as if she'd received devastating news, but she hadn't. She hadn't touched her phone all night and no one had come to speak to her.

Which meant whatever was causing her trouble rested on him. Had he said something wrong? Something that badly upset her? Nothing came to mind. He'd offered financial assistance, but it wasn't the first time he'd done so and she hadn't got upset last time. As she approached the table he stood up to pull out her chair.

Camille shook her head. 'If you don't mind, I'd like to go.'

'No problem.' There was but he wasn't asking here. 'I'll call Alain to bring the car around.'

'Thank you.'

He took Camille's elbow and led her out to sit on a couch by the entrance, where he phoned Alain before approaching the maître d'. 'Dinner was superb.' No surprise there.

Once in the back of the car, Etienne turned to Camille. 'Are you really all right?' He didn't believe her. Never before had he known her to suddenly go so quiet. Something felt off centre and he needed to get to the bottom of it.

'Etienne, I've had a lovely evening. The meal was wonderful. I like spending time with you.' She paused and swallowed hard. 'It's just that it suddenly felt wrong. The atmosphere was special. Too good.' Another swallow. 'We're Elyna's parents, no more.'

His gut tightened. The trouble with asking Camille personal questions was that she gave direct answers, which were often hard hitting. Of course she was right in this instance. They weren't a couple, yet dinner had been intimate. He reached for her hand, but pulled away fast. Touching her would not help the situation. 'You're right,' he told her firmly. Trying to convince himself? Probably.

Her body sagged a little. It had to be because she was relieved to hear him agree with her. 'Would it be too much to ask if Alain could take me and Elyna back to my apartment after he drops you at home?'

He didn't like that. She'd been going to stay the night. 'Do you really want to wake Elyna up to head across the city at this hour?' Besides, he wanted to spend time with his little girl tomorrow.

Guilt filtered through Camille's face. 'You're right. What was I thinking?' She turned to stare out of the window for a moment before turning back to him. 'You're entitled to spend as much time as you can with Elyna.'

Etienne sighed. He really didn't understand what had brought on her abrupt change of mood but thought he understood how difficult this must be for her. 'It's all right. There are going to be times when one or other of us struggles.'

Alain pulled up at his front entrance.

Glad that the restaurant hadn't been far away and they hadn't had to spend too much time in the back of the car feeling awkward with each other, Etienne got out and went around to open Camille's door. Reaching for her hand, he gently pulled her out to stand beside him. '*Merci, Alain.* See you Monday morning.'

Once inside, Camille headed directly to the bedroom where Elyna was.

Etienne followed her into the room and was surprised

to find his mother sitting in the rocking chair. Worry hit. 'Is everything all right?' he whispered.

'Yes, Elyna's fine, just grizzly. She's woken up twice since I put her down so I thought I'd stay with her to see if that helped. Seems like it did.' His mother was also speaking quietly.

Camille went across and leant down to hug her. 'Thank you. You're so special. A lovely grandmother.'

He had to blink. Glancing at his mum, he saw her blinking too. Giving her a smile, he turned to his daughter, and his heart thumped. This truly was his family. The family he'd dreamed of.

'Mama. Want mama.'

'Oh-oh, guess we were too noisy.' He reached over and lifted Elyna up into his arms. 'Come on, sweetheart. Daddy's got a hug for you.'

A tiny fist knocked his chin. 'Dada.' Another tap in the chin. 'Dada.'

A spear to his heart. 'Did you really just call me Dada?' he asked in awe. It was the first time and he was melting inside. Knowing he was her father was huge but hearing Elyna say Dada knocked the floor out from under him. Tears streaked down his face and he couldn't care who saw.

Camille came to stand with them, her arm going around his waist, holding him tight. 'Wow. I'm so happy for you.'

Glancing at her, he found she had as many tears streaming down her cheeks as he did. She meant what she'd said. Not that he'd doubted her. He leaned in and kissed her salty face. 'So am I.'

Whack. Elyna's fist struck his shoulder and he laughed. 'I think we're raising a boxer.' Lifting her up above him, he grinned and blew a kiss at her. 'Hey, my girl. I'd prefer you took up knitting.'

Elyna giggled.

He blew her another kiss.

More giggles, this time Camille adding to them.

Happy families. It was amazing. Looking around, he saw his mother sneaking out of the room, leaving them to this perfect moment. Again his heart melted. His wonderful family had expanded to include Elyna. And Camille. At least in one way or another. That was still to be fully worked out but for now he was so happy he'd let the worries go and make the most of this amazing time.

'You know you're probably waking Elyna up, not quietening her down to go back to sleep?' Camille grinned, all the tension from earlier gone.

He shrugged. 'Who cares?' But he tucked Elyna in against his chest. The giggling stopped as she nestled closer so maybe Camille was wrong and tiredness was taking over.

Camille still had her arm around him so he remained still, not wanting her to move away. Her hand was firm and warm. Her blonde hair fell in waves over his arm. The hip she pressed into his reminded him of lying curled up around her in bed during their fling. Unlike with any other affair he'd had, he hadn't forgotten about their times together.

Camille rubbed Elyna's foot lightly and when she got no reaction, she whispered, 'I think you've charmed her back to sleep.'

'That quickly?'

'Make the most of it. She might wake again later.'

The thing was he didn't want to move. He loved holding Elyna with Camille holding him. But she was right. Elyna needed to get a decent night's sleep.

Within moments they were standing together looking down at their daughter. Etienne felt the tears rising again.

172   PARISIAN SURGEON'S SECRET CHILD

Wrapping an arm around Camille, he held her tight. She had brought him this deep happiness. She was turning his life around. Suddenly, holding her wasn't enough. Turning, he pulled her in against his chest, and lowered his mouth to kiss her. And felt a thrill when she kissed him back, slipping her tongue into his hungry mouth, placing her hands on his chest, heating his blood.

It still wasn't enough. But they had to get out of Elyna's room or she'd wake and all would be lost. Sweeping Camille up into his arms, he headed out of the room and along to his bedroom. The whole way Camille placed kisses on his neck, adding to the heat she'd brought on. Keep this up and he wasn't going to be able to take his time making love to her slowly. And slowly was the only way to go, to pleasure Camille until she was crying out for him. He kicked the door shut, mindful that his parents were here, though their room was right at the other end of the house and they wouldn't hear anything. But they were his parents, and some things were best not made obvious.

Laying her on the bed he knelt beside her and kissed her, as deep as possible, tasting, feeling, wondering at the sensations she was kick-firing through his body and soul. He knew nothing but Camille. The heat emanating off her, the need in her eyes, her strength as she wound her legs around him. Her hands working up a storm in his blood as her fingers touched, caressed, pressed into him. He was lost.

Except he wanted Camille to know the same, to feel him deep within her, mentally and physically, to know how much he cared for her. To experience the wonder pouring from him to her. Rolling off her, he began removing her dress, only to have to stop and let her help get it over her head. His breathing stuttered when her lace-covered breasts appeared before him. Leaning in, he licked her nipples through the black fabric. And smiled when she gasped, then cried out. They were together, as one.

Slowly working his way down her body, over her stomach to her sex, he took his time until Camille was shivering with need. Still he didn't stop, tasting, licking, lighting her up, until her hands gripped his head.

'Etienne, I need you. Now. Don't wait any longer,' she begged.

He obliged, diving into her hot body, taking his fill of heat and need as she came fiercely around him. Moments later he followed her into a pleasure-filled oblivion.

CHAPTER NINE

CAMILLE GROANED AS she rolled over. Her body ached in a delicious way. That had been the night to beat all nights with Etienne. The man took over her mind when he made love to her, stopped all thoughts and reasoning, turned her on and let the wonder take over.

As she reached out to the other side of the bed, disappointment rose. He wasn't there. The sheets were cool so he must've got up a while ago. Guess that meant no sex this morning.

She gasped. Of course. Elyna. She'd be awake and wanting food and attention. How had she slept on as though she had no one else to think about? No one had come to tell her Elyna was up, to ask what she ate for breakfast. Or had Etienne seen to Elyna? *He doesn't have to tell you. He's her father. That's what he would do.*

A sense of being overwhelmed gripped her. This was reality. Exactly what she'd hoped for and now it was here she felt she'd lost something precious. She was alone. Etienne had a family to turn to for help. He had asked her to join him permanently and she'd turned him down. Should she change her mind? No. Her heart hurt enough now. Imagine how that would feel living in a marriage without love. Impossible.

She crawled out of bed and went to stand under the shower to wash away the aches that moments ago had felt wonderful. She'd been wrong to make love with Etienne. It wasn't making anything easier. She felt lonelier than ever. Because she knew what it was like to be held in his arms, to touch him and be touched in return.

Back in the bedroom she was relieved to find her bag on a chair. 'Thanks, Etienne,' she muttered. Always thoughtful. Hauling on jeans and a jersey, she headed down the hall to the kitchen dining area. 'Morning, Etienne. Sorry I didn't hear Elyna call out.'

He was sitting at the table doing something on his computer. 'Glad you got some sleep.'

Looking around the room, she couldn't see Elyna, nor hear her. 'Where is she?'

'Gone out with Mum and Dad for breakfast and a trip to the market.'

Leaning against the counter, she crossed her arms under her breasts and breathed deep. This was something she had to get used to. Elyna was part of a bigger family now and decisions weren't always up to her. But, 'Why didn't you wake me?'

'I figured after all last night's activity you'd enjoy a sleep in for once.' He smiled slowly.

'Thank you,' she snapped. 'But I like to know what's going on with Elyna.'

Etienne came across and placed his hands on her shoulders. 'From the moment I got her up she was happy and giggling non-stop. It seemed ideal for her to go out with her grandparents for an hour or two. It's what you've indicated you want for her.'

176 PARISIAN SURGEON'S SECRET CHILD

Of course, he was right. Didn't make her any happier though. 'I suppose.'

His smile dipped, then returned. 'You and I can have breakfast together, maybe talk about what to do with the rest of the day, since I'm going away for a couple of days.'

He sounded so reasonable, yet she felt tense. Everything was going well so why did it feel as though it was all slipping through her fingers? Raising Elyna as she'd done so far was changing too fast for her to keep up.

'Coffee? Bagel?' Etienne asked.

She nodded.

'What's wrong, Camille? Are you having regrets about last night?'

'No, yes. I don't know.' It had been wonderful but she'd crossed the line. Etienne didn't love her, end of. Now he looked as though she'd kicked him in the gut. Well, her gut was aching too. 'We can't have a relationship that's not permanent, and that's not happening.' *Because you don't love me.*

He'd made love to her last night as though he cared deeply for her. But she loved him wholeheartedly. No doubt whatsoever. Therefore it was time to step up and say it as it was. 'Etienne, I care about you a lot. You can trust me to do the right thing for you and Elyna. But that's as far as our relationship goes.'

A punch in the stomach would've been easier to take. The end to what had seemed an idyllic night together. 'I see.' The hell he did, Etienne thought furiously. Here he'd been reveling in the warm feelings their lovemaking had engendered and Camille was saying they couldn't do it again.

'I don't think you do,' she said pointedly. 'We're meant to be talking about how we're going to raise Elyna, not getting carried away in bed.'

She couldn't mean that. Except he knew she did. It wasn't in her to lie. He trusted her that much. That didn't mean he could let go all the restraints around his heart. Too risky by far. Even if Camille could love him, how long would that last? They hadn't spent a lot of time together until now and that wasn't enough to really know what was happening between them. He wouldn't factor in that he was falling in love with her. He daredn't. 'Camille, I'm sorry. I thought you were happy to go to bed with me.'

He saw the pain filling her eyes. 'I was.'

That had to be positive, though maybe not, as she was pulling away from him again. He cared too much for her and that was frightening. He was afraid to tell her how he felt. Silence fell between them.

Finally it was Camille who broke it. 'Etienne, I'm sorry but I can't continue what we started last night. I understand you still have issues accepting any woman might like you for yourself, and not want anything else. The way I see it, you need to move on from those fears or you're never going to know real happiness. You have so much to give. You're kind and caring, gentle and generous. You could have it all if you'd let go of everything holding you back. Be strong and go for what it is you long for.'

True. He should, but he couldn't. It was ingrained in him to look out for his heart. That wasn't going to change overnight. He couldn't do what it took. He'd got closer with Camille than any other woman, even teetered on the brink of taking the final leap, but it seemed it wasn't in him to hand over his heart once and for all. 'You think?'

'I know.' Her gaze locked on him. 'I behaved similarly after my ex, Benoit, hurt me badly. Then I met you.' She paused as though waiting for him to say something.

He didn't.

'I called off our fling because I liked you—a lot. Too much. I knew where that was headed, and I didn't want to be hurt. You have a reputation for not getting involved with the women you date. I've no argument with that. At least you're honest. But I also learned that I could open up my heart again, that it hadn't turned to dust after what Benoit did.'

'I'm happy for you, Camille.'

She turned away, headed for the door. 'I'll grab our things and walk to the market to join the others, then catch a cab home with Elyna.' The door closed quietly behind her.

They might be going to spend quite a bit of time together with Elyna but he'd just lost Camille. He'd never really had her because that was the way he liked it. Used to like it. Now he knew he was wrong, but still couldn't seem to risk telling her. 'Goodbye, Camille,' he said to the empty room. Leaning his head back, he closed his eyes and thought about the future. Or lack of, as Camille would say. It didn't look wonderful from here.

Camille was never going to go away. They had Elyna between them. But after this they'd be strictly parents sharing a role, not lovers or even friends.

So much for avoiding pain. His heart was in tatters.

Nice turned on a clear blue sky and a warm winter day for the start of the surgeons' two-day conference. Etienne didn't want to go into the room with the crowd of general surgeons all talking at once. He'd much prefer to walk along the beach and soak in the warmth, but that wasn't possible. He had a talk to listen to.

Warmth had been missing in his bones and his heart since yesterday when Camille had spelt out so clearly just how badly he was screwing up his own life. She was right. He was. But admitting it and knowing what to do about it were so far apart he was lost. Even after she'd said she cared about him and that he could trust her, he was struggling to take that last step into what could be a wonderful life. He was afraid.

'There you are, Etienne,' called a familiar voice over the heads of colleagues. 'Over here.' Fillip waved.

Groaning under his breath, Etienne pushed through to reach his pal and give him a rough pat on the back. 'Good to see you.' It had been a while since they'd last caught up. He had yet to tell Fillip he was a father. Not that he'd ever be ready for the jibes and teasing that would follow, but he did want his closest friend to know. 'How've you been?'

Fillip shrugged. 'Same old, same old, as the Brits would say. I'm glad you could make it down here. I hope you're staying on after this is over so we can properly catch up.'

'I'm due back in Paris on Wednesday afternoon.'

'Then we'll have a late night tonight.'

They sat down and spent time swapping news on what they'd been up to over the months since last seeing each other. Etienne decided to avoid the subject of Camille and Elyna—Fillip would be onto that so fast it'd be embarrassing.

'How's Torrie?'

Fillip smiled. 'Pregnant again. We're so excited.'

'Congratulations.' He felt a pang in his chest. He was a father himself now and already being away from Elyna was getting to him. He wanted to cuddle her until she grinned at him. He'd love to see her mother too, cuddle her till she grinned and kissed him. That wasn't happening again.

'What's causing that look of woe?'

A bell rang, and the talking around them subsided in an instant.

Etienne sighed. Saved. He'd been about to blurt out what was going on in his life and now really wasn't the time for that. 'I'm fine,' he said and sat back as the first meeting got under way.

Except he couldn't concentrate. The speaker appeared to have everyone else enthralled about a new surgical technique he was using for removing part of the liver, but not him. Instead Camille's words about how he needed to be brave if he really wanted to have love and a family in his life were taunting him. She was right. It was up to him to sort himself out. No one else could do it for him.

The room became airless, his chest tight. Looking around, Etienne saw a way out without upsetting too many people and quietly left the table. He couldn't stay here for a moment longer. He needed fresh air and space around him.

At the hotel entrance the doorman nodded. 'Morning, Doctor.'

'Morning,' he replied as he strode outside. Crossing the street, he headed along the Promenade des Anglais, hauling sea air into his lungs. Never before had he known

SUE MACKAY 181

claustrophobia, but now he understood those who did. It flattened him, made him want to be anywhere but stuck inside with all those people. It'd been brought on by the perpetual voice in his head telling him to make up his mind about what he was going to do with his future. Every question, every thought, came back to Camille. He couldn't imagine life without her, even though she wasn't fully in his life at the moment.

Did he want her to be? Yes. No hesitation. He did.

Was he prepared to tell her that he loved her? That she held his heart in her hands? It would be the biggest step to take. The step that would win him everything—or lose it all. A step he had to take.

He walked faster. Camille went with him. Her smile cutting through his mind, warming him throughout. Worrying him throughout. This was crazy. Camille had taken over, filling him with hope and yes, damn it, love. Turning around, he aimed for the hotel. He needed to return to the meeting and get on with what he'd come for—to listen to colleagues talk about improved techniques or incredible cases. To be there when Fillip spoke. To be a general surgeon, not a man who didn't have a clue how to front up to what was tearing him apart.

Somehow he got through the rest of the day and the dinner that followed. If anyone had asked him what he'd learned during the talks he'd have struggled to come up with a reply that made sense but somehow he managed to avoid that snag.

Fillip did mention a couple of things and then shook his head at Etienne's lack of interest. 'Sure there's nothing wrong, my friend?'

PARISIAN SURGEON'S SECRET CHILD

There was plenty wrong, but he wasn't about to tell Fillip. 'I'm good.'

So good that when people started leaving for the night, Etienne returned to the promenade and took off his shoes to walk along the sand at the edge of the water. He hadn't heard from Camille since she'd walked out of his house yesterday, not even a text to say Elyna was doing fine. Not that he was surprised. She'd been firm about where they were at with this unusual relationship. But he'd like to hear about Elyna. And to hear Camille's soft, caring voice.

What could he offer Camille except to hurt her by not being able to admit he loved her? She deserved better. How about telling her the truth, saying he loved her and wanted to share their lives? She didn't want the tangible things. She wanted love. His? Did she want what he was afraid to place in her hand and wrap her fingers around—his heart?

If she ever said she loved him, he knew she'd mean it. He was afraid to admit how much that would mean because again he'd be vulnerable. If he told her how he felt there was no going back. Which he wouldn't want to do, but he'd been there once, and he *had* survived the pain and anger brought on by Melina trying every trick in the book to keep him. He was here, thinking about Camille all the time, which showed how much he had moved on.

He stopped to stare out to sea where the moonlight made the water sparkle. Beautiful. Breath-taking. Just like Camille. She was not only beautiful and breath-taking. She was real. She could turn his life around. Face it, she already had. She'd given him a daughter whom he adored. She'd shaken his determination to remain aloof with women. She'd burrowed into his heart and wasn't in a hurry to leave.

He had to talk to her. Now. Which was impossible. They were at opposite ends of the country. He couldn't just drive around the corner to ring the bell at her apartment. Nor was he going to phone her. That wouldn't feel right. He needed to watch her face when he opened up his heart. If she was going to turn her back on him, then he needed to see her do it so he'd know for certain where he stood.

Camille said she'd stopped their fling because she'd begun to like him too much. Hope flared under his ribs. Could she possibly love him? Would she believe he loved her? Was he setting himself up for a big fall? Only one way to find out and the sooner the better for his heart. He had to talk to her. To lay his heart on the line. It wouldn't be easy. Managing to breathe while he waited for her reaction would be difficult. But carrying on living the life he had now would be pathetic. Who knew? As Camille had said, he might be able to have it all.

'I do want it all. More than that, I want to give all I've got in my heart to Camille, and Elyna.'

To hell with the conference. There'd be plenty more of those.

There was only one chance at love. Now all he had to do was convince Camille how much he loved her.

Camille laid Elyna down for her afternoon nap. Her wee girl was very tired so hopefully she'd soon fall asleep. It had been a couple of days since she'd walked away from Etienne for the second time. The ward had been busier than normal, which helped keep her focused on work. At least Etienne hadn't been there but he'd be back tomorrow. Working together wasn't going to be as comfortable as it used to be.

She'd annoyed him when she'd spoken her mind about letting go of his hang-ups. So what if she'd been out of line? She loved him so much she'd had to try to make him see there was a chance at a wonderful future if he was prepared to take a risk. Of course, that probably wouldn't be with her. More than likely he didn't care for her beyond a friend who happened to be the mother of his child, and went to bed with him too easily. For her, being blunt was the only way to approach him. She was amazed he hadn't done a runner when she'd told him she cared a lot for him. Instead he hadn't acknowledged her declaration. That hurt beyond belief, but she'd known to expect it. He wouldn't leave Elyna though, so their relationship was going to become a strained mess.

Would she ever find a man who loved her? First she had to get over Etienne and that wasn't going to happen overnight. Nor be easy when they'd see so much of each other around Elyna and at work. It might be wise to change her job. Except she enjoyed working on the ward, liked the other staff. But to always be knocking up against Etienne when he filled her heart wasn't on. The future looked lonely. She didn't want much, just Elyna and a man to love and be loved by. Etienne.

Out in the kitchen she turned on the coffee maker. Something to eat would be sensible but her appetite had taken leave over the past two days.

There was a knock on her door. Who could that be? Maree was at the hospital visiting Jules, who was making slow progress after his stroke. Peering through the peephole, she gasped. Etienne. He was meant to be in Nice. What did he want? Was this when they got down to the nitty-gritty of how and where Elyna was raised because she'd walked away from him after an amazing night making love? Only one way to find out and she wasn't going to put it off—even if her heart was going into overdrive with worry.

Wrenching the door wide, she said, 'Hello, Etienne. You're back early.'

He looked terrible, as though he hadn't slept at all. 'Camille, can I come in?'

Stepping back, she nodded. 'Of course. Elyna's only just gone to sleep though.'

'She's not the reason I'm here.'

Closing the door, she led the way to the kitchen. 'Would you like a coffee?'

'Okay.' Etienne stood by the counter, looking around. His back was straight, his shoulders drawn back, but there were shadows under his eyes and his cheeks were pale.

This time she wasn't rushing in to ask what was wrong. He'd come here to see her, so she would wait until he was ready to talk. As long as he didn't take for ever. 'Sit down, Etienne.'

'Camille, I need to tell you something.' He looked very serious.

The most serious she'd ever seen him. What was wrong? Had something awful happened? The cup shook in her hands so she put it down. Coffee would have to wait.

Etienne drew a long breath. Then another.

Camille waited, her heart beating like crazy. What was he about to say? Would it be good or bad?

PARISIAN SURGEON'S SECRET CHILD

'You were right. It is time I got on with living, and stopped hiding behind what Melina did.' Another long intake of air. 'You've never treated me in the same way. Never. I've always appreciated that while at the same time looking for hidden trouble.'

She sank onto the nearest stool, putting her clasped hands on the counter in front of her.

'You're nothing but honest. Telling me to get over myself was the right thing to do.'

She waited. There was more to come. She knew it by the tension rippling off him in waves, by the way he was looking at her as if he were about to step into a minefield.

'Camille, I love you. I think I have from the moment you walked away from our fling. Even before then you were in my head all the time, annoying me with the suspicion that you might be the one if I could only stop and take a long look at what I was doing to myself by hanging onto the past so determinedly.'

'You love me?' she croaked over a suddenly dry tongue.

Etienne was in front of her, reaching for her. 'Yes, darling, I do. I love you with all my heart. I'm sorry it's taken a while to tell you but first I had to tell myself.'

She blinked at him, totally lost for words. Etienne loved her. She could see it in his eyes, his face and that delicious smile on those amazing lips. *He loves me.* A solitary tear slipped out of the corner of her right eye and slid slowly down her cheek. 'Phew,' she choked out.

He laughed. 'Is that all you've got to say?'

She nodded. Then proved herself wrong. 'I love you too, Etienne. So much it hurts.'

'I need to kiss away that ache.' And he proceeded to

do exactly that. Followed by making passionate love on the nearest couch.

Followed by taking her hands in his. 'Camille, will you marry me and be with me for the rest of our lives? I promise to always love you and cherish you and be at your side no matter what life throws at us.'

Marry him? Of course she would. It was all she'd wanted—Etienne to love her as she loved him and to have that family together that she'd always dreamed of. 'Try stopping me.' This was so different from the first time he'd asked her. This was real. 'Yes, Etienne, I will marry you. I love you so much. I've loved you since we had our fling.'

'Mama, wake,' shouted Elyna from down the hall.

Etienne swung off the couch and grabbed his pants. 'I'm coming, little one.' Leaning down, he kissed her hard. 'Camille Beauregard, you've made me the happiest man alive.'

Two weeks later Camille did a pirouette in the middle of the lounge in Etienne's beautiful home. *Their* beautiful home. 'Now I feel I'm truly home.'

Etienne laughed. 'More than when you returned to Rue Roy?'

'Yes.' They'd spent the last few hours shifting her few possessions from the apartment to here and setting up Elyna's bedroom with all her books and toys that had finally arrived in the container from Montreal. 'This is beyond anything I'd expected when I returned to Paris and I couldn't be happier. I'm not just talking about living here but living with you. I love you so much, Etienne Laval.'

'I know you do.' He swept her into his arms and kissed

188 PARISIAN SURGEON'S SECRET CHILD

her. 'Love you back, Camille. You have changed my life for ever. I couldn't be happier either.'

'Mama, Dada. Look.' Elyna crawled around them waving a colouring book that had been in the container.

'Never a quiet moment with you, is there?' Etienne lifted her up and plonked a tender kiss on her head. 'Have you got some crayons in that box on the table?'

'There should be some,' Camille said. 'Though she's not really up to speed with colouring in yet.'

'Doesn't matter if she's happy.' Etienne sat Elyna in her high chair while Camille found the crayons.

She felt unbelievably good. All her dreams were coming true. Etienne was wonderful. She still had to pinch herself that he loved her. Not that he didn't show it all the time, but she couldn't get her head around the fact he really had moved on from the past. As she had. Passing over the crayons, she stared at her ring finger. No, she stared at the gold ring with a beautiful sapphire and diamonds on each side. Her heart melted for about the third time that day. It was always melting. Etienne did that to her.

He put his arm around her waist, gave her a light squeeze. 'That sapphire matches your eyes perfectly.'

'So you've mentioned.' She grinned.

'You know my mother's already started planning the wedding, don't you?'

'She has mentioned one or two ideas, which I take to mean she wants to organise everything.'

'Don't let her rule it all.'

'You know what? I really don't mind what she does as long as I get some say in the planning.' Basically she wanted a small wedding with family and their closest friends, which for her meant only Liza, and she was happy with that.

'Are we going with the vineyard setting?'

'What do you think?' It suited her, but if Etienne wanted something more formal here in Paris she'd go with it.

'I'm more than happy. I just want to marry you. Have I told you today that I love you, Camille Beauregard soon to be Camille Laval?'

'Maybe. Tell me again to make sure.'

'I love you, Camille.'

Life couldn't get any better.

* * * * *

If you enjoyed this story, check out these other great reads from Sue MacKay

Brooding Vet for the Wallflower
Healing the Single Dad Surgeon
Paramedic's Fling to Forever
Marriage Reunion with the Island Doc

All available now!

MILLS & BOON®

Coming next month

RISKING HIS HEART FOR THE ER DOC
Traci Douglass

'Remember, team. Secure knots mean the difference between a successful rescue and... Well, let's just say we all prefer happy endings here,' he said, earning chuckles from the group. 'All right. Everyone ready to start?'

Andy avoided Jules's gaze as he moved among the team, double-checking their equipment himself to ensure they were all fastened properly. 'Good. Let's start the simulation.'

'Excuse me, Dr MacDonald?' Jules asked from behind him, and Andy closed his eyes, taking a deep breath for fortitude. 'Could you double-check my alpine butterfly loop again, please? It's been a while since I've done one and I want to make sure I have it correct.'

Andy took another breath then stepped back in front of her, his gaze fixed on the knot as his fingers brushed hers and that odd spark that always seemed to happen whenever she was close flared to life inside him again. He snuffed it out fast. He'd put all that behind him a long time ago. He didn't want to bring it into the present now. Especially since she was on the team and also starting in the ER at Teton Memorial, which meant they'd be seeing more of each other there, too. And he knew personally what a bad idea it was to get involved with a colleague in any way beyond strictly professional.

Continue reading

RISKING HIS HEART FOR THE ER DOC
Traci Douglass

Available next month
millsandboon.co.uk

Copyright © 2025 Traci Douglass

COMING SOON!

We really hope you enjoyed reading this book.
If you're looking for more romance
be sure to head to the shops when
new books are available on

Thursday 25th September

To see which titles are coming soon, please visit
millsandboon.co.uk/nextmonth

MILLS & BOON

MILLS & BOON TRUE LOVE IS HAVING A MAKEOVER!

Introducing

Love Always

Swoon-worthy romances, where love takes center stage. Same heartwarming stories, stylish new look!

Look out for our brand new look
COMING SEPTEMBER 2025
MILLS & BOON

FOUR BRAND NEW BOOKS FROM
MILLS & BOON MODERN

Indulge in desire, drama, and breathtaking romance – where passion knows no bounds!

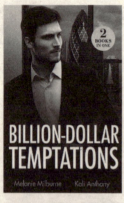
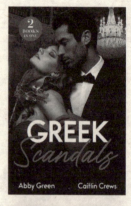
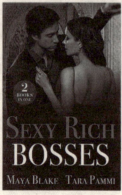
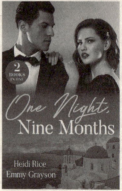

OUT NOW

Eight Modern stories published every month, find them all at:

millsandboon.co.uk

Afterglow Books is a trend-led, trope-filled list of books with diverse, authentic and relatable characters, a wide array of voices and representations, plus real world trials and tribulations. Featuring all the tropes you could possibly want (think small-town settings, fake relationships, grumpy vs sunshine, enemies to lovers) and all with a generous dose of spice in every story.

♪ @millsandboonuk
◎ @millsandboonuk
afterglowbooks.co.uk
#AfterglowBooks

For all the latest book news, exclusive content and giveaways scan the QR code below to sign up to the Afterglow newsletter:

afterglow BOOKS

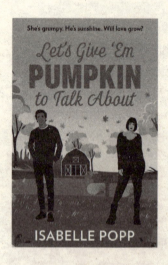

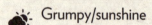 Grumpy/sunshine

 LGBTQ+

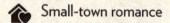 Small-town romance

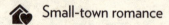 Small-town romance

 Spicy

 Spicy

OUT NOW

Two stories published every month. Discover more at:
Afterglowbooks.co.uk

OUT NOW!

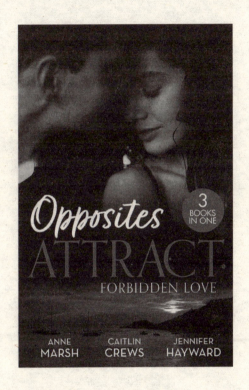

Available at
millsandboon.co.uk

MILLS & BOON

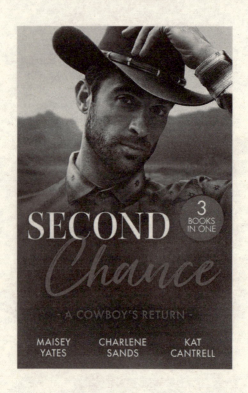

OUT NOW!

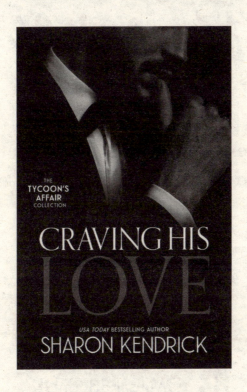

Available at
millsandboon.co.uk

MILLS & BOON

LET'S TALK
Romance

For exclusive extracts, competitions and special offers, find us online:

 MillsandBoon

 @MillsandBoon

 @MillsandBoonUK

 @MillsandBoonUK

Get in touch on 01413 063 232

For all the latest titles coming soon, visit
millsandboon.co.uk/nextmonth